THE
GIRL WHO
FELL INTO MYTH

Published by Winterset Books
www.kaykenyon.com
ISBN 9781733674638 (paperback)

Published in the United States of America

Cover by Deranged Doctor Design

Visit www.kaykenyon.com and join the author's newsletter for a free short story, and find out about new releases and reader perks.

ALSO BY KAY KENYON

Watch for *Stranger in the Twisted Realm,* the next book in The Arisen Worlds quartet: *In a war-like realm, Yevliesza fights for her freedom as a ruthless leader hunts down the truth of her hidden power.*
Coming Fall, 2023.

Fantasy Novels

THE ARISEN WORLDS QUARTET

The Girl Who Fell Into Myth, Book 1

STAND ALONE NOVELS

A Thousand Perfect Things

Queen of the Deep

THE DARK TALENTS TRILOGY

At the Table of Wolves, Book 1

Serpent in the Heather, Book 2

Nest of the Monarch, Book 3

Science Fiction Novels

The Seeds of Time

Tropic of Creation

Rift

Maximum Ice

The Braided World

THE ENTIRE AND THE ROSE QUARTET

Bright of the Sky, Book 1

A World Too Near, Book 2

Collections

PRAISE FOR THE WRITING
OF KAY KENYON

THE
GIRL WHO
FELL INTO MYTH

BOOK ONE OF THE ARISEN WORLDS

KAY KENYON

WINTERSET BOOKS

The Nine Powers

Foreknowing
Manifesting
Creatures
Warding
Healing
Verdure
Aligns
Elements
Primal Roots

PART I
THE DARK EMISSARY

CHAPTER 1

L iesa flew. With the highway forty miles in a straight line to the horizon, her 1981 Celica Supra with its inline six and rear spoiler could hit one hundred mph in no time. It was like flying.

With the sunroof open, her hair lashed at her face and the desert air met her like a blast wall. She and her father might have been stationed anywhere in the world, but they got Barlow County, Oklahoma, bisected by one of the most important *aligns* in North America. If they'd ended up in St. Louis or Tampa, there wouldn't be any forty-mile straightaways, so Oklahoma felt like a little bit of heaven.

The thing about Barlow County was that you could see the weather coming for hours. The winds blew west to east, and sometimes distant clouds humped up in dark towers, trailing skirts of rain, pushing outlier gusts ahead of them like warning shots. Looking out her driver-side window, Liesa caught sight of a big system moving so slow, she knew she could outrace it and be home with store-bought rolls and coffee before it hit the consulate.

Consulate. What her father called their house, beat up as it was, and with the sand that seemed to blow through the atoms of the walls.

Slowing to a mannerly twenty-five miles per hour, Liesa cruised into the village where they got their supplies and parked in front of Rolly's Stop 'n Shop. Just outside, one of the locals was smoking and gave her lovingly cared-for Celica a respectful glance. He nodded at her as she went in, with a terse but neighborly acknowledgment. One of the open-minded ones. They'd had plenty of time to learn to say *Numinasi*. It had been twenty years since the Accord. But most fell back on the more familiar word, the one that was easier to say. Maybe not trying to be mean. But still, they'd mutter behind her back: *witch*.

"Liesa," Rolly said from behind the counter when she walked in, giving her a smile. He tapped a box containing the groceries she'd texted to him that morning. She looked around the store, spotting a few of the locals pretending to shop but watching her.

"Shane ain't here," Rolly said, real casual, but knowingly. "Out to the ditch. Workin' on the irrigation pump."

Liesa wouldn't have minded seeing Rolly's son. Behind the usual grime on Shane's face, he had the kind of features that leaned toward handsome, especially his mouth and eyes. The grimier he looked, the more he stirred her. Matching his Barlow look, she'd taken to wearing ripped jeans and a faded t-shirt when she came to town. As though she could ever be Barlow's own.

"Storm's comin'," Rolly said, glancing west, the wall with the chips and soda.

"Looks like."

"You'd best get back. Put up the shutters. Shane'd help you, but."

"We got it, though. Can you throw in some gummy bears?" She pulled out her father's credit card while Rolly tucked in the candy.

"How's Ansyl?" Rolly always asked after him. It had been

years since her father came into town, and Rolly knew he was poorly. Knew her mother was dead, too, so there was lots of the poor orphan treatment, a little too kind, especially from Rolly. The town knew her father was someone important, but they couldn't figure why he'd be living out past L-Road eight miles from nowhere. Answer: Because the *aligns*. Barlow County had one running smack up the middle, not respecting county lines or riverbeds or highways. Most folk didn't believe in the aligns—you couldn't even *see* them, they reasoned. But the Numinasi knew that all the worlds have deep paths, even worlds without much in the way of powers, without more than a bit of magic. Sometimes mundane people created great cities on the aligns. Cities like St. Louis. They assumed they'd chosen the place because of being on a river, and they sensed—a hunch, they would call it—that it would be a good place.

"Is your dad feeling better?"

"Yeah, he's been grand lately. Working in his garden."

Except he wasn't, not these days. A few years back when her father had begun complaining that nothing would grow, when he began misplacing tools, flooding the rows with water or not watering at all. When it was dangerous for him to be around a stove, much less drive.

Rolly carried the groceries to the car.

Three young guys stood around the Celica, one of them caressing it like it was a girlfriend. They backed off when Rolly eyed them, taking positions leaning on a windowsill or the drinks machine, one of them saying to her, "Sweet rig."

Witch or no witch, she could of had that boy with only a jut of her chin. *Jump in, why don't you? Little spin?*

A distant rattle of thunder, like an eighteen-wheeler roaring by. Clouds charged across the sky, on the move and spoiling to get in on the action. Tornado action.

Smiling at the boys, she swung into the car seat—all low to

the ground where the Celica liked to keep its driver—and cranked the ignition. It fired up real sweet, and she could tell by the expressions on those boys' faces that they knew real beauty when they saw it. Those classic lines, maybe from a bygone era, but never beaten.

Giving them a nod, she flipped up the headlights, letting the Celica strut for them. They grinned at that, knowing she was showing off and liking it.

She pulled into the street. The day had taken on an orangey tint, how the sky sometimes went when dust got kicked up. But in the direction of home, it was still all blue and hot.

The Celica knew the way.

꧁꧂

"IT'S ME," LIESA CALLED OUT, KICKING OPEN THE BACK SCREEN door, balancing the box of groceries on her hip.

The kitchen was dead quiet, like she'd let in the muffled air from the flats where the storm was getting into position. From the kitchen window, a little flick of sheet lighting over the distant hills. No wind yet, but the crickets had gone to ground. Even the ag ditch down the road had been silent, running swiftly, like a video with the sound muted.

From the office down the hall her father's chair squeaked as he shifted his weight. He would be at his desk where he used to have real work, with the missions sharing diplomatic concerns and plans. Over the years there'd been less and less of that. Fewer missives from St. Louis. And then none. The exchanges had mostly been about the Nanotech Accords, where a bunch of countries agreed on curbs and things to protect the hidden realms from microscopic machines. Because no one knew how easily nanotech might penetrate the Mythos.

You didn't want to mess with the Numinasi. There was no

telling what their powers really were, so an accord came together and everyone was happily co-existing. Even if they tended to hate each other.

Therefore the consulate in Barlow County. But why hadn't anyone stayed in touch with her father? A few times her father allowed as how the Numinasi center in St. Louis had been quiet lately. And then he started saying that it was time to report in person, and she'd go too, they'd make a trip of it. Liesa was dying to go, but knew that with the way her father was drifting it would never happen.

She found him at his desk, surrounded by disordered piles of paper, some of which were just flyers and ads. "Liesa," he said, looking up and patting his thick hair as though looking for something.

"Groceries are put away. We'll have meatloaf tonight."

Thunder gargled in the near distance.

"Your mother will like that." His gaze slid away from her. "Now where's my pencil?" he said, worried.

"Behind your ear."

He found it and pulled a yellow pad of paper closer. "Notes will be expected."

"I can bring you a nice cup of tea. And I have gummy bears."

Her father shook his head and pulled down his waistcoat over his flannel trousers, the ones that hung flabby on his dwindling frame. "No time. I'm in a hurry . . . so much to do."

"We could have a cup of tea and plan the day," she suggested, seeing that he was starting to get wound up.

"But the visitor," he said, glancing toward the front of the house. "He'll expect a report."

Liesa couldn't help but look toward the parlor, wondering for a second if maybe Shane had come after all.

Noting her glance, he said, "Not in the house! In the yard . . ."

"Who is it, then?"

"Who?" He frowned in concentration. Then in Numinasi, he said, "He gave his name, one of the old names."

She and her father spoke in Numinasi as well as English, and lately it had more often been in the home language, which seemed to comfort him.

"Shall I go and see?" If no one was there, Liesa would just say they must have left. Then they could have tea.

"No!" he shouted. "Go upstairs, it's got to be handled . . . handled . . ." He looked up, his eyes wide. "Did he see you?"

"I came in the back door." She was starting to feel alarmed, herself.

"Well, something must be done," he said. "Clearly."

"I can talk to him. See what he wants?" She rose from her chair. "I'll be right back."

Her father got up too, holding the notepad full of jottings, some underlined for emphasis. She looked at her father standing there. Something was wrong. Terribly wrong.

She made her way to the front screen door. Beyond it, the dust blew in curtains, coloring the sky like a bruise. A lone figure was out there, a stone's throw from the house, partially obscured by the old flatbed truck they didn't use anymore. So far the figure was nothing but a black silhouette, hair lifting in the wind as though alive.

Stepping down from the porch, she approached but stopped a few feet away from the stranger. He wore a quilted coat with silver clasps and grommets, and boots with leather thongs wrapping them tight to his calves. He was tall and clean-shaven, with jet-black hair. She was close enough to detect that marker of the Numinasi people: a faint violet cast to his dark eyes.

"Your name," the man said softly, in the Numinasi language.

Her voice stuck in her throat. She knew what he was, what he must be, but it seemed like a dream, a bad one. She should have gone upstairs, should have taken warning, but it was too late now. He had seen her.

"What is your name," he repeated.

"Liesa."

"We know nothing of a . . . Lee-za."

He waited for her to explain herself. To say how an envoy from Numinat could be living with a girl whom he no doubt already guessed had to be a daughter.

"My father and I live here. My mother is dead."

The stranger studied her face. He could not fail to notice the Numinasi violet-black of her eyes.

"I have come to take your father home."

"He can't come with you," she said, wishing the storm would come down and swallow them all.

"He is ordered home."

She began to be afraid. This man seemed determined to take her father. Her thoughts skittered to find a plan to stop this, to get away. They had to get to the Celica. A Numinasi would not approach a machine, not one that was turned on. They would run to Oklahoma City, or Denver, or . . .

Seeing her father come out onto the porch, the stranger strode toward him. Liesa rushed to her father's side.

The man came to the foot of the porch. His next words were laden with accusation. "You did not say a child had been born."

"I wrote, I explained it . . . Or Natia, she did. It was all written down, somewhere."

"No one has ever heard of a child."

"Well," her father said peevishly, "here she is in any case!"

The man turned to her. "You must come also."

She looked in alarm at her father.

"Liesa," he said from the porch. "I should have sent you back. Long ago."

The stranger narrowed his eyes in what seemed incredulity. "Why . . . why did you not?"

Her father stood, his arms hanging helplessly down at his sides as though there was nothing left to say or do or fix. A fist of wind lifted the dust on the porch and snatched it away. The three of them stood unmoving until her father finally answered.

"I forgot."

CHAPTER 2

The stranger gave Liesa one hour to prepare. Thoughts of escape rattled through her mind, but the man wore a short sword at his belt and she had no doubt he was willing to use it. He demanded that she impress upon her father the importance of obedience. Otherwise, he said, it would be noted. She was to change her clothes. He was explicit: she should wear something decent and dark. Also strong boots. She hoped tennies would do.

Her distraught father was stacking papers and looking in boxes trying to set things in order. She helped him, all the while whispering that they should call for help. She spent precious minutes trying to get her father to concentrate, to acknowledge that the man waiting for them in the yard could not command them. Finally she said she would call the local sheriff, even Rolly —but at that her father became alarmed and made her swear not to oppose the princip's courier, as he called the stranger.

"But why just let him take us? We're happy where we are!"

Her father swallowed. Taking her hand, he said, "It's where we come from. It's the only place you can be happy. Your own country, you see?"

"But—"

He squeezed her hand, searching her face for understanding. "And if we don't return—if *you* don't—it will be a great . . . disgrace."

"Why didn't you send me back? You said you forgot. But early on? When you remembered better?"

He slid his gaze away. "I don't know. There must have been a reason."

Liesa shook her head in frustration. "Why do they want us so much now, when they never did before?"

"The ways," he muttered. "Numinasi ways." He brightened then, as he sometimes did when the fog parted for him. "Your power. You need to receive your power." His eyes pleaded as he said, "Tell me that you'll go, promise me . . ."

Numinasi had mystic powers. All peoples of the Mythos did.

With only minutes to decide, she looked at the expression on his face and couldn't say no.

Her father asked the courier for time to put his affairs in order —whatever those affairs were—and the man agreed, saying that in two days' time they would send someone to guide him home. But it was best that Liesa go immediately. When she balked, her father pinned her with a frantic gaze, shaking his head. Was he in his right mind to be sending her off? She couldn't know, but his newfound conviction swayed her.

She was going, really going, to Numinat, a place that she had come to think of as a story, or a distant country that would always be remote and mysterious to her. She had said she would go, but as she rummaged for the clothes the courier had told her to wear, the weight of her decision pressed down on her with a cold hand. The urge to escape vied with her father's wish to avoid disgrace. Minutes passed, with her mind caught in an endless loop. At last the thought occurred that surely she could return here, if things didn't work out. Yes, she would go. For now, for her father's sake, she would go.

By the time the hour was up, Liesa had put on a navy-blue plaid shirt and almost-new jeans. It was the closest she could come to something dark and decent. The Numinasi looked at her skeptically but managed to nod his approval.

Her father walked with them to the equipment shed, where the stairway was. Outside the shed, he embraced her for the first time in years. She clung to him as he kept whispering, "I'll join you soon. Soon." Gently, he pulled away, patting her shoulder, trying to make everything seem not so bad, like a fall from a bike. He gave her a shaky smile.

The storm was receding into the distance, flickering with sheet lightning and grumbling as though it had been unfairly driven away by the dark emissary.

"Tell them I'm coming," she heard her father say as he backed away.

And then she was inside the shed, the courier behind her. He ordered her to clear the path, to move the noxious machines like the leaf blower, electric generator, even flashlights, so that he would not pass close to them. Machines disrupted powers; it was why magic had faded from the earth, why her father's gift of perceiving the aligns had fallen into a weak reflection of what it had been. Envoys accepted this diminishment, knowing it only lasted for the term of their service in the mundane world.

This must be why the courier was in such a hurry to leave. He could feel his powers blurring.

The door was still open. Her father smiled at her, urging her to continue. To repair the disgrace that they had somehow incurred.

With a last, faltering smile at her father, Liesa turned to the courier. The trap door was still open from when he had arrived. The depths beneath it glowed faintly, making it seem that in the murky shed they were about to leave a darker, lesser world and enter a more vibrant one.

They descended the stairs and entered the paths between. With the shock of events, she had not even begun to think of what was to come. She would enter the *crossings*, the network of branching tunnels between the realms. She had no idea what to expect.

Except for the fact that she had been there once before. When she was eight years old, and against her father's warnings, she had gone into the shed where the entrance was. Ordinary citizens wondered how to access the crossings, but no one thought to search for them in humble, even rundown places. In Barlow County, the entryway was in a shed that her father had built twenty-some years before.

She remembered her dread as she had lifted the hatch in the shed floor, curiosity pushing her like a strong hand against her back. And the moist, yeasty smell as she descended the short staircase into the tunnels. Although she had brought a flashlight, she didn't turn it on because the tunnel glowed softly from everywhere at once. Then she heard—or maybe imagined—muffled, echoing voices. Turning, she fled back to the stairs, taking them two at a time. She was never so glad to see the flat, open desert that met her as when she burst through that shed door.

And now here she was again, in her twenty-first year, deep in the unmistakable, heavy air of the crossings.

Liesa stood in the strange tunnel, with its gloaming light and the fecund odor she remembered so well. The Numinasi was patient as she took in her surroundings. The ground beneath her feet—and the whole tunnel—seemed to be a rubbery material she could not begin to identify. It was pale gray, pebbly, and hard; the high ceiling, roughly rounded. No clear source of light, yet she could see all the way to a distant turn in the path.

As they walked, and things were no longer in a rush, she recognized the clutching feeling in her chest for what it was. Fear.

Fear of what waited for her. Her father had said that the Numinat had renounced machines. She was going to a place that would be almost primitive. But her father always spoke of it fondly. A simpler life. A better one. She tried to believe it.

The tunnel narrowed. It had been twice her height and wide enough for four or five to walk abreast, but now it was half that size. Her breath came in little gasps and her heart sped. She went into a crouch and held her head in her hands.

To her surprise, the courier—the guard as she now thought of him—sat down beside her, handing over a leather pouch shaped like a bladder. He urged her to drink. The cool water helped her disordered thoughts to subside. In that stunned quiet she heard faint clanking noises like someone carrying a boxful of bells, some of which clinked together and others rang softly.

For comfort, Liesa rubbed at her smart watch beneath her shirt sleeve. A forbidden object, no doubt, since it would likely be considered a machine.

As she sank into the first peaceful moments since the stranger had appeared in their yard, she considered what kind of trouble her father was actually in. Was it just that he had been out of touch, or were envoys not supposed to have children? By the guard's attitude, she wasn't sure the mistake was a small one.

Her father had kept his daughter a secret even before senility began stalking him. Then the truth of it came to her. He had done so because he didn't want to be alone. Her mother died giving birth to her. And she was all her father had.

"Did I have a choice?" she asked the Numinasi, unsure if he would allow a real conversation. "About coming with you?"

"Your father chose."

"Could he have chosen otherwise?"

"Yes. But he chose well." He stood up. "We will continue."

"What is your name?" Liesa countered.

"I am in service to the court."

So no personal details. "Why are we in a hurry?"

"The princip sent me. She wishes your father to be brought back from the mundat. You also, since you have . . . happened."

Mundat. Their term for the regular, mundane world, where magic was nearly dead. She handed him the water skin and they walked on. And that word, *princip*; she didn't ask who the princip was, not wanting to reveal her ignorance.

The corridor at times branched off at odd angles, and some of those branches were more like caves, because she could see to the end of them. Others led into distances, perhaps to places that were not Numinat, but the other kingdoms of the Mythos.

Liesa tried to remember her father's tales of the Mythos realms. As she grew older, she had come to understand that they were—and also were not—stories. That the Mythos worlds came from the closely held legends of the mundat. And while they did really exist in their way, they were called forth by the engines of magic and, once formed, retained those connections to the origin world. The world she had just left behind.

She allowed herself a growing curiosity to see something of these realms. Their wonders, the places of wizardry, realms that were related to, but forever altered from, their former home.

Out of nowhere, like a long-forgotten song, a childhood recitation came to her: The chant of the Nine: fore-*knowing,* mani-*festing,* ward-*ing,* heal-*ing,* crea-*tures,* ver-*dure,* a-*ligns,* el-e-*ments,* prim-al *roots.* The nine powers. One of these would be hers, now that she was to be in the Mythos. She held her breath for a moment, testing to see whether a flicker of enchantment lay somewhere in her being, especially her left hand. But there was nothing.

They came to a side tunnel leading upward. To her relief, it spread wide as though it were more heavily used. The main one continued on, but they would depart here. The Numinasi went ahead, confident that she would follow.

As she trailed after him, she carefully pulled up her shirt cuff to check the time on her watch. The screen had gone dead. The time readout, gone. Email gone. Internet gone.

She was on her own.

THEY EMERGED INTO A FORTIFICATION. LIESA TOOK IN THE HIGH walls of mortared stone, soldiers wearing quilted jackets and fur-wrapped leggings. Swords at their sides, gleaming in a dusky light. Her guard exchanged a few words with one of them, and they passed through into the fort's courtyard. From walkways on the walls, soldiers watched them, as though she and her guard—and not whatever was on the outside—were the enemy.

He took her to a low wall behind which was a trench. By the smell, she knew what it was for. She had expected simple ways, but *this* . . . Perhaps the primitive sanitation was just at this fort. Though she had expected medieval, she hadn't really grasped the likely conditions. The lack of conveniences. When she finished relieving herself, a female soldier approached. She wore the same quilted jacket and trousers as everyone, and her hair was pulled into a bun at the back of her head. Small knives crisscrossed through it. She held out a bulky pile of clothes.

Unfolding the stack, Liesa noted that it was a long, heavy dress. Incredibly, she was supposed to wear it.

She was tired, hungry, and cross, and now required to wear a ridiculous gown. "What is this *for*?"

"It is how one dresses," the soldier said in Numinasi as though explaining the obvious.

"It's not what *you're* wearing," Liesa said, hoping to talk her out of the dress.

With some kindness, the woman responded, "But you are going to Osta Kiya."

There was no hope for it. She had to wear the dress, a situation that irked her all out of proportion. But she was in their world now, and if she was going to make demands, it wouldn't start with what to wear.

The gown was a dour shade of dark gray, with a voluminous skirt and tight sleeves and fitted bodice with a high neck. "Help me, please," Liesa said. The buttons were in the back and she thought she could get lost in all the folds of material.

When the woman had finished buttoning her up, she handed Liesa leather ankle boots, fur-lined gloves, and a water bladder with a sling to carry it crosswise over her chest. Liesa drank greedily as the soldier led the way out.

It was twilight, and Liesa wanted nothing more than to lie down and sleep, but instead her guard took charge of her again and led her out of the fort onto a hillside where grasses swayed in the wind. Overhead, clouds raced across the sky as though fleeing something. The soldiers on the wall were still looking down at the courtyard.

"What are they watching for?" she asked the Numinasi.

"Raids."

"But they're not looking out here." Liesa turned her gaze to the prospect before them. They were on a low saddle between two rocky outcroppings. The land sloped to an immense plain bearing, in the distance, tall buttes like ships upon a calm sea.

"If the Volkish come, it will be through the crossings," he said.

"The Volkish?"

"Well, we would have no need of a garrison without enemies."

Something moved on the near hillside, startling her. A great hump of glistening silver.

The hump was alive. Stepping quickly backward, Liesa caught her breath. A huge creature, twice the size of their old flatbed truck, slowly lifted its wings and lowered them, catching the last of the sun on its scaled body. Grass hid what looked to be four legs.

It swung its head around to regard them with a baleful stare and, as though it had been asleep, yawned, exposing teeth and a bright red tongue. Its elongated skull bore a sharp crest, and as the animal stretched its wings to their full length they were as wide as a small airplane's.

"A dactyl," the Numinasi informed her.

Alarmingly, on its back it bore a rigging that looked like a saddle.

৯১৯

THEY FLEW. THE GUARD WHO HAD ESCORTED HER FROM THE mundat was seated in front of her on one of the two saddles. On her own saddle, she lay flattened against the heavy leather out of sheer terror.

On the hillside the guard had asked her whether she would like to be tied into the saddle, and she had nodded numbly, resigned to flying on the back of the dactyl, a beast that mythology had termed *dragon*, but that here, actually existed.

"In a *dress?*" she had asked plaintively.

In answer, he handed her a long, heavy coat.

She asked how far they had to go. He said that it would take half the night to get to their destination. To Osta Kiya, presumably. Whatever that was.

Evening came on as they flew over a prairie with, here and there, clusters of homes amid plots of cultivated grain. Low green hills in the distance grew as they approached. In the deepening night, Liesa looked down on a ridge and spied a pack of wolves loping along, wild creatures knowing their territory and commanding it. This was the realm of the Numinasi. This was the place they had fled to when people of the mundat could not tolerate them, hated their strange ways and their magic. They had called themselves Numinasi or Numina, a term that alluded to the connection between matter and spirit, the land and the heart. But to the mundat they were witches. Liesa looked down on the hills, wanting to sense that numinous connection, but feeling only apprehension.

The moon was full or nearly full—it was the same moon as earth's, she noted—and it turned the land into black and white shapes and vistas. She hung on, hunkering down to stay out of the wind. The guard steered with reins attached to the dactyl's great head, held in place by a webbing of braided leather.

As the dactyl flew on, her legs and groin grew sore from her unnatural posture. The heavy wool ropes that tied her were loose enough to allow room to move, and she bent her legs so she could form herself to the dactyl's back. Her exposed ankles scraped against the creature's scales, but they were also radiating heat, since the dactyl was apparently warm-blooded.

Clouds moved over the sky, erasing the stars.

Liesa dozed, waking now and then, always startled to find herself flying far above the landscape, but even that danger could not keep her awake for long. Once, she heard thunder and then again as she fitfully slept.

A shout woke her. It was raining hard. The guard yelled for her to hang on to the ropes, as the dactyl's great wings beat harder and faster than before. Lashing rain glistened against the creature's scales and against the coat they had given her, which so far had kept her core mercifully dry. In the downpour, with her body plastered flat, all she could see was the saddle and a small portion of the dactyl's upper body. The storm was very near. Soon they were in the midst of it and, with the roaring thunder, she clung in terror to the saddle. She was learning in those moments what terrified her the most, and it wasn't heights or the prospect of death. It was sound, the roar of the sky, beneath which one could only cower. Because they were in the throat of the storm, and it was howling, broken now and again with the most terrible bellows she had ever heard, including in Oklahoma.

Oklahoma. It was Liesa's last thought before the entire sky turned neon blue and the air around them shuddered and screamed. She was thrown upward and, suspended for a moment in midair but held by the ropes, she saw that the edge of the saddle was in flames, and as she crashed down to the dactyl's back, she knew how, in that deluge, she would die.

By fire.

CHAPTER 3

Kirjanichka, listen to your friend Dreiza: These are the things that I dare tell no one else, only you. It relieves my heart to speak of these things, even if only in a whisper. My great friend, I knew what was coming to Numinat. Yes, I knew, but my foreknowing was blocked by attachment, my desire to have things remain the same. I had my circle, I was of the circle, and could not imagine being out of it, and so my sight was clouded.

You, Kirjanichka, who live a solitary life, will find it hard to understand how I could have been so foolish. Oh, it was so very easy. I had lived seventy-eight years, only half of my allotted time. I had a handsome husband, I had standing in the court and the regard of the new princip, who in her youth had no interest in my supposed past mistakes. I lived in this great city-palace of Osta Kiya, far from the drab lives of the outlying polities. Life was sweet and my days lapped gently on my mind.

Then came the girl in the storm. She blew in as though on a gust, pathetic and broken. She had no power and we all pitied her. Well. Everyone but Nashavety, who hated her on sight. When she arrived, life changed for so many, and not just for me.

Yes, yes, I am getting to the point, you need not give me that look!

But it comes to me first to speak of circles. Of how during leavings and arrivings, the circle is broken for a brief time. Reforming the circle usually makes the bonds stronger. But sometimes it is fatal to the old circle.

Every story ever told is about someone entering the circle, usually unwelcomed. I did not welcome the mundat girl, why should I, who had so much to lose? Here is what you do not know, Kirjanichka. Even old women want things. Why does everyone think the old are ready to let go, to quietly release? It is not so. Embers can burn as dearly as fire.

So, as I said, the girl came amongst us.

CHAPTER 4

S he bent over the dead girl for a closer look.

"It is just as well," Nashavety said. "Bravely done, no doubt, to ride a dactyl through a storm, but as she is ugly, she will be happier dead." She looked at Valenty, who was also peering at the body. "Do you not think so?"

"Of course, lady. But there is a problem."

Nashavety waited for the insufferable Valenty to go on.

"She is not dead."

Nashavety looked more closely at the envoy's daughter, laid out on the bed in the poorly lit room. "Not dead?"

"No. She is severely burned, but still breathing. At least her chest rises and falls. That means she is alive, I believe?"

Valenty made it a point of pride to know little, and even worse, to brag about it. Nashavety looked the girl over more carefully. Yes, she was breathing. She was thin as a wraith and her skin, ashen. Her long, dark hair lay in filthy gobbets around her face. By the healing gauzes that wound around the girl's body, Nashavety surmised that the burns covered her lower back and right shoulder as well as her neck and just over one side of her jaw. Other than that, the girl might be said to be attractive. A high forehead, a pleasing oval face, and a generous mouth. Her long neck was without a sag, and could have been her best feature if it had not been ruined by lightning.

"Someone must pay for what has happened," she murmured.

"Yes, of course. Who would you suggest?"

Ignoring this question, she peeked under the blanket that covered half the girl's body. The legs, thin and bare, were pale as an ocelot in winter. The healer had left one foot bare, but the other still bore a leather boot that had melted onto her foot. She replaced the blanket. "Perhaps," Nashavety said hopefully, "she may yet die."

"Perhaps," Valenty replied, having looked away as Nashavety inspected the girl's lower regions.

Nashavety's mood darkened. It would have been very agreeable if this young woman had died. It would have been an omen against foreign adventurism. She had been imagining a speech to that effect for the next court assembly. By the Nine, this turn of events was aggravating.

She looked down at the newcomer. This young woman—Yevliesza, it must be, since Liesa was not a proper name—would have a freakish nature. She was a child of Numinat, but mutilated, one in whom the Deep did not run. After they disposed of her father, she would be without family. Something would have to be done about the creature. She would put her mind to it.

A noise at the door. The royal personage entered, leaving her entourage behind. Nashavety and Valenty lowered their heads in a bow to Princip Anastyna. A petite frown of worry crossed the royal's face as she saw the disfigured creature lying before her.

Nashavety would have to counter the impulses of pity and horror that the princip would likely spread amongst the court. Is one horrified to put down a sick horse? Does one pity a clumsy and erring Numinasi struck by lightning?

She felt a sneer begin to form on her lips, but managed a

respectful calm instead, as Anastyna bent closer to the girl to see what fate had wrought.

◈

LIESA DREAMED. THE STORM WAS COMING AND INSTEAD OF charging down the road toward home, the Celica lost more and more power the harder she pressed on the gas pedal. The sky bloomed orange and brown. Small funnels dipped down to test their power, snapping back up. The big one was sucking all the energy up into its hulking, immanent self. Her father was alone at the house with the shutters not yet up. Shane appeared to be driving, resentful that he'd had to leave Rolly behind at the store. She was in the back seat trying to flatten herself against the rear bucket seats, but there wasn't enough room and one foot was sticking out the window. It hurt. She called out to Shane, but he could barely drive in the rising wind. Voices calling her, father asking what was for supper. Liesa had forgotten to buy supplies, so there wouldn't be anything to eat. The car pierced a wall of wind, dust, and debris. Everything blew sideways within it. TVs, a shovel, laptop, hubcaps and a dog. Her father stood by the side of the road trying to catch his papers. At the house, someone opened the car door for her, but instead of helping her out, the person, a woman with a metal cuff around her neck, shook her head. "You'll be safer in the car. There's no room in the house." Her foot hurt, and alarmingly, also her back and her arm. She asked Shane if they'd been in an accident. He said, "Yes, and someone has to pay."

Liesa rose and fell, rose and fell, from sleep to consciousness and back. Voices. People touching her. Sleep contained tornadoes. Waking brought pain through her whole body.

In the dark, a candle. Someone was urging her to drink. She

sat up with the help of the person with the candle. The pain had subsided. They held her shoulders and offered a cup of water.

It took a great effort to swallow, but she felt better for it.

"What is this place?" she whispered. It was hard to see in the gloom, but she sensed around her massive, cold stone walls.

"Osta Kiya, of course."

The words didn't register. Already she was sinking back into Oklahoma. "Is there room for me?" she asked.

As she fell back to sleep, she heard, "We must await outcomes."

CHAPTER 5

Days and nights came like unwelcome visitors. One, loud and bright, pushing into the room and demanding attention; the other a vast darkness filled with skittering, random thoughts and gong-like warnings. A young woman changed her bandages and sometimes rubbed the bad side of her, ministrations that should have hurt—even turning on the bed hurt —but instead softened the pain.

When Liesa's thoughts at last cleared, she asked where she was—*Osta Kiya, as we have told you*; Was her father here—*yes*; Can I see him—*no,* with a frown; Would her wounds heal—*yes*. She learned that the courier had not fared as badly as she. He was well, considering what had happened.

She continued to ask where her father was and if she could see him, but no one would answer her. One of the women who came in to check her bandages had the grace to act regretful about not giving her information. But not regretful enough, apparently.

One day Liesa was able to practice walking. She had done well until she tried to stand on a table near a high window. As dizziness struck, she steadied herself against the wall, leaning her forehead against cold stone. With her eyes closed, the storm came back to her: the wind yanking her clothes and hair, even, she swore, lifting the scales on the dactyl. It seemed to her that it had been the same storm as at home. There on the plains it had hovered and then moved on; but it touched down as she flew toward Osta Kiya, in whatever correlations the two worlds shared. It gave her comfort to think that the worlds had a connection besides cramped tunnels smelling of yeast.

When the dizzy spell passed, she leaned out the gap of the window—there being no glass pane—and at last took in the view.

Osta Kiya was a castle, or a fortress, more like, built on a steep outcropping. She had been told that it sat on the rocky summit of a massif and that it had many levels, chambers, wings and towers. It was not only a castle, it was a city, with dwellings and pathways clinging to the hillside.

Across an enormous courtyard she could see another wing of the castle, four stories high with sloping roofs, piles of chimneys and, framing the roof, very serious-looking battlements. It was a harsh view, darkly feudal, and not at all what she had hoped it would be. Yet they had cared for her, helped her to heal. It might yet be what her father had promised. A home.

She and her father still had to answer for the transgression of not returning to Numinat. Liesa herself would have refused to return, but her father had a loyalty to Numinasi ways. He said it was a matter of honor, but it was an honor that he had managed to ignore even before dementia made him forget.

One day a young servant came to her room with a dress. She filled a basin with water and with wet cloths helped Liesa wash her hair and bathe. After that they began the methodical work of getting her into the dress which was much like the one she had received at the fort, except beautifully made. The sleeves were tight all the way to her shoulders and soft as down. The skirt, gathered and full, fell to the instep of her new boots. The gown's dusty blue fabric was quilted across the snug chest and swooped up to form a frame around her neck. She expected the tight bodice to hurt, but her burns only itched. The girl combed her hair around her shoulders, patiently detangling the knots.

"Where is my . . . bracelet?" she asked. But the girl knew nothing. It galled her to think they had felt free to take her watch and no doubt destroy it or bury it or whatever they did to machines.

The purpose of the bath and the dress was soon apparent, as the servant told her that royal household guards awaited her. The two guards wore brown velvet tunics to their thighs with finely tooled leather belts and close-fitting trousers tucked into leather boots. Emblazoned on their chests, a white circle.

The guards didn't say where they were taking her. It might be to a judge or a coven of witches—a term she knew better than to use here. Her father had said it showed ignorance and contempt. It was a mundat word, from people who feared what they didn't understand.

They ascended winding stone stairs from the lower floor to one with soaring open-air windows and lofty ceilings webbed in shadows. Here she saw many inhabitants of the palace, with a variety of skin tones, light and dark. Most of them wore clothes of fine materials, women in deep blues, purples, blacks and grays, men more colorfully, but all, men and women alike, richly dressed. People back home wondered if men could be witches. And of course, they could be and were.

But a different question had been looming in her mind: what was *she?*

The long dress that she wore made her feel less of a foreigner. That, and her black hair, though one woman's hair shimmered with a deep violet color. Liesa was certain it didn't come from a bottle.

One man outright stared at her, and when she stared back, he touched his mouth with the little finger of his right hand. It was a rude gesture. Her father had taught her never to raise a little finger, and particularly not to her face.

"Keep your eyes lowered," one of the guards ordered. They came to a tall foyer dominated by massive doors of carved wood, inlaid with bold strands of metal.

"The princip?" she asked.

"She receives you in the Numin Room with the sacred pool," he said. "You will find yourself before Princip Anastyna and some of the *fajatim*. Do not lie or argue. If you stand tall and calm, it may go well."

She held onto his words, and as she entered the room where all the faja-whatevers stood waiting, she managed to keep her expression bland.

The room held a small group of people milling and chatting near a low half-wall. Some of them turned to regard her, with flat, appraising gazes. A woman in an elaborate silver-gray gown stared at her as though she were a giraffe in the court of an English queen. Next to her, a strikingly handsome man with whitish-blond hair wearing a long cloak over court garb.

A ripple behind the low wall drew her attention; it was a circular pool of water about fifteen feet across. Above it in the ceiling was a small round opening that allowed a shaft of light to strike the water.

The knot of people parted to reveal a young, pale woman dressed in a dark grey dress sparkling with glitter or precious stones. Her face was heart-shaped and in place of the high neck-lines of the other women, she wore a silver choker. Curiously, on one arm she wore a long glove.

"Yevliesza," this person said to her.

In the silence that followed, Liesa realized she was supposed to respond. "I don't know that word, ma'am."

A long-faced woman dressed in midnight blue murmured just loud enough to be heard, *"Ma'am?* Is the princip to be addressed so?"

A man in a blood-red jacket turned to Liesa and said with a moue of distaste, "In proper manners, you will say 'My Lady Princip.'"

"My Lady Princip," Liesa said, feeling the air thicken around her, swirling with curiosity and malice.

The princip nodded. "Very well. And so." She made a pleasant smile. "You will be called Yevliesza, a proper Numinasi name."

"But my name is Liesa."

A guard strode up to her and struck her across the face. Pain radiated in every direction. It was not a serious blow, but Liesa staggered, holding her stinging cheek.

"She is a visitor," someone said, disapproving of the slap. The man had a commanding aspect, wearing, over dark suitings, a long sleeveless coat of brown and yellow. "She is of the mundat, and one hears they have no royals there and because of this no need of proper address." He spoke Numinasi with a heavy accent and when he frowned, as he did just then, he looked like someone you wouldn't want to displease.

"It may be, Lord Chinua," the princip said. "But she is here now." She flicked her hand at the guard, who retreated a few steps. "And so. What is your name, young woman of the mundat?"

Liesa paused. These people could kill her. Drown her in that pool behind them, or take out their anger on her father. "Yev-lee-za," she managed to whisper.

The princip, who had been standing this whole time, seated herself on the edge of the pool. As she did so, a bird flew down from the skylight and landed on her fist. It looked like a hawk or a falcon. Once it settled, the princip addressed the group. "Now that Yevliesza has come amongst us, who will board her? She must have a household to speak for her."

The woman with the long face and midnight blue gown said, "No one here need take her in. Send her to a village to learn our customs. And manners."

Liesa's heart crimped. These people intended to keep her. "I am the daughter of an envoy," she said, hoping not to receive another blow but not caring a lot.

Long-face said, "A daughter who is in a ruined state. Plain."

"My Lady Nashavety," Red-jacket said. "Powers do come in degrees." He spread his arms, inviting people to agree with him. "Perhaps her degree is *none?*"

Someone tittered, and Long-face swung around to note them. Turning back to Liesa, she said, "You, who were born of Numinasi, are not Numinasi."

"If I'm not, it's not my fault nor my father's. We were abandoned in . . . the mundat."

Anastyna said, "That is a fair point." Absently, the princip petted the bird's head.

The man in red flattened his lips into the smallest of smiles, as though starting to enjoy the show.

Lady Nashavety continued, "Did you ever try to come home? Back before you were too old, when you could have welcomed your natural Deepening instead of being bereft of power?" A smile twitched at the corners of her mouth.

There it was then, the sticking point. Her family's misstep or insult. She should have come to Numinat one way or the other. Then she would have received her power, and now—if she gathered what the woman was saying—she was too old.

The question came again. "Did you ever try to come home?"

She had not, but she thought it best to keep silent.

Long-face sighed. "Not very bright, then." She looked around at the others, trying to draw them in. "Did you even bother to learn about your true people?"

"Yes. A little."

Now her adversary allowed a sneer to cross her face. "And still, never sought them."

Liesa felt the weight of the moment press down on her. "I . . ." She considered the guard's warning about lying. "I never thought about it."

A raised eyebrow from her inquisitor. "Then not very loyal, either."

The princip held up a hand. "Enough. We have learned what we had need of. Therefore let us decide which polity she can be sent to, in order that she can become more suitable."

"A polity can easily be found, My Lady Princip," Red-jacket said. "But someone here might keep her."

"But who, Lord Valenty?" the princip asked.

"I will do so," he said. The group stirred, several sliding glances at the woman in midnight blue who looked at this Valenty person like a wolf at a rabbit.

The rabbit turned in Liesa's direction. "I have no great Hall, but we can supply refuge for a visitor such as this who will need to"—he waved his hand, fluttering his fingers—"learn how to dress and comport herself, things of that sort." He turned a cheerful look on Nashavety. "What do you think?"

The woman opened her mouth to let him know, but the princip rose, interrupting her.

"Lord Valenty, this is graciously done. May not a young girl's mistake be excused, given her imperfect upbringing?" She rose and, with a small lift of her arm, let fly the falcon which skimmed close to Liesa's head, forcing her to duck. Several of the nobles chuckled as the bird swept up to the rafters. "You may proceed, Lord Valenty," the princip said.

He came forward, taking Liesa by the arm.

Things had concluded quickly, before she could give her side of things. Was Valenty's household a good place to be? At least he didn't seem hostile, like the rest of them.

With the lord gripping her arm, she repressed the urge to yank away. Nashavety was watching her, everyone was.

Anastyna fixed Lord Valenty with a narrow gaze. "We will expect her to know the ways and customs, my lord."

"Yes, Lady Princip," he murmured, patting down his hair, which was combed behind his ears.

The princip considered Liesa with a doubtful expression. "She has far to go."

Long-face smiled. Maybe she had never learned how to smile naturally, because it didn't look good on her.

The meeting had not gone well. She was leashed to a man she didn't know and though she had just gotten there, she had already made an enemy. Bitterness welled up at the unfairness of the hearing. Her captors were barbarians. They lived in what appeared to be the Middle Ages and spent a good deal of time frowning over outsiders while demanding that they come to see you.

Still holding her arm, Valenty walked her out of the room, leaving the guards behind.

She risked a question. "My father is here. Please, may I see him?"

"Asking for favors already," the lord murmured with an air of hopelessness.

"Where is he, though?" She knew she was pushing. But calmly, calmly.

"He is held in confinement."

The thing she had feared. "But he's been sick for years. Please, at least let me see him, show him that I'm all right."

"All right?" the lord said, propelling her down the corridor. "Do you imagine that you are?"

"No," she hastened to say.

"Good," he said, nodding graciously to some of the women they passed. "A little common sense from the wench, then."

She took a slow breath of stone-cold air. She despised him already.

CHAPTER 6

N ine days after her encounter with the princip, she woke as dawn slithered through the narrow lancet windows. Her bed in the dormitory was furthest from the windows, bordering the hall to the latrine. Point made. She was a disgraced Numinasi, who had failed to report home even if she had never known where home was.

They saw no mitigating circumstances about her upbringing, because who in the thirteenth century, or whatever year the Numinasi planned to stay in permanently, had ever heard of dementia? They didn't want her here, and she didn't want to be here, so it should all work out grand, but obviously it hadn't.

Sitting up and slipping into her underthings and shift, she made her way to the latrine which was, thankfully, at least a little like a bathroom. She used the hand pump to splash water on her hands and face. It surprised her that water pipes or channels ran through parts of the castle, a modern convenience she hadn't expected here.

Pulling her shift down, she brought a handful of water to her neck and side. Her burns had healed, or almost healed, but she suffered from bouts of dizziness and worst of all, itchiness. She didn't know how bad her burns looked because they were on her back and on areas of her upper arm and neck that were impossible to see. And there were no mirrors.

It could have been worse, Liesa reminded herself. The lightning could have struck her face and she would have been deformed, or more likely, dead, like the poor dactyl.

So far, her days began with lessons on the *Book of Ways and Customs*, all the hundreds if not thousands of rules of Osta Kiya that included laws, obligations, customs, governance and, of course, manners. There were other books in the lord's collection that she was not to touch, not when her tutor Master Grigeni was around, anyway. An exception was the grimoire, Valenty's project that he had everyone working on. It was a compilation from his grandmother's time on the uses of small powers in a household, such as banishing dust (warding), keeping mites and spiders away (creatures). Valenty's grandmother had collected the household uses of powers all her one hundred and forty-seven years. Numinasi lived a long time, one hundred and fifty years, if it could be believed, and at that milestone it was considered polite to expire, which most did, or shortly before.

Aside from ways and customs, Liesa had learned a smattering of history, a subject she had always loved. So some days she enjoyed her lessons. Yesterday she had asked how big the realm was, and were there other kingdoms in it besides the one that Anastyna ruled. Her teacher had said that no one quite knew how large the realm was, because it was still growing. As to growing where, the answer seemed to be the primordial lands—wild, recently formed places. And yes, the princip ruled the entire populated area and always would. As to how the realm could be growing, Grigeni had scrunched up his face and answered, to his satisfaction but not hers, "It grew in the first place. And continues."

On her way through Valenty's apartments to her lessons,

another bout of dizziness welled up. She steadied herself with a hand against the wall, and it passed.

The noise of a door closing brought her back. A young woman hurried down the corridor toward her. More footfalls as a man caught up with her, taking her arm. She turned to him and they fell into an embrace, enjoying a long, groping goodbye. When the man pulled away, she saw that it was Valenty. The girl scurried past Liesa, straightening her disheveled clothes, not noticing the witness in the shadows.

The lord was sleeping with a servant. Liesa considered how there might be advantages to being covered with ugly welts.

She made her way toward the household kitchen, the only room that was ever warm. Eyeing the bread rising on the shelf over the fire pit, she received a narrow glance from the cook who pointed to a bowl of fruit on the work table. Liesa took an apple, thanking the cook, and was still devouring it when she arrived in the scriptorium where she had been helping to mix dyes. There the steward informed her that she was summoned to Valenty's study and would have to change her clothes and net her hair suitably.

Back in the dormitory Liesa found her hair net had been gnawed on by rats or cut with a knife.

She decided that haste was more important than formality—and it would be better not to complain of vandalism in the household—and so she presented herself to Valenty as she was.

Woven tapestries covered the walls of the lord's study and a finely patterned rug softened the floor. Valenty sat behind an ornate table that served as a desk. This was the second time she had seen him—third, if she included the tryst in the hallway—and this time he was dressed in brown velvet suitings and a vest of burnt gold ornamented with silver clasps. His dark hair curled tightly, barely restrained by the ribbon that tied it into a queue in back. On a tanned face, his dark brows slashed over his eyes, and his mouth often skewed to one side in a dismissive smile. He was handsome in an aristocratic way, with an air of amusement as though he found life trivial and preferred it that way.

A man in a cape stood at Valenty's side. It was the man with blond-white hair she had seen in the Numin Room. He had the kind of face that made you want to look just a little longer than you should. She found herself scratching her neck, not the deportment she wanted to show in front of these men, but the burns made her crazy.

"I was not expecting you in such haste," Lord Valenty said. He looked at her dress and hair with dismay.

"Promptness is a virtue," the other man chided him. His skin was very pale, but a healthy blush on his cheeks gave him a vibrant aspect.

The lord of the household drawled, "Who could expect promptness, Lord Tirhan, since it took her twenty years to pay a visit to her cousins?"

"Yes, but with the treatment she has received, can she be blamed?"

"I'm not afraid of getting blamed for things," she ventured to say. "As long as they aren't true."

That drew a wide smile from Valenty's guest. Though she wished to make a good impression on both of them, an itch on her shoulder overtook her, and she discreetly rubbed at it.

"Woman," Lord Valenty said, "stop scratching. My household will be accused of harboring fleas."

The white-haired lord rolled up a scroll that he had been showing Valenty. "I will leave you to this most interesting discussion, my lord. Thank you for making time for me so early in the day."

Valenty yawned. "I was told it was of the utmost. As it happens, it is the same problem you seem always to have and are under the strange impression that I can assist you." He said this lightly, but, it seemed, with warm regard.

When they were alone, Valenty said, "Now then, Yevliesza, how are you faring? As well as can be expected, given the circumstances?" He leaned back in his chair, looking quite comfortable with himself. She supposed he had a right to be, since he had taken her in to his household.

"I am surviving," Liesa said. She felt she should be grateful to him, but the way they kept her and her father apart was distressing, especially as they had come to Numinat willingly.

Hearing her answer, his eyes narrowed, having no doubt wanted to hear *as well as can be expected.* "The dactyl you rode on died, however."

"I heard."

"It was one of our best. It took thirty-five years to train it, so you must forgive the court if some wish it had been you instead."

Her fault, then. The list was growing.

After an appraising silence, Valenty rose and paced to the great window behind him, looking out into the massive central enclosure of Osta Kiya.

"How do you manage," Liesa asked, "with all the uncovered windows? If it rains or gets cold?"

He half-turned toward her. "Warding. Some of us are very good at it." He flicked his left hand at the window aperture, clouding it, then filling it with what looked like stone. The lift of a finger, and sunlight burst in again as though it had been penned up behind the window.

He examined his fingernails in a show of boredom.

"How is my father? Have you seen him?"

He turned, sizing her up. How much trouble she was going to be. Whether he might make some midnight use of her. "Your father. Well. He presents a problem. My own opinion is that the man was brave to accept envoyship to the mundat. He failed, but he did try. I will make sure it is known."

It was important to stay calm, she knew, but her pretense dissolved. "Don't bother, Lord Valenty," she murmured.

A bemused look crossed his face.

"It really won't do to tell it that way. You people forgot him. If you'd bothered to communicate with him you would have seen the state he was in." Tranquility forgotten now, unquiet fury took over. "You're punishing him for what you did, messing with me because I'm the closest thing on hand to blame this on. Even your queen doesn't believe the story."

Since he hadn't struck her yet, she went on, falling into all the words that had been gathering: "I'm still alive, but wondering how long I will be, if I've failed to learn some ancient custom from the book because I was in the wrong world and the wrong century and hadn't gone into the big tunnels and somehow found my way to this delightful place. So if you want to make the truth known, that's it right there."

Valenty came slowly around the desk like a panther. She braced herself.

Instead of the slap she expected, he put his hand under her chin and lifted her face as though to examine it. He tilted her head to one side to look at the scarring under her chin, his face quiet, showing nothing, then pinned her with a black gaze.

Finally he said, "On your way then." Releasing her, he flicked his hand at the door. "Do not wander too much. Once I lost a servant in the far reaches of this place for a tenday. She was from the polities and made the mistake of too high a self-regard."

❧

"WHAT IS THAT CONSTRUCT UP THERE?"

Liesa stared out the window at the beginnings of a narrow

stone bridge that, precariously, and high up at the fourth-story level, hung a quarter of the way over the central compound.

Her servant guide, Pyvel, looked to be about twelve. His energy and ready smile was a welcome relief from the mostly staid Numinasi—or at least the Numinasi she had met. At his age he still had his black hair cut short, but with an unruly fall of bangs. "The new bridgeway, miss," he answered. "The Bridge of the Moon. With all the work of the aligners, it gets a little bit longer every day."

To Liesa it seemed a very bad idea for it to get longer, as it had no supports except for a heavy buttress on the castle wall that anchored it. "Where will it lead?"

"Across the courtyard." He pointed up in the air. "It is on an align."

"An align in the air?"

"Aye. Sometimes. And wherever they are, aligners prefer to build along them. It is a custom, to go along with the world."

Going along with the world had made a jumble out of Osta Kiya, she thought, but kept it to herself.

Over the last few days Pyvel had taken her on tours around the city-fortress, into a bewildering array of wings, halls, balconies, galleries and staircases. They passed vaulted rooms, each with great fireplaces and furnished with divans and chairs. They paused at the opening to a chamber called Waxing Moon, where a glowing mosaic in the floor slowly shifted from new moon to full and back again under the care of manifesters.

On these tours she had learned that the place extended beyond what could be seen from courtyard windows, with accretions of annexes and rooms hugging the hillside like the legs of a great, exhausted creature. Today's tour took her through the spacious forecourt of Raven Fell Hall, one of the great houses presided over by Nashavety, the *fajatim,* or what they called speaker of the hall.

But through all of their wanderings, Liesa had not yet seen the thing she most needed to.

"Pyvel," she said at last, "show me the prison."

Pyvel looked at her skeptically. "The prison?"

She had delayed asking him, knowing that they were trying to keep her away from her father.

"I can show you the door. And it is not the *prison*, but the *nethers*."

"OK," she said, using the English word.

Pyvel squinted at her. "Oh-key?"

"Oh-kaay. A mundat term. It means sure, why not?"

A grin took over his face and off they went, descending a short staircase and then one more, in the castle's pattern of connecting just two floors at once. At last they stood before an unadorned double door. The nethers.

"Can we go through?"

He sized her up. "It is a hard place to be. Everything is mixed up, from the times when the First Ones built it to confuse enemies. It takes years to know your way."

"It's where Lord Valenty's servant got lost."

"And," he said, relishing the story, "she was half-starved when they found her."

"Right. So I'm only going if you're with me."

Pyvel grinned. "O . . . K. But just a little way in." He opened one side of the double door and they stepped through. A cold draft met them, smelling of soil and rot.

After descending a long stairway, they stood in a murky passageway with walls that looked to have been carved out of rock. Pyvel lifted his left hand, bringing a fringe of light that gilded his body and threw a soft glow on the walls.

"How did you do that?"

"My small power. Manifesting. There are nine of them—"

"I know. But that one is amazing."

"Nay, just crow power." His voice filled the space around them, clearly, wistfully. "If my Deepening had been a noble power, I would train to be a *harjat*. But I can go for a common soldier. They use manifesting to confuse the enemy."

"Powers come in degrees," she murmured, remembering that Valenty had said so.

"If you have a full hand—noble power—you can train in an arcana. Even a servant can, if they have a high gift."

"Arcana?"

"A group of three, and you have a guide. But not for the likes of us."

Nashavety had said that she had missed her chance of Deepening into her natural power. She wondered what it would have felt like to have magic slowly grow within her? She flexed the fingers of her left hand: open and closed, open and closed.

Pyvel traced his hand in the air around her and then Liesa was emanating the same cold light. The corridor surged more brightly, revealing rough cracks lined with moss and trickles of water.

"I love this," she whispered, marveling at what he had conjured.

He shrugged. "Some people even have two powers. Better ones than mine. Lady Nashavety has both elements and creatures."

"Lord Valenty?"

"Warding. A high gift."

"What about the princip?"

"She has creature power. In fact, she is so close to her falcon that it has become her *sympat*, seldom separated from her. It is never hooded and always calm around her."

"I've seen it. But it dove at me."

Pyvel smirked. "Then she urged it to."

As they walked down the passageway, they crossed a number of connecting tunnels, leaving her disoriented, but Pyvel moved with certainty. They passed deeply shadowed alcoves and closed, rusted doors. It was a place that had long fallen into disuse, except for rats that scrambled out of their path. At times a putrid smell arose. She had not known that her father was being kept in such a foul place. She had begun to think that these people could be decent, but how could they be with this almost casual choice to keep her father in filth?

"Where is my father's cell?" she asked her young guide.

"Somewhere here, they say. But miss, we cannot go to him. You need permission."

"I'm really worried about him. What would be the harm?"

"I will get in trouble. Please, miss. We should leave."

She had no right to endanger him. Her heart sinking, she relented and followed him as he retraced his steps.

"Does Numinat have capital punishment?" she asked as they went. "Death as a penalty?"

"Best not to think of that. We should hope for the best."

"If they kill someone, how is it done?"

Pyvel whispered, barely audible, "By falling. From the heights."

When Liesa got back to the household, her tutor was waiting for her at the entrance. Holding her gaze, he said that a servant of the envoy Lord Tirhan had brought something for her. Grigeni handed her a small package, raising an eyebrow to make clear that a gift from Lord Tirhan was most unusual.

To annoy him, she waited to open it until she was in the dormitory.

It was an earthen jar of ointment. A note in Numinasi, which took a great deal of time to decipher, read: *Please accept this salve from the Alfan people who use it with benefit for sores of the skin.*

She lifted the cover and raised the jar to her nose. It smelled gloriously of pine needles, eucalyptus, and rain.

CHAPTER 7

Kirjanichka, look, I have brought you a gift. Figs from Nubiah, your favorite.

So, my friend, where was I? Ah yes, the girl who fell from the sky.

Her arrival was unwelcome to me. I admit I was not fair to her, allowing resentment to grow like a mold. I know, Kirjanichka, I know. In my seventy-eight years I had time to prepare for tribulation. Who can be so foolish to think that life will not sometime bring suffering? But I had long ago found refuge with my Valenty and felt unassailable. At one time we had a princip who despised me, who wished to see me fall from the great tower and push me over herself. Then I came to Valenty's household, taking refuge with a man of noble lineage. Even the princip could not touch me once I was under his protection.

Then the girl of mundat arrived at Osta Kiya. She came to us sopping wet and half dead. We found her to be deformed, rude, and disruptive. She was very young, but fully grown, so she had the wits and determination to cloud our peace in many small ways. Ways that became like a crack in a rock, a seam that could

48   KAY KENYON

fill with icy doubts. Our visitor knew better than to confront us directly. Most times. I wanted to like her, but it was not easy.

Nashavety especially did not approve of her, and from the very start, which was to be expected considering her distaste for outsiders. She had a way of dismissing Lord Tirhan of Alfan Sih, and she even dared to show her disapproval of the Nubiah envoy Lord Chinua, whom everyone knew Anastyna had grown to admire. The fajatim dared much and, of course, much more as the days darkened into winter.

A part of me felt compassion for the mundat girl, but she was old enough not to make things worse for herself. She could have accepted us and bided her time. Instead she made enemies. And mistakes, grand mistakes.

But, truly, the whole matter was the princip's fault, or the old princip's, anyway. Naturally no one wanted to take responsibility. And so it fell completely on our visitor's shoulders.

I did what I could to help the girl, despite my vague fore-knowing of what would come and all that would be lost because of her. My intimations of the future taught me to be cautious, but not cruel. The visions formed and deformed, and what came to my hands remained cloudy. If I had heeded my power with true skill, I could have fended off the worst outcome. I could have forbidden her to enter our household. Valenty would have acquiesced—he is without foreknowing, so he would have listened to me.

But I said nothing, demanded nothing. I know, Kirjanichka, it is hard to believe your old friend Dreiza could be so timid. Yet I was. I watched her carefully, fearful that she would crack things open at Osta Kiya. I never imagined that it would be me who cracked.

CHAPTER 8

Yevliesza stood in her shift before a maid who held a voluminous dress collapsed into a heap that somehow would go over her head and fall into place.

She had finally accepted the name Yevliesza. If she had no other authority she could at least decide how to think, whether to allow a name to discount her or to divest it of its pain. Nearly three weeks had passed since her crossing, and she was beginning to find her stance in this city-palace: self-contained, calm and strong and watchful for any chance to push against Numinasi constraints. Secretly, she wanted to find her way back to the fort with access to the crossing, but it wouldn't be easy. At that moment it seemed impossible.

A person she hadn't met before, Lady Dreiza, supervised. Her household status was signaled by the richness of her dress, velvet with tiny jewels sewn in. The woman's hair, heavy with threads of grey, was bound into a twist at the back, netted in gold filigree.

Pulling the shift off Yevliesza's right shoulder, Lady Dreiza made a close inspection of the damage to her back. The silence wasn't a good sign.

"How does it look?" She had high hopes for the magic of

Numinasi healing. When she first arrived they had dressed her wounds with potions and pressed their hands against her back and neck. The pain always subsided under their ministrations. "Are they fading?"

"Do not worry," Lady Dreiza said in a worried tone. "The gown will cover them sufficiently. And if you are to be disfigured, you could take the pale, I suppose."

"What is that?"

"Become a *satvar*. A renunciate."

Yevliesza rolled her shoulders, unused to the close-fitting bodice and sleeves. "Maybe we could try something more loose-fitting?" Lord Tirhan's ointment had soothed her sores, but she had never worn tight clothes before, and she longed for sweat-pants and a hoodie.

Dreiza's face hardened around the creases of her face. Numinasi women were merely middle-aged even in their seventies and eighties, so no telling how old this high lady might be. *"Loose?"* Dreiza asked sourly. She flicked a gesture at the servant, and the gown descended over Yevliesza's head. Cascading down, the skirt fell in elegant gathers from her waist. As the servant buttoned up the back, Dreiza adjusted the high-necked collar.

Yevliesza trailed her hands over the metallic threads of the bodice's stitchery. "Fancy," she pronounced, hoping that a dress this fine might signal an improved status.

"You cannot be seen in drabs," Dreiza said. "Or so Lord Valenty will have it." She stepped back to view Yevliesza, nodding approvingly. "Our household reasons that perhaps if you have the apparel, the manners will follow."

Not an improved status, then. But Yevliesza maintained an untroubled expression. The guard's advice was proving to be an anchor. Act as though you are peaceful, and you may be peaceful, or at least deny your captors the satisfaction of distressing you.

When she was buttoned into the gown, she turned in a circle, letting the garment flow around her. "No mirror," she said in disappointment.

Dreiza frowned. "Mirrors cause mischief. It is all too easy for a manifester to send a vision into them." She gave a lopsided smile. "Some of those visages you would not wish to see."

The servant pulled Yevliesza's hair into a net, securing it with pins. As she did so, Yevliesza murmured, "I'm sorry that the dactyl died, Lady Dreiza. I know some people blame me for it. If the accident had happened in the old world, I would have called doctors to save it. It was a grand creature."

"That is ridiculous," Dreiza said. "You lived in a barbaric state, without kinship to the world. Without a power flowing through you. If this had happened in the mundat, I assure you, you would *both* be dead."

She wondered if that were true. Had she been saved by magic? "If the healers saved me, then I thank them for it." The old woman sniffed, not mollified. "Lady Dreiza," she dared to ask, "do you know why I'm not allowed to see my father?"

"Are you not allowed?"

"I've been asking, but Lord Valenty pushes the question off."

Dreiza scowled in what might be irritation at Valenty—or at her, for asking.

"My father is ill—in his mind—and if he's done something wrong, at least we should take good care of him. If my mother was alive, would she also be unfairly jailed?"

"She would be severely disciplined. And it would be fair." Dreiza held up her hand to forestall an argument. "You do not yet understand. With time you will learn how it is that a kingdom can be assailed by the outside world because it resides in a fragile cradle. And you would understand your error that neither your father—who was not always without his senses—nor you yourself when you came of age, came home for what forgiveness and healing might have been offered."

"So I can't see him," she said, refusing to concede.

Dreiza looked at her a long time. "Being right can be a heavy burden, Yevliesza. When you are poised on the ledge of the tower, you must watch your step."

"Why do the Numinasi hate the mundat?" Yevliesza blurted. "You'd think that it would be respected as the origin world, wouldn't you?"

Dreiza's face fell into a moue of exasperation. "Respected? We had to flee from its persecutions. And they were not satisfied with torture and murder. No, they must have their heavy and inimical machines that crippled our powers. And now, the small machines that can blow in on the wind. I think it is understandable that we are wary of them."

"But there are agreements, treaties . . . I think you're protected."

"My dear." Dreiza took a deep breath. "We do not hate the mundat. But in your case, people are alarmed that you are cut off from your birthright, your power, whatever it was to be. To us, that is an unthinkable misfortune. And for many, they do not see beyond that. They do not blame the mundat. But they do your father."

Yevliesza was about to come to his defense when there was a knock at the door.

When the servant opened it, Valenty stood on the threshold. "Dreiza, there you are! No one knew where you were, but lunch is served." He nodded at Yevliesza, then turned to Dreiza. "I have not had the honor of your company today."

Dreiza smiled indulgently and off they went, linking arms.

When the lady had gone, Yevliesza asked the servant, "Is Dreiza Lord Valenty's mother?" The woman had spoken of *our household*.

The girl's eyes widened. "Oh, nay, miss. She is his wife."

Back at the dormitory, and changed into her everyday dress,

Yevliesza managed to stuff the new gown into the chest near her bed. In a small drawer she placed a new hairnet decorated with garnets.

To her surprise her watch lay in the drawer. They had returned it. Maybe they didn't know what it was. Pulling up the sleeve of her dress, she strapped it on her right hand. The face was a rectangle of dark glass that resembled a stone in a bracelet. She rubbed the surface like a talisman. Her eyes grew hot with the memory of the place where such a screen would bring her the company of the world.

"ENOUGH," NASHAVETY TOLD HER STEWARD, DARALISKA. RISING from her chair behind the table piled high with scrolls, Nashavety stretched. If the work of the day could not be finished in two hours, then matters could wait. After six hundred years, Raven Fell had not yet collapsed from unfinished paperwork.

Her steward sniffed. "We are not done."

"No, but I will see my niece. What was her name, again?"

"Sofiyana," Daraliska responded with a droll look. "Of Karsk polity."

"Ah yes. What does she want?"

"Your sister has sent her to apply for arcana after she refused to marry as directed."

Hells. "In other words, my lady sister wants to be rid of the trouble of a headstrong daughter."

"I am afraid so." Her arms full of scrolls, Daraliska looked even wider than usual. But her bulk made her strong and capable of taking on the endless details of the Hall.

Dismissing her, Nashavety left the day-study to enter her formal office where the girl from Karsk stood waiting.

"Ah, Sofiyana, a pleasure." Nashavety took a seat behind her desk, with her back to the window, leaving her niece staring into the glare of the day. "You have grown up."

"Yes, my lady *fajatim*."

In fact she had grown beautiful. Small, inoffensive features— not the finest, but the glory of her hair made up for all, her profuse ringlets intensely violet.

"And how is House Cherev and your lady mother?"

"She prospers, my lady, and wishes to prosper more."

That earned the girl a pointed stare.

"Or, I mean, she manages the family with skill." Seeing that the *fajatim* was not yet satisfied, she added, "She has arranged matches for my brothers and has considered one for me."

"Whom you find unsuitable."

"Well, but he is old. And bald."

"And you prefer handsome, no doubt." Nashavety wished, with all her elemental gift, that her sister's crops be visited by torrential rains, to have sent such a simpering girl to Raven Fell.

"Did you make the journey by carriage or horseback?"

"Oh, carriage, my lady."

"So you do not ride." Nashavety kept her expression neutral, but any woman of birth who did not know how to ride . . .

"Which languages do you have?"

"I know a little Norslad."

Very little, Nashavety guessed. She played with the ancestral ring on the second finger of her left hand. Perfectly preserved within the amber stone was a tiny claw from an immature dactyl. She was tempted to send the girl home—by horseback.

"What is your birthright power? Or, perhaps more than one?"

"Aligns, my lady."

Everyone wanted the aligns. Following the crowd, this ringletted, shallow girl. She fixed her niece with a cold gaze that over years she had sharply honed. "Sofiyana. Given your few skills, I think I shall send you back to your household in the outlands. You have insulted your mother and her choice for you."

Sofiyana had the sense to look stricken and remain silent.

"Unless you bring honor to Raven Fell I have no use for you."

"But my lady aunt—"

"You will address me as Lady Nashavety. Surely you see that I do not wish to claim blood ties to a hapless girl from the polities?"

"Yes, lady. But if I could take arcana training, it would teach me the discipline I lack. And I would dedicate my gifts to the practice and to the Hall."

Nashavety sighed. "But the align arcana? To spend your days tracing the lines, building and creating along them. It is hard work, exacting work. Have you the fortitude for it?"

"I have a sense of the aligns. They speak to me . . ."

Every youngster with even the slightest crow power thought they had a mysterious way with whatever left-handed gift. Why did so few understand their limitations? Well, she would see if Lady Byasha would take her on, if a triad could even be put together.

"Who vouches for you, child?"

"My lady, the magister of the town who himself has the aligns in abundance."

Nashavety rose from her desk, beckoning to the girl, who joined her at the window.

"Look at the compound stretched out in the center of our great edifice. Do you discern an align?"

A long pause as Sofiyana's gaze gripped the scene with desperation. She swallowed. "My lady, I . . ."

"Sense nothing?" Nashavety murmured savagely.

"There is power in the courtyard, of course, but I would need to walk it."

"And thereby miss the greatest align of all." At Sofiyana's

frown, she pointed to the sky. "That bridgeway stretching toward us up there. It is called the Bridge of the Moon. Do you see it?"

"Yes . . ." the girl whispered.

"That—" Nashavety pointed at the bridge with a finger of her left hand, causing the girl to quail. "*That* is an align, piercing the air. An align so profound that our gifted practitioners can summon stones high above the ground and fix them into place." Nashavety could not help but smile. "And you missed it."

The girl looked like she had just tripped and fallen flat on her face in the midst of an important gathering. As indeed she had.

Well, that ought to put the fear of the Nine into her, Nashavety thought. *A good beginning.*

CHAPTER 9

Yevliesza sat with her tutor at the long table in the library. Through the window, she saw great stacks of clouds herding by in the brisk wind. The window opening must have been warded because the air in the room didn't stir.

"Why am I too old to develop a power?"

Grigeni had been expounding on the Numinasi practice of *satva*, taking vows of seclusion and contemplation later in life, but her mind had strayed far away.

"And why, Master Grigeni, are there only nine powers? Are they the same abilities all over the Mythos?"

Her tutor did not answer at once. He was thin, with straight black hair and a beaked nose. He reminded her of a crow, though he had what they called *a full hand*, noble power, when it came to manifesting.

At last Grigeni indulged her. "You are too old because the body must be trained to accept the Deep when it is malleable. And yes, the same in all the realms."

"And are you sure there aren't ten—or twenty—gifts?"

"After a thousand years, one is sure of the number. And now to the *Book of Ways and Customs*—"

"But what *is* the ninth power? What does primal roots mean?"

He tapped the nub of a feather pen against the wood table. "Last question, and then you will submit to the lesson?"

When she nodded, he pulled the *Book of Ways and Customs* to a prominent place in front of them, and before opening it, answered, "Primal roots refers to the Deep source from which all powers arise, even as the Mythos arose from the origin world, and sons are delivered of their mothers."

"So," she began, and seeing his frown, added, "same question . . . the ninth is not a distinct magic."

He blew out a harsh breath. "*Magic* is a word of the mundat and is in error. *Magic* is a misleading name for Mythos power which seems to those of the mundat like an outside thing, even an impossible thing. The Deep is our term because the powers are in our bodies and in our land." He pointed the feather at her. "Do not use the word *magic* here. And as for primal roots not being a usual power—that is a proper insight, Yevliesza. In the early times primal roots was added in to balance the eight powers and bring their number into proper correlation."

He noted her blank look. "Even numbers are not favorable."

"So there are only eight powers."

"No, there are *nine*, Yevliesza. Who is the teacher and who the student?"

Though she had more questions, he was determined to control the lesson and opened the book in front of them. It was very thick.

The class stretched on until a servant came to announce that Lord Valenty would have Yevliesza attend him. At last they would bring her to her father.

🙚🙘

HOLDING A SPUTTERING TORCH, VALENTY LED YEVLIESZA INTO the nethers. Against his better judgment he had consented to take her to see her father. "Watch your step, here the ground is jumbled."

"I can see my way."

"And I said, *watch your step.*"

"Yes . . . my lord," she whispered in the dark just loud enough to escape criticism.

Stubborn, this Yevliesza. It galled him. Still, it was his job to shelter the creature and make something of her. For some unfathomable reason, Dreiza wanted to indulge her in this visit.

The farther they went, the darker. The girl's right foot had almost cleared of the wounds, but the healers had said she should be careful. He took her arm so they could walk abreast in the light of the torch.

"Pyvel said the dungeon was the original fort," Yevliesza said, "built long ago. Who was the enemy?"

"The kingdoms. Raids, skirmishes, towns plundered." As they went, Valenty watched for the runes on some of the walls. Without them, he would not be able to find his way. "Things are generally peaceful now."

"Which kingdoms attacked?"

"Various ones. Testing us."

"Which ones are close to you?"

She would not think to say *us*. Making a point. "They are all close. But in the past, we had to confront Nubiah—the Lion Court. Sometimes Norslad, or Arabet. Various. But now there are ties of diplomacy with some. Others have cut off all contact: the Indigene Nations. Closed to us. But the Volkish, they test the boundaries. They are new."

"New arisings in the Mythos?"

In places the passageway narrowed so that he had to lead the way, with Yevliesza following. The smell of ancient water and crumbling stone filled the tunnels.

"How new?" she persisted.

"Very."

"But—"

Her questions circled him in the dark confines like flies. He hoped they were almost to Ansyl's cell. "Half a lifetime ago."

"And who are your allies? The Alfan?"

"Yes. Thus you may charm the envoy as much as you like."

"So you're watching me."

"I watch everyone. Quite entertaining."

"And why have the . . . Indigene Nations . . . cut off contact? Does that mean the crossings do not reach them?"

Was Grigeni teaching her nothing? "The crossings once did. But without use they have atrophied. As to why they do not wish interaction, it comes from experience in the origin world."

"Contact was a disaster."

"Indeed." He stopped, looking around. "Here is the cell, I think."

The barred chamber looked empty. But a shadowed form slowly emerged from a corner. "Who's there?" came a voice in a mundat language.

"You will speak Numinasi," Valenty said.

Yevliesza rushed to the bars. In Numinasi, she cried, "Father, it's me, Liesa."

"Eh?" Ansyl kept back. The stench from the waste pail and centuries of mold clotted the air. "What do you want? Come for the letters, I warrant . . ." He scowled through the gaps in the bars.

"No, Father, it's me. The courier came for me, remember? And took me to Numinat." She stretched out her hand, but he remained out of reach. "That's where we are. In Osta Kiya."

"I don't have time for a meeting, can't you see? Nothing is arranged. Nothing is where it should be."

Yevliesza turned to Valenty, her face stricken. It was the first time he had felt moved by her condition. "Not a good day for your father," he said. "We will return another time."

"No." She turned back to grip the bars. "Father . . . I wanted you to see that I'm well. It's not so bad where they keep me, but I worry about you. We'll get you out of here, I promise."

"I would not promise that," Valenty murmured behind her.

Ignoring him, she reached past the bars. "Take my hand. You'll see it's me." Then switching to the mundat language, she began talking to Ansyl in soothing tones.

That would not do. If others heard them, it would not go well.

Valenty approached the cell. "Ansyl, you are here for failing to bring your daughter back to Numinat. It was a grave error. But your daughter has not been mistreated."

Yevliesza nodded. "It's true. I am well. Do you have enough food? What can I bring you?"

"Go away," Ansyl said, retreating back to his pallet. "I cannot think with everyone chattering. And you, dressed like a Numinasi. What will your mother say?"

Yevliesza put her head against the bars as though she needed help to remain standing.

"You used to wear American clothes. And you studied with me, remember? When did Oklahoma become a state? Liesa?"

"Father, we have only a few minutes . . ."

"Or no television. Say it."

Her voice went throaty. "1907."

"Yes, correct. Very good. You were always good at history." He wandered back to his corner. "History . . ."

Valenty took her arm and urged her to leave.

"I'll come back," she said to her father. "I will, I promise."

Valenty guided her a few steps away until he felt her relent, and then she fell into step beside him.

"You are keeping him like an animal," she hissed. "I should have brought food. Look how thin he is." She yanked away from him, staggering. Crouching down, she held her head in her hands. "I can't walk. Dizzy."

He let her settle. She had her little fits, reactions to the world she found strange and intimidating, just as Numinat judged the machines of her world threatening. Machines that, if tiny enough and allowed to proliferate, might traverse the crossings and sicken his world. If she failed to recover, he wondered if Anastyna would send her back.

"How do you people stand this place?"

"As long as we avoid trespass, we live well," he snapped, tired of her carping.

"Trespass," she spat back.

"In a land of Deep powers, we learn what is dangerous and what is merely unpleasant. You are slow to understand the difference."

When her fit passed, she rose and they continued through the labyrinth of corridors. After a time he said, "If you are determined to wither, you will bring yourself nothing but misery."

She muttered, "Do you really think I can ever be happy here?"

He bit his lip. "Hells, woman. It is not about your happiness. It is about the immemorial ways and customs. Without them we have no code, no meaning."

"Well, screw your ways and customs."

He grabbed her arm and pushed her against a wall, pressing her into it as she tried to free herself from his grip. His face was very close to hers, so that she could not look away. "Say that ever again and I will have you whipped. And I will do it myself, gladly." He released her and walked on ahead.

After a couple turnings in the route, he heard her stumbling behind him.

Anastyna and her serpentine plans, he sighed to himself. He never should have taken Yevliesza on. Not that the princip had given him a choice.

Pyvel followed Yevliesza down a hallway leading past the Waxing Moon chamber. "Stop," he said, trying to keep up with her. "You will miss lunch."

"I'm not hungry." She needed to get out of the palace, away from the nethers, the household, the stifling corridors of the place.

"We could visit the horse stable or take the Long Valley staircase. You can see all the way to Ivasa. And I saved you an apple." He thrust it out to her.

"No, Pyvel, not right now." She began climbing the first stairs she found and turned to look down on him. "Go have your lunch."

She raced up the stairs, losing him. Her conversation with Valenty circled around again. *It is not about your happiness, it is about the customs. . . . You are slow to understand. . . . I will have you whipped.* He felt no outrage for her father's condition, no understanding of her predicament. And she was completely in his hands.

Oddly, he had seemed different today. Not the fussy, shallow noble. More direct, and an inch more engaging. Until he threatened to beat her.

On the next floor she walked down a corridor where the windows were smaller and the hall more narrow and plain. But everywhere, the brutal stone walls like the throat of a dark beast. She longed to walk out under the sky but the courtyard was too public for her mood. She thought of home. Often, her memories came in small, random scenes, laden with pining.

Need help with those storm shutters? Shane, leaning against his truck. Dusty, tight jeans, sunburned face with an easy smile, hands with permanent grime. He'd driven all that way out on her account. Felt like a courtship, maybe just to her.

As she walked she drew stares from people, even the lowly among the residents. The Numinasi were quite content with themselves. They didn't have a father in the dungeon, they weren't wracked with dizziness and the urge to vomit. She was sick of them all.

A maid was scrubbing the floor with a pail of soapy water. Among the many Osta Kiya absurdities, one maid, one bucket, and one hundred miles of stones. A black cat with white paws sat next to her as though supervising.

"Where can I get out in the air?" she asked.

The woman, looking entirely too old to be scrubbing a floor, took her in with a long gaze. On her left hand, her little finger was missing.

"I'm sorry to interrupt you," Yevliesza said. "But I'm new here and I need a little sunshine."

The woman gave the faintest of smiles, as though she knew the feeling. "You want the Verdant," she said, pointing to an obscure door farther down the corridor.

Thanking her, Yevliesza found the unmarked door and, opening it, discovered a small, winding stairway. Up and up, and then the last door, and she was through and onto the roof.

A cool breeze met her, wafting from a lush, green garden that appeared to cover half the palace roof.

A few people walked amid rooftop trees and flowerbeds. Here, free of walls and ceiling, was the wide outdoors she had craved, rich with gardens and wandering paths. In a sky tall with cumulous clouds the sun shed a glowing warmth.

She felt as though she had not breathed for hours, but now, glorious fresh air and the scent of verdant grasses and trees. Far below, wooded, jagged hills leading to a shadowed, distant valley. Osta Kiya was at the top of the world.

Passing a grove of trees she spied three men standing in a circle around a tall evergreen tended in the shape of a bear rearing on its hind legs. Using the gift of verdure, they made pushing and twisting motions with their hands. Whatever changes they were unfolding in the bush didn't immediately appear. Verdure's trans-formations were slow.

She spied a fountain near the parapet. It beckoned her with its steady cascade, falling and plucking at the water's surface. At the perimeter bench with a view to the far valley she sat and let a sudden peace envelop her. If she had only known about this place earlier, she might have maintained her calm instead of goading Valenty, who didn't think much of her to start with.

"You have found the fountain, I see," came a man's voice.

It was Lord Tirhan. He was accompanied by another man who stayed back on the main path.

She smiled at him. "I didn't even know there *was* a roof. Not one like this."

Tirhan wore his hair in a tight queue in back, but even so it gleamed pale gold in the sun. "It is one of my great pleasures, to come here."

"To the fountain?"

"To the Verdant. It gives relief from the hardness of the castle. Where I come from, forests hold sway."

Far down the valley, a dactyl soared, its scaled hide flashing in the sun like a lantern signal from a ship at sea.

"May I interrupt you to sit?"

"Please. And your friend, too?"

"Caden is my lieutenant," he said by way of not inviting him. "An adjutant."

When he took a seat, Yevliesza wondered if they would be noticed sitting together and if this would go in a report to Valenty, who watched everyone, he'd said.

She remembered to thank Lord Tirhan for his gift. "Thank you for the salve, Lord Tirhan. It smells like pine trees."

"Is it helpful?"

"Yes, very soothing." She didn't want to tell him that the jar had been stolen. "What made you think to offer it?"

"By the grace of the Deep, I have the gift of healing," Tirhan said. "I practice it when the occasion comes to me."

The patter of the fountain seemed to cleanse her of worry and tension. "How do they bring water for this fountain?" she asked. "Where I come from, it would be . . ." She glanced at him, wondering if she should mention technology. "It would be done with machines."

He noted the word, but overlooked it. "You have seen the river at the base of the mountain?" When she shook her head, he went on. "The water from the Kovna River is brought up by element power. Up the cliffside in a constant stream. It has gouged a crevice in the rock over the centuries."

A stream that ran against gravity. She would have to see this. "It must take great power. And constant attention."

"Nay, many small powers. When children begin to receive element power, people say they have water power, since when grown they will all help bring the river water up. For those with an affinity for elements, it is a regular, but minor duty. You have heard the term 'crow power'? One crow leaves no trace across the sky, but a flock can block out the sun."

They didn't need pumps or mechanical rooms to bring water a thousand feet high. They had a different kind of power. It brought new meaning to the expression *to lend a hand*.

Tirhan gazed into the valley. The dactyl, still distant, was circling as though looking for something in the dark folds of the hills.

She was curious about this man who was an outsider like her. "You're a diplomat? An envoy?"

"A second son of my father the king whose heir is my older brother. But of all the envoy postings, this one is pre-eminent."

A real prince. He looked the part. "In Alfan Sih you live in a forest?"

He smiled. She thought it looked well on him. Actually,

terribly handsome. "Alfan Sih *is* forest. My father's court is of timbers and lodgepoles. So different from here."

She hadn't thought much about Alfan origins, but now it came to her. "On the mundat we would call your people . . . perhaps elven?"

"Yes. I think that is the English term of the mundat. Many of your . . . nations . . . had names for us. From what you might call overlapping legends. And we have become our own version."

"I would love to see your realm. Numinat is . . . hard to get used to. But you think it's the best post?"

He quirked a smile, as though knowing that she thought it must be more like the worst. "I have the challenge to forge an alliance with Numinat. To ally against the Volkish, who look to fight, to enlarge their holdings."

"Do they threaten you?"

"They are not so bold. But together, this realm and mine can be stronger. My work progresses slowly because some here oppose this."

She lowered her voice. "Lady Nashavety doesn't like the outside."

Tirhan nodded. "A small summary for large things."

They watched as the dactyl approached the city-palace, great wings beating, and between the wings, someone in harness. They flew into the pens, hidden by the castle's bulk.

Tirhan turned to her. "The lady is afraid for her people. When the crossings are used, they grow larger and . . . more lasting. Every crossing augments them. And then they become routes for enemies as well as friends. But she lets that thought color all. Color you."

"I thought no one could see that."

"Perhaps it takes an outsider to hold certain thoughts." He rose. "I thank you for the pleasant visit."

"Could I . . ." She hesitated. "Could I have another jar of Alfan Sih salve?"

He smiled, part pleasure, part conspiracy. "It shall be done."

As she watched him leave the Verdant, she thought, *Father, I think I've made an ally.*

She explored the rest of the roof, and her mind wandered to her conversation with the Alfan lord. Was he attracted to her, or just being kind? Undoubtedly, it was kindness. Nonetheless she found herself smiling as she descended to the lower floors.

As she passed the Waxing Moon chamber, she heard the chatter of voices. Heading in her direction was a group of women, nobles by their dress. She stood aside to let them pass and found herself making eye contact with one of them. Nashavety.

"Ah, our foreign visitor," Nashavety said, stopping and turning to Yevliesza. The others paused in surprise, the silken threads of their gowns and the gem-studded hairnets winking in the light of tall windows.

Yevliesza made a short bow. "Lady Nashavety."

Nashavety smiled at her companions as though a pet had accomplished a nice trick. "Yevliesza. How are you finding our mountain fastness? Is it not a wonder?"

"Yes, Lady Nashavety."

"You must acknowledge my companions, who are *fajatim* of great Halls." She turned to a pale woman with curly, iron-grey hair. "Lady Ineska of Red Wind Hall." She nodded in the direction of a spindle-thin woman, with skin a deep shade of mahogany. "And Lady Vajalyna, *fajatim* of Wild Hill."

"My ladies," Yevliesza said with another bow.

Nashavety came closer. Her long, thin face made her look very serious, no matter if she smiled, as she did now. "The gown becomes you, Yevliesza. I hear you now have accepted the name that our princip bestowed upon you."

"Yes, my lady." She had made it sound as though Yevliesza had considered *not* accepting it. Which was true . . .

"The gown is well done. It is what a guest of Lord Valenty's household should wear." She touched the high neckline ruffled with lace. "Perhaps the collar could be somewhat higher, to cover all. But it is well. And the sleeve cuffs might drape to the full extent." She examined Yevliesza's wrists. "Except, what is this . . ."

Pulling back one cuff, she exposed the watch. "What is this circlet with the strange stone?" She turned back to the *fajatim* of Wild Hill. "Lady Vajalyna, have you ever seen the like?"

The woman came close to examine it. Her eyes flashed to meet Yevliesza's, even as she moved her right hand across her chest in a sign of protection.

"I have asked you a question," Nashavety said.

"It is . . . a plaything. A memento."

"By the Deep, is it from the mundat?"

"Yes."

"Perhaps a device such as one has heard of, a machine to mark time?"

"It's broken. Only a keepsake now, my lady."

Nashavety inclined her head, as though accepting this. "Broken." She turned back to the *fajatim* and their attendants. "That is well, or we could have suffered trespass here. But—" She paused as though confused. "Might it not suddenly become unbroken, in the way of mundat machines?"

"No, Lady Nashavety. It's broken."

"I see. So it is just an insult to our ways, not a trespass. That is well to know."

They left her there, her tongue dry and sticking to the roof of her mouth like a trapped bird. Nashavety had let her go, sweeping out of view with the other *fajatim*, none of whom had ever seen a machine nor wanted to. She had feared for a moment that they might have reacted fiercely. But Nashavety seemed content, having made her point. If this was the end of it.

When she got back to the dormitory, she took off the watch and securely tied it in a scrap of paper that Lord Tirhan had used to wrap the jar of salve. Then she went in search of Valenty. Finding him gone, she left the watch with his steward, accompanied by a note.

I kept this broken mechanical timepiece because I did not know it was an insult. Lady Nashavety found me wearing it. I am sorry for the mistake.

It was not exactly true that she didn't know it was an insult. She might have guessed. She *did* guess, but this was no time for honesty.

CHAPTER 10

Yevliesza entered the nethers. Tied into a scarf, a leg of chicken, half a loaf of bread, and an apple. With a candle she had lit from a fireplace, she put the flame to one of the torches stored at the foot of the stairs. Before she got in trouble for having the watch, she would bring her father some decent food. It was little enough that she could do, and perhaps he would really see her, look into her eyes, and know who it was.

She didn't doubt that it was Nashavety who had sent her the watch. So that she'd wear it and be exposed as a rule-breaker.

In the wavering light of the torch, she examined the passage-way, its hewn walls and turnings. Yes, right turn here, she remembered. Down one passage she glimpsed someone, but they disappeared. It hadn't occurred to her that the nethers might be dangerous. Since she was alone, best to be quick about her mission. She hurried onward.

When she found her father's cell, he was dozing, sitting propped up against the bars of his prison.

"Father."

He woke with a start and staggered to his feet.

"Father, it's me."

Turning, he looked at her with no sign of recognition. She gave him the food items one at a time, cajoling him to talk, but he didn't meet her eyes. Still, she pressed him. "Did you belong to a noble Hall when you lived in Numinat?"

"A Hall?" He frowned, glancing to the side as though searching for the answer there.

"Did you live in one of the great houses? Like Red Wind? Wild Hill?"

"Ah, Wild Hill . . ."

"Was Wild Hill yours?"

From the gloom of the cell his voice came like a memory. "No, no . . . Dust and Wind. That one. I think they are all gone now."

There was no Dust and Wind Hall. Maybe he was thinking of the dust and wind of Barlow County. She stayed as he ate, but he only picked at things. By his gaunt face, he wasn't eating much.

"Please eat. It'll do you good. Remember how you always wanted me to clean my plate?"

"You used to be a good cook," he murmured. "Now you bring me cold chicken."

"I'm sorry. It was all I could find."

His eyes met hers. "Are you well, Liesa? You don't look it. Welts on your neck . . ."

Sometimes he spoke with all his faculties. It both comforted and distressed her, to see him become himself only to lose himself again. "I'm well, truly. I live in the household of Lord Valenty."

"Ah. That's where you've been. We must take a trip, just you and I. To St. Louis. We should have gone . . . before. I kept putting it off. Sometimes I think I forgot to go." He looked at her, begging her to understand. "Forgot, Liesa. Forgot."

"It's all right. No one blames you." A horrid lie.

He turned away, leaning against the bars, his head tipped back as though he was resting his eyes. At his side, a rat daintily chewed on the bread.

As he stood gazing into his cell, she knew he was no longer with her. She whispered to him, "I'll come back. Soon. As soon as I can."

Returning along the route, she walked with a sad knowledge. Her father was worsening. She wanted to blame Princip Anastyna, but considering what Dreiza had said, the cultural pressures made her father's harsh punishment inevitable. So then she could blame all the Numinasi. And did.

When she emerged from the nethers, Pyvel was waiting for her.

"Yevliesza!" He sprang from the floor where he had been resting. "What are you doing?" He took her by the arm and urged her away the door. "You cannot be seen here. People will think you are trying to free your father. You could be whipped."

She nodded. "I know. Worth it."

"Yevliesza. You do not understand . . ."

Turning to him, she planted her feet. "I do understand. It's not only Numinasi who know things, Pyvel. You can learn from me as well." It was time he got that straight. "OK?"

He gulped. "OK." As they walked back to the household, he asked, "But what were you doing down there?"

"Visiting my father. I brought him extra food."

"You *saw* him? How did you find him in the passageways?"

With Pyvel's face so full of worry, she had to laugh. "I was fine."

"You could have gotten lost. Did you? How long were you there?"

"A while, a long while." He continued to act confounded. "Pyvel, Lord Valenty took me there yesterday. I know the way."

"It cannot be as easy as going once."

But she did remember the route she and Valenty had taken.

Perhaps it was not so much memory but an instinct for direction. She had backtracked a few times . . . "Maybe I have some crow power," she said, as a possibility rose in her like a green shoot through a crack in cement.

Pyvel's eyes narrowed. "Maybe you have . . do you think you have the aligns?"

The aligns, the nether ways were along aligns. But it hadn't felt like some kind of Deep power. No rush of understanding, no tingling, no visions of shimmering lines.

Pyvel went on. "The whole nethers is true to the aligns. That is why it is so jumbled. The First Ones cared only for the aligns, no matter what paths might have worked better."

"What does it feel like," Yevliesza slowly said, "when you use manifesting?"

He glanced at her, his face shining with excitement. "Oh, it feels like . . . well, it just feels natural."

She concentrated, searching for the imprint of magic inside her, a wisp of color, a carving on her bones, a trace of writing on water, but all she found was herself.

"Say nothing about this," she admonished. "Not one word."

She didn't want to claim a power, only to have it be nothing.

When she and Pyvel entered the household, Grigeni was waiting for them.

❦

YEVLIESZA WAS TO GO TO VALENTY'S PRIVATE CHAMBERS. Grigeni accompanied her, grim-faced. Now came the confrontation about the watch. *Let him do his worst*, she thought, needing, trying for the dignity that she had entirely lost in the hall outside Waxing Moon.

When they stopped in front of carved double doors, she recognized them. The room where the young servant had rushed out, rearranging her hair.

In the enormous bed chamber, a cozy fire flickered in the fireplace. Valenty sat on a divan, wearing relaxed trousers and a soft, quilted jacket of moss green. By his side, Dreiza, in a rich blue-grey dressing gown. Her hair was gathered casually in back, with wisps hanging free.

Valenty looked up to acknowledge Yevliesza's presence. "Our guest has emerged from the nethers," he said with wry humor.

"Yes, thank the First Ones." Dreiza rose and looked at Yevliesza, frowning.

Valenty gallantly rose when she did, taking the cup she still held in her hand.

Dreiza approached her. "So, my dear, did you consider, before you went hunting for your father, that getting lost down there might be an embarrassment to Lord Valenty?"

"I didn't think I would get lost, though, my lady."

Dreiza shook her head. "Stopping to consider is not one of your strengths. How shall we ever protect you if you spend all your time warding us off?" She turned to Valenty. "Good night, my lord. Try to talk some sense into her."

Valenty went to an elaborately carved sideboard bearing a soft, icy sheen. It was likely built from Alfan Sih silverwood at great expense. Pouring red liquid into cups, he came back to the sitting area, gesturing her to join him. This was friendlier than the reception she had expected. Maybe too friendly. She hesitated to take the proffered cup.

He smirked, understanding her reluctance. "We could have our conversation in the cookery, or in the courtyard if you prefer."

"I'm an envoy's daughter. Not a servant to be played with."

He rolled his eyes. "We are here because this conversation needs to be private. You may keep your clothes on, but please discard the attitude. My interest in you is . . . political, nothing more, I assure you." He put her drink on the table between two chairs and sat opposite her.

"Political?"

He watched her for a long moment, as though summoning patience. "Yevliesza. I shall lead this discussion. You will listen respectfully, taking care to feel grateful that I do not intend to punish you for keeping the watch."

He took a sip of his wine, if that is what it was. Rain pattered against the windows, the sound of pebbles hitting paper. "How was your father?"

"Poorly."

The abrupt answer annoyed the lord of the household, and he made her sit in silence for awhile. Outside, she heard the sluice of water from the gargoyles, collecting rain from the slopes of the roofs.

"I am having your father taken to another place, a better chamber, higher in the castle." He snapped a look at her. "You are not to see him."

She nodded, grateful to think of him free of the nethers.

Valenty regarded her, noticing that she hadn't touched her cup. "Have a sip of wine, as a concession to me. I am trying to change the tenor of things."

He was indulging her, showing a considerate side of himself. No doubt it was because he wanted something. She took a drink, the first alcohol of her life. Bitter and heavy, but she swallowed it.

"So," he began, "here is what you do not understand: We are —Osta Kiya is—troubled by a delicate problem. You. Allow me to explain. Six years ago, the previous princip died. She was only one hundred and five, but her time had come.

"So, the role of princip. It is always a woman, at the election of the *fajatim* of the Halls. Men typically form the military, and women, governance. It was the only way the Numinasi could bear to settle in mixed company, that if men had the arms, women would say when they would be used.

"The old princip, Lisbetha, had approved four envoys to your former country, and yes, she lost track of one of them. The envoys in Sant Loois and Sea-tal—I pronounce them correctly?"

"Well enough."

"At these stations, they did not hear from your father, neither did they receive answers to their letters. They thought he had been recalled. He was, as you have said, forgotten.

"When Princip Anastyna received the torc—" He noted her confusion. "Her silver collar of state. When the torc was conferred, she began to clean up affairs. Eventually she discovered the error and sent a courier to release your father from his assignment. But her courier found you there. The problem arises from the fact that because your father kept you in the mundat, you were past the years of your Deepening. You have twenty-one years, a grown woman. So to most Numinasi, you can appear as nothing except a ruined figure."

The rain came heavier. At one window a rivulet of water intruded and threaded down to puddle on the floor.

"Now comes the part you do not understand." He frowned at her almost untouched cup. "The wine displeases? We could have a servant bring a cup of savory, but it would mean waking them."

She took another sip.

He went on. "We have had relative peace in our realm for three hundred years. But then came convergent threats: From Volkia, and also, from the mundat, the virulent technologistics of very small machines. We are under threat, with two outcomes presenting themselves. Close up and shut the doors on interaction with others. Or form agreements with other realms for mutual protection. Some of the *fajatim* favor the former, thinking nothing good comes of interaction. But Anastyna wishes to consider alliances. Who knows if she is right?" He shrugged. "It is not my place to say. But know this, Yevliesza: she wants you to succeed. She wishes for you to be a good example of outside, especially since there are those who will point to you as an example of ruin and even trespass.

"You know the term *trespass*?"

Nashavety had used it.

"It is a diabolic use of noble power. The three offensive uses of power are: reach, infestation, and selfhood. To cast influence over wide territory; to engender sickness or blights; to invade the mind or body of another. These trespasses are forbidden throughout the Mythos, except for violence against persons in war. It can be argued that the mundat invaded your heart and mind, stealing from you your rightful power and—note this carefully—your love of Numinat and your care for it."

"But I wouldn't be *ruined* if you hadn't brought me among you."

Valenty shot her a dark look. "You will remain silent until I finish. I am not relating what I think, nor even what most people think about you. I am relating how things could be twisted by a few who find these interpretations useful to their purposes. Like the *fajatim*. They can depose a princip. Imagine, if you will, who might then be raised to the torc."

She nodded, thinking of the one with the long face and nasty smile.

Distant thunder rumbled outside the windows. "The princip would like to avoid such an outcome. Even I do, though I have nothing to do with politics and barely understand what the fuss is all about."

"But you took me in . . ." She dropped her gaze, remembering to be silent.

"Yeesss, because the princip directed that I do so. It was privately settled before your audience with Anastyna."

That set her back. Valenty had acted on orders from the princip. Secret orders. She bit her lip, stifling the urge to ask a question.

Valenty sighed. "You may speak."

"Why are you telling me this now?"

"Because the stakes are very high. And you are playing the game as though it was about fairness and"—a long-suffering look —*"happiness."* He examined his fingernails. "I considered whipping you into playing the correct role, but I had the feeling that not even that would curb you. So then, since you are the daughter of a diplomat, I am testing whether you have any gift whatsoever for diplomacy and the . . . dissembling it requires."

He raised an eyebrow, soliciting a comment, but for once she had nothing to say. She needed to think about all this.

"So, Yevliesza. As to unfair or illogical, this is not a useful perspective. You are a political problem—or opportunity. How you thrive or fail will be used one way or another. And there is the added disadvantage that if you fail, *I* will be seen to fail, and I would rather avoid the embarrassment."

He tossed off the last of his wine. "I intend to watch over your father's welfare as best I can without being *seen* to do so. But do not count on his situation being resolved soon. Anastyna wishes for the matter to fade, the gossip and outrage to subside. Then she will pronounce the atonement required by what, in her noble prerogative, will be deemed your father's missteps." He shrugged. "Your situation may not resolve to your satisfaction given how we are at present. I believe your expression is, walking through eggshells. But you see how rebellious *mementos* and midnight wanderings work against your interests."

"Yes. I see." She did wish he had told her this sooner, but she supposed he hadn't yet trusted her with secrets.

"And can I expect your help, given that we both have things to lose?"

Help. What exactly would that entail besides accepting whatever happened? But if her father's situation were going to improve, she might need to show the people who feared mundat —feared anything from the outside—that they were wrong.

She did like Valenty better. But she didn't believe he wasn't political. He was in the thick of it.

"I'll try," she said. "If you'll try to keep me informed."

"Splendid." Valenty rose from his chair. "Now get some sleep and so shall I."

Standing, she said, "There's something that I'd like to ask for, though. I would like my own room." At his raised eyebrow, she went on. "In the dormitory my things are getting . . . lost."

He pinned her with an ironic gaze. "A room with a nice view? Your own maid?"

"I have simple needs, my lord."

"That is obviously untrue." He held the chamber door open for her. "But I will set Grigeni to it."

"Will Nashavety punish me for the . . . memento?"

He snorted. "She has already punished you. That little drama in the hallway was carefully planned."

He noted her dismay. "Yevliesza. We are far from done." His gaze was clear, tinged with something she thought might be kindness.

She nodded, and feeling lighter than she had in weeks, slipped out the door, hearing it close behind her.

CHAPTER 11

K irjanichka, you must not blame Valenty for my circumstances. He has done his best for me. How unfair it is for him always to be entangled with difficult women! Yevliesza, of course. But first, me.

Oh, kindly do not tremble your wings at me. I have not forgotten your figs! Here, your favorites, the large purple ones. And see, I have removed the stems.

So, Kirjanichka, I come to talk of Valenty. Of how we came together, the handsome young man and the middle-aged woman under a cloud of disapproval.

His family was one of the great houses, making him powerful and beyond most dangers. So it happened that he could offer protection to me when I offended the princip. In those days it was Lisbetha, and she hated me. She intended to ruin me, but her hate gnawed at her from within, and she died before her time.

I was the wife of Valenty's brother. When he died in a border skirmish, Lisbetha's oldest son declared himself for me, and I could have married into the highest of noble families. He and I were of an age, both with seventy-two years, and he was decent enough. But I did not love him and rejected his suit. He killed *himself. In a most terrible and public way. The Tower. You remember Kirjanichka. You saw it.*

Lisbetha wanted revenge and wove her plots. Seeing that I was in danger, and out of respect for his brother, Valenty offered to marry me. I took refuge in his protection. So I suddenly was, instead of his sister by marriage, his wife. Thus Lisbetha became an enemy to both of us.

But she died, Kirjanichka. My happiness was complete. I had married a wealthy and handsome man and, over time, even if I was much older than he, we grew to love each other. I insisted he take his ease as often as he wished with the women who offered themselves to the virile young man with the old wife. But as we grew in our bonds, he found himself wishing to honor me and never to doubt his devotion. Though I did not ask it, he vowed that he would never take a mistress whom he loved. So that I would know, if a woman came to his bed, he did not regard her seriously.

Then the princip directed us to house and instruct the girl of the mundat. Anastyna's wishes had to be served. Valenty and I discussed it and agreed between ourselves. We would take the girl in and do what we could for her. My foreknowing warned me that she would undo many hopes and plans. But I thought they would be of great things, of the struggle of fajatim *against princip. I did not see that the girl would undo . . . me.*

Oh, Kirjanichka, I tire you. I will leave you now. Yours is a world untroubled by desire and regret, and my story is full of these. Have your sleep. I would rest against your warm side, but there would be no end of scandal. Lord Valenty's wife sleeping in a dactyl pen!

You smile despite yourself. I am glad I can still amuse you, my old friend.

CHAPTER 12

In her new quarters, Yevliesza spread out her things on the small bed set into an alcove: One change of everyday dress, two plain hairnets, two sets of underthings and stockings, and a good gown with fancy hairnet. A new jar of salve, hair pins, comb, and soft cloths for moon days. They all fit into a wooden box at the end of her bed.

In deference to her sensitivity to the cold, shutters on her windows, and a fireplace with a bucket of coal.

A door with a key.

It was heavenly, but marred by the thought of where her father was kept and how he had no luxuries like these. Unless Valenty could secretly arrange things.

Valenty. She'd had two days to begin doubting him. What would she gain by becoming a good citizen of Osta Kiya? Valenty could point to his project—her—as a success, the princip might be closer to fashioning alliances . . . but what did she herself want? To stay and work to gain acceptance? If her father gained his freedom, it seemed likely he would want to stay, if he understood his choices. In any case, for him, there was no going back to the old world. She found herself looking at Numinat in a new light. This place might be her only future.

A knock at the door. Pyvel arrived.

"A grand room!" he enthused, opening the shutters to look out. "You can see the whole courtyard and . . ."—he leaned out the window to look down the side of the palace—"the Tower."

Yevliesza was glad her view didn't face the Tower. She wondered if the hidden side of it, the one that faced the plains, had bloodstains.

She closed the door and leaned against it. "Pyvel. I have something to ask of you. Something risky."

◌⋈◌

IN THE END, HE AGREED TO TAKE HER BLINDFOLDED INTO THE nethers. Very far into the nethers. He had carried a load of small stones and, on their way, marked intersections so that he could find his way after leaving her. As a test, she had to find her way out. If she wasn't out in three hours, Pyvel would inform Lord Valenty.

Now it was at least an hour since he had left. The marking stones Pyvel had brought were gone, and she was on her own. Her torch threw a wavering light on the ancient walls which everywhere looked the same. She wouldn't find her way out by sight, but by the aligns.

The route was easy at first. She could remember the last few turns, whether to the right or left, and reversed them, but soon she ran out of memory. The nethers were chopped into several corridors, some of which passed through rooms and gathering spaces. Adding to the challenge were the several aligns that crisscrossed here, so it was not just a matter of following an align, but of following the correct align.

At intersections she closed her eyes, concentrating, trying to sense the mysterious trajectories. When she could strongly visualize the door to the upper palace, she chose her turn.

But what if those subtle intimations were just her imagination? In the flickering torchlight, it was easy to let her hopes create an urge for turning one way or the other. If she lost her way, Valenty would have more proof of her recklessness. But if she got back to the upper palace on her own, it would suggest that she had an affinity for the aligns.

If she had a power, it would prove that she wasn't an unnatural Numinasi. A proof that Anastyna would welcome, a proof much greater than the princip had reason to expect.

She wanted the aligns. For her father. And even for herself. She thought of Lord Tirhan, and the idea of leaving with him for Alfan Sih swirled in the background. The idea was ludicrous, but her imagination conjured it. He couldn't want a woman with a half-burned body and a bad history. Yet, when Tirhan had sat with her in the Verdant, there was something in the way he looked at her. She thought it was attraction.

But she wasn't going to marry a prince, for God's sake. She wasn't going off to live in an enchanted forest.

Why couldn't things be as they had been, why couldn't she just open her eyes one morning and find that it had all been a dream: the troubling arrival of the courier in the front yard, the flight of the dactyl through the storm, the burns, the witchy *fajatim* in indigo blue, her father's dungeon, and the strange Numinasi name, *Yevliesza, Yevliesza* . . . It would make her crazy to think of all she had lost, the very earth she had thought— though she had known better—was the only world, and her cozy life with her father in their comfy old house in Barlow County.

On and on she walked and, with each step, trying to unwind her thoughts from their tangle.

Had her former life been cozy? Isolated more like, if she was honest. No friends, no schoolmates, a foolish longing for any boy who flirted with her, there being only one to choose from. Then her father, withdrawing into a private world, and she, stepping in more and more to fill in the blank spaces for the only person she had ever loved. No, it had not been a hazy, perfect childhood. It had been a slow crawl of days punctuated by tornadoes and trips to the Stop 'n Shop.

She was *here* now. What would she make of it, if this was all there was? Would Numinat open even the slightest bit to let her in?

The torch had burned out. She had been walking in darkness. Fear cloaked her in a cold, heavy embrace.

A stab of pain as she stubbed her toe on something. A staircase going up. By God, she had done it. Exultantly, she climbed, and at the top found the wooden door. She pushed it open.

Pyvel was waiting for her. "Yevliesza!" He rushed to her, eyes alight. "The aligns, Yevliesza, the aligns. You have them!"

She let the sudden rush of cool, fresh air envelop her. She had done it, had emerged from the underworld.

"It helps not to try," she murmured. "You have to trust them to speak to you. They lead you as long as you don't want it too much."

He looked at her like she was babbling. He carefully enunciated, "We can go home now?"

"Do you have something to eat?"

Out from his pocket he took out a small item wrapped in thin cloth. A hunk of cheese. She devoured it as they went.

◈

HER HAPPINESS DID NOT LAST. SHE HAD ALMOST FELT A KINSHIP with Osta Kiya, almost had believed that Valenty was an ally. But none of that mattered, not even her likely gift of the aligns.

Numinat became a dark, sad foreign land. Because her father was dead.

Valenty came personally to her room as a grey dawn leaked through the shutters. After speaking to him through the door she hurriedly dressed, wondering what news could bring him to her and so early.

He had brought a candle in a holder, though he could hardly have needed it in the lit halls. It was for her, she realized, a flame to keep her company for the time it would take to accept what had happened. Her father had died during the night, his heart having come to the end of its thousands of beats. Valenty said this as though her father had been destined to die after a certain number, when in fact Numinat had broken him, killed him.

When the candle was half gone, Pyvel came to the door. She didn't answer him when he called to her.

By the time the candle guttered, she heard a clatter on the other side of the door. "Miss, please open for one moment." Grigeni's voice. A tray of bread and fruit. She thanked him.

The room, the castle, pressed down on her with its endless weight of quarried stone. Her chest seemed reluctant to rise, if her father's did not. She wandered up to the Verdant to find a few breaths.

A hard rain had come and the roof was deserted. Making her way to the central stand of low trees, she entered the copse and found a refuge in a dry spot by a trunk. Through a gap in the branches she could see dark clouds bulking, torn by rainfall. It gave her solace to look into the roiling clouds, as up-close things were impenetrable. Her father dead. Dying alone, and maybe not understanding what was happening or why his daughter wasn't at his side.

She was wet and shivering when Dreiza found her.

A fur cloak came around her shoulders and Dreiza led her

down from the roof. "We could not find you. My dear, it is our custom to remove the body as soon as death comes."

"The body," she whispered, remembering that it was her father's.

"Yes. He has been consigned to the elements." In her room, Dreiza said she must take off her wet dress. She would bring her a dry one. The dress fell around her feet in a soggy pile, and she climbed into bed, pulling the covers up. And slept. She stirred when Dreiza came in to leave dry clothes for her, then slept again.

When she woke, she found a dress in plainest black lying at the foot of the bed. Removing her shift, she wrapped her left hand around her rib cage, feeling the rough welts on the right side of her back. Reaching over her shoulder she traced the scars up to her neck and under her chin. Here was the record of her visit to this place: scars that would never heal. She was glad she had them, so that her father had not been the only one to suffer.

The simple gown had laces up the front. After dressing, she made her way to the latrine, down the shadowy halls dim despite the manifesters' lights.

On the way back, Lord Tirhan was waiting for her outside her room.

"Yevliesza." He paused. "I am saddened to hear about your father." He looked at the door to her room. "I may come in?"

"No, I'm sorry. You don't need to comfort me. Please don't." She felt herself losing her grip. Her eyes grew hot as the unwelcome embarrassment of crying hovered near.

"There can be no comfort for sadness in a foreign land."

The words pierced her, and fathoms of water began to rise in her chest. When she put her hand on the wall to steady herself, to find the cold relief of stone, he folded his arms around her. She allowed it, then relented and pressed against him, hating to be weak in front of someone she hardly knew.

"He's gone," she whispered, glad her voice was steady, or almost.

"Let the tears move through you, Yevliesza," he whispered.

But she did not. She would not cry in Osta Kiya. She would not give them any more reason to despise her. Pulling away from the embrace, she said, "Would you take me to my father?"

He frowned. "Numinasi custom is to make a funeral pyre. Unless it is raining and then burial."

"They buried him?"

"Yes." He looked at her with outright pity, and she wished he would stop. "Do you know where they buried him?"

"I can take you there."

They made their way out of the castle, down the narrow halls and great ones, down the staircases. Tirhan's servant caught up with them, and the Alfan lord put him to finding long cloaks against the weather. Once outside on a covered porch, he insisted they wait for his man to return. When he did, Tirhan took one of the cloaks and placed it over her shoulders, folding the hood carefully over her hair.

THE GRAVE WAS AMONG OTHERS ON A TERRACED LEDGE OF THE hillside. An inscription charred into wood said, ANSYL OF IRON RIVER HALL, TWENTY-FIFTH DAY, NINTH MONTH, YEAR OF THE HERON.

So their heritage was of Iron River Hall. For what it had been worth.

The rain stopped. A gusting wind blew the clouds into piles, letting a stream of sun fall into the near valley. She kneeled in the mud.

When she tried to say to her father that he was home at last, the words wouldn't come. It seemed wrong to say such a thing when home had killed him. But the longer she spent on her knees, the more she felt it was true, that he had been born here, had been a member of a Hall that had discarded him, but still, a home for all that.

She had come to the grave for last words with her father, perhaps to find a moment of comfort. But all she felt was loss and anger. They had made an example of him and if it hadn't outright killed him, it had hastened his death.

Numinat was a brutal place. Placid in some regards, but ruthless when its customs were unheeded. To survive here you had to be strong. They were all strong, especially the women, women who ruled the kingdom and decided who would fall from the Tower and when to go to war. If she had to be here, if she was to survive, she would have to be like them. And when she had walked out of the nethers, she had known that she *was* like them. The Deep had come into her, and it wasn't in a small power, but full-fledged.

As Tirhan stood by, she whispered, "Father, I have the aligns. They said I was too old, but it came to me in bits, when I was softened by spells of dizziness. Or maybe the spells were caused by the power entering my body."

Rain began again. Lightly, relentlessly, with a will to erode the great hill and all its stones.

She went on. "I'm going to claim my right of arcana training. I think it's the only way I can earn respect. I hope it's what you would have wanted. I hope you approve." She placed her left hand in the mud of his interment. "I will always love you and I will always miss you." She got to her feet.

She and Tirhan had to cross the central courtyard on the way back. A thousand windows were lit, like the faceted eyes of an insect. "I tested myself in the nethers," she told Tirhan. "I went hours in, blindfolded, and came out again."

"To have the aligns is a splendid gift. If you lived in my land, people would honor you."

She had the feeling there was much about Alfan Sih that was more welcoming than this place. "But maybe it's crow power."

"If you went alone far into the nethers, I think it is a high gift. Have you told Lord Valenty?" She shrugged in answer. "He is the only one that can speak for you, for the arcana. I would do so, but I have no influence here."

"Even if you don't, you're an ally."

"I am that. At least that." Saying this, he smiled. She noted how not many people smiled in Numinat, and how thoroughly stirring it looked when he, in particular, did. Then the reality of what the day had brought clamped over her, and she turned to go.

"Thank you, Lord Tirhan, you've been very kind." He made a small bow, and she left with a determined step. To find Valenty. To say what was due her and why.

She found that Pyvel had already told him. And that he would be delighted to speak for her arcana training.

She would have a triad. Valenty—or Anastyna—would make sure she did.

For a week she wore the black dress that Dreiza had given her. And then a new gown, of finer cut and detailing that Valenty provided for her. It was dusky grey with a shimmer of lavender and small yellow stones sewn into the quilted bodice. She thought of refusing it. But every move now had to be made with calculation. She would wear the dress, because it showed that she had risen in the world.

Her new gown sometimes looked grey and then, in the next moment it had a ghost of lavender. She wondered if the color came from an expensive Numinasi dye, or if that shade of violet was magic, and if so, was it low magic or high. There was so much she didn't know. And had to learn. If possible, quickly.

PART II
THE BRIDGE OF
THE MOON

CHAPTER 13

Byasha stared up at Yevliesza, who was a full head taller than her. "We will begin by you finding an align. Proceed."

A thick fog filled the woods, turning everything to shades of grey except Byasha's hair, a shade of red never seen in nature. Behind them the hill sloped up to the horse stables, lost in murk.

"I think over there?" Yevliesza pointed to the right.

A sigh came out of Byasha's rotund body as though from a bellows. "That is, in your opinion, an align?"

"Yes, lady." She was guessing. A deer path threaded into the trees and, by the power of suggestion, it had become an align.

She began to fear Byasha's coming test. The first form of align arcana training was discerning the aligns. The three kinds of discernment were perception, touch, and sight. Although touch and sight were beyond her capabilities for now, in the nethers she had experienced *perception*. But where was perception now?

"Let us proceed to the align then." Byasha pulled her cloak more firmly around herself and stamped through the underbrush to the place her student had indicated.

"So now, which direction?" Byasha's stare intensified. "Well?"

"I . . . I can't tell, I think further into this stand of trees."

"Or perhaps curving toward the gully? Or passing in front of us?"

Yevliesza's mind was as clotted with murk as the day with its fog. It had been ten days since her father's death and she could not yet fix her mind on her training.

"Silence is no answer when I ask you a question," Byasha declared. "You may pull your moods on Lord Valenty's household, but not with me. The align arcana is not a horseback-riding class, it is a lifelong practice, and it begins humbly. As for the fog, the woods, none of this is your concern. Only the aligns, if you can even find one. And?"

"Here is the align, lady. It runs straight into the forest."

Byasha rolled her eyes. "No, it is not here. Nor does it run into the trees."

Yevliesza's noble power had gone shallow. Or perhaps it had never existed.

"Do you discern an align *anywhere* before you?"

Yevliesza began walking, trying not to try, calming her striving mind. They entered the dark, dripping trees, stepping over fallen logs that tugged at her skirts as though trying to show her a different path.

"The fog distracts me. It's difficult to concentrate."

Byasha planted her feet, hands on her wide hips. "It is an extra barrier, to be sure. But if I am to take you into a triad, I must gauge your readiness and today is the day I judged best to begin the task. So I will give you a start." She tramped off downslope, and after a few minutes they reached an overlook. She pointed. "There, the tallest pine, the one with the great nest. That is where you are to go. You understand?"

"No, my lady."

A great, foggy sigh. "The align leads to the tree. You are standing on a major align. Follow it to the tree. From here I shall watch how you proceed."

"The align?" Yevliesza struggled to sense it. She felt it pulling away from her, burying itself.

"By all the First Ones! Do you not discern it? Sofiyana grasped the task—not without some prodding, but she was not *helpless*. This is what I feared from your unnatural growth of powers, coming in bouts of sickness—"

"I wasn't sick, just dizzy."

Byasha looked back to the castle, as though help might come from that direction. Turning back to Yevliesza, she said with the voice of strained patience, "Coming in bouts of *dizziness*." She studied her student's face for a few moments, perhaps considering whether to give up on her. Then her face relaxed. "Close your eyes, Yevliesza. Empty your chattering mind. Set aside hope and imaginings. Allow the forest to simply be. Allow the align to enter your awareness."

After a moment, she had it. Like a murmur in the ground, like a rustling beneath her feet: an align. She began to walk along it. The forest floor sloped gently down. The align didn't follow the gully next to it, but angled off with a mind of its own. The tree trunks were covered with velvety moss, the air richly scented with pine needles and pungent sap.

The trance worked for fifty steps before she lost the align.

Then, again, she found it, sometimes appearing like a length of rope on fire.

Lost again. She looked back to see if Byasha was watching, but she couldn't see her arcana guide. Not that Byasha was her arcana guide. Not yet. This was her interview for the position. Apparently one member of the potential triad had interviewed very well. Sofiyana, whom she had not met. In a snarl of worry, she lost all concentration.

The fog thickened into woolly clots, frustrating her efforts at perception. She stopped to rest, leaning against a tree with a deeply grooved bark. Closing her eyes, she tried to free her thoughts in the way Byasha instructed.

When she opened them, a large wolf stood fifteen paces away. She went very still. Its black fur was strange, seeming to blur into grey. Luminous green eyes stared at her, unblinking. With a lurch in her stomach, she remembered that she should not meet its gaze, because years ago she had read somewhere that you don't stare into an aggressive dog's eyes. In the next moment the wolf turned and in a few strides, disappeared into the fog.

When her heart slowed, she took up her quest again, keeping an eye out for wolves.

An hour later, as the trees cast long shadows, she saw in the distance a flash of crimson.

As she drew closer, she saw that Byasha sat under the great lone pine. She was chewing on a sausage and didn't even look up at her student.

"You will do," Byasha said to her sausage. "You have barely passed, but as a favor to the lord, I will take you on." She wiped her hands on her cloak and stood.

The news, even delivered with criticism, buoyed her greatly. She thanked Byasha.

"Lady Byasha, there are wolves about. I saw one back there, quite close."

"What foolishness. You are just nervous to be in the woods. You girls all worry about meeting wraith wolves. Soon you will see them behind every tree!"

"It was probably fifteen feet away from me."

Byasha gave her a droll look and sighed dramatically. "This is what happens when we have converse with the mundat. Our powers are mixed with . . . dizziness and too much imagination."

Weary of the disdain and tired from the long walk, Yevliesza complained, "It wasn't my imagination."

Byasha snorted. "It would be better to perceive the aligns than the wolves. But by the grace of the Deep your power found you, and I will do what I can to provide guidance. Are you willing, despite all?"

"Yes, lady." She held Byasha's gaze, determined not to show annoyance. "If you'll give me a chance."

Byasha began ascending the hill, waving for Yevliesza to follow.

NASHAVETY PULLED UP ON THE REINS OF HER HORSE, A FINE black stallion. She patted its neck, as she watched Byasha and her charge head back to the castle.

With all of Yevliesza's blundering about in the woods, it was clear the girl was inept at aligns. That, at least, gave her some comfort. If Nashavety could not prevent her from taking training, at least she could assure that she was at the bottom of the triad. Byasha would not be hard to influence. She no more approved of Anastyna's decision to bring her to Numinat than Nashavety did.

To her consternation, the Deep had come into the girl. But how could it be in any way natural, given that Yevliesza was an adult when it ripened in her? Her power was bound to be twisted, her abilities stunted. In time, this would become clear. With a little help from Nashavety.

She raised her hand, closing her fingers, all except the smallest, and dismissed the heavy fog. It began to thin, first into a scrim of grey and then a mist, tattered by shafts of sun. Heavy fog created obstacles to discerning the aligns. But Byasha was correct not to delay the assessment just for that.

Now that Yevliesza was accepted into arcana training, certain people might breathe easier, knowing that she was not ruined after all. But those hopes would be dashed. Poison could not be wished away, it must be washed away.

She had not quite decided how to assure this cleansing. Small steps, and then the wider view would open up.

One small step had already proved efficacious. She had sent Daraliska to suggest to the appropriate guards that the envoy be harried in matters of food and water and also emotional peace. Sleep interruptions and hints of coming punishments. The men had been more than willing to do their part. The result had been satisfying, even if the outcome came somewhat close to trespass of person.

Ansyl had already been sickly when he returned to Numinat. It could not reasonably be said that a simple diet and a few disturbing comments from the guards had killed him. Nashavety felt confident that she had kept to the ways and customs.

No one should depart from them. The First Ones had decreed it so.

CHAPTER 14

Valenty stood in the library doorway, seeing that Yevliesza was at her studies with Grigeni. Amongst other duties, Grigeni was the household Keeper of Books, a position he relished and that prepared him for a role as tutor. His thin, hunched back was to the door, and although Yevliesza saw Valenty enter, Grigeni did not, continuing his lesson on penalties for crimes and trespasses.

"Thus for minor missteps, the house may correct the miscreant, but for large transgressions, the Lord High Steward decides. And . . . for trespass?"

"The sacrifice of the left-hand small finger, or the princip can order casting from the Tower."

"And if sacrifice of the finger, could a noble affinity come back?" He tapped the *Book of Ways and Customs*.

"Probably it could, in time?"

"No, it could not. Without a full left hand, noble power fades and in its wake comes a small power, the shadow of what had been."

Grigeni started to go on, but Valenty came forward, saying,

"Could you not find a more pleasant topic for early morning studies, Grigeni? Bloody fingers and jumps to the death. Enough."

The tutor stood. "My lord."

"Grigeni, my thanks, and I will school our guest this morning."

"The *Book of Chartings* was to be next."

"I shall bear that in mind." Grigeni had been his man for a long time, and he was indispensable, but now and then the pedant came out.

When they were alone, Valenty noted Yevliesza's wan look, her eyes in shadowy sockets, her skin dull. "You are well, I hope?"

"Yes, my lord." She played with the collar of her dress, tugging it up, though it rose no higher.

Valenty knew she was aware that her burns drew the eye, even if they were noticeable only at close examination. From what he could see of the scars under her chin, they did seem to be fading.

"I thought I would drop in on your study session. I was across the hall, examining the work in the scriptorium." He did not owe her an explanation for his actions, except this time, perhaps. Even Grigeni had found his presence odd.

"The work on the grimoire?" she asked. "When will it be complete?"

He laughed. "Oh, never. 'As to the uses of small powers,' he recited, 'they are as many as the feathers of birds.'" If the grimoire was ever complete, he would lose his purported life endeavor, and people might begin to wonder what else he did. It was not easy to appear useless, and he hoped not to have to redouble his efforts.

"Let us open the *Book of Chartings*." He took a seat next to her. "You have looked at it before?" Though his copy was quite old, new folios had been recently added.

"A few times. It's got maps of the known aligns. Ones that are on the ground, anyway."

Valenty opened the thick tome. "It is not possible to memorize every one, but practitioners have a natural interest in recording what they know." He slowly turned the pages, some with minor crosshatchings of lines and some with complex assemblages.

Yevliesza pointed to a page. "That one looks like the Numinasi letter A."

"Yes, I see it." The aligns sometimes seemed to form configurations of a pleasing sort. Like the stars that one grouped into constellations, the aligns appeared to have, yet did not have, symbolic form. "But do not become one of those practitioners who find patterns everywhere."

She dropped her gaze, offended.

He had meant to put her at ease. They had a different understanding between them now. But it was early for him to say he understood her. She was closed off to him, not working to offend him as before, but not opening to him, either.

Turning to the back of the book, Valenty drew it closer. "This section is the codex of the crossings. Our couriers must know these routes. It presents a particular difficulty as the tunnels are very much alike."

Her hand traced the routes. At the joins to the separate kingdoms she leaned in to read the inscribed names. Arabet, Alfan Sih, Jade Pavilion, Volkia . . . "But the other page showed a different version."

"Because over time they change. It is why the crossings can be dangerous. A traveler might end up somewhere unfriendly."

"Like?"

"Depending on which places one has dealings with. Friendly or unfriendly dealings." He turned the book over and began untying the back cover from the bound pages. "The chartings are often updated, so more folios are added." He worked at the bind-ings until he had one of the sections pulled out. "This is the one we will use today."

It seemed her mind was elsewhere. "The guard who brought me here," she began. "Do people blame him for the dactyl's death? Should we have landed or sought shelter?"

"Ah, that one. He has no blame. But the man was greatly disturbed by the dactyl's loss. He is a *harjat.*" He noted her frown of confusion. "The Numinasi warrior order. Even so, he resigned his post."

"Oh, I didn't . . . I didn't know." It sounded like a heavy penalty, even if self-imposed.

He stood up. "But we must think about the future, not the past. Come. And take this folio with you." He handed her the sheaf of pages. "I presume you have not been to the Tower yet."

She reacted with a spark of interest.

"Are you up for a long climb?"

⚜

THEY ENTERED A SECTION OF THE CASTLE THAT HAD BEEN LONG abandoned. Here the great halls soared high, as though built for a greater people. The windows were merely slits, keeping the region in gloom. Owls roosted in the roof timbers and, stirred by the visitors, gently hooted.

"Why doesn't anyone live here?" Yevliesza asked.

"Over many years the castle expanded, and some areas were considered less desirable. I think no one wanted to spend time so near the Tower."

"Because it's the place of execution."

"The resistance is not to death, but to the trespass that earns the sentence. That aversion is profound in the Mythos. It is not as resilient as the origin world. We are sustained by powers, but can also be destroyed by overreach."

"Are we . . . is the Mythos that fragile?"

"Life is fragile."

"And some fears are overblown? Are Nashavety's?"

"I want to say yes. But she is not wrong to be cautious." He could not place himself against Nashavety, not openly. "Volkia is cause for worry."

"I hear about this, but what have they done?"

"What is it called, in mundat, when there is much talk of conflict but little done outright?"

"Saber-rattling."

"Perfect. They have a disturbing goal, that the Mythos kingdoms should allow open mixing; few barriers. Our custom is that realms approve or deny outsiders to enter. The Volkish wish for what they call *Miderhom*. Freedom of passage."

"Maybe they're right?"

"Lady Nashavety says it is a subterfuge, hiding their wish to extend their control. There are those who agree with her."

They came to a circular staircase. Blackness hovered around the curve, and Valenty wished he had brought a torch, but he had not been here for years and had forgotten how the Tower had no windows except at the top.

"The stairs sometimes have debris from the wind, from birds. Take my hand lest you trip."

"I won't fall."

She was overconfident as always. "Take my hand," he repeated, trying for a gentle tone.

Her hand came into his, and they went up.

"Why are we here, Lord Valenty?"

In truth, he had carefully worked out an excuse to spend some time with her. To get to know her, as Anastyna expected him to do, so that he could advise her and keep her from trouble. He preferred to do this without people gossiping, without household staff whispering that she was favored for his attentions. The Tower was private.

"Tomorrow you begin the arcana. I have an exercise that may be helpful."

Her steps became more assured as her eyes adjusted to the black throat of the Tower stairs.

"The arcana," she mused. "I could fail it. I might not have a strong enough power."

"There is no failing the arcana, although the teacher can dismiss the arcana. In any case, you take instruction, and your power—however great or small—becomes closer to you, more true."

An eruption of wings from above them. Yevliesza's startled jump made her miss the step, and Valenty pulled her toward him, steadying her. He had almost put his arm around her waist for a better support, but decided that might be misinterpreted.

As they continued to climb, she asked, "Could you have had an arcana? For warding?"

"Ah, no. My gift is small."

"It didn't look small to me when you demonstrated in your study."

The windows. He carefully steered her away from that line of questioning. "It is your arcana we are focused on today. You will see when we get to the top."

They went on, once stepping over the bones of what might have been a bird.

At last the spiral of the Tower lightened to grey and then to brighter day.

The room at the top.

"Oh . . ." Yevliesza pulled back. She surveyed the three windows, seeing that they were from floor to ceiling and without railings.

"It is all right. We will not go too near."

"This is far enough."

Now he did have good reason to put his arm around her and did so. "We will go just far enough to see most of the courtyard."

She leaned into him as they took a few steps.

"Which one is . . ." She paused.

"Behind you, that one." He turned with her, and they faced the Trespass Door. To his surprise, she took a few steps toward it, pressed tight to his side.

They looked down. Very far down, for the fall from the Tower through this door was not only to the base of the Tower but three times that far, down the rock cliff to the bottom.

"It's a wicked punishment," she whispered.

"For the wicked." He sometimes forgot she was of mundat and had not the hardness of Numinasi women. "But now, Yevliesza, let us talk of the aligns."

She let him lead her to a different window, the one facing the central compound. He took the codex from her and after a moment found the page he sought. "Here is the record of the great courtyard. The aligns that traverse it."

They gazed intently at the page for a few moments.

"Six lines," she said. "Two are long, major ones."

"They might be major, but length does not signify strength, so I am given to understand. Now, look down and imagine the six lines occupying the courtyard." They took a step closer and then one more. She had gone closer to the window than he would have taken her, but he held her firmly.

"I don't see them," she said, squinting in the sunlight.

"Perhaps not, but now you can imagine how they run. And when you walk in the courtyard, you can remember."

"It's wonderful, Valenty." Her eyes seemed focused very far away, as though taking something in that could not be explained. "Six lines. The worlds have corridors of magic."

"What runs through the rocks of the land runs through the

bones of the Numinasi."

She leaned into him. "That's beautiful."

He shrugged. "A saying."

They stayed long minutes, transfixed by the view from the opening. For her comfort he could have warded the openings with clear glass, but she needed to harden.

A Numinasi should not be afraid of heights.

YEVLIESZA CAME TO RAVEN FELL TO MEET BYASHA. THE HALL of Nashavety was large and deep enough that some of the rooms —like the one she stood in now—lacked windows and lay in soft gloom, except for light globes that hung near the ceiling like moonlets.

She and another woman waited outside a large archway that gave onto a parlor with a fireplace large enough to drive a golf cart into.

"I'm Yevliesza," she said to the other woman.

"Rusadka." The broad-shouldered woman, in a belted, quilted jacket with silver buttons, wore her dark, springy hair tightly pulled back by a clasp that looked to be made of iron. She was military then, by her bearing and severe hairstyle. Maybe even *harjat*.

"I take it we are both to be in the triad," Yevliesza said.

"Likely."

As there seemed little chance of further conversation, Yevliesza noted her surroundings more carefully. The lower part of the walls were dressed in polished wood. She saw that just through the spacious arched doorway, the room's floor was laid in an intricate mosaic.

"Nashavety is a wealthy woman," she murmured to herself.

"She is a *fajatim*." Rusadka didn't seem to possess more than one blank facial expression. Or more than four words at a time.

Three figures approached from down the corridor. One was Nashavety. The other person was a slim young woman in a fine gown. A very large dog walked at Nashavety's side. Its back was not much lower than Nashavety's waist.

"A thrall," Rusadka muttered. "Since she has the gift of creatures, she can control it."

This was hardly reassuring, as Nashavety might as easily sic the beast on her as restrain it.

"Lady Nashavety," Yevliesza said, making a bow of courtesy, just creasing her waist.

Rusadka bowed stiffly. "If I may make myself known, Lady Nashavety, I am Rusadka, of the *harjat* order."

"Welcome. And now," Nashavety said, "you must greet Sofiyana of Karsk Polity, House Cherev, who is joining you for the arcana." Next to Rusadka, Sofiyana's face looked pale as a fish belly, though her features were attractive. The trait that drew attention, however, was her violet hair, tightly and profusely ringletted. Wisps of hair charmingly escaped her hair net.

Nashavety gestured for them to enter the great parlor.

When they had settled before the cold fireplace, Nashavety pointed to a spot at her feet, and the dog—or what Rusadka had called a thrall—lay down, one paw possessively over the lady's right shoe. It watched the three women with bright, disconcerting interest.

Nashavety took in her guests, each in turn. "I am pleased to host an arcana in Raven Fell. Because it is an arcana of aligns, however, most of your work will be out of doors. Still, you are welcome here. It gives me particular pleasure to welcome Sofiyana, who comes to us from Karsk polity with the highest recommendations. She has already made a favorable impression on your arcana guide, so I have confidence that your efforts will bring success."

Byasha appeared at the door and was waved in. The thrall raised its head, ears forward, and tensing as though hoping for a chance to demonstrate speed.

"Lady Byasha," Nashavety said in welcome. "Please make room, ladies." Rusadka jumped up to give Byasha her seat. At the abrupt movement, the thrall snapped around to look at Rusadka who dared to curl her lip at the beast.

Sofiyana spoke up. "We are so honored to be led by Lady Byasha. Her name is known as far as my polity."

Byasha scowled, but seemed pleased.

"We also welcome Rusadka, who is in *harjat* service," Nashavety said. "And, as well, Yevliesza . . . a newcomer amongst us, I think would be the best way to say it." Nashavety's expression was only slightly warmer than the thrall's, which seemed to reflect stark hunger.

Flicking a glance at Yevliesza, Nashavety said, "Do not look at him, my dear." She sighed. "Now you have taught him to distrust you. Ways and customs, ways and customs." She appealed to Byasha. "I leave them to you, with apologies for the task you have ahead of you. We must depend on Sofiyana to help her triad sisters, shall we not?"

Byasha nodded. "I expect them to help each other, of course. Even if it is bound to be one-sided. A triad is a triad."

Sofiyana murmured, "I am sure they will help me as well. My own mother could not do a thing with me, so I very much hope to earn their friendship."

Byasha chuckled. "That is why a mother never leads a triad with one of her own." She rose to her feet. "With your permission, my lady, I would like to begin immediately. May I take my girls now?"

At Nashavety's nod, Rusadka came forward to take Nashavety's hand, making a small bow as she did so. Then Sofiyana. With her turn, Yevliesza made sure not to step on the thrall, and took the *fajatim's* hand. Nashavety's prominent amber ring drew the eye, resting on the third finger of her left hand like an exotic bird's egg. The thrall watched every move with bright, fierce eyes, tinged—if Yevliesza was not imagining it —with red.

Nashavety's face was placid as she looked at Yevliesza. "I trust your fits will not interfere with arcana instruction. Byasha will keep me informed if it is too rigorous for you."

"I will try not to let you down, my lady *fajatim*," she responded, determined to copy the neutral expression and to pretend she had not just been insulted.

As they left the room, Sofiyana leaned in to Yevliesza and whispered. "I thought the thrall beast was going to kill one of us for fun!"

Yevliesza whispered back. "If only she had *fed* it ahead of time."

Sofiyana chirped a laugh, which earned a frown from Byasha as she led them out of Raven Fell. Sofiyana composed her features with difficulty. It seemed that her hair was not her only feature that tended to escape confinement.

"HOW MANY POWERS DO YOU HAVE?" SOFIYANA ASKED THE other two.

Byasha had left them to practice first form on their own in the great courtyard where, she had said, the aligns were very strong, and thus there should be no difficulty in finding connection.

"Oh." Yevliesza frowned. "I never thought I had more than aligns." She looked to Rusadka.

"One."

Sofiyana laughed. "Well, good. Then we do not have to be jealous of each other. Because, me too. We are all starting out the same. Except, do you know, Byasha will rate us every day as to whether who is first, second, or third."

"Plenty of time for jealousy, then," Rusadka said.

Sofiyana rolled her eyes.

They were carefully, slowly, strolling on the central path which Byasha had said was purposefully built on an align. They edged around several great blocks of stone that the high practitioners of aligns would lift into a secure place on the Bridge of the Moon. The women looked up at the jutting first section of bridgeway. They all knew there was a great align above their heads.

"Who feels something?" Sofiyana asked.

Yevliesza thought that claiming a perception might chase it away. She had felt the bridge align immediately when she entered the courtyard. There was a shimmer in the air of its intended path.

She answered Sofiyana. "Let's just stay quiet and see if it wells up."

As they walked, they neared the Great Circle, the disc of grass surrounded by a beaten path where Numinat rites were observed. Yevliesza remembered how from the Tower, she visualized three of the six aligns crossing the center of the circle. But they wouldn't walk into the circle; no one did except for high ceremony.

"There are three approaches to connecting with the aligns. Perception, touch, and sight. And I have to admit, nothing is reaching me." Sofiyana complained.

"A lot of words, though," Rusadka muttered.

"Well, we are not on army patrol right now. We are a triad; we are *supposed* to talk." In a few more steps, Sofiyana said, "I am not having any luck. I will try the align that runs through the copse of trees over there." She latched onto Yevliesza's hand. "Come on."

Once inside the stand of trees, Sofiyana turned to Yevliesza. "Rusadka does not like me. I strike some people that way. That is the reason I was sent to live with my aunt." She shrugged and plopped down on a bench.

"Nashavety is your *aunt*?" The thought of that woman being part of a family was startling.

"Please do not tell Rusadka; that will just make things worse. I mean, my aunt does not even like me, in fact she thinks I am pathetic. Arcana is my only chance to do something useful." She patted the bench. "Oh, just sit. Because this is a really good place, I can definitely perceive the align. Try it."

Yevliesza sat and waited. Despite Sofiyana's chattiness, she felt a stirring. Something swept up from her feet into her chest, a warmth that was also like knowing. Having a moment of what she thought was true perception lightened her heart. It struck her how infrequently she felt truly happy and how it was always in the presence of other people: Pyvel, Valenty, Tirhan, sometimes Dreiza. And now Sofiyana. For the first time in her life, she was surrounded by people who knew her, at least a little.

Sofiyana turned to her. "Tell me about the mundat. Tell me everything."

"Machines. Democracy. Guys in blue jeans."

"I love it already. What are blue jeans?"

A movement to one side caught Yevliesza's attention. A man had entered the clearing and paused, regarding them. He wore a grey-green, well-tailored army uniform, and over his jacket he wore a belt with a ceremonial sword.

"Good day to you, young misses." Heavily accented. Likely a court envoy.

"And to you, sir," Sofiyana said breathlessly.

Yevliesza continued to take the man in. His uniform was strange. Oddly modern, with what might be called riding trousers, loose at the hips and tucked into high leather boots. His brimmed hat looked like what any mundat army officer might wear. It did not go at all with the feudal world around them.

"A fine day to enjoy the trees, yes?" The officer looked around. "I come here as well. My favorite bench there."

"Oh!" Turning to Yevliesza, Sofiyana said, "Perhaps we should move on . . ." She stood.

Yevliesza saw no reason to give up their place. "But we have been walking for hours."

Sofiyana latched onto Yevliesza's arm and pulled her to her feet.

The man watched them with some humor in his face, but it did not soften his aspect.

As they retreated down the path, Yevliesza glanced behind to see that he had taken a seat on the bench.

"That was the Volkish envoy, Count Gautrik," Sofiyana whispered.

"How do you know?"

"Who else could it be, dressed like that? I was so nervous! He made me quite uncomfortable. What did you think of him?"

The modern uniform was startlingly out of place. She had accustomed herself to this society, which seemed, in her limited knowledge of history, to be thoroughly feudal—however with deep powers. But in this soldier she saw a different century, a recent one. The envoy almost looked as though he might have come from Fort Sill in Oklahoma.

"Well, what did you think of him?" Sofiyana persisted.

"His manners were lacking."

"He is an ambassador and a Count," Sofiyana protested.

"No excuse."

Sofiyana smiled conspiratorially. "You are right. Do you always say what you think?"

"Well, only to friends. Best to avoid whipping."

"Whipping! No one would dare."

But Yevliesza knew that wasn't true.

CHAPTER 15

L ying awake hours before dawn, Valenty considered his dream of the raven with a head of a dactyl, circling, circling. The leather straps of its saddle hung far down, trailing knives.

It was only a dream, but he could not shake it.

He got out of bed, taking care not to tug the blankets. Swathing himself in a robe, he paced to the fire pit and back, several times stopping at the window to detect how near dawn was. Not a hint of light in the sky.

With the fog of sleep dispelling, the raven at last came to perch. Valenty recognized the visitation and how it had embodied his fears. The raven stood in for Raven Fell and Nashavety. The raven had grown powerful, dactyl-strong, knifing those it wished ill. As the *fajatim* had cut Ansyl down. He could not prove it, but he had awakened in the heart of the night knowing what Nashavety had done.

Dreiza stirred. "Valenty," she murmured, "come to bed."

"I will. Go back to sleep."

Nashavety was an enemy to Anastyna and therefore to himself. And she was a zealous one, without fear.

Dreiza sat up and propped the pillows behind her. "Come. Talk to me."

He climbed in and sat beside her, pulling her into the crook of his arm. "Nashavety is growing daggers for teeth."

"You are just noticing? She has tried to make trouble, but she has failed to discredit Yevliesza. The worst she could do is spread rumors that our guest wore an unsightly bracelet."

"Not the worst." He told her his suspicion that Ansyl died from neglect or mistreatment by one of the guards. At the *faja-tim's* urging.

Dreiza bit her lower lip. "Anastyna must be told."

"Yes, but the guard has left the city. Nashavety had to make sure he would not be questioned."

Dreiza threw off the covers and got out of bed. "How could she have dared? By the eight hells . . ." She shrugged the night-gown from her shoulders and began to dress. "She grows bold, that woman."

Her nakedness was still pleasing to him, especially when she was unselfconscious. Her body was strong and mostly smooth, but even her lines of aging were unable to dull her as a woman.

"Oh, stop looking so hard," she tossed back at him, smiling and pulling her shift over her head.

"A man may look at his wife," he countered, happy for the distraction, glad to think that she would share the pre-dawn with him, foregoing sleep.

"All the young things that you have in my place, Valenty. Do you not tire of me?"

This was her familiar question. And though he did have lovers, his answer was always the same. "I do not tire of you, my love."

She brushed her hair into order, making a quick plait over one shoulder. "Then, as to Nashavety, how shall we handle this matter with Yevliesza?"

"With Yevliesza?"

"I mean"—she sat on the edge of the bed—"do we tell Yevliesza how her father might have died?"

"We tell Anastyna our suspicions. As for Yevliesza . . ."

"Valenty, my dear. She has asked you to share information with her. This is rather big information."

"There is no proof. And Yevliesza has enough trouble comporting herself without a gnawing hate for a *fajatim* she must often see."

"And she might turn on us."

"Might?" When Dreiza said *might*, she sometimes knew how it would be, sometimes catching a moment from the braid of time, a time to come.

Dreiza persisted. "She might well. If she discovers that we withheld knowledge of Nashavety's role in her father's death."

Anastyna would not be pleased. Nor did *he* want Yevliesza to feel betrayed. But whether he told her or not, there was a chance she would blame him. Blame him for not doing more for her, for her father . . .

"It is for the best," Dreiza pressed on. "To be open with her."

As he thought through the implications, his wife watched him struggle. "Valenty? Surely you are not hesitating?"

"I will tell her," he casually said. At some point, he would tell her.

۞

IN THE MIDDAY SUN, RUSADKA HELD UP A HAND TO HELP Sofiyana manage one of the stairs cut into the cliffside, a tall stair and, like them all, without a railing. "Next time you might try sturdy boots," the *harjat* said.

The triad was halfway down the hillside, passing cliffside dwellings tucked in like bird nests in a tree. It hadn't occurred to

Yevliesza that the aligns would run vertically. The alarming steepness of the stairs had utterly blocked her perception of the supposed align hereabouts. To make matters worse, in places the stairs were wet from a trickle of water that slid up the mountain side to augment the palace water.

Sofiyana thanked Rusadka for the help, but looked down the remaining stairs with apprehension.

In second form, they were assumed to have mastered align *connection* to some extent. Now Byasha had introduced *elements* to show how the mediums through which the aligns progressed could be anywhere, in land, water, or air.

"We're thrown off by investigating the hillside," Yevliesza said as she managed a few more steps down. "It's easier to find aligns on the flat."

"What if it is in the air around us?" Sofiyana asked.

"The point is not to guess, but to know," Rusadka said.

"Well, if I knew, I would have said so," Sofiyana threw back as Rusadka led the way. At times people passed them on the narrow stairs, moving easily and faster than seemed wise. "Perhaps we should rest. Movement might distract us."

"Close your eyes," Yevliesza suggested.

"I shall not," Sofiyana proclaimed. "Or do you wish to see me plunge headlong into the valley?"

Rusadka chuckled. Then she sobered. "I think it is close to us. But I cannot sense it firmly."

Yevliesza felt the same way. But Byasha might have lied about there being an align nearby in order to test them.

"I am going back up," Sofiyana declared. "We may have missed aligns that run horizontally along the cliffside." She lifted her skirts and began the hike back up. "I will call down to you if I find something."

As she left, Yevliesza sat on the stairs, over to one side to allow the flow of people to bypass her. Rusadka sat on the step just below her.

Many common citizens—field workers, tallow makers, launderers, tanners, weavers and others—lived on the cliffs in ancient quarters hewn from rock and wood, all cunningly fastened to the hillside. A few broad ledges served as plazas for shops and industries like iron working and tallow making.

Yevliesza's feet ached from the past week of walking the aligns, or trying to. She pulled off a boot to rub her foot. "I wish I had a pair of those *harjat* boots," she groused. Hers were of fine leather workmanship but they weren't made for hiking.

"I will bring you a pair."

They gazed out on the vast, folded hills of the valley. At this height it reminded Yevliesza of her view from the dactyl's back, and she wished she had paid more attention instead of cowering against the saddle.

"How do you bear Sofiyana?" Rusadka was asking.

"I know she can be trying. But she livens up our work. I'm never quite sure what she'll come up with next."

"She is afraid of hard work. And makes light of Byasha's teaching."

There was something about Sofiyana that Yevliesza admired, and it came to her that it was her rebel streak. Rules were suggestions to her. But unlike Yevliesza, she seemed to know just how far to go.

Rusadka had learned discipline in the army, and even more so as a *harjat*. Sofiyana must be a constant annoyance to her. Yevliesza turned to her companion. "Do you have a—leave of absence, from army service?"

"I am under discipline at night and in the mornings. But the arcana lasts only as long as Byasha says I am progressing, which might not be for long."

"She's not pleased with anyone. I think we're an extra duty she could do without. The work on the bridge is her priority."

"But the Bridge of the Moon has other practitioners. They raised more stones yesterday." She turned to look at Yevliesza. "Have you tried lifting anything? The third form is control, but we should be able to lift at least a pebble."

"Have you?"

Rusadka smirked and pointed her little finger to a small stone at her feet. It wobbled, then slowly lifted.

"Wait—" Rusadka rose to her feet. "If I can raise a stone, then maybe we are on an align!" She looked back at the cliff face. "Oh, that is it, then." She nodded to herself. "That *is* it."

Yevliesza got up. "What?"

Rusadka leaned over and put her hand in the trickle of water making its shallow way up the hillside.

Then it was clear. A veil which Yevliesza hadn't even known was there, lifted, and all the nerve endings in her left hand and in her arm up to her elbow zinged. The trickle of water. That was the align.

"Rusadka!" Yevliesza exclaimed. "It was in the water all along, and we just ignored it." Yevliesza put her arms around the woman for a quick hug. "You did it." To her surprise, Rusadka hugged her back.

They savored the breakthrough for a few moments, grinning, and then began the climb back to find Sofiyana.

At the summit they found her engaged in lively conversation with Lord Tirhan.

He saw the two women approaching. "Oh, so these are your triad companions." He smiled in greeting at Yevliesza. Sofiyana introduced Rusadka and heard of the water align, but Sofiyana's attention was on the Alfan lord.

"Had I known that you were at your studies," Tirhan said, "I would not have intruded. Please forgive me."

"This is not the army, my lord," Sofiyana laughed. "We can take our ease. The arcana is intense and one must turn away from the effort at times lest one become trapped in too much striving."

"That is wisdom, perfectly expressed," he said, pinning her with his attention. "But I fear I must leave you or I will have to answer to Lady Byasha." He bowed and they watched as he walked away.

Sofiyana murmured, "Now there is a handsome man."

Rusadka was not impressed. "And one who may safely toy with affections since he will no doubt be returning home."

"And might bring a wife with him when he does," Sofiyana tossed back, still watching him. "And, anyway, it does not stop the princip from her dalliance."

"With Lord Tirhan?" Yevliesza asked, surprised.

"No, she has taken as a lover Chenua of the Lion Court."

"That is just a rumor," Rusadka said. "It is not an open thing."

"Yes, and the further rumor is," Sofiyana began, her eyes sparkling with the gossip, "that she is besotted with him." As they made their way back to report to Byasha, she added, "When we consider Tirhan and Chenua, maybe they have the allure of what is different."

Yevliesza muttered, "I never knew that being different had allure in Osta Kiya."

"Nor I," Rusadka agreed, smirking.

CHAPTER 16

Three nights ago I looked for you, Kirjanichka. I was disappointed not to find you. The stabling girl told me that you had a several nights' duty to patrol the gorge, and though it was an important task, I was sad not to see you for so long.

You were looking for Volkish intrusions. I hope that you will never find them. It comes to me that their dark fingers are reaching for Numinat, but I prefer to banish these premonitions. The princip has the foreknowing of greater adepts than myself, and for me it is too troubling to think upon. Change is coming, but we can survive it, despite Nashavety's fears. It is said the Volkish are not only new—their kingdom arose very close to the day I was born—but that it is their way to have a sense of aggrievement. In the past they would conduct small raids, stealing what they could find. We must be watchful even now, lest they come in stealth, slipping past our defenses. It is more likely that they would try to muster a great force, but they must hesitate to confront an army such as we have.

Here are your figs, Kirjanichka.

You see how I dote on you! But you should not eat them all at *once. Savor them, my dear. That is the secret of happiness. Trea-sure what you have, for who knows if it will be snatched away in an hour, in a breath. Yes, I am thinking of such things again. Wondering how a woman of my years could forget to treasure things.*

I know it is a mistaken impulse to try to make sense of it all. Life happens moment by moment and then we impose a story upon things as though there was a pattern that was too large for us to see at the time but, later, all too plain.

To foresee a great pattern is beyond my gifts, surely?

Oh very well, Kirjanichka. I will tell you what I see, or think that I see:

The weave of the world set out to trap Yevliesza.

Look at the pieces that waited for the girl of the mundat. Imagine her in the middle of a circle of power. Not in the circle, but in its center. Some of the players are clear. Anastyna is there, of course. She had need of the girl as an emblem of the wider field, beyond Numinat. And if Anastyna is there with hopes, then of course Nashavety appears to ward off those hopes. Then, here is a surprise: The girl Sofiyana. She came from the far reaches of the kingdom with her simple hopes that could never remain so. And so we have three points of the circle occupied. Then Volkia, for four. And because numbers that are even are without power, here is the fifth presence. Valenty.

They stretch out their arms, and without touching, without true alliance, they create a circle. A potent one, infused with ambition, envy, and desire to fully entrap the girl who fell from the sky.

You see, Kirjanichka, why I do not blame the girl. When she came to us she was a sparrow. And in the circle a few of them were hawks, circling, circling . . . and they were hungry.

CHAPTER 17

Yevliesza stood barefoot, wearing only her shift of soft cotton trimmed in lace. She leaned out the window of her room watching the preparation for the Ninth Moon Festival. In the vast central courtyard, people were laying out tables of food, setting up tent shops, and creating arbors from poles and branches.

Her best gown was on the bed, the one Valenty had given her, grey-lavender, the bodice glimmering with small amber stones. Sitting down next to it, she trailed her hand along its intricate stitchery, remembering her dismayed reaction when she had been told at the fort that she had to wear a long, old-fashioned gown. That had been nearly six weeks ago. Wearing a long dress had been inconceivable then, back when all she had known were jeans and loose shirts.

She wondered if she would ever go back to the place where she was raised and, if she did, if there was any future for her there. She might live with Shane in a tidy homestead surrounded by cottonwoods. He might start an irrigation company. She would do the books, help Rolly in the store. The image carried an idyllic patina, but it faded like smoke in a breeze.

Her father wasn't there; and just as she had made the mundat bearable for him, he had made it so for her.

When a servant came in to help her dress, she was resting her elbows on the windowsill, looking out.

"Will anything be happening out there yet, Masha?"

"Just preparations, miss."

"When will the sky painting start?"

"Not until full dark. But you cannot see it from here. You must be in the courtyard, for it will play out in the north."

A knock at the door. It was Rusadka, looking quite imposing in her blue dress uniform with grey velvet cuffs and gilded buttons.

"Rusadka!" Yevliesza exclaimed. "You look wonderful." The blue of the jacket set off her flawless dark skin, and she wore the uniform with elegance.

As she pulled Rusadka into the room, Masha looked askance at the *harjat*. She was carrying a sturdy pair of boots, which she quickly explained was for the arcana, not for the night of the Ninth Moon.

Yevliesza tried the boots on. "Perfect," she pronounced. "Thank you."

Rusadka ducked a nod. "My team leader sends them to you for the arcana."

"Please convey my thanks." She added with a smirk, "Sofiyana will be so jealous."

Rusadka looked down at Yevliesza's gown, lying on the bed. "Such a grand dress," she said doubtfully.

"If it's too much, I'll wear something else. Masha has come to button me in."

But Rusadka insisted she would help instead, and after dismissing the servant, they began to cinch the dress into a pile to go over Yevliesza's head.

"Your scarred flesh . . ." Rusadka murmured, as she stood behind Yevliesza.

"But it looks better, doesn't it?"

"It does not look like any burns I have ever seen. May I touch your shoulder?"

After a few moments, she said, "This is peculiar. Most healed burns pucker at least a little, despite the healers. But yours are smooth."

"Still pinkish and angry, though?"

"In places, but in others . . . in the center of your back and on your neck, the scars are grey and even a low shade of blue." Rusadka touched her upper back. "And here, tiny lines spreading out like a spider web. Most peculiar."

Yevliesza tried ineffectually to turn her head to see. "Have you ever seen lightning burns, though?"

"No," Rusadka admitted.

When she was finally buttoned in, she looked down at the full skirt, the shimmering folds, and the delicate silk of the bodice gathered in diamond patterns. She tugged at the high neck to be sure it covered all. "Well?"

Rusadka nodded. "Very good. You make a noble figure. Except . . ." She stifled a grin, pointing to the hemline. "The boots may not go well."

❦

IT WAS LATE IN THE NINTH MONTH, THE MONTH THAT IN HER previous home she would have called September. Dusk came on earlier now, and lavender shadows softened the courtyard. Twenty feet above the walks, small glowing circles hovered, lighting the grounds, a service of manifesters who inconspicuously plied their arts from scattered posts. Household guards stood at intervals along the courtyard walls, looking splendid in formal dress, black trousers and dark red tunics bearing the white symbol of the torc.

Finery was the dress code for the festival. The women's gowns in silvery grey, blue, black, and deep violet contrasted with the brighter colors of the men's jackets: Dusky orange and reds, burnt gold, and every shade of green. Dark blue *harjat* dress uniforms wound through the crowd, and a few officers in tailored black uniforms stood out as members of the Volkish mission.

Lord Valenty and Lady Dreiza left Yevliesza in company with Sofiyana as they traversed the grounds. People stared at Sofiyana. She had flouted convention and wore a pale yellow gown that made her look fatally beautiful. Unless it was her hair, looking more violet than ever, and framing her face like a crown of magic fire.

Sofiyana's skin glowed with pleasure. "My mother told me what the Ninth Moon Festival would be like in Osta Kiya, but this is more than I can stand!"

"Will there be dancing?" Yevliesza asked, suddenly wary because she didn't know how to dance.

"Oh, Liesa, dancing? If one dances it must be in rites."

She had called her Liesa. "Don't use that name." Yevliesza whispered.

"Why? I asked you to call me Sofi."

"But in private!"

Her friend pulled her toward a food table. "You worry too much. About everything!"

Younger people circulated through the crowds carrying trays of special liquors and punches. One of the servers caught Yevliesza's eye, and she left Sofiyana to greet Pyvel.

"A cup of serpent's blood, miss?" He flashed her a wide smile.

"Is that what they call it?" She took one, noting to her relief that it smelled of spices, not blood. "Where were you for our game of cards yesterday?"

"Pressed into service. We have all been working on the observance for days." He leaned in. "I hear gossip from folks. Some is about you."

She sipped the drink, finding it over-sweet like pure honey. "What do they say about me?"

Their attention was drawn by a shimmer in the sky near the Tower. For a moment a woods appeared in the north sky, a scene of trees flickering an unnatural blue. Then it melted into dusk.

"I did that," Pyvel said. "My manifesting is getting deeper." He laughed at her expression. "Nay, that is Master Rostov, teasing us for what comes later."

"What gossip, then?"

"That the girl from mundat is in a triad. Everyone is surprised. And that Sofiyana is first, because she is Lady Nashavety's favorite. And that Lord Valenty gave you a dress fit for a *fajatim*."

She wouldn't care for Nashavety to see her in a dress above her station. She wanted to change, but her first impulse was to confront Valenty about this. Thanking Pyvel, she plunged down one of the walkways, scanning the crowds for her patron. She found him in a two-sided arbor where Dreiza was seated, deep in conversation with another woman.

"What were you thinking?" she demanded of him under her breath. "This dress is too fancy for me!"

"You are welcome," he said good naturedly. "You look quite good in that color."

"But it might make me an object of scorn to . . . to . . ." She hesitated to say the woman's name out loud.

"Yeess," he murmured beside her. "But she must see clearly that you have standing in my household."

As though their talk had conjured the woman, they both saw her as the crowd parted. But she stood with her back to them.

"Dreiza had the dress designed, so if you hate it, take it up with her."

His cavalier attitude annoyed her, but she decided that she had to make the best of things. Perhaps the gown was not so showy.

Two Volkish officers approached, and Valenty turned from Yevliesza to greet them, speaking in Volkish, one of his languages. She supposed that in such long lives there was time to learn several of the many tongues of the Mythos. It satisfied her that she already knew two. If English counted.

Yevliesza continued her stroll, not eager to meet the rude Count Gautrik again.

The great circle of grass came into view. The only place in the courtyard without adornment. There, Tirhan found her.

"Yevliesza, good evening." He narrowed his eyes as he noted her expression. "Not enjoying the evening?"

"Yes, of course. It's splendid. But I had a cup of serpent blood, and it didn't sit well with me."

"Never imbibe a Numinasi festive drink," he said with amusement. "How are you faring in arcana? You are meeting with Lady Byasha's approval?"

"Barely. Sofiyana is always first, that's clear. I'm probably third."

"Someone must be third; it is no shame in a triad. I barely survived my triad, but at least the score I earned was my own, prince of the realm or no."

So he *was* a prince. And was it fair that he was also alarmingly handsome? Especially in that dark, velvety green tunic with the coffee-brown cape. "You look well, Lord Tirhan. Very much a dashing noble."

Another trial manifestation colored the sky and fell away like a passing thought.

He raised an eyebrow. "Dashing? Well, if we are allowed to compliment each other—and I would not presume to, as it is not an Alfan custom—I will say that you are the loveliest woman on the grounds tonight."

"That's too grand."

"And humility makes you more so."

"If you're so stubborn, then that might be why you had trouble in arcana," she said with a smile. "But I suppose a prince can do as he wishes."

"If you but knew. Princes least of all."

Overhead more stars had joined the great field of the sky, emerging like bright, exotic creatures leaving their camouflage behind. She identified Orion with its bright belt. "How is it that everywhere the stars are the same?"

"Could it be otherwise for the Mythos kingdoms? We arise from the origin world."

"But then, where *are* we? Maybe a foolish question, but do you ever think of it?"

He pursed his lips. "On the mundat did you ever think of where you were . . . in that sense? Where in infinity your world was?"

"Ninety-three million miles from the sun."

"But I think it would not satisfy you to say that Numinat is ten thousand steps from the origin world. It is closer than that. It is the alter-earth." He looked up at the section of the sky where she had been gazing. "In Alfan Sih we call that constellation the Silver Queen. And you?"

"Orion the Hunter."

"The worlds exist overlapping."

"But it was a long way through the crossings to get here."

"Like the journey from youth to old age, it is a passage without a distance."

It was an idea that her father had spoken of, too, but it had always made her uneasy, as though she could slip from her world at any moment. "You are a philosopher, Lord Tirhan."

"Yes." A wry grin. "A bad one."

Over his shoulder, she saw Sofiyana approaching them. Before she could mention it, Tirhan had taken her by the arm. "Walk with me. But only for a moment."

It was rude to walk away from Sofiyana, but Tirhan hadn't seen her, and perhaps Sofiyana didn't know that Yevliesza had. "A moment? And not two?"

"Then two, if you would have it so. But we should not risk gossip."

"Can't you talk with Numinasi women?"

"Oh, certainly. But you cannot talk with Alfan men." He bent his head low to murmur, "Nashavety would see it in a certain light."

The light of foreigners showing their true loyalties. "I'm afraid that we may have snubbed my triad partner," she belatedly said.

"Then we shall include her."

Turning around as though to take in the sights, she beckoned to Sofiyana who stood some way back on the path. Sofiyana brightened and approached them. Yevliesza was glad of the decision, though she would have preferred to have Tirhan to herself.

The prince of Alfan Sih made a bow, and Sofiyana returned a deeper one. She was effusive in her comments about the evening. But it couldn't hold Tirhan's interest for long, and eventually he excused himself.

"He did not compliment me," Sofiyana complained. "Not even in the most careless way."

"The Alfan don't compliment people on how they look. It's not customary."

"Oh." She frowned. "How do you know?"

"I thought everyone knew. Anyway, you obviously are stunning."

"I chased him away."

"You worry too much," Yevliesza said playfully.

Sofiyana smiled. "Yes, you are right. We must grab one of those cups." She started off towards a serving girl with a tray. Once they had fresh cups in their hands, Sofiyana insisted that Yevliesza drink hers empty. The world grew hazy around her.

They sat on a bench to give Yevliesza a rest, but Sofiyana couldn't remain still for long, and left her just as the sky began to turn a neon, glowing green. The sky painting had begun.

In one quadrant of the sky a black shape solidified, like a high, flat cloud. By contrast, the sky below it still lay in gentle dusk. From the flat cloud, a vivid blue began to stream down like paint leaking from a can. Joining this trickle, yellow spilled, then many other colors, some merging into brown and green and all the colors of the spectrum. They began to form into shapes, until the northern sky became a tableau. It showed many people gathered in a courtyard, gazing up.

Applause broke out, as the crowd, now settled into many chairs and benches provided for the sky show saw a version of themselves and their courtyard. Then the scene transmuted into a vast chamber where hundreds of people were enjoying a feast. The story was underway.

Yevliesza held onto the edge of the bench to keep it from swaying. Tirhan had been right about Numinasi liquor. If Pyvel had been in sight she would have asked him to help her to her chamber.

Someone was approaching her, a person looking a lot like Valenty. He sat next to her.

"You should be mixing with people, not sitting off to the side-lines," he said.

"Umm . . . OK."

He looked more closely at her. "Yevliesza, everything you do is watched. We have discussed this."

"OK." The sky painting now depicted a ferocious dragon

which had somehow entered the doors of the feasting hall, and was upsetting tables and batting soldiers aside.

"Stop using that word." He watched the sky story for awhile, then murmured, "You know, you should not be seen with Lord Tirhan like that."

"Like what?" It was important not to appear drunk in front of Valenty. If drunk is what she was. Her head felt full of dried leaves and her tongue was not under strict control.

"Walking with him and having a long chat."

No walking. No chatting. "OK."

His voice fell into a tone of rebuke. "Half the women of Osta Kiya are in love with him and a good number of the men. It may appear that you have succumbed as well. If you are lonely, find a Numinasi man to warm your bed. Being too close to an Alfan will set people to saying that you are not returning to your roots, but . . . experimenting with who you will be."

In the sky story, one man stepped forward and spoke with the ravaging beast. At first it appeared that the dragon would summon a breath of fire to kill him, but instead, it narrowed its great yellow eyes and listened.

"Jealous?" she blurted, and then wished she hadn't. She took a deep breath, trying to clear her head.

He laughed. "I think not. In fact there are times when I would gladly ship you off to Alfan Sih where you could happily live for your remaining years. Which are likely to be half as long as Tirhan's, since you cannot be sure how deep Numinat flows in you." He stood up. "I will send Dreiza to you. It appears you have drunk too much."

She had missed part of the story, and now the man was riding through a forest. A pack of wolves secretly followed him. The horse kept looking back nervously, but the man was oblivious. Dreiza was on her way. Yevliesza didn't want to face her and, feeling a little more clear-headed, she made her way into the crowd.

Against the east wall of the compound tents displayed a dizzying array of wares: brooches, pendants, pottery, wovens, and from the iron forges, buckles, buttons, nails, and sheers. There were also leather goods like packs, belts, shoes, vests, and saddles. One seller had a table displaying great lumps of amber and finely wrought jewelry made from it. But few people were browsing since most were watching the sky painting. She kept her eyes averted from the show since it had been making her dizzy.

A merchant with a long, braided beard tried to interest her in a bronze bracelet set with opals.

She had a few coins in her pocket, but she declined the bracelet. She couldn't remember the values of the coins. When Grigeni had given them to her, he had explained that coins were for small needs. There were also things like stored credits of what they called *numining* from the use of their powers in service to others. The credits were reported to and recorded at the guilds, one for each power. Of which she had none, since her align power could not yet be of benefit to anyone.

As another wave of unsteadiness coursed through her, she asked the merchant if he had a chair she might sit in.

He brought two of them and sat next to her, giving up on the prospect of a sale.

"Where is the painter? Who's doing the show?" she asked.

The merchant pointed to the Tower. There, in the window facing the courtyard, the man stood, perilously close to the opening.

"Isn't he afraid of falling?"

"Afraid?"

"Such a long fall."

"Aye, but the Numinasi do not fear doing their job."

"Or death?"

"When it is not here, there is no reason to fear. When it comes, you are beyond fear."

"Um. Could you repeat that?"

A hand on her shoulder. She had been dozing. It had to be very late, but the sky was lightening. The orb of the full moon had risen over the east ramparts. Rusadka stood in front of her.

"Wake up. The Circle is forming." She helped Yevliesza to her feet. "How could you fall asleep?"

"Wasn't sleeping."

Rusadka shook her head. "Some brews should be avoided."

"I wish you had told me. I wish *someone* had told me." They approached the wide stretch of grass where, in a circle thirty yards across, people were joining hands. They were nobles and commoners, men, women and youngsters. A great crowd was assembling around the circumference.

"Who gets to be in the Circle?"

"The princip gave a nightbloom rose to ninety-one citizens, and they are different ones every year. If you get a rose, you are in the Circle."

Through the crowd Yevliesza could see Anastyna standing in the Circle, joining hands with an old man in drabs and a young girl in minty green, the kind of pastel color reserved for underage children. Someone began a chant. Yevliesza could make out only a few of the words.

"It is old Numinasi," Rusadka said. "The ancient tongue. The chant speaks of the chain of ages, the circle of kinship, the bonds of the Numinasi to each other and to the land."

A shudder took hold of the circle, as someone dropped the hand of the person next to her. It was Anastyna. She had turned to listen to someone who had come to speak to her.

The crowd shifted uncomfortably. Those in the circle dropped their hands to their sides. The circle was broken. A long wail on a horn sounded from far away, causing a few people to hurry from the field.

"I have to go," Rusadka said. "The warning call has gone out." A man hurrying by paused to speak to Rusadka. Turning back to Yevliesza she said, "Alfan Sih has been invaded. One who escaped was just here and told how the kingdom fell. It was conquered in a single day by overwhelming numbers. They say the king was slain."

"Slain by who?"

"The Volkish. They are on the march." And she was gone.

CHAPTER 18

In the brisk dawn, Valenty walked along the battlements with Lord Tirhan. They watched as a contingent of soldiers marched off, heading for the boundary gates to strengthen the forts there. Riders had left on dactyls to alert the regional forts three nights before. The Volkish envoy and his people were gone, banished and given transport by dactyl to the nearest boundary gate.

"They march with discipline, my lord," Tirhan said. In the cold of the morning, he held his cloak around him.

"Aye, they are well-trained," Valenty said. He had not seen Tirhan since the invasion, and he offered his condolences now. "I was shocked and saddened to hear of your noble father's death. And your brother's. Heavy losses, my lord."

Tirhan fought to keep his composure. "They died with many other warriors, defending the land."

"So I have heard. They set a brave example for all those who remain at arms against the invaders."

Tirhan could not speak, or chose not to. Valenty knew he must fiercely wish to go back, but now, as the presumed king, to enter the realm would just put him in the hands of the enemy.

After a pause, Tirhan returned the conversation to the Numinat army. "If Volkia tries to make an incursion here, they will find your forces a daunting match."

"Perhaps. But for three hundred years our army has been practicing without a major enemy." Valenty was trying to prepare the Alfan lord to hear that Anastyna did not plan to send help. But he knew that he would be pressed hard on it.

"The Volkish believe," Tirhan said, "that none of the realms have a military to match theirs. But Numinat clearly does. And Nubiah."

Valenty shrugged. "A trained army can be admired, Lord Tirhan. But if it does not fight . . ."

Tirhan turned from the parapet and regarded him. "You must fight, my lord. You can choose to do so in Alfan Sih, or you can wait until they bring arms against you."

Valenty had many opinions on this subject, but he could not be seen to support Tirhan's cause. Court opinion was in turmoil, many believing that Volkia was done with expansion, and that nothing could be salvaged for Alfan Sih in any case. To some, the way forward must be a defensive one, making the boundary gates unassailable.

"What answer does the princip give?" Valenty asked. Tirhan had been pleading his case with her already.

"To wait and see." He gazed out at the ranks of some seven hundred soldiers raising dust under their boots as the line snaked into the distance. "The Volkish have succeeded in conquest because they are uniquely prepared for war. They do not fear the other Mythos kingdoms because those armies are small. Now that Volkish intentions are clear you are like ducks tucking your heads underneath your wings."

Valenty snapped, "You are a guest here, my lord."

"My apologies. But it is true first and foremost of my own

land. We failed to defend ourselves. I would not like to see Numinat incur the same fate."

He went on. "There are rumors leaking out of Alfan Sih. That Volkia has new weapons, ones that disturb the general sensibilities, that undermine ways and customs."

"Who makes such a claim?"

"One who escaped. He fled to Norslad, and they have sent word to me. All this I told the princip. I believe their ruling prince, Albrecht, has . . . unnatural ambitions."

Valenty chewed on that. Perhaps Lord Tirhan was imputing dark imaginings onto his enemies. But Anastyna herself had always been deeply suspicious of Volkia. Still, if Tirhan was saying these things freely to others, he would not long be welcome in Osta Kiya.

Tirhan went on. "If you are to act, Anastyna would need support. She needs the *fajatim* to express willingness to stand against the invaders. Without the Halls behind her . . ."

"She is the princip," Valenty said. "She can decide to fight." At her word, the army would go to war. But she would not be princip for long. Perhaps Tirhan only cared that she send a force now. He was a desperate man.

"Lord Valenty, would you be willing to speak to some of the *fajatim*?"

Valenty raised an eyebrow. "I am not invited into their circle."

"But even one *fajatim's* voice could be influential."

"Those *fajatim* of my acquaintance have never heard me utter a word about matters of state. They consider that my strengths lie in managing my household poorly and my wardrobe supremely well."

"At least seek out leanings. If there is any chance . . ."

"It pains me to say that I do not support an armed response, Lord Tirhan. We have never been at war. Our forces have fought skirmishes, and those long ago. We are not ready."

Tirhan narrowed his eyes. It was the look of man taking another's measure. Deciding whether this Numinat lord was as sanguine as he appeared.

He was not, but Tirhan meddling with the noble Halls was the last thing Anastyna needed. Nashavety would love to have a warlike princip. She would bring her down faster than a hawk on a limping prey.

"I am sorry, my lord," Valenty said. "But we must wait and see." Tirhan now knew him to be either witless or a coward.

Sometimes Valenty hated himself.

⚜

WITH OSTA KIYA MOBILIZING FOR DEFENSE, BYASHA SUSPENDED the triad. Rusadka stayed busy with castle duty, and meetings of one sort or another took Valenty away. Yevliesza was on her own. She wondered how Sofiyana would fill her time, and the answer came one evening with a knock at her door.

"Are you ready to get out of here?" Sofiyana wore an everyday gown but managed to look striking in it.

"Where to?"

"The courtyard." She leaned against the door frame and critically took in Yevliesza's sparse chamber.

"Half of it's been taken over by soldiers," Yevliesza said. "They've put up temporary living quarters."

"I know. Grab your shawl."

Soon they stepped into the autumn night, and crossed the courtyard. Sofiyana led the way, taking them into the opposite wing of the castle, but refusing to say why.

A column of house guards came down the middle of the corridor with glowing globes lighting their way. Sofiyana pulled her into a recess to let them pass.

"Why are we hiding?"

"Because we must keep to the shadows for the next part."

"That doesn't sound good," Yevliesza said doubtfully, but intrigued anyway.

"Do you ever just cast aside the rules?" Sofiyana asked. "I thought coming to the city-palace would mean at least a little excitement, but I am stuck in Raven Fell. It is all so somber, I feel like I am in the lair of a malwitch!" She turned a worried look on Yevliesza. "Oh. I should not have used that word. Please do not tell anyone."

"No, of course not."

They ascended three flights of stairs and finally found themselves in front of a heavy iron door. "The bridge," Sofiyana pronounced.

She slid aside the bar securing the door, and then they were standing high above the courtyard, looking out onto the upper reaches of the castle's western side. A short stone walkway jutted out before them.

"The Bridge of the Moon." Yevliesza whispered.

"What there is of it. Come along," her companion said, stepping out onto the stub of the arched bridgeway. "Do not worry," she whispered. "It has these low stone walls for most of the way."

Yevliesza watched as Sofiyana crept along the short span jutting into the air, growing shadowy as the night enveloped her. Stepping out on the bridge bed, Yevliesza clutched her shawl around herself against the cold. The night sky was vast above her head and almost crusted over with stars.

By the dim light reaching her from the numerous palace windows, she could see Sofiyana sitting at the end of the bridge stub. She moved to join her, feeling as though she walked on the air itself.

Taking her cue from Sofiyana, she sat and let her legs dangle over the end of the bridgeway. The view of the castle, with its many lit windows flickering from fireplaces within, gave Osta Kiya a grandeur and mystery that thrilled her.

"It's fantastical."

"I knew it would be! Someday coming up here will be commonplace, but tonight, we are the first to have seen such a sight."

Muffled sounds of soldiers' voices came from small cook fires that dotted the courtyard's opposite end. She and Sofiyana sat entranced.

"It is so quiet," Sofiyana said, "compared with the Ninth Moon gathering. I wish it had not ended as it did. My mother will be worried."

"The Volkish wouldn't dare attack Numinat, so Lady Dreiza told me."

"Perhaps. But with Alfan Sih occupied . . ."

Yevliesza thought about Tirhan and the concerns he must have. And what he would do. Now her conversation with Valenty about not being seen with Tirhan seemed nothing but petty. The more she thought about it, though, the more she wondered if Valenty had in fact been jealous of Tirhan. The conversation was hard to recall exactly.

"Will Lord Tirhan leave soon, do you think?" Yevliesza asked.

"Oh, no, he must not leave. He is the next in line, and the Volkish would immediately apprehend him. He has an older brother, but they say he also died." Her friend gave her an appraising look. "I suppose you are in love with Tirhan."

"Of course not. But we are both exiles, now. Both of us far from home, with little hope of returning."

Sofiyana put her hand on Yevliesza's. "But surely you do not still feel like an exile? At least, not completely. I hope you do not."

Remembering Valenty's caution about being seen as an

outsider, she responded. "Well, at least I hope to become less of a stranger."

She thought their voices were getting too loud, and she pulled her legs up to be less noticeable. "Don't dangle your legs. The soldiers might see you."

"There is no light up here," Sofiyana responded, content to stay where she was. They sat in the quiet dark for awhile. In some of the lighted windows, shadows passed within. Yevliesza saw an owl glide into one of the Tower doors.

"I used to fear Numinat," Yevliesza said. "Long ago, when I was a child."

"Because you did not know us."

"Right. I didn't know much, except that they might come for me. Once I saw a man . . . a stranger. He came up through the crossing access near our house. I was very young. I knew he was from Numinat because he came out of the shed. I hid in my closet. There were voices downstairs, and I stayed hidden until I heard the front door shut."

"I would have been afraid, too!"

"From things my father had told me, I knew he would want me to go with him. But I wasn't sure why. I just knew that I was afraid."

"Well, you are very brave now. With all you went through and your father, too."

Yevliesza barely heard her. There was an align below, and it plowed through the courtyard like a furrow that had uncovered a river of molten silver. She stared, wondering if it could be her imagination, or if it was true align sight, that aspect of the first form that she had yet to experience.

She was about to mention it, when Sofiyana suddenly scrambled away from the edge of the bridge. "Hells!" she whispered. "A soldier has seen me! He is making for the door."

They sprang to their feet and, ducking down to try not to be seen over the bridge's stone barrier wall, they rushed to the end.

"He doesn't know there are two of us," Sofiyana said. "We have to split up. Find a different staircase. He can only catch one of us."

She grabbed Yevliesza by the shoulders. "If either of us gets caught, we swear there was no else, all right?" Starting to back away, she said, "Promise."

"I promise!" Yevliesza raced down the corridor. As she ran, she faintly heard the sound of a baby crying, so thin and far away that it seemed to come from another world. A distant door thudded closed. The memory came to her of being in the crossings when she was small, and the panic that overtook her, though nothing had been in those strange tunnels except the faraway sounds of voices and clanking, almost out of hearing range.

Reaching the staircase and descending, she slowed, keeping her steps soft so that she could hear if the soldier was coming up from the other direction.

At the bottom, she paused at the door to the courtyard. Going out now could alert the soldiers camped there to her unexplainable presence in the courtyard in the middle of the night. If only they had not gone up there! But the urgency of her situation began to pale. How bad, really, was sitting on the end of the bridge? Nothing had been damaged, and no one had ever warned them against going there. But Byasha would likely be furious.

Voices approached from down the corridor. Stepping behind a pillar, she made herself small, gathering her skirts to slim her profile. As she heard the door to the courtyard open, she peeked out and saw a soldier leaving with Sofiyana.

OVER HER MORNING MEAL, NASHAVETY HEARD FROM DARALISKA of a girl sitting on the end of the unfinished Bridge of the Moon in the dark hours of the night. Not just any girl, but Sofiyana, who now cowered in her room after a severe talk from Byasha, who threatened to dissolve the arcana. Fortunately, Nashavety convinced her it would be too harsh a penalty. Not the least because—although she did not put it so blatantly to Byasha—it would embarrass Raven Fell.

"Had she fallen . . ." Daraliska shook her head slowly. "Some align practitioners would have refused service to the bridge. Because of the offensive correlation."

The Bridge of the Moon was the most ambitious undertaking in Osta Kiya for hundreds of years. Nashavety inwardly groaned at the prospect of being identified as the family of the one who had sullied it.

She picked up her plate and turned to Gorga, sitting patiently by the veranda window, salivating after birds. The thrall jerked its head around as Nashavety put the plate of food on the floor.

She narrowed her eyes at the thrall as it twitched.

The beast became calm.

She flicked her left hand in the thrall's direction and it sprang to the food and began to feast.

Leaving Daraliska to pick up the plate when she dared, Nashavety left the table thinking how provoking Sofiyana's behavior was. The only reason she had supported the align arcana was the likelihood that Yevliesza would fail, as Byasha predicted. That would put an end to pretensions of the girl's normalcy. And now Sofiyana might earn expelling from the triad instead. And worse, it came at a time of the fall of Alfan Sih, when Nashavety should not be distracted by other matters.

The Volkish had proven their true nature: craven, deceptive, rapacious. They wanted mastery of other realms, not *Miderhom*. Open crossing, indeed! Her lip curled in disgust as she thought how Count Gautrik had stood in court, smiling and talking about relations and trade, and thinking as well, how Anastyna had been charmed by him. The princip was not only without sound bearings, she was bedding the envoy of Nubiah and no doubt talking to him of treaties between bouts of lust.

When she threw open the door of Sofiyana's chamber, her anger had stoked so high she had to hold her left hand behind her lest she do harm to the girl.

Sofiyana rose, looking like a fox cornered by a bear. She bowed. In a voice pitched high, she managed to say, "My lady."

"Explain yourself," Nashavety said in the soft tone she usually reserved for terrifying a servant who had erred.

"My lady, I did not know it was forbidden. I meant to see the stars, no more, but now I see it was a bad mistake, and I have once again shown my . . . silliness, as my mother says."

"A pretty speech. 'Out to view the stars.' And what if you had lost your balance and fallen to your death? How would I answer to your lady mother?"

"She would never have blamed you—"

"And how to answer the princip when she heard of an offensive event on the Bridge of the Moon? To think that I had been proud of your standing in the arcana. You have consistently been rated first in the triad. Now that will certainly change, if . . . *if* I can persuade Byasha to continue. Rusadka is a high second, and she will now supplant you. Even Yevliesza is improving. Did you think you would be first no matter what you did?"

"Probably," Sofiyana said in a beaten whisper.

Nashavety hooted a laugh. "Ah! So you know yourself to be a spoiled and simple-minded girl?"

"Yes, lady," came the voice of a mouse.

"Well. A start, then. You are my niece, and you will do my Hall proud, turning your attitude around so fast it would break the neck of anyone watching you."

Sofiyana's face turned hopeful.

"Yes. I will fix this situation for both our sakes. You will act properly chastened, but not beaten down. You will take any punishment Byasha delivers, without self-pity. You will earn back your first position. Do you understand?"

"Yes, lady." She was practically fainting with relief.

"But in return . . ." Nashavety's mind had been churning with options during this exchange. "In return, you will be mine. To serve me. To honor me. To do my bidding *whatever* it might be." She cocked her head at the cowering girl.

"Yes, Lady Nashavety. I am yours."

"Indeed." She drew herself up. "And there was no one up there with you?"

"What?"

"On the Bridge of the Moon."

"Oh! Well . . ."

"A lover? Was it a tryst?"

Nashavety stared at the girl, daring her to lie.

"I am not supposed to tell," Sofiyana said miserably.

"Except you will."

"It was Yevliesza. She was with me."

Well, now. Nashavety's mind began its turn into twisty corridors. Another delicious misstep from the ruined girl.

"She was afraid to go." Sofiyana said with satisfaction. "She has no courage at all."

Then it came to Nashavety that whatever stigma attached to Yevliesza, the same would fall on Sofiyana. She could not position it as a prank from one, but an insult from the other.

Nashavety sighed. "We will say no more about this."

"But she should be in confinement as well!"

Indeed. At the very least. It went against Nashavety's better nature to let pass an opportunity to abuse an enemy. But let it pass she must. The manner in which the mundat girl was offending the ways and customs was bound to deliver up further prospects.

CHAPTER 19

F ar below on the plains, Numinat fighters stood in formation, fifteen soldiers across and several ranks deep. They advanced. Officers led them forward, but at a shouted order, the formation began to change.

Pyvel pointed to the ranks as they began a methodical movement to the sides. "They are forming a square."

"But why?" Yevliesza asked. "Why a square?"

"To fend off attack from the rear. The center remains hollow, and the wounded from the square are pulled there for protection." He watched the maneuver keenly. Several other people, too, had gathered to observe the drills.

Here on the west side of Osta Kiya lay the great plain stretching almost as far as the Numin Mountains, out of sight to the north. Below, the army could muster and drill. Fields of wheat and rye had been harvested, now converted to a mock battlefield. From where Yevliesza stood on a jutting slab of the massif below the main castle, the fighters were so small they could hardly be distinguished from each other.

"Lord Valenty does not approve that I want to go for a soldier when I am older," Pyvel said. "They value manifesters. But he wishes for me to remain with the household."

"He wouldn't stand in your way, would he?"

Pyvel gave her a worried look. "I would always do as Lord Valenty wishes. Would not you?"

She smiled in answer. Yes, she would do as Lord Valenty wished. Within limits. Obedience did not come easily to her given the way she had grown up, with few rules and little supervision.

On one of the fields, dozens of archers practiced with bows as long as they were tall.

Seeing Yevliesza look in that direction, Pyvel said with enthusiasm, "An arrow from a bow like theirs can go right through a person."

"It is enough if it pierces the heart," someone said from behind. Rusadka had joined them with a smile of greeting.

"I thought you'd be down below," Yevliesza said.

"Castle duty, alas," Rusadka said. She was dressed in uniform as usual, but today her hair was pulled into a bun with stiletto-sized knives stuck through it. She wore a short sword at her side. "I would give much to see action," she said as she watched the maneuvers. "My officer says I must finish arcana training first, so I must report to Byasha. We are back."

Pyvel asked to be excused as he had duties in one of the kitchens. "Can you find your way home, miss?" Yevliesza assured him that she could. It was a long climb up an unfamiliar side of the hill complex, but she was not so new as to lose her way.

When he had gone, Rusadka asked, "Is our third aligner released from confinement?"

"She is." Not that it had been much of one. Confinement to her quarters, except for meals and when she sneaked out. "We were just waiting for you, Rusadka."

Yevliesza hated that Sofiyana had taken the bridge trouble all on herself. The one time she had been in Sofiyana's presence, it was clear that she didn't want Yevliesza to bring it up, even privately. *A promise is a promise*, she had murmured.

"Going up there was stupid," Rusadka said. "Sofiyana cannot accept rules."

Yevliesza caught sight of Lord Tirhan coming into the viewing platform.

As he joined them, Yevliesza bid him good morning.

Rusadka bowed to the Alfan lord, receiving his in return. "I must return to my duties," she said with a sly look at Yevliesza.

Did everyone think she was smitten with him?

When Rusadka left, Yevliesza said, "We are all saddened by what has happened, Lord Tirhan. I'm so sorry. Your father and brother. Your land. It's awful."

"We will fight back," he said, watching the maneuvers on the valley floor. "If not today, then soon. It is very hard to stay in Numinat."

"Of course you want to be there."

He seemed deep in reflection and didn't answer.

After a time, she said, "I'll leave you to your thoughts. If there is anything . . ."

"Please forgive me," he said. "Stay a few moments, if my company is not too dark." He turned a smile on her, but it was a forced one.

"You can't go to your kingdom where they need you. It must be so difficult for you to remain here."

"It is eating away at me. I am told that the fact that I am alive and in Numinat gives my people hope, and I am trying to believe it."

On the valley floor, some of the units were leaving the field, marching to the castle and the two thousand steps up the side.

"I'm sure they do find comfort in that," Yevliesza said, "because they have to know that someday you'll return."

A smile started to form, but stopped halfway. "Thank you, Yevliesza. It will be soon, if I can find a way."

They watched the soldiers drill for a while, until Yevliesza recalled Valenty's caution about being seen too much with the Alfan lord. She made her excuses, leaving Tirhan to watch the maneuvers, dreaming of a chance to strike back.

☙❧

IT HAD BEEN A MONTH AND A HALF SINCE YEVLIESZA HAD arrived in Osta Kiya, and during that time she had become some-what familiar with the castle, though she felt she would never know its farthest corners. It was not clear where Osta Kiya left off and the cliffside city began, since regions of the castle hugged the massif where it was perched. But when she decided to look down on the courtyard at night—to test whether she could see the aligns in the dark, as she had on the Moon Bridge—she had a few choices about where to do it.

One option was the Verdant. She decided against it as there might be people up there, and she needed quiet to concentrate.

But the Tower would be perfect.

She set out at dusk, bringing a candle in a holder. In the cooler autumn evenings she had seen children, the ones coming into elemental power, lighting the fireplaces as one of their duties. Without matches, she'd need to light her candle at one of these fireplaces. She didn't want to attract attention by asking someone in the Valenty household. It would seem strange for her to need a lit candle, and she wouldn't want to mention the Tower. People didn't visit it.

She stopped in one of the common rooms closest to the north end of the castle, where a fireplace was burning, and lit the candle without drawing too much attention to herself.

Hesitating before the darkness of the abandoned chambers

near the Tower, she raised the candle and made her way in. Here, night fell quickly as the trickle of light from the few windows hardly penetrated. From the rafters, the rustle, coo, and scuttle of the current occupants fell around her ears like a distant party to which she had not been invited. In the last light of the day, a veil of spider web drifted down past a window like a jellyfish into the depths of the sea.

A sound came to her ears. A soft thudding almost out of hearing range. She realized that she had been hearing it for some time, but only now registered it in that way the mind had of not informing one of everything it knew. Facing the direction it might be coming from, she listened. Yes, something was there. Maybe a small animal that had gotten in or a *sympat* straying from its person.

Holding up the candle, she peered into the darkness, but the light barely reached to the nearest wall. She wouldn't have given it much more thought, except after pausing again to listen she noticed that the sound stopped with her. Someone was following her.

She had never felt threatened in Osta Kiya, not even in the nethers. Oh, worried that the princip might have her killed, yes, but not a common danger from an enemy or a criminal. The castle had seemed safe, but she had never been in this abandoned area alone. The best idea was to leave, but that would bring her closer to whoever followed her.

Quickly, she considered whether she was close enough to the main hall to call out for help, but couldn't bring herself to shout.

The noise came more loudly. If it was a friend—but who could it be?—they would have called out to her by now. Breaking into a run, she turned for the Tower stairs. Foolish, because the Tower had no means of escape, and in her long dress, she could hardly defend herself without tripping over her skirts. Fear drove her forward as she looked around for something to use as a weapon.

She had just reached the stairs when, with a crash, her pursuer rushed toward her. Jumping to the second stair to gain a height advantage, she found the candle still in her hand and raised it to peer out.

Standing before her, a leap away, was a thrall. She was looking directly into its eyes, incandescent in the candle's light.

With stealth forgotten, the thrall slowly advanced. She could only ascend the stairs, and as useless as that was, she found herself retreating. Up and up, with the thrall following one stair at a time. By the expression on its heavy face, she thought it was growling but she couldn't hear it.

As she backed up another step, the beast remained where it was and hope bloomed that it would leave. Until it crouched for a leap. She plastered herself against the stone wall, arms over her face, eyes shut tight, heart lurching.

"Be gone!" someone yelled from below.

Opening her eyes, Yevliesza saw the beast leaping, but moving through the air in slow motion. Its form wavered, greyed. And vanished.

Valenty emerged from the shadows at the bottom of the stairs. He placed a torch in a niche in the wall and came up to her. "Yevliesza," he said, putting a steadying hand on her arm, "it was a *zemya*, a creation of air. It was not in body."

Her heart still pounded, threatening to leap out of her chest.

Valenty put his arm around her shoulders. "Come."

The thing had gone, but even so, she was shaking. "It came after me," she said. "I was going to look for aligns and then it followed me. Jumped at me . . ."

"That is how it seemed," Valenty said, "but it had no will, being like a sky painting." He gently urged her to walk down the stairs.

Her legs were finally working, and she let him lead her down the stairs where he retrieved the torch.

"You chased it away," she said. "The thrall."

"It was not a thrall. It could have done no bodily harm."

Holding her firmly by the arm he began leading her back to civilized light. "I would give you my jacket," Valenty said as he noticed her trembling, "but that would draw attention in the halls. Let us act as if nothing happened."

He brought her to his den, where a fire in the grate glowed with embers. With a small movement of his hand, he shuttered the windows, tiling many pieces together to form a complete barrier. The impressive display hardly registered with her, as her mind seemed to have gone into a pale retreat.

He settled her in an oversized chair strewn with pillows. Over her he laid his jacket. "Warm enough?"

She nodded.

Across the room Valenty had produced two glasses and was pouring a liquor.

"How could it be imaginary," Yevliesza said, "if I heard its feet padding behind me?"

"You did not hear the thrall. You heard its controller. The one manifesting."

As he brought her the drink, she asked, "But who?"

"Someone working for an enemy who wanted to frighten you."

"Nashavety," she murmured.

"Perhaps." Narrowing his eyes, he said, "Almost certainly."

When she set the glass aside, not trusting Numinasi drinks, he went to the hallway door and spoke to someone outside.

"Andrik will bring a cup of pear savory."

"You are very unmoved, my lord." He seemed so composed. So Numinasi.

"I am not unmoved." He sat on the footstool by the chair and reached to take both her hands in his. "I assure you, I am quite the opposite."

After a moment he released her hands. "Move over?" He glanced at the chair, which was large enough for both of them.

She nodded. He moved next to her and, turning in the chair, pulled her gently into his arms. She allowed herself to fall against him as the embrace began to dispel the shock of the almost-attack of the thrall. The warmth of him ran through her, and she put her arm around his chest, resting her head on his shoulder.

They sat unmoving in the silence until a knock at the door.

"Yes, enter."

Andrik, who was not entirely a servant, but not a man of standing—she had not figured out his exact role yet—brought a cup of something steamy and floral-smelling. He put it on the side table next to the chair and left without speaking.

Valenty disengaged himself far enough to reach for the cup and see that she took a sip.

"Does it please you?" he asked. "I know you are particular."

"Yes," she said, smiling. "So much better than serpent's blood."

Carefully, he placed the cup back on the table, leaning over her to do so. Once his hands were free, he cupped her face, framing her face with his hands. Now was the time to pull back if she wished to. He gave her time and when she leaned into him, gently kissed her. Her arms came around him and she kissed him back. His mouth on hers became more insistent, his teeth nipping at her lower lip. She opened to him and he felt it, becoming more insistent. Then his mouth was on her throat as he threw his jacket off her. He rose from the chair, pulling her to her feet. She closed the small gap between them, clinging to him.

His hands went to the buttons on her dress.

Voices outside the door. He pulled back, taking a deep breath. He tucked a lock of her hair behind her ear.

A knock.

"I will talk to Dreiza," he said. "Wait here, I beg you."

Valenty went to the door, and opening it wide, revealed Dreiza standing there.

Yevliesza heard only a few of their words: Tower, *zemya*, the raven.

Dreiza nodded, answering him.

When he closed the door, they were alone again. She began to collect her thoughts. Maybe it was a good thing to have been interrupted, when she hardly knew what to think about what they were doing. Obviously, the mood was broken. He stood apart from her, combing a hand through his hair.

"I took advantage of your frightening event," he finally said. "I should not have. Please excuse my behavior."

She didn't like his sudden formality. But Dreiza had seen her. So his wife wasn't so relaxed about his habits. Maybe Yevliesza shouldn't have been so relaxed, either.

His voice was gentle as he explained that Andrik would take her to her quarters, and soon the man was escorting her away. He was muscular and compact, a man who could be a servant but also a bodyguard. At her room he told her to lock her door from inside.

The night's events replayed in her mind. She had been in Valenty's embrace. The kiss. And there had been a thrall. Or the ghost of a thrall. Sent by Nashavety. But more to the point, Valenty had kissed her. He wanted her, something she had guessed at the night of the Ninth Moon festival. Valenty had lovers. She had seen for herself that he wasn't faithful to Dreiza. If Numinasi even valued that concept. But he didn't want her to be at a disadvantage. Maybe it was up to her to say what she wanted when she had a clear head.

One thing she was coming to know about the Numinasi. They could have an extraordinary attraction. She had been pushing Valenty away by side-stepping him, keeping her own counsel. Because she had been both attracted and afraid of his powers. And not his powers of warding, either.

CHAPTER 20

The next evening Yevliesza stood on the roof with Dreiza overlooking the battlements. A few people strolled through the gardens and, by a gazebo, a verdure practitioner cultivated a graceful shrub sculpture of a dactyl landing.

Dreiza had come for her after supper in the dining hall. Though Yevliesza knew that fidelity wasn't expected in Numinasi marriage, she was nervous to face Dreiza. She could imagine how the scene in his study had looked the night before. She was certain they would talk about it.

Did Valenty love his wife? She had the impression that he did, unless it was just friendship. Despite being seventy-eight, Dreiza was still handsome. Her dark hair was threaded with white, and her face lined but still lovely. Still, she was twice Valenty's age.

Marriage in Numinat was an exercise in building strength and position at court. In the past, Numinasi women and men had lived separately because of issues around dominance and control, and apparently these days marriage did not bind partners in most personal matters. So Grigeni had told her. She had also heard that Valenty's marriage was said to have been a way of protecting his brother's widow from the anger of a former princip. So perhaps their union wasn't heartfelt, even in the Numinasi sense.

But at the meeting Dreiza made no mention of Valenty. She said she wanted Yevliesza to have a chance to discern the aligns at night—as she had tried to do in the Tower—and it was best that for a time she should not venture out after sunset alone.

It was very hard to concentrate on aligns with Dreiza nearby. Down in the courtyard occasional shouts came to her ears as a stone at least two feet wide hovered near the bridge stub. Byasha stood on the bridge deck, working her power from above, as two others concentrated from below. The aligners were just finishing their work as light seeped from the courtyard.

And then, as twilight darkened into night, she saw them. Faint glowing cracks. She leaned over the parapet, riveted.

"Do you see something?" Dreiza asked, as Yevliesza scanned the ground below.

"Oh," she breathed. "The aligns!" The six great aligns of the courtyard pierced the surface like tiny streams of fire. Every time she had an intimation of her Deepening, she felt her heart stutter in her chest.

She was eager to tell Byasha of her night perception. A small victory, but at least it was something.

Dreiza drew nearer. "My dear. Something I need to discuss with you." She kept her voice low. "The *zemya*. You understand who sent it. But we must not let it be known that we suspect who it was."

The malwitch, as Yevliesza had begun to think of her. "She's too powerful?"

"Of course. If it becomes known how we perceive things, then this person—Raven, as we prefer to say—may claim that a shadow has been cast upon her reputation. And, failing to offer proof, you will appear disruptive."

"But why did she try to frighten me?"

Dreiza looked out across the courtyard and the eastern arm of the palace, sighing. "To harass you. But that she would go so far as sending a *zemya* is a surprise to us."

But how surprised had Valenty really been? Had he anticipated how Nashavety's malice would erupt, and if so, had he been following her? Last night she had not thought to ask him, not after those feverish moments in his arms.

"Yevliesza," Dreiza went on, "*are* you frightened?"

"Well, it's over now."

"And, unfortunately, it might reoccur at any time, you see?"

She did see. Nashavety was without pity when it came to her goals, her stance toward the outside. There might be more *zemyas*, perhaps worse ones. "But does she think I'm so easily frightened?"

"Her plan is to disturb you. To make Numinat uncomfortable for you, perhaps offensive. So that you become unhappy. So that you will go back. And, my dear, we do wish for you to stay."

Because Anastyna wished it. So despite the *my dear*, she knew herself to be a political asset. One that had to be polished. She knew because Valenty had told her so. But she thought that she might be something else to him as well. He hadn't wanted to take advantage of her. But he had wanted her.

"I won't let her scare me off," Yevliesza said. In fact it was better to know the woman's hate so she could be prepared for it.

Dreiza seemed to be as political as Valenty. Whatever her personal feelings, her duty to Anastyna came first. It didn't mean, however, that Dreiza was happy about Valenty's attraction to someone else. But if not, then why was she up here on the Verdant talking with her about staying?

One thing especially stood out in what Dreiza had said. How much she hoped that Yevliesza would not give up and go home.

It startled her that this thought had not entered her mind for weeks.

A ROCK HOVERED IN THE AIR ABOUT A FOOT ABOVE THE GROUND. It was a good size this time, larger than a man's boot, and Sofiyana was exultant. "See! I did it!"

Yevliesza, Rusadka, and Byasha stood in the *harjat* training yard practicing third form: control, lift, and hold.

The rock plopped back down.

"You did the lift," Byasha said, "but not the hold. Try again." Her attitude was even more jaded than usual, her patience barely up to the task of teaching what she clearly felt were inadequate students.

"Rusadka. Lift that shield lying over there. And hold it." They were standing on a small align, through which they could control objects.

Rusadka licked her lips and brought her left hand up in front of her chest. Her eyes narrowed in concentration. Slowly, the heavy iron shield rose from the ground, wobbling.

"Control!" Byasha demanded.

The wobbling stopped.

"Now guide it over here. And by the Mythos do not drop it on anyone's feet!"

Slowly, the shield began to turn in the air. "Oh, wrong direction!" Sofiyana whispered.

"Silence!" Byasha hissed, sending a scowl her way.

The shield began to move horizontally. Then, picking up speed, it flew toward them, causing the group to scatter. It fell to the ground with a crash.

Rusadka took a long, slow breath, keeping her face *harjat*-stoic, looking as though chiseled from stone.

Several soldiers were watching the display and smirked, but Byasha exclaimed, "Excellent work! You both could learn concentration skills from Rusadka. See that you do." With that, she wiped her hands on her work apron and left the yard, leaving them as usual to their own devices.

"So how did you do it?" Sofiyana asked, abashed.

"Concentration." Rusadka headed toward a corner of the yard that held a pile of staves. "We can try adding staves one at a time."

Sofiyana gave Yevliesza a long-suffering look. They had been in arcana third form now for a few days, but had yet to discuss the bridge incident.

With Rusadka out of hearing range, Yevliesza said, "Does Nashavety suspect anything?"

"No! She thought I might be seeing a lover up there. I can think of a few I would have been willing to meet, you may be sure. But she does not know anything. As I promised. Besides, it was not so bad. Except now I am in last position, and guess who is number one?"

"Rusadka."

"Maybe after today. But I heard it is you!"

"Will wonders never cease."

"That is so clever, 'Will wonders never cease'!"

"A mundat expression. Better not use it."

They smiled conspiratorially as Rusadka waited for them to join her at the staves.

They all built up to eight staves. Yevliesza thought she could have gone higher, but she was so grateful to Sofiyana for not outing her to Nashavety, that she claimed she was at her limit.

As they left the yard, with Rusadka going her separate way to the barracks, Yevliesza asked her companion, "What will you do when the arcana is finished? Will you stay here or return to your village?"

Sofiyana gave Yevliesza an ironic smile. "That depends on whether I meet someone I can tryst with on the bridge."

"What if they're married?" Yevliesza asked.

"You ask the strangest questions! But I have decided who I will marry."

"You have?"

"I have an intimation of who it might be." Lowering her voice, she said, "Lord Tirhan. If I can even get him to look at me."

Yevliesza did not say how unlikely she thought that goal. "So do married people care who else they sleep with?"

A laugh. "Whyever would they?"

"To know who a child's father is, for one thing."

"Any woman who allows herself to conceive, and any man who allows her to without full agreement, is no Numinasi. Did you not control such things in the mundat?"

"With devices or medicines."

Sofiyana raised her right arm and lay it over her chest in a warding motion. "They are unnatural. But—did you not know, Yevliesza—here women control their bodies, as do men. If you are going to enjoy a man, you had better know how." She looked eagerly at Yevliesza. "Are you thinking of someone? Not Tirhan!"

"No, no. Not thinking of anyone, but I'm curious about how it's done."

"You admire someone!"

"I wish," Yevliesza said in her best forlorn voice. "But no, no one." Changing the subject, she said, "Do Numinasi women ever worry about sex being forced?"

Sofiyana's eyes widened. "A man may try to make a woman accept him—by persuasion. But by force?" She snorted. "A Numinasi woman would destroy such a man. It is the way and custom."

"Kill him?"

"If need be, but certainly destroy his capacity. For as long as the offense deserved. And it would not be trespass, either." Sofiyana shrugged. "In any case, it never happens."

She and Valenty hadn't yet had a chance to speak of the night in his den nor had she even seen him. Perhaps their moment together had been a fleeting hunger, there and gone. But it was becoming impossible to forget kissing him. She found herself looking forward to seeing him again. Well, it was beyond looking forward. Quite a bit beyond.

❧

AS HE HAD SO MANY TIMES, VALENTY WALKED THE NARROW backway, the cramped secret way to the princip's meeting chamber. For generations there had been a passageway accessed through a door in the household scriptorium. He summoned a small warding to keep the dust and spider webs at bay. It would not do to attend Anastyna covered with cobwebs.

He needed that walk through the dark tunnel. The close, cold stones helped him to concentrate and stop thinking about Yevliesza. He had to brief Anastyna, and she must have his undivided attention.

Coming from a long line of hidden agents of the princip, Valenty knew his duty and, especially for this princip, cherished it. She was young but wise. Open to what was new while steeped in the traditions and ways. As princip, she had a delicate task to balance these. So did he.

In her service he controlled a number of informants. Grigeni. His indispensable attendant Andrik. As well, Elivasa, his sometime bed partner with whom he had never been intimate. She was his best operative, shrewd and creative, with a fine ear for gossip. His father had warned him to limit the number of his private band. Keep the circle small, he had said. He had also ensured that Valenty had arcana instruction, but under the guise of a long sojourn in a far polity where an aunt lived. Valenty had, through strict practice at his father's side, learned how to present his deep warding gift as crow power. So that nothing about him would seem admirable. And if the princip ever critically needed him, he could bring his strong warding to bear and take her assailant by surprise.

Of course Anastyna had other warders. His main use to her was as a spy.

Arriving, he opened the door and pushed aside a tapestry. She was waiting for him in the usual airy small room, sitting in a plain chair with her needlework in hand. Her heart-shaped face was almost child-like, her skin, rosy. But no one would ever mistake her for fragile. The torc around her neck was the rigid collar of state, made of ever-shining silver and never removed.

"My Lady Princip," he said with a small nod of his head. In private they dispensed with formality.

"Valenty," she said distractedly as she yanked at a thread. "You have found me with a knot in the pattern. The harder I pull, the worse is the knot."

"Perhaps I shall take it up. To become better at fixing knots."

"Oh, please tell me that you have something pleasant to report about our stratagems. What do I pay you for, if it is all knots and problems?"

"You do not pay me, my lady."

"You refuse payment, but even without your permission my *numiner* tallies your contributions to the royal welfare."

He bowed in acquiescence. "But I have done little for the royal welfare of late."

"Nashavety is causing disorder again?"

"I regret to say that she is."

At the slit window he noted Anastyna's *sympat*, Evalanja, perched quietly, ruffling its neck feathers.

As Valenty settled himself in a chair opposite Anastyna, she said, "Was it not enough that Nashavety encouraged Ansyl to die? There is more?"

She would not use the word *murder*. It meant trespass, a grave matter, which must be brought to public view and judged. "I believe she sent a manifester to harry Yevliesza with a *zemya*."

She put her needlework aside. "What, in your very household?"

He explained how Yevliesza had been intent on practicing the aligns from the Tower window that night.

Anastyna touched her right hand to her heart. "In the *Tower*?"

"I had taken her there once for that purpose. She is unaffected by the correlations of the place." Or was. "I have no proof it was the Raven, my lady. Perhaps best if we find no proofs?"

"Perhaps. But what form of *zemya*?"

"A thrall, which Yevliesza already fears, having seen such a beast in Nashavety's company."

"So forward she becomes," Anastyna brooded. She raised her hand to summon Evalanja, and it swooped onto her jeweled leather arm band.

Nashavety was a longstanding problem. The solution had always been to appear to be influenced by her. It was an indirect strategy and might no longer be sufficient in case of hard decisions about Alfan Sih. But Valenty did not take the lead in this matter. It was for Anastyna to decide when to strike back at her.

"She has two high sisters by her side, Valenty."

"More besides Wild Hill?"

"To my dismay, I believe she has the Hall of Storm Hand."

He let out an angry breath. Of the five Halls she now had a majority. For Anastyna, Iron River would be loyal, and she usually could depend on Red Wind. Thus the princip had support of two, but Storm Hand's defection was a blow.

"Raven Fell pushes us to make a judgment," Anastyna said. "To close our Numinat crossings, permanently. All that I have worked for, gone in one Volkish invasion, all my hoped-for alliances, gone."

She did not say, Chenua of the Lion Court, also gone. But any closing of the crossings would mean never seeing him again.

Rising, she took Evalanja to the window and released the *sympat*, watching it beat a path into the sky. "I perceive a darkness on the Mythos," she said, her voice small. "Worse than the nanotechnologics, much worse." She turned to face him. "Because who can understand the Volkish, why they wish other realms? It is a Reach trespass of the highest order."

Since she had risen, he also got to his feet. "They were ever covetous, from the beginning."

"They must be dealt with, Valenty. I must decide how to aid Alfan Sih, if at all."

Chenua might persuade Nubiah to a joint expedition with Numinat. Others might join. The Jinn Court of Arabet. The Jade Pavilion.

She turned from the window, her shoulders relaxing from a sigh. "And so. Let us speak of other matters."

"We have a small success," Valenty said. "Yevliesza has sometimes been in first position in her triad. She does especially well in align perception."

"That is well. Finishing last must be avoided. But I have been informed that the *harjat* Rusadka is first in rank today."

"Your better spies precede me, My Lady Princip," he said in good humor.

"Ah, Valenty. I could not do without you. Your protection of our guest of mundat gives me great confidence. But." Her eyes narrowed. "I would not have you share Ansyl's manner of death with the girl. It would weaken her bond to us. And in truth, it is not proven that the Raven harried him."

He paused at this injunction. But only for a moment. "Yes, my lady."

"You must keep her close to us," Anastyna pressed.

"It is my pleasure to do so."

She leaned against the windowsill, considering him. She had caught his mood. "Do you . . . admire her, Valenty?"

"I have sworn to Dreiza."

"Ah, your vow. To share your bed with any, but no one that you love." She shook her head. "Only someone like you would think of such a promise. Impossible."

She touched the silver torc at her neck as though thinking of her own difficult promises as sovereign. "But perhaps for the best in the circumstances. Be careful, Valenty."

CHAPTER 21

The dactyl raised its great silver wings, stretching them nearly to the ceiling of the shed. Its nostrils flared, noting newcomers nearby. Dreiza was familiar, but Valenty was not.

"Kirjanichka has just awakened, Lady Dreiza," the shed girl said. "She has been on continuous patrol for two nights."

"Thank you, Vara," she responded. "We will not stay long. Please open the gate so that she may stretch her legs."

The girl paused, but knowing her visitors were high in rank, she obeyed, pulling the wheeled gate aside, exposing the vast ledge where the prize dactyls could sun themselves.

Valenty admired the beast, with its fine scales the color of tarnished silver, the great yellow eyes that were said to read a Numinasi and accept or reject a rider, shed girl or even a princip, based on whim or wisdom. No one knew. Except that they preferred women. And figs.

Only one other dactyl occupied the ledge, a dwarf indigo racer. Kirjanichka slowly swayed into the opening, darkening it, and lumbered onto the platform. It turned to Dreiza, whiskers lifted.

Valenty's wife smiled in pleasure and opened the basket she carried. She approached Kirjanichka but did not touch or pat it, as one might a horse. Dactyls did not perceive affection from touch. If so moved one might sing to them, but never in the presence of a shed girl, of course. Instead, Dreiza had brought treats and hand-fed it something from the basket.

Valenty had not seen her so happy in quite a while, cooing at the beast, her face shining. He knew he had been neglecting her. It was difficult to be around her when he was convinced that she had noticed his attraction to Yevliesza. Such things usually prompted teasing and remonstrations about how to please a woman in bed and make her feel appreciated. But it had been three nights and still silence on that topic.

Looking down the length of the castle wall, he noted the Elemental Balcony. Four men and a woman stood there, watching the distant mountains where clouds stacked dark and long. If the clouds approached, practitioners would raise a rain inundation, he supposed. The work of several hours. His mother was an elementalist and loved nothing better than a good storm, whether it was useful or not. He had not seen her in many years, since his father died and she went home to Norslad, a realm he had never seen. He spoke the language, for his mother thought no child was well-educated unless they spoke at least three.

He walked to the rimless edge of the great shelf and looked down into the gorge of the Kovna River, so far below, its torrents came to him in a whisper.

Dreiza joined him. "I do not approve of having the dactyls worked so hard. A waste. Only for show."

"Most are quartered at the crossings now, but Anastyna needs a demonstration of strength."

"Well, she can do it without my Kirjanichka driven to exhaustion." Dreiza scowled at the line of clouds over the mountains, which had not moved.

"Kirjanichka is strong."

"How heartless you are," she murmured, linking her arm in his. "If you are in such a sober mood, take a lover. It is no good to work so hard."

Since the Volkish incursion, he had often been late in meetings with Anastyna. He did not contradict Dreiza's conclusion that he was somber because of the crisis in Alfan Sih.

"Perhaps I will," he said.

"I believe there is a line waiting," she said indulgently.

"I already look like a wastrel," he said. "But if I have them all?"

"Well, you have spent thousands of days painting that picture. You must be true to your course."

True to his course. Yes, but which course? Being known as shallow and worthless or keeping faith with Dreiza? He could not do both, for if Yevliesza agreed to be his lover he would then be with a woman he might care for. Dreiza had never asked for the vow, but he had been happy to give her the reassurance. Now, it presented him with a dilemma. If he did not take Yevliesza, and Dreiza having no doubt guessed his attraction, then she would know his feelings were not casual.

"Perhaps a woman is the answer to whatever you called it . . . my sober mood?"

"We are all sober these days with our soldiers gone to the gates." She looked back at Kirjanichka who was keeping close watch on her as she stood near the ledge. "If she goes to war, I will be bereft."

"Dreiza. I have had a conversation with the princip. I did not tell you because I wanted to be sure it was possible."

"What was possible?"

"That you can have Kirjanichka. That you will manage its service to the realm, whether for patrols or no."

He noted her look of wonder and doubt.

"How can this be? The cost . . ."

"There is no cost. I asked it of Anastyna, and she granted me the beast as an honor for long service."

"Oh, Valenty!"

"Anastyna knows it is my desire to give Kirjanichka to you. And so, he is yours."

"But, what, otherwise you would have paid from the household purse? Such a sum . . . it would make beggars of us."

He shrugged. "The guild does not hold my *numin* reckonings. The princip's *numiner* tallies my work. We have wealth beyond our needs."

Dreiza looked at the dactyl, her eyes glistening.

"Thank you, my lord," she whispered.

It would have given him the greatest pleasure to give her this gift, but he knew it was not given totally out of love.

He was considering taking Yevliesza if she agreed. He could offer her more protection from Nashavety that way, for one thing. Nashavety might turn her intentions elsewhere. Might. But even with that benefit, it was hard to think how he could have Yevliesza as a mere paramour. In fact, he could not. And even though he would not invite her to share his bed, he knew he had already betrayed Dreiza in his heart.

He gazed out at the view into the valley. The long rank of storm clouds had risen high into the sky and, riding a new wind, slowly approached the massif of Osta Kiya.

There were days that he felt himself standing on a ledge in a strong wind. With the next step, safety or a great fall.

❧

THE SERVANT WHO BROUGHT HER BATH WATER WAS UNHAPPY.

Yevliesza avoided the women's baths because she was self-conscious about her scarring, even though it was apparently fading. The only other bathing option was to have a couple of buckets of water brought to her room, since she didn't have running water in her chambers.

"But miss, to bathe so often, every three days, it is unnatural." Floris set the buckets down, but could raise no response.

"Please undo my buttons, Floris." She had one gown that buttoned up the front, but she could not wear it every day.

Floris unfastened the buttons and took her leave, sighing.

Yevliesza sponged herself off, letting water dribble onto the floor. She ran her hand over the scars behind her right shoulder, feeling the indentations. But the puckering had lessoned. Once clean and rinsed, she applied her Alfan ointment as best she could and, lying down on the bed on her stomach, she let herself dry.

She wondered where Valenty was, what he was doing. They hadn't spoken since the night of the *zemya*. She had hoped to see him, but maybe he was too embarrassed by what had happened, given that he thought he had taken advantage of her. There was a time when he'd been an arrogant, distant protector. But from the night she found her align power he'd become a different Valenty. He had begun to guide her in Numinasi customs, and advise her, console her. Around others he was careful to be offhand, but not in private. Why he adopted a different persona in public, she didn't know, but he had depths he showed to only a few, and she was attracted to those depths.

She remembered that he hadn't liked to see her with Tirhan. *Find a Numinasi man.* Had he meant him?

Picking up her front-buttoning dress, she began pulling herself into it, worrying about her scarring and how she would look to a man.

On the way to her triad session, she passed the scriptorium. She spied Valenty looking over the shoulder of a man who was illuminating the grimoire text. She passed by, but before she had gone more than a few steps, Valenty was at her side.

"May I walk with you?"

She nodded, and they strolled down the corridor. Valenty didn't say anything more and, if there was to be silence, she didn't want to be the one to break it.

At last he said, "All this must seem strange to you."

"I'm not sure how it seems." Her heart was skittering.

"I should not have pushed you," he said. "That night. I could not be sure what you wanted."

"I thought it was clear."

He paused. "But you do not know me."

As they passed a side corridor, Valenty guided her into it. No globes illumined the recess, and he put his hand behind her head, gazing at her, his face in shadows. "Yevliesza," he said. "I have no right to pursue you."

Why not? she wanted to ask, but didn't.

"There is Dreiza to think of." The words hung solidly in the air between them. "She is a part of this."

"Yes. I know."

"My actions did not suit me. Or you," he said. "It would not be possible, even if you decided to have me."

Her first reaction was surprise. The second was acute embarrassment. Keeping her voice flat, she said, "I think you're saying we made a mistake."

"Yes, I am sorry to say. Under other circumstances, I would want to . . . to offer you companionship. But I am not free to do so."

Her emotions circled, now adding confusion to embarrassment.

"Not free . . ."

"No."

It seemed that Lord Valenty was trying on a new set of habits. To be true to his wife. It shamed her to feel so struck down, to have believed, even for a moment, that Numinasi did not care about faithfulness. All she could think of at that moment was to put distance between them.

She turned from him and slowly walked away. She didn't blame him, how could she? Entering the main hallway, she hurried to arcana training, dragging Valenty's words behind her.

❀

"EVERYONE HATES THIRD FORM," SOFIYANA DECLARED AS SHE looked at the scattered remnants of bricks and rocks the triad had been practicing with. It had been raining, and now, as the sun reappeared, mist rose from the grassy courtyard.

Though Sofiyana disliked the last segment of their training, control, Yevliesza enjoyed having something to think about other than what had happened with Valenty.

"At least I kept the rock lifted for three breaths," Sofiyana said.

Rusadka shook her head. "Two breaths. We are counting for each other."

Yevliesza was distracted by a glimpse of Nashavety walking with her steward, Daraliska, deep in conversation. At one of the castle entrances, Nashavety turned briefly toward Yevliesza. Even at a distance, her dark gaze could cool a heart. *Malwitch* suited her so well.

"We are, are we not?" Rusadka asked her.

"Are what?"

"Counting for each other."

"Well, you can stop now," Sofiyana snapped. "I shall count my own."

Trying to bring her attention back to the arcana, Yevliesza raised her left hand in front of her, taking her turn at a large stone. All her concentration sank into her fingers, then into her small finger, which she pointed at Sofiyana's rock and guided it a yard above her head.

The others looked at this display in stunned silence.

Seeing their expressions, Yevliesza felt herself losing control. The stone hovered too close to Rusadka. As sweat broke out on her face, she attempted to guide the stone a few feet away, and did so, but then it crashed to the ground with a horrid crunch. Her relief at missing Rusadka made her weak in the knees.

"Splendid! Splendid!" came the unmistakable cry of Byasha, who was hurrying toward them, as fast as her short legs could carry her.

"Well done, Yevliesza," she said as she approached, accompanied by several other align practitioners in work clothes, three men and an older woman. Turning to her companions, she said, "This is our mundat girl, and she surpasses a *harjat* and a niece of Raven Fell." She looked at Rusadka and Sofiyana. "Do not be downcast. Celebrate what each of you does well. Tomorrow it will be someone else." Nodding pleasantly at Yevliesza, she walked onward with the other aligners in the direction of the Moon Bridge.

"You might have chosen a different stone," Sofiyana said, abashed. "It was the one I held for three breaths."

"Oh, I didn't mean . . ." Yevliesza began. "I didn't think . . ."

Rusadka pinned her with an impatient look. "Ignore her. Be confident!"

Later in the afternoon, Yevliesza and Sofiyana took their midday meal on a bench across from the great circle. Rusadka had seen *harjat* companions and went with them for lunch.

Sofiyana was over her pique. "Byasha has finally praised you. I am glad she did." She chewed thoughtfully on a piece of buttered bread. "And Rusadka is right. We must build up confidence, especially when we do something well."

She smiled at Sofiyana, grateful for her friendship. And it was a good reminder not to let her emotions interfere with her gift. The aligns. Her success with the stone today had been fueled by anger—after seeing Nashavety—but that was also when she had lost control. Valenty's rejection didn't help her mood, either.

She reminded herself that today she had flown a large stone into the air above her triad companions' heads.

⚜

AT THE CORRAL ON THE VALLEY FLOOR, A MAHOGANY-COLORED horse with a white blaze on its head nuzzled through the fence at her hand. Yevliesza had come to the corral a few times, finding it peaceful and often empty of people.

As the horse delicately took one of the apple quarters she had brought, she thought of her father. Her memory was bright with an image of him, in the times when he had been wholly himself. She imagined asking him: *Is the arcana the right way for me? Will I ever be Numinasi or will I always be halfway?*

Numinasi, he answered. The look on his face was certain, peaceful.

She hoped he was right. This was no time to be doubtful. She put her head against the rough fence post as the horse nudged at her pocket.

A stiff breeze greeted her as she lifted her head. She inhaled the wild smells of the valley: clear and rich with turning leaves and warm earth. The mahogany horse had wandered away. Across the corral, she saw Lord Tirhan talking with a stable hand. He spotted her, and leading his horse by the reins, approached her.

The horse was a magnificent grey, with black mane and tail.

Tirhan was magnificent himself, dressed in tan and brown and high riding boots.

"I did not know you rode," he said after greeting her.

"I don't, my lord. I've never been on a horse. But I like them."

She brought out a piece of apple and held out her hand to Tirhan's horse. It regarded her with huge brown eyes and then took the apple piece from her with a soft brush of its lips.

"Oh. I should have asked you before feeding your horse," she said.

"No." He smiled, "It was enough that you asked *him*." Dismounting, he looped the reins around a slat. He joined her in watching a stable hand exercise a horse. "This is the place I feel most at home. With horses. In Alfan Sih they are entwined in our lives."

"The further I am from the castle, the more at home I feel."

"But do you come down here, then? To the valley?"

"The corral, sometimes, but I haven't explored the valley."

"I could take you for a ride, if you like. You could ride in back."

"But my reputation, Lord Tirhan," she said in mock admonishment, and they laughed. But they did have to exercise restraint.

They watched the horse and rider come around the paddock again in a fast trot. She wanted to ask Tirhan about things at Alfan Sih, but she hadn't the heart to bring up the painful subject.

"Is all well for you, lady?" he asked, as though he had glimpsed her mood.

"Oh . . . it's just that sometimes I have to find my way through household politics. It's not always a happy place." It had been a week since Valenty had decided that kissing her had been a mistake.

"You can depend on the young lad Pyvel," Tirhan said. "He is all for you. And Master Grigeni has spoken highly of you."

"Has he?" She wasn't sure she had been an A student except in reading, which she had taken to quickly.

"His opinion of you is high. And Lord Valenty is your defender, no matter his carefree manner. I am sure he is your supporter." He patted his mount to calm it as the horse fretted at its tied reins. "It is not the Alfan way, to take many lovers, so I do not pretend to understand the man. Lusiana told me he is very kind in that regard."

"Lusiana?"

"His new consort. I know her through the court. It is a happy match for her."

Somehow there was a rock in her stomach. She forced a smile. "You know things I would never have imagined."

"My knowledge is superficial, but it is my job to understand Numinat."

Valenty had taken a lover.

Tirhan went on, "His household is devoted to him, which leads me to believe there is more to the man than what appears."

"Or perhaps less?" All she could think of was that being Valenty's lover was a happy match for Lusiana.

Tirhan cocked an eyebrow, but remained silent. Finally he said, "Come dressed for a ride tomorrow and we will go into the valley."

She looked into his handsome and serene face, framed with hair that turned white in the sun. "I'd like that very much. But it would feed my enemies."

"Well, they will gorge on their malice no matter what you do." His smile gave her heart.

"At three-quarter day, then?" she said. Without her watch she had to become aware of how high the sun was at any time. By late afternoon, arcana would be finished for the day.

"I will be here," Tirhan said.

She walked back to the palace, hardly seeing where she was going. Valenty wasn't bound to his marriage. He had cast her aside. Unless he expected her to get in line.

CHAPTER 22

The afternoon sun blazed over the central enclosure of Osta Kiya. The city-palace, though thoroughly drenched by the rain, now regained its warmth. The stones dried, the parapets glistened, and people flocked to the courtyard to enjoy the sun. Women barely needed to lift their skirts, so carefully had the verduralists kept the grass at the proper height.

Yevliesza had come back from the stables and joined the crowd, most of whom were watching another addition to the Bridge of the Moon. Over the last few days aligners had worked with builders to extend the massive shaved timbers that served as temporary decking. Now more shaped stones were being raised to rest on top. Once the entire bridgeway was finished, the timbers would be removed, and the force of rock against rock would fasten all in place. The aligns made this great feat possible, allowing the stones to be raised and adjusted.

Surreptitiously, Yevliesza scratched at her neck, a habit by now. Scratching at her upper back with one hand over her shoulder was something she only did in private.

Scanning the crowd, she looked for a young woman named Lusiana, even though she had no idea what she looked like. A strange feeling fed her search. Not envy. She was too hurt to worry that the woman had found a *happy match*. The truth was that Valenty cared nothing for her. His excuse about Dreiza's feelings was just a ruse to be rid of her. And in fact, Dreiza was standing by the central copse of trees laughing with a friend, looking totally content.

The crowd stilled as a great block, larger than any others, began to rise from the ground. Byasha stood with several other practitioners, forming a circle but with half of them facing outward, toward the stone. Two others stood on the bridge deck, and the great block rose steadily, a fine display of power and affinity. It approached the wood struts and very slowly moved a few feet above them, to approach its interlocking place.

Then a child shrieked and ran after a pet that had escaped a leash. The piercing scream caused a ripple in the circle, and the great stone slipped to one side, hanging at a wrong angle. The aligners forced it higher, so it wouldn't damage the wood forms.

But Yevliesza saw that it was out of control, wobbling. Then it started to rotate, gathering speed. Now almost under the bridge, she rushed forward, jamming her left hand into the air, willing the stone to steadiness. It held. And rose higher. And higher. But then she felt her control flounder, and it came crashing down on the exposed planking. Wood erupted into splinters and the finished strut of the bridge began to shudder and bend down. It fell.

People came down with it. In the billowing dust, a timber hurtled toward Yevliesza. Something hit her in the side of the head with enough force that she went sprawling. A few final pieces of the bridge came down with grinding impacts.

She lay in a white-out of dust. Sounds came from every direction. Shouts, a last groan of twisted wood. Then silence.

Long minutes passed. Perhaps hours. Consciousness came in flickers, riding waves of pain. The ground she lay on jabbed at her. Voices came near. Someone was at her side.

"Do not pick her up. Her foot is pinned down."

Whose foot?

Then a slice of aching pain in her ankle. In the next moment, she felt herself lifted up and carried. So much dust. The bridge . . . It fell. She remembered a great stone hitting it, shattering it. Voices rose around her, and when she was able to keep her eyes open, she saw only swirls of color as people moved in and out of her vision.

A man was laying her down somewhere inside. People were sitting and lying in the corridor.

"Can you hear me?" A great bearded face peered close to her. "You are injured. Stay still until a healer comes. Do you understand?"

Her tongue would not work. By the time she summoned a yes, he was gone.

It was pleasant to be lying on the floor. She could breathe, which was a very good thing. She tried to remember what happened. Oh. The bridge. Something terrible had happened.

A voice behind her. Opening her eyes, she saw a wall very close. She was lying on her side. Someone leaned over her, saying her name. Tirhan.

"Yevliesza," he said. "Speak to me."

"The . . . bridge . . ."

He rested his hand on her shoulder. Then his hands went to her forehead and throat. She remembered that he was a doctor. Not the right word.

"Where does it hurt?"

"Ankle." She groaned as he touched it.

After a few moments he said, "It is not a bad injury. It will quickly heal."

"So cold," she whispered.

"Your dress has torn," he said.

She felt his fingers on her bare back.

"It is a work dress."

"Yes . . ." He pressed the torn back of her dress into place.

A woman's voice. "How does she?" A shadow fell over Yevliesza. It was Nashavety.

"She is not badly hurt. But stunned, my lady."

"We shall send a healer straightaway."

"I have sent word to Lord Valenty, my lady. Others have more need."

The shadow retreated.

"She is gone, Yevliesza. I am going to move you onto your back."

The move hurt, but the pain was nothing compared to tangling with lightning.

Someone came by with water. Tirhan helped her to sit up and held a cup for her to drink.

"Was anyone killed?" she asked, dreading the answer.

"Yes. I do not know how many. Everyone will have care."

People had died, and she had caused it. "It was my fault."

"Your fault? But no one is assigning blame. For now, I need to take you to your quarters. You need to leave before a healer takes charge of you."

"Leave?"

"Get to your room. Do you think you can walk with my support? It is important."

She thought she could. When he helped her to stand, she wobbled, but it passed in a few moments.

In the confusion no one noticed their passage. At her room, she produced a key from her skirt pocket and Tirhan opened the door. He brought her to the bed so that she could sit, then went to the door and threw the bolt. After closing the shutters on her window, he opened the small armoire where her dresses hung.

Yevliesza watched him in confusion. "What's going on?"

Holding up one of her plain gowns, he said, "You can change into this."

"Right now?" She was filthy and wanted to call for a servant to bring water.

He placed the gown on a chair and leaned against the deep reveal of the window. From the courtyard came a few shouts of people working to find the injured.

"Yevliesza," he began. "The scars on your back are not scars. They are something else."

"Turning dark as they heal?" Rusadka had said so.

"No. They are a different thing . . . a tracery of lines. They curl and connect with each other in a kind of pattern. A blue-grey pattern."

"But Rusadka saw them and never said . . . a *pattern*."

"How long ago?"

She thought about it. "Three weeks? I mean, maybe twenty days ago."

"They have changed, perhaps, since then."

"Is there something wrong with me?"

He shook his head. "I think there is something right with you. There is something etched into your back. Something I have never seen before. A tracery." Noises in the hallway drew his attention. "I should help you to dress. Quickly, if you can manage to stand."

Her ankle throbbed and so did her head. But she nodded. When he tried to raise her to her feet, she swayed. Still supporting her, he said, "I need to rip the back of your dress. The buttons are entangled."

"OK."

With one hand he tore the dress down to her waist. Then he

helped her pull the sleeves down her arms. "Do you have another shift?"

"In the chest."

Fetching the undergarment, he returned to the bed and gently laid her down on it. He pulled the torn dress over her hips and legs, leaving it in a heap. Then he removed her slip which was shredded and stained with blood.

"Where is the ointment?"

She directed him to a drawer, and soon he was patting the salve onto a few spots on her shoulders that he said were abrasions from the accident.

He helped her into the clean shift, doing so easily, as though he was used to dressing patients.

Since the clean dress was an everyday one, the buttons were in front, and she began on them. "Tirhan. What is really happening to my back?"

"I cannot say what it might be, but I believe it is part of you, part of what you have come to in our world." He touched the right side of her neck. "This is not a scar like most. It is a reveal of something within you."

"But what?"

"I do not know. Something profound." He put his hands carefully on either side of her face. "And the tracery is beautiful, Yevliesza. You cannot see it for yourself, but it is very beautiful."

She wanted to believe him. And she did. He was of the Mythos, and he was saying her . . . *tracery* was a good thing.

He took her hand. "I will leave you now. Will you be all right?"

She said that she would. She needed to rest, but she had survived.

At the door he turned. "I believe that this is a gift of our world. In some way, it is a gift."

"But no one must know?"

"Keep it secret until you know what the tracery is and if it protects you or jeopardizes you. Do not let them use it against you."

And he was gone.

PART III
THE EMBRACE OF THE MALWITCH

CHAPTER 23

A day later they came for her. Byasha reported that Yevliesza's interference had contributed to the Bridge of the Moon disaster. Nashavety wasted no time in demanding Yevliesza's imprisonment while evidence could be gathered.

As Yevliesza waited in a cell in the nethers, she tried to work out what had happened and why.

She had interfered with the aligners at their job, but whether disastrously or not, she wasn't completely sure. The stone might have fallen even without her interference, fallen onto the jutting end of the bridge with the same awful result. She knew that the aligners below the bridge segment had lost their hold on the rock before she had joined their effort, but it was hard to deny that she had acted recklessly, even if she had meant to help.

She deserved to be here. It was harsh treatment, but her dark cell matched her self-assessment. Two people had died. They might not have if it hadn't been for her.

Why had she rushed forward like that? Someone new to arcana training had no business trying to lift such a massive rock. But she hadn't decided, it was a spontaneous thing, to try to help.

The sickening thought kept intruding: Or had it been to prove herself?

Now, after a sleepless night in the nethers, she stared vacantly through the bars, wondering if they would place all the blame on her and if they did, how they would punish her.

A noise down the passageway. Someone was coming. "Pyvel!" Yevliesza cried out softly.

Around him hovered that soft manifesting glow that she had seen him use before. It brought welcome relief from the permanent dusk of the dungeon.

"Lady Yevliesza," he said, his voice breaking.

"I'm no lady," she said, smiling, "As you see."

"Well, I think you are."

He had no reason to feel such loyalty to her. But she felt a surge of tenderness for him, almost like an aura all her own.

"You shouldn't be seen here," she said. "I'm a bad influence." She hadn't heard from anyone since the guards had taken her from the household, despite Valenty strongly objecting.

"I do not care what they think. And no one actually said I should stay away." He produced an apple from his trouser pocket which she gratefully accepted.

"What are they saying about me?"

"Well, high folk. What do they ever say? But cook, and Floris and Grigeni, they are upset for you." His aura of light dimmed as though reflecting his worries. "It will be all right, will it not?"

He was twelve years old, soon to be thirteen. Not a young child, and he deserved not to be coddled. "Some people need me to fail. To be an example of what happens when you deal with outsiders." He mustn't stay long and she still had so many questions. "How are the injured doing? And Byasha? I heard she broke her arm."

"Both her arms are broken, so she will not be doing aligns for a while. Who the other wounded are, I have not heard, but I could find out."

"No, Pyvel, don't. Don't let on that you support me. I'll see you soon, all right? You should go before someone sees you."

Eventually he relented and she watched as his shimmering form disappeared down the passageway.

Standing had made her ankle throb, sending threads of pain up her leg. She hobbled back to her pallet. One good thing about a small prison cell was that if you had a bad ankle, you didn't have far to walk to get anywhere.

Outside the bars of her cell and several yards away was a hovering globe that allowed her to see in the gloom, so that she wouldn't trip over her waste pail. A shadow down the passageway caught her attention. Someone had been watching her and now left. She hoped whoever it was wouldn't report Pyvel.

Despite her circumstances, a bright hope was circling her, coming into view from time to time to buoy up her thoughts. The tracery. She must get someone, maybe Rusadka, to sketch the pattern for her so she would know what it looked like.

As to what it meant, she thought she knew. It came from the lightning strike.

It was how her power had come to her, saved up over twenty-one years and ready to find her. Her healers had claimed that the lightning must have hit the dactyl, not her, and that was why she was only slightly burned. But what if it had hit her directly and somehow been softened by the Mythos? What if her align power had ridden the lightning? This was the conclusion she had come to, even if was unlikely, and even if she couldn't prove it.

Her natural power hadn't come to her through moments of dizziness in those first weeks after her arrival. It had come all at once, and as a result she was imprinted with a pattern, a carving on her skin. One that people hadn't seen before—or at least

Tirhan and Rusadka hadn't—because no Numinasi had ever been kept from their power until fully grown.

This idea sustained her, even if she didn't know what the strange initiation meant for her align power—whether it was stronger as a result, or in some way distorted. Nor did she know what people would think if they knew. One thing was certain: It was *not* going to be according to the ways and customs.

Tirhan thought that her—tracery, as he called it—was a sign that the Mythos had accepted her. It heartened her to think that it might be true. She hoped it was, because there was no place else for her.

When she looked up she saw Valenty. For a moment her heart lifted. But only for a moment.

"Yevliesza," he said. Someone was with him, a heavyset woman she did not recognize.

"Lord Valenty."

"Yevliesza, I am working to get you out of here. I hope the night was not awful for you. How do you fare?"

"I am well."

"Come closer to the bars, will you?"

She managed to stand without wobbling and approached him.

"We will get you through this, I promise." His dark hair fell in front of his face, and he swept it behind his ear. Since he normally wore it in a queue, she wondered if he had just awakened. If Lusiana had been with him.

"I have brought a healer to look at your ankle."

"How is Byasha doing?"

"She will recover."

"And her left hand?"

He leaned his forehead against the cell bars. "Yevliesza . . ."

"Is her hand damaged?"

"No. Not damaged. But we must be sure your own injuries are

healing properly. I would like to come in to allow this healer to examine you."

Tirhan had urged her to keep her tracery secret for now, and she thought it was good advice. "That's not necessary, though. I feel much better."

"But can the healer attend you?"

"Is it up to me?" This could turn ugly if they just came in. She would not undress for a healer.

"Yes, if you insist."

"Valenty. What will happen to me?"

He murmured to the healer and she withdrew to the far wall of the corridor.

"Lady Nashavety believes you misused your align power. Byasha concurs. But I do not believe the princip will impose a harsh penalty. It may yet be well."

"Is what I am accused of . . . is it a trespass?"

"No, Yevliesza! Trespass is misuse of power with mal intent against people or against nature." He shook his head. "Have you been thinking this is about trespass?"

It had crossed her mind. It was frightening to consider, even without the worst outcome—the Tower. They also had a nasty tradition of the removal of the smallest finger on the left hand. To be sure you didn't misdirect your power again.

"I have to ask you," he said, lowering his voice. "Did you bring your power to bear on the stone?"

"I tried to keep it from falling. I saw the stone rise higher when I raised my hand, but then it fell."

"You may not have been the one to raise it higher. You cannot know, so do not say it. You tried to assist, but you could not help the aligners who were struggling to manage it. That is what you must say. Not that you lifted it higher."

"OK." It was not becoming easier to be around him. He upset

what little peace she had. "Would you bring me something? The *Book of Ways and Customs*? I'd like something to read."

"Yes, of course."

From somewhere a skittering sound. She had seen rats and sometimes fast, hard-shelled beetles. "Did the princip send you down here? To be sure I can still be of value to her?"

He sighed, acting as though she was the one who was unduly formal. And maybe she was, but she simply didn't know what was the right way to be around him.

Finally he said, "I would have come in any case."

"How is Dreiza?"

A pause a heartbeat long. "She is very well. Concerned at your treatment."

"Please thank her for me." All this calmness was impossible. She felt like throwing something.

"If you are sure you won't have a healer . . ."

"I'm sure."

"If you change your mind . . ." he began, and then with nothing left to say, at last he left.

Part of her hoped that he would come back later. And part of her hoped she would not have to be around him at all anymore. Because now that she couldn't have him, she could only think about what it would have been like if she had.

That sort of thinking would have to stop.

CHAPTER 24

I t was a terrible day, Kirjanichka, the day the Bridge of the Moon fell. Two aligners died and others were badly injured. But worse, the noble undertaking of the bridge along the great align was abandoned. What remained were the offensive correlations, strong enough that the bridgeway endeavor would always remain in disrepute. People would remember the failure and associate it with mal influences, which, to make matters worse, were seen as precipitated by our guest of the mundat. And so the great align of the air, the dream of our former princip and adopted by Anastyna as a show of continuity, would never be a pathway in Osta Kiya.

A terrible day.

Everywhere in the household, people were talking about the young woman we had taken in. Everyone had an opinion. That disaster had come because Yevliesza had brought a small machine to wear on her wrist; about how it was the kind of thing that would happen when you try to make a Numinasi out of a foreigner and not just any foreigner, but one who was not of the Mythos but of the origin world. All the false notions broke out. Yevliesza, who had begun to redeem herself, was a stunted figure once again.

Valenty was sorely distressed that they took Yevliesza to the nethers. He tried not to show it. My Valenty, so good at dissembling! But he was not sleeping. After a few days I knew that he had a great weight on his heart.

I should have foreseen that Yevliesza would push beyond her limits. But I had failed to foreknow. Oh yes, the premonitions—I did have those. But I did not come close to perceiving the particulars.

It was then that I began my retreat. I felt the need to think things through. How a shadow had fallen on Osta Kiya and why it oppressed me so. Yes, Valenty and I appeared to have failed to teach Yevliesza our ways. But that was not the whole of it.

I went to my rooms and did not mingle. I sat alone with myself and listened to the currents of my mind. I did not try to piece together explanations or dwell on past signals that I had missed. How could I be blamed, if other adepts of foreknowing had not seen the warnings either?

It was not a happy time. As days passed I saw how far my power had gone from me. But I knew that high gifts do not disappear, so I remained quietly faithful to my training and waited. One with my affinity learns very young that foreknowing cannot be forced or even prompted. It is the ground of one's being, and because this is so, one must listen for the future, like a far-off voice calling out in the forest.

Valenty came several times to ask after my well-being. I told him that I was worried about Yevliesza and that we might be blamed. That was only part of the truth.

Because I began to think that it was not the future that I needed to understand. It was the present.

Though I had resolved not to analyze too much, the question kept flitting through my mind like a lost bird:

Why had I lost my way?

CHAPTER 25

Valenty stood with Anastyna in the Numin Room with its round pool and, above, the matching ceiling eye that brought sunlight to the pool. With them were the princip's high steward, Lord Michai, as well as Lady Byasha—seated in a chair in respect of her injuries. And standing by her side, Nashavety.

"So the stone," Anastyna mused, having heard Byasha's recital of events " . . . it was the stone that brought down our hopes of the sky align."

Valenty thought it bold of her to call it the stone's fault. Like all her difficult meetings the princip knew the positions and the facts before she entered the room. Her hope was to absolve Yevliesza, but she could not appear to have decided in advance.

"Yes, My Lady Princip, the stone." Byasha answered. "There was the scream in the yard, and we suffered a momentary lapse of our aligners—and then the student's disruption of our efforts to prevent the stone from falling."

Lord Michai asked, "How can it be said that one in an arcana training had the depth to disrupt the endeavor? Was not the stone above the bridge at the time?"

"She did not lift the stone to so great a height," Byasha said. "But once we had brought it high, she intruded on its positioning."

Valenty kept his face impassive, but the direction of Byasha's testimony was worrisome. He believed Yevliesza when she said she had tried to help, and he had told Anastyna this. The princip intended to play this as an unfortunate accident.

Nashavety asked Byasha, "Why would she even attempt to intrude?"

At that, Byasha leaned forward, careful not to move her arms swathed in bandages. "Oh, she was a desperate one, our mundat girl. She was consistently in third place, and her self-importance could not countenance it. Because I made no effort to downplay Sofiyana's success, I believe the girl could tolerate it no longer. She was envious."

Valenty softly coughed.

Anastyna turned to him in annoyance. "And so?"

"What makes you think there was envy?" Valenty asked.

Byasha flashed him a look of contempt. "Her triad partner, Sofiyana, can tell you how she suffered the girl's hostility."

Anastyna pursed her lips in thought. "Would you, Lady Byasha, as an expert aligner and guide of the arcana, think it possible that Yevliesza could have any control over the stone?"

"In a moment of overarching excitement . . . I believe it could happen."

Valenty interjected, "But have you ever before seen such a thing?"

Byasha looked down. She did not want to say.

"Answer," Anastyna commanded.

"It would not be usual." Byasha murmured. "Until that day I had not seen it."

"Then," Anastyna said, "it is unlikely. And even if true,

should we not consider how we failed to see such power developing in her and did not properly guide her?"

"She could not be guided if she hid her ability," Nashavety said.

The room grew quiet. A ripple appeared in the pond as though it were troubled. Valenty had known Nashavety's hostility to Yevliesza ever since the night Yevliesza arrived unconscious, strapped onto the dactyl's saddle.

Anastyna asked, "Why would she hide such a thing?"

"Because," Nashavety replied, "she has always despised us. She cannot help what power she has, but she hates our deep gifts."

In the circumstances he could not respond to such a poisonous statement. He became very still and hoped it looked like boredom and not the anger that he felt.

"Bring the girl," Anastyna told her high steward.

By the time Yevliesza arrived, Nashavety had sent for Sofiyana. The two women stood across from each other, by their respective houses: Yevliesza by House Valenty, Sofiyana by Raven Fell.

Yevliesza had not been allowed to change or clean up, but she stood straight and composed. Valenty felt ashamed at her treatment; not only her imprisonment but the indignity of appearing at court unwashed.

He had mishandled so many things. He had shown his desire for her—all unplanned, but which in honor he could not act upon. Lurking in the back of his mind, too, was Anastyna's injunction against telling Yevliesza the suspicion that Nashavety had hastened her father's death by persuading the jailers to harass him. And so he had not told her. But he felt complicit in the deception. And now confinement in the nethers, and these accusations. They were driving her away, in body and spirit.

Lord Michai took charge. "Yevliesza, you are accused of

misusing your align gift and causing the collapse of the Bridge of the Moon. Lady Byasha claims that you brought forth your align power to the ruin of all. How did you think to help, when your ability has up until now been challenged to lift even small objects?"

She should have looked at Lord Michai, but her eyes met Byasha's, seeming to plead. "I . . . I don't know."

Nashavety watched her with cold concentration.

"I wanted to help and I had only a moment to decide."

"Yet you may have altered the course of the stone, sending it higher over the abutment. Did you think yourself able to help in a situation where others of your station would have fled to safety?"

"I had no time to think. And I can't absolutely say that I *did* have any influence on the stone."

Michai went on. "Did you harbor a hope to do something important?"

"I didn't think of anything like that. People were going to die. I tried to help."

"Were you envious of Sofiyana, of her place in the triad?"

Yevliesza turned in confusion to look at her triad companion. "Envious?" Sofiyana's face was blankly innocent. With her sweet face and lush violet hair, she presented the image of a woman who could well inspire jealousy.

"Were you envious?" Michai insisted.

"No. I wished for her . . . to succeed."

Byasha snorted.

"Did you have reason to think that you could help what experienced aligners were failing to do?"

"I didn't think. And now, remembering it, I still don't know why I tried to help."

Byasha began, "Such pretense—"

Anastyna held up her hand. "Enough. I have heard enough."

Valenty thought Yevliesza had done well. By admitting what

she did not know, she made herself more credible. Anastyna might well be able to pardon her.

Nashavety spoke up. "May I have permission to let Sofiyana tell of something that calls the accused's integrity into question?" She rested a hand on Sofiyana's shoulder as though to steady her.

This was something saved for last. What did she know?

"She may speak," Lord Michai said.

"Explain what Yevliesza told you," Nashavety directed her niece.

Lord Michai held up a warning finger. "Let there be no pettiness to cloud our deliberation, Sofiyana."

"Yes, my lord. Once Yevliesza told me that she had never wanted to come home to Numinat. She feared the Numinasi and knew that she should return, that she would in fact be required to return and she did not want to."

Valenty objected. "A person cannot be faulted for their feelings. Only their actions."

"She told me . . ." Sofiyana's voice went low and Michai demanded that she speak up.

Raising her voice, Sofiyana said, "Yevliesza told me that when she was younger a messenger came to see her father and she chose to hide in a closet so that she would not be exposed as a Numinasi. So that she would not be taken away."

A terrible quiet descended on the room.

Lord Michai looked at Yevliesza. "Is this true? You hid from a messenger of the princip, taking advantage of your father's declining judgement?"

Yevliesza looked at Valenty for the first time. A fleeting expression of pain shadowed her face. "I was a child of not more than eight." She paused. "But yes, it's true."

Nashavety waited a few beats before she drove the point home. "She never loved what she was, never wished to know Numinat. When she was finally recognized by the princip's next

messenger, she had no choice. But she has always despised us."
She turned to Anastyna. "It is what some of us have feared from
the start. Now you see what indulgence has wrought."

"We must hope to find a resolution," Anastyna carefully said.

Nashavety answered in a chillingly calm tone, "I join you in
that hope, My Lady Princip."

Anastyna dismissed them. Yevliesza's fate was now solely in
her hands.

Valenty wanted to warn Anastyna away from any rash moves,
but he could not be seen to linger and he left the Numin Room. In
the corridor he watched as a guard led Yevliesza away.

He approached Nashavety, putting on a perturbed expression.
"What do you think the princip will do?"

"It is hard to predict," Nashavety said. "She does not often
share her thinking with us." Belligerently, she looked into his
eyes. And she had said "us," reminding him that she was a *fajatim*
and had support of influential others.

He broke off his gaze, putting on a weary expression. "I had
no idea it was all going to be so . . . complicated."

Nashavety murmured, "Perhaps we can ease your responsibil-
ities, my lord."

※

BACK IN HER CELL, YEVLIESZA SAT WITH HER NEW WORRIES. THE
visit of the first Numinasi messenger. Foolish, so foolish, to admit
such a thing. Sofiyana had betrayed her. She didn't think that she
had told Nashavety about being on the Moon Bridge, so Yevliesza
was surprised that her supposed friend told about her hiding from
the messenger. Thinking back on how she had shared that secret,
she winced at her naiveté. Of course hiding from the courier
would be seen as disloyalty.

She turned her attention to the book in her lap. Valenty had brought her the *Book of Ways and Customs*, where she had been searching for any reference, no matter how obscure, to scarred or patterned skin. But the early sections of the book were written in a different dialect; the older the entry, the harder it was to decipher.

She was also looking for passages describing how align power might flare or respond to emotion.

In the courtyard she thought she'd seen the building stone stop wobbling when she directed her attention to it. And then it rose, at least for one or two seconds. It was possible someone else might have done the stabilizing. But she doubted it.

Some of the older align discussions concentrated on perceiving aligns and using them in setting boundaries and building. In the early days especially, aligners were called upon to scout locations favorable for defense. Osta Kiya had been chosen for its formidable nexus of aligns. The intersections made it a place of strong align power. But nowhere was there mention of surges in power.

When Pyvel came to her, she had been slumped on her bed, sleeping with the book in her lap.

Waking at the noise at the bars, she groaned. "I hate this book, Pyvel." She limped over to the bars, carrying the book.

"Lady?" He extended his manifested circle of light to include her.

"I need to learn more about the *ways*. As everyone has been telling me from the start." She sighed. "Is there any news?"

He shook his head, looking glum.

"Pyvel, do you know the old tongue? Can you read it?"

Glancing at the book, and recognizing it, he gave a lopsided smile. It seemed he, like everyone else here, had language skills drummed into them.

She asked him to find pages dealing with the aligns and how the powers worked. Pyvel sat with the book, back against the prison bars, and started paging through the tome which spread across his lap almost from knee to knee.

❦

"AND IF OUGHT SHOULD BE PLACED IN THE WAY OF A CHILD'S . . ." Pyvel squinted at the page. *". . . a child's natural Deepening, by dark intent and to the detriment of the child, then it is considered a . . . diabolic interference in nature, a trespass of selfhood whereby the person acted upon may suffer grievous harm."*

Perhaps they had only imprisoned her father because it wasn't clear that his *interference* had been done with *dark intent?* And people considered it not just an unusual situation, but *grievous harm?*

She stared at the stone wall of her cell, her back resting against the bars so that she could hear Pyvel clearly. "What is the Deep, exactly?"

"Aye, the Deep," he repeated. "It is where the powers come from. The source."

So everyone kept saying. But she'd never been clear on it. "Is it like God?"

He looked at her blankly. "God?"

That would be a bigger conversation than she had time for. "Never mind. But why call it the *Deep*?"

"Because it is deep inside us. Deep in our bones."

Valenty had once said that what ran through the land ran through his people's bones. Their connection to the natural world, the land. If it wasn't worshipped, it was at least revered.

Pyvel's finger moved along the lines on the page. "Here is something," he said. *"Occurrences arise of the Nine combining . . ."* He glanced up. "The nine powers it means: foreknowing, manifesting," he continued in a chanting cadence, "warding, healing, creatures, verdure, aligns, elements, primal roots."

"Yes, I remember." It was her childhood chant.

He continued reading. *"Occurrences arise of the Nine combining in a child of the Mythos, with the result being a two-sided affinity, wherein one is vital, and one is subsidiary. It is efficacious then to provide guidance in both arenas—"*

"Wait. Read that again?"

He did so. Then he paused. "Do you think you have *two* gifts?"

"No. Nothing like that, Pyvel. You mustn't even think that. I'm just trying to understand."

"Because if you *did* have—"

"I barely have one power. I was last in my arcana, OK?" His light aura shrank, barely covering his shoulders.

"But you are not really last, are you?"

"That's what Lady Byasha says."

But her thoughts had moved far beyond Byasha. She had suddenly become very focused. Two powers. It was not uncommon. Nashavety had two: elements and creatures. So if she herself had two powers, and her align power was subsidiary, what would be her vital power?

She ticked off the powers, one by one.

It was not foreknowing, that was certain. She didn't have the slightest advance warning about anything that had happened to her in Osta Kiya. Nor did she have experiences of warding—creating barriers or preventing aggression. She had never created a manifestation, nor did she remember having any sort of a green thumb. Although her mother had been a verduralist, so her father had said. But a person didn't inherit a parent's powers.

Thinking of the thrall she had met in Nashavety's library, she was sure she had no affinity for creatures. Elements empowered you to influence the surroundings, especially weather, but how did one sense that power? Had she called down the lightning strike on herself by mistake? That deserved more consideration.

Lastly, the primal roots power was said to be the ground of all powers. It implied an influence over all the others. Apparently this power was experienced in the early times, but she had found no information about it. Grigeni had said that even among the First Ones, primal root power came to very few. But what exactly it was, he didn't really know, or if he did, he couldn't explain it. All she had gathered from him was an assumption that it referred to the source of powers. In any case, clearly she had no affinity for *all* the powers.

And apparently, not even two.

Turning to Pyvel, she said, "That's enough for today. I don't think I'm getting anywhere just yet."

Pyvel passed the book through to her. Along with it, a kerchief tied together and containing nuts. The image came to mind that she was like a pet squirrel, with Pyvel always bringing her food.

CHAPTER 26

Valenty woke in the third quarter of the night, always the worst time for considering problems. The moon shone onto the bed and showed his companion in a gloaming light. He raised up on one elbow and studied Lusiana.

Her elegant black hair splayed across the pillow, framing her exotic face. She had thrown off the covers, and he took the moment to regard her closely. Her full breasts and narrow waist. The sculpted neck. She was beautiful in a way that few women were, young and firm and flawless. And utterly vacuous.

As he gazed at her, he began finding fault. Were her lips too thin, as though she had often flattened them in impatience? Was her chin weak, like a child's? Strangely, she did not please him, though for comfort he had been less exacting. But in truth there was no one who could stir him tonight. It was not her fault that he was so unmoved. Dreiza would tell him it would cool his fire to think too much.

Eight hells. He rose from the bed and quietly dressed.

In his adjacent study the embers in the fireplace could not be coaxed to life, and he sat in the great chair staring at the black firepit. If only Yevliesza had told him about hiding from the

Numinasi messenger when she was a child. He could have prepared Anastyna for this revelation, and they would have played the interrogation differently. Nashavety's surprise accusation that Yevliesza's actions sprang from contempt could not be ignored. In a dark mood he considered how Anastyna would have to pronounce some penalty, and it could not be minor.

If the princip came around to sending Alfan Sih relief, she needed support amongst the great Halls. Anastyna must adopt a show of unflinching justice in the small matter, in order to call for backing in the great one. He feared for Yevliesza.

The Volkish could not have an unassailable position yet in Alfan Sih. They were outnumbered, perhaps over-stretched. They relied upon the isolation of the realms and the kingdoms' habits of self-sufficiency. And they were not wrong to think no one would stop them. It had been fourteen days since their forces had overcome Alfan Sih, and aside from a missive of protest, Numinat had not acted.

But pressure was building, as more reports came from Alfan Sih of brutal suppression of opposition, even executions. Nashavety called these claims lies, fabricated with the hope that Numinat would intervene. But Anastyna believed them. If she decided to send a force of arms, it would firmly establish her reign—or topple it.

In the midst of all this, Yevliesza was a fallen branch carried headlong down a surging river.

He went to the window, willing the sun to rise so that he could reasonably begin his day's work. A glow in the east, a blush of light on the horizon.

Today Dreiza would leave to spend a few days in retreat, taking Kirjanichka to Zolvina. She had been deeply affected by the bridge collapse and Yevliesza's part in it—whether out of fear for Yevliesza, or guilt that they had not mentored the girl properly. *I cannot do without you for long*, he had told her, for he knew she was at a low ebb. *Only a few days*, she had said. *Kirjanichka needs a long flight.*

The Zolvina sanctuary was almost a full day's flight away. He wanted to send a rider with her, but she bristled at the idea that she could not handle the dactyl on such a journey. It was no time to suggest that her stamina was not as it once was.

🙦🙤

YEVLIESZA'S NEXT VISITOR IN THE NETHERS ARRIVED SHORTLY after her breakfast porridge. Two men came bearing torches and with them a woman in a midnight-blue dress.

Nashavety.

Yevliesza rose from her pallet. Though she had cultivated an automatic stance and expression of equanimity among the Numinasi, it faltered now. But, she reassured herself, Nashavety couldn't harm her without Anastyna's permission.

She set her bowl aside and stood. "My lady *fajatim*."

"I have come to rescue you from this gloaming cell." The woman's face was in shadow, as the illumination globe was behind her. "You must thank me," she said in a droll tone.

Yevliesza suppressed a shudder. Something about Nashavety told her that the woman had won. "Thank you, my lady," she murmured.

One of the torch-bearing men unlocked the cell with an iron key the size of a hammer.

Yevliesza paused at the threshold. "Where are you taking me, my lady?"

Nashavety nodded to the nearest guard, who took her by the arm and pulled her into the corridor. The woman gestured for the other guard to lead the way, and they set out.

"We are going to Raven Fell," Nashavety said, at last answering her question. "You are mine now. It is Princip Anastyna's will that you be given over to my care, as a mercy considering your ignorance and as we have seen enough blood because of you." She turned toward her prisoner. "Your correction will now be at my hands, relieving Lord Valenty of the onerous task."

The guards, or one of them, must have had aligns, because he easily led them through the twisting nethers. They might have been entering some chasm of the underworld, so thick was the murk around them and in Yevliesza's heart. She was going to be in the malwitch's care. Anastyna's will. Lord Valenty relieved of the task. She tried to absorb it, to place it somewhere in the confusion of events. Anastyna gave her to Nashavety. So much for Valenty's theory that Anastyna needed her. When the pressure was on, the princip had simply tossed her aside.

The torchlight made little impression on the close stone walls, with their footfalls the only proof that they made any progress. Part of her wished for the nethers to keep them, for days, forever. And part of her wished she could have taken the book of customs with her. It seemed she would enter Raven Fell with nothing, least of all her freedom.

They emerged into the light of the upper castle. At first they were alone, making their way through a narrow passageway. Around them came a draft of cold air, like a forlorn sigh, the exhalation of an impossibly old corridor hollowed out by forces of nature no one could remember.

But then there were people.

Many were about at this early hour, standing in knots and then making way for the two women and their guards. Some nodded to the *fajatim* as she passed, receiving a smaller nod in return. Others placed a small finger on their cheek in a warding gesture against a woman whose clumsy powers killed two Numinasi. Yevliesza looked down the corridor ahead of her, spying some faces she knew. Pyvel among the first, looking ashen. Andrik, Valenty's steward, his dark face rigid as jet-black stone. His eyes met hers and the look gave her courage. They passed by the Waxing Moon chamber. Standing in the entrance was a fiercely scowling Rusadka. Then, Lord Tirhan with his lieutenant. She didn't look into his face, because if it was kind, she might lose her resolve to show no emotion.

When they came to the great facade of Raven Fell, she had to strictly command her expression. She remembered she had been here once before. It was just a section of the castle. Inhabited by a dark and twisted woman and others who could bear to live with her.

As they passed through the tall arched doors, she told herself that they couldn't kill or maim her. She would survive.

Still, she took a good look around for the thrall.

৩৯৩

THE BEST PLACE TO WALK OFF FURY WAS ON THE CASTLE ROOF IN the forest of chimney stacks, water cisterns, and weapon sheds. In the chill of the morning Valenty paced beside the parapets with Andrik, receiving his report of Yevliesza's transfer to Ravel Fell.

Between clenched teeth, Valenty asked, "Did they bind her wrists?"

"No, she walked freely. With a guard on each side and Nashavety leading the way with a face that could scare the Deep out of small children. A goodly number of people assembled to watch. They kept their thoughts to themselves."

Andrik, who ostensibly had the title of steward in his house-hold, dispensed with formal address when they were alone. He was Valenty's primary spy, and no one better.

"How did she look?"

Andrik knew who Valenty was most interested in. "As though she was out for a stroll. Not so much as a frown at what was happening."

Valenty was not surprised. He had seen her display such calm before. If he could have advised her, he might have suggested that she look at least a little contrite. It would be more satisfying to those who feared her. She would have to learn how to let go of some things—unfortunately, including pride—now that she was Nashavety's.

Anastyna had done what she believed she had to, and her decision showed how desperate her position was. She had to take a stern position. He wished that she had asked for his counsel, but she had not. Now he could only hope that Yevliesza's sojourn at Raven Fell would be brief. And it could only be brief if Yevliesza submitted to Nashavety. He would suggest that she do so at the first opportunity, but he feared he no longer could influence her.

They skirted around an embrasure projecting out from the ramparts where hot oil could be dumped on an attacking force.

A bird had been circling overhead, and now steeply descended, flapping into one of the crenelations in the parapet. It was a great female stormhawk, Andrik's *sympat*. Andrik murmured something to it as they passed, a greeting, a term of affection, or a command. Only Andrik and the hawk knew.

"You are sure the guards did not mistreat her in the cell?" Valenty asked. He had assigned Andrik to keep close watch on her in the nethers.

"Yes, well enough. I could not tell what they fed her, but she ate it."

By now they were on the east wing of the castle, the side facing the valley. Fog curled in the ravines, masking the river and any enemy that might lurk in the mist.

"Tomorrow will be a good day for a long ride," Valenty told his spy. "Take my dappled gelding if you like."

Andrik nodded, waiting to hear what the task would be.

Valenty had been considering a certain undertaking for some time. He had been waiting to find Anastyna in a favorable mood, but now he would send Andrik out to accomplish this without the princip's sanction. He trusted that she would forgive him, or get over her annoyance quickly. In any case it was time to send Andrik on a journey. Though he would rather have kept him close during this fraught time, there was no one better to find a missing person than Andrik.

And once he found his quarry, his considerable aptitude in persuasion could be brought to bear. Valenty presumed Andrik's *sympat* would go along, perhaps aiding him in his quest.

CHAPTER 27

W e have come so far together, Kirjanichka. But you have been in this place before. Zolvina.

When I asked if you fancied a leisurely flight to the Numin Mountains, I saw your excitement over the prospect of the journey. It was a fine day, warm enough for me and cool enough for the one who would be doing all the work.

It has been many years since we have been to Zolvina. So long ago that in fact I cannot remember much about the trip to keep vigil over my grandmother's dying. I remembered how my mother was annoyed that her mother chose to die so far away. And how I was strapped behind her in the saddle. And how warm my mother's back was when I left off craning my neck to see the sights.

You and I, Kirjanichka, we were both young then. But I knew that you loved me. You tolerated my mother, as was your duty, but you accepted me completely. The reason is not to be known, except by your kind. But I am, and have always been, deeply grateful.

So you and I left Osta Kiya, and this time I was seventy years older. The only ones who knew we were taking a journey were your shed girl and Valenty. I had no need of permissions because *your role is no longer to serve the Numinat court. I think you felt as free as I did that day, lifting into the wind, leaving the stony castle and the solid world behind. Those who have never ridden in the sky cannot know how it is that the lesser self falls away and the truer self abides in perfect stillness.*

I could have traveled for days on your strong back, but soon we came to the foothills and the short ascent to Zolvina. It is not the largest satvary, *but the oldest, built on two aligns intersecting at right angles and famous for the fact. My mother dismissed the significance of this as superstition, and she may have been right. But all I hope for at Zolvina is a little detachment and peace. Is not this why Numinasi in the last quarter of their lives so often repair to its quiet halls?*

We circled the compound, showing our flag of request. They would know my colors because my grandmother had richly endowed the sanctuary. She spent her last years here and died promptly at 150, which was considered proper, even elegant. I was present at her death, but alas, I do not remember it or her final words which were, apparently, "Now you know." *Mother sniffed that we knew nothing because she had not told us anything, but I am not sure she would have understood any trans-missions of wisdom from a* satvar. *My mother always loved the duties of the court and had served in its chambers until the end. She considered renunciation a waste of time and often said that to wear the pale was all very well if one wished to live without cares. However was caring not the point of it all?*

I am so happy we have arrived safely here, Kirjanichka! I should have come sooner, because already I feel a great stillness pervading me. Some of this comes from the Devi Ilsat, *the High Mother, who welcomed me like a beloved child. It was exceed-ingly kind of her to spend so much time with me, offering a cup of hot barley savory in her apartment. After all, the High Mother oversees not only Zolvina, but five other* satvaries. *She asked many questions about goings on at court. Though she had not had news of Osta Kiya for some time, she did not appear surprised by anything, not the arrival of our guest of the mundat or the fall of the Bridge of the Moon. We talked of Yevliesza's power coming to her once she arrived amongst us, and she seemed to very much approve. In her kind manner, I could see that she was disturbed to hear that the girl was being tutored by Lady Nashavety, even if she would not openly say so.*

Kirjanichka, how strange it is to feel like a beginner at my age! The Devi Ilsat *has more than a quarter again as many years as I, so that must explain why I raptly listen to her, almost inhaling her wisdom and serenity.*

They have given me a lovely, small room with a narrow window looking into the courtyard where satvars *dressed in their pale uniforms of long tunics and trousers pass to and from the well. They do, for the most part, look sincerely happy, even if the oaten color of their garments to my eye seems bland indeed. They are excited that a dactyl will be staying for a tenday at least, so please tell me if you tire of their frequent visits, and I shall explain to them that it must be your retreat as well as mine.*

I suspect there will be an abundance of figs, my dear, so there is that.

CHAPTER 28

Yevliesza leaned on her shovel and looked up as a great shadow passed over the garden. It was a giant dactyl with its gleaming scales and elongated head crest. It pumped its wings to gain altitude. Holding the reins was a rider wearing a skirt.

"Keep on, now, we still have eight rows to do." The gardener didn't seem happy to have her help, though he was so old he had trouble getting up from a crouch, much less shoveling soil.

The Raven Fell vegetable garden had been harvested, but now they were digging it up to alter the rows along aligns instead of facing the sun. It was a foolish idea but old Jeder was keen on the project, especially if she did all the digging. He had a sack of black rocks and when he threw a handful into the air, they would fall along aligns, so he swore. Now they had a lot of rocks in the garden as well as new ditches which must be made ready for planting come spring.

"Ah, here is a goodly line," Jeder said staring at the bare ground. "I knew it, for old Treshia told me, and she it was who taught me all I know about planting." He held her gaze with his one good eye, the other being at half-mast due to an unnamed condition. "You see it, do you not? You who have done the arcana?" His smirk drove home his opinion of her align powers.

The problem was that there weren't any aligns in the garden, but when she had suggested this, Jeder had become so angry that she finally acknowledged that there might be an align or two.

"You can learn a few things," he muttered, "if you are not so full of yourself." He reached in his bag for more marking stones. "She warned me, the lady did, and she was not far wrong." Nashavety could not even let her dig in the garden without an enemy at her side.

At midday, she stacked their tools under the colonnade and scurried off to the servants' dining hall and, on the way, the privy next door to the household baths. Emerging from the surprisingly clean and vented toilet she found someone waiting for her in the corridor.

"Rusadka!"

Her friend took her by the arm. "Come, before they see us."

"How did you get in?"

"My officer sent me with a message for the Raven Fell *numiner*. I have taken my time leaving."

"Tell me the news," Yevliesza said. "I hear nothing. How are you, are you going to a boundary fort or staying? I hope you're staying, but I know you don't want to."

Rusadka guided her through an archway into a shadowy room with scrolls stacked on a table and the windows warded to block the sun.

Her arcana partner's broad, dark face was hardly visible in the gloom, but her presence raised Yevliesza's spirits. "You are a sight for sore eyes, Rusadka."

"I make your eyes sore?"

"If my eyes were sore, you would be good for them." Impulsively, she reached for her friend's hand, and Rusadka smiled at this, squeezing back with a grip like a crescent wrench.

"How are things with you?" Yevliesza asked, desperate for conversation.

"I came to see how *you* are doing. But for me, I am being considered for a promotion to third rank. I have been appointed adjutant to the commander here."

"That is wonderful, Rusadka!"

Her friend's face did not reflect pleasure. "Osta Kiya is impregnable. There is no action here."

Selfishly, Yevliesza was happy Rusadka hadn't left for the gates.

"Is the arcana still on, without me?"

"Still on. You have been replaced by Grenavel, a skinny girl who has limited affinity, but who has supporters. Sofiyana will likely get her triad victory." Rusadka smirked. "But my power is with me lately, so she may have to settle for second place."

Yevliesza felt a grin break out. "I've missed you so much!"

"Is it bad here? Do they bother to feed you, you look as thin as Grenavel."

"Nashavety doesn't dare mistreat me. I have to fail all on my own, or she'll lose face."

"The woman could do with a better face." She glanced at the doorway arch. "Do you have messages for anyone?"

Who was there to give a message to? "Tell Pyvel I'm well and miss our card games."

A door that she hadn't noticed before began to open. She and Rusadka hurried from the room. Rushing into the hall and turning a corner, they found themselves passing an open-sided stairway.

Sofiyana was just coming down.

She paused for a split second, then joined them at the bottom of the stairs. "I suppose you hate me," she said to Yevliesza, her face closed.

"First, tell me, was it your plan to win me over so you could betray me, or was it just a passing urge?"

Sofiyana's lips flattened. It was startling to see such an expression on someone who had always seemed airily happy. "Once you told me about hiding from us, I had the *urge* to reveal an enemy amongst us."

Rusadka's voice was a dangerous rumble. "She always treated you with kindness. You betrayed her to win favor with your aunt."

"I had nothing to gain. I spoke only the truth."

Yevliesza knew they shouldn't goad her and placed her hand on Rusadka's arm to warn her, but Rusadka pressed on. "Everyone knows what you have done. You betrayed Yevliesza to enslave yourself to the *fajatim*. Now you will rise, and we all know why."

Ignoring her, Sofiyana addressed Yevliesza. "You think I am so bad and yourself so blameless. But I took on all the responsibility for sneaking up on the bridge that night. But there is a limit to how much I can protect you. Look at all you have wrought."

"I've made mistakes," Yevliesza said. "And now I have to submit to the *fajatim's* education sessions. In addition to losing my place in the arcana. Does it satisfy you?"

"I never wanted you to fail. You did that on your own."

"If you see me in the worst light, then we don't have anything to talk about." She turned away, hoping that Rusadka would follow, but the *harjat* could not help a parting shot.

"You are walking hollow, Sofiyana," she snarled. "Hollow."

When Rusadka caught up to her, Yevliesza asked, "What does that mean?"

"That she has lost herself. She has become an empty vessel."

If that was the case, Yevliesza knew who was ready to fill her with a nasty brew.

⚜

SHE SAT ON A BENCH IN THE CORRIDOR OUTSIDE NASHAVETY'S office. Her routine would be to come every three days at dawn. Nashavety would evaluate her progress and correct her as needed. This was the first time. She wasn't surprised she was made to wait.

As the sun finally made it over the lip of the east window, Nashavety's steward, Daraliska, appeared at the door, practically filling it with her girth. She raised an eyebrow, her version of a summons.

Inside, Nashavety stood at the window, looking upward, perhaps in the direction of the great align that once had begun to hold a walkway. "Sit," she said, without turning. Her dark hair, without any grey, was gathered in a loop at the back of her neck and covered with a net fashioned from gold thread. Yevliesza wondered how old she was. But Numinasi life-spans made ages hard to figure out. At seventy-five one was only half through their allotted years.

Daraliska gestured at a chair in the center of the room.

Nashavety turned to look at her boarder. "Humility. Deference. Patience," she began. "These are the basic qualities you must learn. Then we will attend to customs. So, as to ways and customs, you will not be reading of them, nor will any scrolls or codices or books be needed. You see how we will proceed?"

"No, Lady Nashavety. Not really."

A smile slowly cut into the woman's face. "We will begin right there. I have said you will learn three qualities first. Then, customs. You are pretending not to understand. This shows a lack of deference. Do you see?"

"Um, yes?"

"Correct her," the *fajatim* said to Daraliska.

The steward came forward. In her hands was what looked like a slab of wood. With a tug it opened into two halves. She grabbed

Yevliesza's hand and thrust it in, giving the top half a sharp rap with her fist.

Yevliesza cried out in surprise and pain.

"Hostile responses will be corrected," the *fajatim* said.

Daraliska released her hand from the wood device but remained standing at her side.

Nashavety took a seat in the chair behind her desk and continued in a relaxed tone. "Humility will be the hardest for you. You are proud of being different, as though such a departure was a superior attribute. You must learn otherwise." Her mouth flattened into a determined expression. "We will start with whether or not you are Numinasi. How would you answer this?"

Her tongue was poised between a *fuck you* and avoiding pain. With great restraint, she said, "I'm Numinasi. My parents were, and so am I."

"Very good. Then in what way were you and your parents flouting Numinasi laws and ways?"

She saw how it would be. She'd have to criticize her parents in order to show humility. Daraliska hovered just behind her right shoulder. Numinasi would never torture the left hand. "To bear a child in the mundat," she answered. "To keep a child in the mundat."

Nashavety's lips crawled toward a sneer, but never got there. She slowly nodded. So her answer did not earn the wood vise.

"Why do you think your parents bore and kept their child in the mundat?"

"My mother died. My father had a mental illness."

The *fajatim* nodded at Daraliska. She took Yevliesza's hand again. The spike of pain opened a pathway in her body she had never known existed. Eventually she composed her face.

"Why, again?" Nashavety insisted.

It had only taken two slams of the wooden vise before she gave up. "They didn't respect the ways and customs enough."

And at that moment, she didn't either. At some point people here should recognize that they were doing the same thing to her that the mundat had done to them. Punishing her for being different. For not toeing the line on *ways*.

Nashavety stared at her for a long while, deliberating about the correction. Yevliesza hoped her glance wouldn't go to to Daraliska. It didn't.

"That is a beginning. You will spend the next three days probing beneath the surface of *not respecting enough*. Why this was so."

Out the window behind her tormentor, Yevliesza saw a crow sweeping by, gliding free, master of the air currents. In that moment she imagined herself perched on the back of a dactyl and lifting away from this pile of stones.

"May I ask a question, Lady Nashavety?"

She nodded.

"How will I know when my answers are the truth and when I'm just trying to avoid the . . . wooden trap?"

Nashavety rose from her chair and approached Yevliesza. She lifted her left hand, the ringed one with the large amber stone, and tilted Yevliesza's face toward her. "*I* will know which it is," she said from deep in her throat. "I will always know. Let the wisdom of the vise take you further into yourself. It is here to help you."

Her rigid face held no flickers of emotion except contempt. The impression Yevliesza had was of an empty person, filled only with darkness.

A longing for home crept over her. For her old life of caring for her gentle father, flying down the highway in the old Celica, the twice-weekly task of sweeping the dust from the floors and windowsills. Dinners in front of the TV, and watching the tornadoes dip down from the sky, sometimes just a stab and sometimes hell-bent.

To be homesick was a ruthless thing, ripened by the knowledge that you couldn't be there and even if you could, nothing would be the same.

❧

NASHAVETY STOOD ON HER VERANDA OVERLOOKING THE GREAT courtyard. Her nostrils filled with the scent of a coming storm. It would bear half-frozen pellets turning to sleet. Winter was coming. And thank the First Ones for that, because soon it would be a hard season to send out the army. Food, shelter, and so forth. However, it was also true that once into the crossings, they would not encounter the cold. So perhaps winter would not deter Anastyna from a disastrous expedition to Alfan Sih.

And then, the mundat girl. She was lying, of course. It would take time for her to understand the truth. A first step was to be willing to say a truth, even if she did not believe it. Gradually belief must come, aided by corrections, but not so often as to leave lasting bruises. Daraliska was a good judge of the nuances.

It seemed to Nashavety that it had become her fate to teach younger people how to behave, because now she also had Sofiyana to deal with.

Her niece stood before her, ringletted hair framing a troubled face. The girl no doubt expected her to fix whatever in her small world had gone wrong, not understanding that the things one chose to fix defined one's character.

Nashavety gave permission for her to speak. "Well?"

Sofiyana took a deep breath. "Yevliesza. She is here and acting as though she is a real guest. She has no remorse. I am sure that she feels misused. In fact, she blames me."

How could it be otherwise? That is where Yevliesza had begun, but she would learn not to be so satisfied with herself. *Patience, Sofiyana, patience.* Anastyna was watching, after all.

She went on. "Yesterday Rusadka was walking the halls with

her, and she accosted me. My lady, it was insufferable, if you could have heard it."

"Rusadka insulted you? Or Yevliesza did?"

"Both. They said I betrayed Yevliesza to gain favor with you."

"As you did."

Sofiyana had the decency to look abashed. But then she ruined the moment. "She was always so sure of herself. She had forward ideas in arcana—like not trying too hard to perceive an align. . . ." Her voice trailed off to a murmur. "And it was pitiful to watch her flirt with Lord Tirhan."

"Lord Tirhan?" That was interesting.

"Yes, as though he would ever take an interest in a girl like her."

"She admires him, then."

"My lady, she admires everything that is not Numinasi. She even said that strangers are always more attractive than others."

Nashavety looked out at the courtyard. The wreckage of the bridge had been hauled away and the remnants of the decking hewn back, leaving a scar on the castle facade. The Great Circle had gone as yellow as a sunflower, but the verduralists kept it free of weeds. She still remembered the year, not so long ago, when Princip Lisbetha had given her a nightbloom rose, that invitation into the Ninth Moon Festival. If the princip had not died young Anastyna's mal influence would not even be felt.

Bringing her attention back to her niece, she said, "I fear you have strayed from the path, Sofiyana."

"I have, my lady?"

"You have. First, you will leave Yevliesza's instruction solely to me. I do not require your opinions."

Some moments passed. She could not tell if her words had penetrated the wild nimbus of the girl's hair.

"Next, you must learn true strength. The only way is to know what is important and tie your thoughts and actions to them. You will discover this through hard work and mental control."

"My lady, do you say that I am not strong?"

"You are angry. Do not confuse the two. You have succumbed to low hate over a person of little account. Do not, do not indulge this tendency, for it will impede your growth. You must reserve your hate for high things—for your realm, your culture, the true Numinasi ways. When these are in jeopardy. Do you see?"

Sofiyana nodded, looking as though she did not.

Nashavety went on. "If you are to be of use to me, everything you do, every intention, must be in service to Numinat. Not in service to yourself. To Numinat only, through service to me. Go and consider this. Come to me when you understand."

"My lady aunt . . . I understand. I do."

"Sofiyana. That is unlikely in the extreme. You are in Raven Fell now, not in Karsk polity where your pretenses mattered. Much will be asked of you here, under my will. I can raise you up, but only if you are strong in your heart and mind." She tried mightily to remember what it had been like to be twenty-five and of scattered will. "Go and seek out your errors of thinking."

Nashavety watched as the sky darkened with fast-moving grey clouds. She felt the small finger of her left hand twinge in response. Weather always stirred her, especially a grand approach of storms. These winds would bring freezing rain. She welcomed the approach of winter, its hard and vast grip. Perhaps a winter in Osta Kiya would correct Yevliesza, if nothing else would. It was Nashavety's favorite season.

When she turned to go inside, Sofiyana had fled.

CHAPTER 29

O n horseback, Yevliesza and Valenty made their way down the one gentle slope that existed at the foot of Osta Kiya. Gusts of cold wind persisted after a three-day storm, sending remnant clouds flattening into thin, crumpled strips.

"Try to keep your skirt from blowing," Valenty said. "It distracts the horse."

She tucked her dress more securely between her thigh and the side saddle. "You might consider letting women wear trousers."

"It is not our way."

If she heard any more about Numinasi *ways*, she thought she would scream.

After a week in Raven Fell—Yevliesza still thought in weeks no matter how hard she tried to count off days in tens—Valenty had asked Nashavety if her student could be allowed out for a brief spell. Nashavety had granted the request, probably in an attempt to appear less brutal than she was.

When Valenty had brought Yevliesza to the stables, he had found her a horse that looked like its galloping days were over.

His own was a fine, dappled grey which he expertly mounted after he had helped her into the side saddle.

They made their way down the grassy slope where Byasha had conducted her first exercise to determine Yevliesza's affinity for aligns.

"Why are you taking me out here?" Yevliesza was enjoying being on a horse, but she was wary of Valenty.

"To let Nashavety know that I am invested in you."

She had wondered if she was of value any longer to Princip Anastyna. If Valenty was *invested* in her, then the answer must at least tentatively, be yes. In her helplessness under Nashavety's control, even a crumb from the princip felt like a gift. After seven days in Raven Fell, her heart sometimes felt like a small animal curled up, huddling for warmth.

"Can this horse go any faster? Or are you afraid I'll fall off?" A little speed would go well right now. Perhaps a wild gallop down to the meadow.

"Later. After you get somewhat used to riding." He had seemed surprised to learn that she had never ridden before. Once, she had told him about her sports car. The subject had quickly gone cold. Perhaps he had tried to appreciate her love of her car, but was not up to it. Or he might have been thoroughly disgusted.

"How does your sojourn with the Raven go, Yevliesza?"

She paused on the verge of describing how it really was at Raven Fell. But complaints would be seen as weak or rebellious, and she could imagine how Nashavety would turn them against her. "She has me digging furrows in the garden. Except when it rains. The gardener believes there are aligns there, but he is deluded. I have to act as though there are."

"Digging in the garden? Even for Nashavety, that is going too far."

"Not really," she said, thinking of the wooden vise. "I'm not supposed to have any books to read. I hope you got your *Ways and Customs* back."

"I sent Pyvel to the nethers for it." He looked at her with the hint of a smile, which made him look a bit handsome, damn him. "The boy worships you."

"I have that effect on people," she said, meaning to be offhand, but then realized that she had once hoped to have that effect on Valenty. She wished she hadn't sounded bitter. It was impossible to be with the man without excruciating considerations.

"Yevliesza . . ." he murmured.

It was a moment when they might have broached the subject of what had happened between them, but he had nothing to say that she wanted to hear.

"I have some things to ask you about," she said, turning the subject. "Now that I don't have the book." She decided that the ride needed to be all on business, as she had only a short while to be out from under Nashavety. "It's about Mythos powers. My powers."

They picked their way across a flat meadow, her horse swaying under her and unerringly knowing where to put all four of its feet in sequence. "There is something strange about me," she began. She wasn't going to tell him about the tracery on her skin. Tirhan had warned her that it might be the cause of trouble among the hidebound Numinasi, and though she felt it was not likely to be the case with Valenty, he did have the princip's ear. She didn't trust how the woman would react.

"Do you mean because you held up such a large stone?"

"Well, if I did hold it up. But I think I might not have the aligns in a normal way."

They entered a thick woodland, and began following a wide trail rutted with wagon tracks. Heavy shade cloaked them, a suitable backdrop for discussions of magic. Her horse twitched its ears, perhaps picking up sounds she couldn't hear.

Valenty had paused before responding to her and now murmured, "It is possible the aligns are not completely normal in you. Because of how late your Deepening entered you, and how quickly."

"Except . . . I wonder if I have only one. One power. What if I have two?"

He paused, perhaps considering if there was more to her than he had thought. "Yevliesza, I watched for that from the moment you became my guest. There never was much about you that seemed to be the usual case."

They rode easily, letting the new thought—two powers—settle around them. Now and then a shaft of sunlight bored down to the forest floor like a brilliant thought banishing the darkness. The trees grew so close together here, the shade itself looked green. Yevliesza breathed deeply of the cool air, so cleansing after the close atmosphere of Osta Kiya.

"What did you notice about me?" she asked at last.

"That you were sharp-tongued, impatient, and resentful."

"Rather what you'd be like if you were forced to live in Barlow County?"

Valenty bit his lip. "I was going to say that your impatience and anger came from how we mistreated your father and that you were at a complete disadvantage as a stranger amongst us."

"But you didn't notice anything about my gift?"

"I did wonder, after the Moon Bridge, if another power was influencing you. Pushing back your align power and then erratically augmenting it."

"Maybe elements?"

"It could be any one of them," he said. "Any one of them which has not found its way to you, but is trying to."

He stopped his horse and now turned toward her, holding on

to one of her horse's reins. She had his complete attention. "Do you feel an affinity for elements? Affecting moving water, or the arising of storms?"

"No, I don't think so. But now, I'm almost waiting—for something—to come."

He looked at her, maybe hoping she would be more forthcoming. But she had nothing else to say, nothing that she was willing to say. An errant itch crawled through the etchings on her back as though urging her to acknowledge them.

Disappointingly, Valenty said it was time to turn around, and they began a slow walk back along the rutted track.

"If you need some guidance in this . . . we can speak again, Yevliesza."

The last thing she wanted was to have close conversation with him. She didn't like that he had offered it. When he was nice, it made things worse.

It was time to pursue the questions she needed to put to him. "Why does no one have primal root power anymore?"

"Because at one time we needed great powers. These are lesser times."

"But there isn't much even written about primal roots. Not in *Ways and Customs* anyway."

"I have not heard that there are any specific descriptions of it. Only that when Numinat first arose, such a power could be harnessed."

"But what is the power?" she asked.

His horse shied at something, and he stroked its neck, calming it. "Some say it is the primal base from which all the powers arose. I think of it as a reference to the Deep itself."

"So it's not a power as such."

Valenty looked thoughtful. "Maybe a source power? Whatever it is, perhaps the First Ones believed that knowing more about it would be dangerous—for the lesser beings we have become."

"So they didn't write about it. And when the first generations died, no one *could* write about it."

"Yes, that is what we have come to believe."

The field lay before them in brilliant sun. Valenty cocked his head at her, a signal that they might urge their mounts to run.

She felt a smile crease her face. Leaning closer to her mount, she dug into its side with her boot, shouting an encouragement. The horse leapt forward, and soon they were racing over the flat, through the withered grass, kicking up clods of dirt from the sodden land. She slapped up and down in the saddle until the horse reached a graceful, lunging gallop, and then side-by-side with Valenty, she rode, exulting in the power of the animal beneath her and the freedom of speed. With this taste of freedom, she felt strong enough to withstand anything her jailer could deliver.

She would survive Nashavety. And then she would be free.

At the paddock, two stable boys came down to meet them, their faces full of relief that she hadn't fallen. They broke into grins.

"Not bad for a slow horse!" she told them, returning their smiles and jumping down from the saddle with only a little stagger.

❧

YEVLIESZA, SWEATY FROM THE DAY'S GARDEN WORK, THANKED the servant for bringing a basin of water.

"But would you not prefer a full washing, miss? Our baths even have a view of the west plains, and our element workers keep them cozy warm."

"No thank you, Annady. This will be enough." She could not show her skin markings in such a public place. "What news do you hear about Alfan Sih and its troubles?" She was always plying the servants for outside news.

"Alfan Sih is far away. Who can say what troubles they have?"

"Well, Osta Kiya is on alert. Nothing of special note going on? I think you hear more than I ever would."

The maid brightened. "Oh. The lady *fajatim* will host a fine supper tonight, and the Prince of Alfan Sih will come."

"Lord Tirhan is coming?"

"Yes, we will lay a great table, with the *fajatim* of Wild Hill coming also. They say the lord is very handsome and will be a king."

It seemed wrong for Tirhan to attend a dinner hosted by someone who opposed aid to Alfan Sih. But then again, maybe it was the very best thing for him to do.

❧

IN THE FOYER OF RAVEN FELL, MERRY VOICES ERUPTED AS GUESTS arrived, attired in gowns and jackets with jewels, braid, and buttons catching the glittering lights from the many candles.

Yevliesza stood in the shadow of a side corridor, watching. She had found herself wishing to see the Alfan lord again, even if only from a distance. Nashavety was greeting everyone, wearing a gown of swirling grey, its high collar swathed in jewels like a princip's torc. Yevliesza was sure the effect wasn't lost on her guests.

Tirhan looked dreadfully handsome, dressed in dark green and black. His lieutenant, Caden, stood at his side, entranced by the sight of Sofiyana wearing an indigo-blue gown exposing one shoulder, the first time Yevliesza had seen such a thing. Nashavety's close ally, Vajalyna, usually severe-looking, wore a stunning bronze ensemble that set off her deep brown skin.

Yevliesza's feelings alternated between fascination and envy at the glamour of it all. But underneath the gaiety, dark things skittered. Politics, threats of war, ambition—and perhaps, for Sofiyana, envy at what she might have thought was Tirhan's preference in women. Yevliesza herself.

From the corner of her eye, a motion caught her attention. She swiveled to see the thrall just coming into the corridor. It was still a stone's throw away. Reaching into her pocket, she produced a hunk of cheese. Since the beast at times roamed free, she always had something in a pocket to feed it. As the creature stalked closer, she tossed the food in its direction, where it disappeared in a lunging gobble. A moment later a handler rounded the corner and silently commanded the thrall to his side.

The party guests were moving off to the dining hall. As they left, Caden glanced at her, nodding slightly in acknowledgment. She was grateful for it and hoped that he'd tell Tirhan he had seen her.

She remained at her vantage point for a time, listening to the sounds of conversation and laughter from the hall where the dinner was served. Resolving to return later and watch the guests depart, she began to retrace her steps to her room upstairs, but turned, hearing footsteps.

Lieutenant Caden. He closed the distance between them and leaned in to whisper that Lord Tirhan begged to meet her later that evening on the east terrace. Was she able to be there? She whispered that she was, and conspiratorially he gave her a small smile.

A meeting on a deserted terrace. It was a risk, but Tirhan must have something to tell her, something important enough to risk the fallout from seeing her without Nashavety's permission.

It was moonrise before Tirhan arrived.

He joined her near the castle wall where the three-quarter moon wouldn't cast its light.

"Yevliesza," Tirhan said, very low. "Are you well?"

"I am. But I wish I wasn't here."

"There are many who wish you were not, believe me."

"Many?"

He smiled. "More than a few."

"She means to break me, my lord. But she won't."

"No, she will not. This will not last forever. I have asked the princip if you will have your freedom, and she acknowledged it is only gone for a time."

"How are your people?" she asked, "What do you hear?"

"They suffer, Yevliesza. The Volkish have slaughtered whole villages that opposed them, even if only a few people crossed their purposes."

"Whole villages?"

His voice tightened into a near-snarl. "They despise us. They believe they are a purer people. Volkia being the true land of the Mythos."

The thought came at her like a stage curtain parting. It could not be, it *should* not be . . . But the awful possibility swept over her. "Nazis," she whispered, dismay spiking within her.

"What do you mean?"

"On the origin world, there was a time. A time of . . . the Third Reich. You've heard of it?"

He cocked his head, wondering at her intensity. "No, Yevliesza."

She realized that was very probably true. Whatever people in the Mythos knew of the origin world, it might not include much about the twentieth century.

"This can wait," Tirhan said. "I should not stay longer, but for now . . ." He drew out a folded paper from his jacket. "This is for you."

She stared at the paper, trying to bring her attention to the moment and not the revelation that had her in its grip.

"What is it?" she asked, feeling the parchment, smooth and thick in her hand.

"Your tracery," he said. "To the extent my poor artistry could render it. Do not look at it now."

She thanked him, though still preoccupied with what she had guessed about the real oppressors of Alfan Sih.

"Is there anyone you trust to share this with?" Tirhan asked.

That was easily answered. "Rusadka, of the *harjat*. She already knows. A month or more ago she told me that the scars were changing."

"Rusadka. I know of her." He held her gaze. "Tell only those you completely trust."

A muffled sound caught their attention. "I must not stay." He pressed her hand in his. "Be well, and take heart, Yevliesza."

When he was gone, she waited on the terrace, looking out at the palace wing across the central courtyard. Her thoughts were far from whatever markings were on her back. Her personal situation didn't seem so unimportant now. If the Nazis were back, if a version of them was . . . She remembered the uniform of the Volkish envoy that day in the stand of trees when she and Sofiyana had seen him. It was a Nazi uniform.

She leaned against the cold stone of the castle wall. This changed everything. The Volkish were not just a possible threat. They were the worst possible threat.

CHAPTER 30

They walked through the dormant gardens of Zolvina, one woman in iron-grey, the other in the oaten-colored garb of the *satvar*. A brisk wind pushed at their garments as though trying to strip them bare. Despite the cold, Dreiza found the gardens remarkable, with their shaped trees and hedges trained and coaxed and sung into graceful shapes.

The Devi Ilsat spoke. "Your gift of honey from the Osta Kiya bees was gratefully received by the Zolvina circle. Thank you."

Dreiza bowed her head. She had also brought a goodly sum of coin as a gift of Household Valenty, but it was like the High Mother to mention the humble one.

Everywhere within the domicile walls and outside it, the renunciates were busy with preserving the fruits of their harvests, the cleaning and oiling of implements for storage, and the endless task of sweeping and raking even if only a handful of leaves had fallen during the night. Dreiza let the unhurried routines seep into her body, chasing away the gnarls of concern that had brought her here. She would have liked to ask the Devi Ilsat about the threat of war, the sides for and against, and the machinations of

Nashavety, but these things were not in the woman's purview. In any case, it was enough just to be away from such concerns.

"I had thought to see you long before this, my daughter," the High Mother said warmly.

She had known Dreiza's mother and grandmother, and Dreiza always knew a visit would be welcome.

"My thoughts have often come here."

"And now we have all of you," the old woman replied, her face crinkling with pleasure.

They climbed the stairs to the narrow walkway near the top of the wall surrounding the domicile and its outbuildings.

A very large striped cat lay sleeping on the wall next to a bowl of cream.

"The *satvary* cat," the Devi Ilsat explained. "Lord Woe."

"A hard name for such a peaceful cat."

"Ah, but the rats do not think so," the High Mother said proudly.

As they walked, Dreiza looked down into the courtyard, noting the numin pool, a stone's toss in diameter. Some households in Osta Kiya had smaller versions of the round pools, but in the *satvar* sanctuaries they were outside, where vigilance was required to keep them clear. Warders made every effort, but should an errant leaf find its way in, there was always a small scoop on a pole.

A woman sat on the wall encircling the pool, occasionally passing her hand over the water's surface and noting the reflection.

"Who is that?" Dreiza asked. "She looks quite lost in thought."

"That she is. Very perceptive."

"And so young to be a *satvar*." She could not have more than fifteen years.

"Her name is Kassalya. You have noticed her preoccupied

behavior. She is our unique treasure. Her story is that she came to us with a most desperate gift of foreknowing. Premonitions so profound they have unseated her mind, I am sad to say. We watch over her, and no one knows of her except we at Zolvina."

"That is very sad," Dreiza said, well understanding how a foreknowing gift could be cause for distress.

"It has been two years now, and she does no better. Thus we care for her, because the outside world would devour her." They came to the end of the walk along the wall. "Would you like to walk the garden?"

"I would, very much."

They descended an open-sided stone stairway to the courtyard and left through a gate composed of hundreds of thin saplings. Zolvina was not fortified. The *satvaries* were far from the border-lands with their gates where they might be at risk.

"Tell me, my daughter, about your marriage," the Devi Ilsat said as they walked.

It was an odd question for the High Mother to ask. "It is . . . good. Mostly."

"Yes. But start from the beginning."

The beginning was twelve years ago, unless you counted how Valenty was the handsome younger brother of Dreiza's husband Mityan, and how she had often been in Valenty's company in those days, and frequently engaged in interesting discussions. They had an easy way with each other, though he was forty-one years her junior.

"Where to begin, High Mother?"

"You must choose. No one else knows your story so well."

She began her recital as they entered the stand of trees that protected a simple garden, now infused with the browns and yellows of late autumn.

"In my first marriage I had a place at court. My bonded mate was Mityan, under-steward for the old Princip Lisbetha. We were known in the royal household, and that set things in motion."

"Ah, Lisbetha," the High Mother said fondly. "I knew her. And grieved when she died."

Did the Devi Ilsat know everyone? Sometimes it seemed like it.

They walked slowly, following the gently circular path, sometimes winding into a copse of trees and then back into the sun.

"When my husband died I was courted by Alesandrik, the princip's son. I was still young. Only sixty-three, and he was the same age."

"Or sixty-six, I believe?"

"Yes, sixty-six." Dreiza must not underestimate this woman. If she wanted the story, it would have to be a precise one.

She related how she had loved Mityan and her sorrow at his loss in one of the last border skirmishes in the realm. In foreknowledge she had known that Mityan would be taken from her, and she had treasured their days all the more for that. She also foreknew that she would be in a difficult relationship in the future, so when Alesandrik made his admiration known, she shied away from him, seeing all his flaws but none of his good attributes.

So she rejected him and not with any grace.

The princip took insult from her son's rejection. Fortunately she had more than one son, because before long Alesandrik fell into a dark unhappiness and one night he went out the Trespass Door of the Tower and stepped into the air. The suicide shook the whole of Osta Kiya and Dreiza fled to the house of her husband's brother, Valenty.

Nevertheless, Lisbetha worked her revenge. The princip cut off the stipends that were her right as Mityan's widow, and banished her from court and high observances. As time went on she also conspired against Dreiza in other matters large and small, making her life a misery. It was then that Dreiza decided to leave and take refuge with a cousin in a distant polity. But Valenty came to her rooms one night and suggested a marriage between them, one that could stop the princip's trepidations since he had high standing as a noble.

She declined. The age difference was too great, and Valenty was seldom rejected by women he admired. How could she be happy?

As Lisbetha's hostility grew sharper, Valenty told Dreiza that he worried the princip's hatred would follow her even to the far-off polity. That was when he proposed the arrangement that he would never take a lover who stirred his heart. It would be physical, only. Again, she answered no. But when Lord Michai, who was High Steward then as now, came to the door with a parchment tied in the silver cord of the princip, they feared the decree would forbid her to leave Osta Kiya. Valenty and Dreiza paused in the atrium long enough to exchange vows. Lisbetha's decree had lost its power to hurt her and was subsequently rescinded.

The High Mother and Dreiza seated themselves on a stone bench as the sun dipped behind tall pines.

"So this has ever been your agreement?" the Devi Ilsat asked.

"Yes, Mother. And he has been faithful to it."

"Your husband is an ingenious man," the old woman said, chuckling. "Come." She stood and put her hand out to raise Dreiza to her feet. "They will be expecting us at table."

Dreiza was starving. Telling the story had worn her out, as though she had to dig out the memories from frozen soil.

If the Devi Ilsat disapproved of Dreiza's unusual marriage, she did not give the slightest indication, and for that Dreiza was relieved.

"I believe we will have pumpkin soup for supper," the High Mother said. "With barley bread and your good honey."

A BITTER WIND SCOURED THE HILLSIDE. NASHAVETY LED
Sofiyana on the path, one so narrow that at times they must walk
one in front of the other. The wind raked them like the talons of
an owl. Sofiyana had only a thin, hooded cloak over her palace
dress. The path was called the Stone Torc, as it encircled the
mount on which Osta Kiya perched.

"Go on," Nashavety said. Sofiyana was relaying her experience of isolating herself and thinking on her shortcomings.

"I see that I have been full of myself. Absorbed in my comfort
and status. My fears. It is a relief to pull back, to become . . .
larger."

"And to become more important?" The cold bit at Nashavety.
She might have put her elemental hand to the calming of the
wind, but she would not. Hardship would strengthen the girl.

"If I am larger," Sofiyana said, "it is in relating to the realm,
which is the largest thing, save only the Mythos itself."

They continued on, passing through stacked homes clinging
to the mountainside, where the path became for a time a cobbled
street. Sofiyana had exceeded Nashavety's hopes. She had
found, in three short days, humility and a glimmer of purpose.
Now if she could complete the circuit of the hill without
complaint . . .

She interrogated the girl. By the end of their walk Sofiyana
looked half frozen, her skin taking on a shade of grey like a
wraith. And not one word of protest, nor any deviating glances to
judge how far they had yet to go.

Nashavety paused on the great west stairway. They would not
ascend before completing the last thing.

She nodded for Sofiyana to join her on the stair. "Sofiyana. I
would grant you a high honor. If it is your will to serve me absolutely." She held Sofiyana's gaze. "Is it?"

Her lips parted but at first nothing came out. Then, she whispered, "My lady, it is my will."

"Then from this day forward, Sofiyana of House Cherev, you will be of Raven Fell. And you shall be Right Hand to me in all things. Swear to me."

"I pledge service to my lady *fajatim* with my full heart, body, and mind."

Nashavety looked into her black-violet eyes and held her gaze, for this was a vow that could not be withdrawn. "Do you say so?"

"In all honor, I do."

A smile tugged at the corner of Nashavety's lips. "Then let us get out of this hellish wind."

Sofiyana nodded, and as she joined Nashavety for the climb to the castle, her hood fell back, freeing a riot of violet curls.

Something would have to be done about that hair.

۞

IT WAS NOT A GOOD NIGHT TO BE NAKED. THE GREAT STONES OF the castle had lost their warmth, and the night winds lashed at the outer walls. Yevliesza sat by the small fire in the grate. Having shed her gown and her shift, she was trying to stretch her left hand across her shoulder to feel the pattern on her back.

She imagined she could feel the branching and rebranching lines that comprised the tracery on her back. But the scars had subsided; what remained was invisible to touch.

Tirhan's drawing lay before her. The blue-grey lines swooped upward, splitting into two, sometimes three graceful filaments and then moved outward, repeating a lovely, simple pattern that reminded her of textbook drawings of veins and capillaries. If only she had a mirror to see for herself. Even on her neck the pattern remained out of sight, though it reached nearly to her jaw.

She folded the parchment into a small square. There was one person she could be honest with and whose opinion she valued. Rusadka. And she was secretly meeting Rusadka tonight.

When the household was utterly quiet and the moon was two hand-widths above the east castle wing, she made her way down three twisting staircases into the underway of Raven Fell. She had taken the route during the day to be sure of the way, and good thing, because the last stairway was dark as tar and the underway itself little better except for the occasional manifester's globe.

The fragrance of roasted meats still lingered in the main cookery just ahead. Her mouth watered. The adjustments to life in Osta Kiya had been many, but one of the most difficult was having nothing for snacks. No doubt this lack was why people ate as much as they could when meals were laid.

A click behind her. Heart lurching, she spun around to find a dark form standing there.

"Do not cry out!" Rusadka whispered. "You are as skittish as a mouse under an owl's shadow."

In relief, Yevliesza said, "If the owl comes, we're toast."

Rusadka took Yevliesza's hand and led her past the kitchens. "Let us hope the owl is asleep. I would not like to be toasted." Down the narrow corridor they found a small room where glowing coals still surged in the fireplace. "How do you fare?" Rusadka asked. She had already seen the swelling on Yevliesza's right hand and had decided that someone had to watch over her lest she sustain permanent injury.

"Do they still use the vise?" She squinted at Yevliesza's bruised right hand. "I will go to Lord Valenty."

"No. Don't. Not yet." Yevliesza still planned to let Nashavety think she was winning.

"By all that is Deep," Rusadka muttered. In the glow from the fireplace, her face was grim, a harsh look on this woman who normally showed little expression, no matter the circumstance.

Yevliesza took the folded drawing from a pocket in her gown. "Lord Tirhan gave me this drawing of what is on my back."

Rusadka raised an eyebrow and took the parchment, unfolding it. She held it up to catch the firelight. "These are your scars? They are . . . not what they were. But how did Lord Tirhan . . ."

Yevliesza told her how Tirhan had helped her after the Moon Bridge collapse, when he'd glimpsed the tracery on her back and then seen the full extent of it when they were alone in her quarters.

"Rusadka," Yevliesza began. "This is what my burns have become. Tirhan told me that as a healer he had never seen this before, and that it must be a message. A sign that I'm more than healed of burns, I'm being given an assurance of . . . acceptance."

"Acceptance? By what?"

Yevliesza hesitated. But the words came out. "The Mythos."

A creaking sound came from deep down as though the stones of Osta Kiya were settling an inch or two—or trying to adjust to such a claim.

Her friend studied the drawing. "It looks like roots," she murmured.

"Oh . . ." Yevliesza gazed at it. "Yes, I see it. The roots of a plant . . ." Her mind lifted away from the drawing, from the room. She stood utterly still as the thought seeped down on her like rain into a thirsty garden.

"Primal roots," she whispered.

They stood in silence for a few moments as the full import bloomed in her mind. "I have a second gift. What if it's *roots*?"

Rusadka frowned, trying to follow.

"What if primal root power doesn't refer to the source of all powers. What if it *is* a power?"

"But what power?"

"Have you ever been in the crossings?" Yevliesza murmured, shaken by this new idea.

"I have heard them described."

"Well, I was in them. They're like paths, that's how I thought of them, how everyone thinks of them. But what if . . . what if they're more like roots? What if the first Numinasi thought of them as roots? And primal roots, because that's how they first arrived here from the mundat."

Rusadka stared at her. "They used the ninth power." Her voice grew incredulous. "And you think you have it?"

"Because there's a picture of it on my skin."

"That is a far stretch."

"Far stretch?" Yevliesza asked. "What about this wallpaper on my back?"

"Wallpaper?"

"Never mind, but couldn't it be an explanation?"

"To have both powers . . . aligns and primal roots . . . they would make a good pairing because the crossings are on aligns. Maybe you only have crow power in aligns. If you have the ninth power, then that one is the major power."

Yevliesza barely listened to this analysis because a fear had fallen over her, an urgent one. She took the sketch from Rusadka and hid it up her sleeve.

"What?" Rusadka asked.

Yevliesza whispered, "What does one *do* with root power?"

"Create the crossings. Alter them. Grow them."

"Oh God," Yevliesza moaned, bringing her hands up to her face and covering it.

Her friend frowned in concern. "Yevliesza. Do not worry. If this is true, it is an honor greater than any."

Yevliesza shook her head. It was an honor she didn't want. After a few moments, she looked at her friend. "Something you could do for me."

"Ask."

"Tell Tirhan what I'm thinking the tracery on my skin means."

"Tirhan? He is not even a Numinasi."

"I trust him. He might advise me what to do. Please, Rusadka."

"Your heart has been captured by him."

"That's beside the point. He has wisdom in these things." She gripped Rusadka's hand. "Tell him what we've discussed. And tell him . . . that I'm afraid. Will you?"

"Of course. But Yevliesza, why are you afraid? If you have this great honor, it is a good thing."

Yevliesza felt an almost hysterical laugh trying to form. "No. It's a terrible thing."

She looked up at the ceiling, thinking whose house this was and who hated the connections to other realms. *She will kill me*, Yevliesza thought. *If I can grow the crossings, she will make sure I don't live long enough to try.*

Looking wildly around, she felt as though there might be a secret door out of Nashavety's basement. She had to escape.

But there was no place to go.

CHAPTER 31

It was a warm day in Osta Kiya. The air didn't move, nor clouds form, and the stones of the city-castle basked in the sun, hoarding its warmth against the coming season.

In the vegetable garden Yevliesza wore what she thought of as her mud dress, and the solid boots that Rusadka had given her during arcana training. All that was left of garden chores was the removal of the smaller rocks in the soil. After hundreds of years, only pebbles remained.

As she picked up a few more, she shoved them into a pouch tied to her belt and followed the furrow to the arches that formed a facade around the garden. There she noticed that Jeder was taking his ease against one of the stone columns. He was asleep. At his side, slumbering also, Jeder's *sympat*, a scrawny orange cat with a tattered ear and a missing patch of fur on its side.

When she turned back to her chore, she saw Tirhan standing on the other side of the garden in the deep shadow of the arcade. In his moss-colored cloak he was almost invisible.

She hurried to join him in the shadows of the sheltered walkway.

"You shouldn't be here!" she whispered. "The gardener is asleep, but—"

Tirhan put a hand softly to her mouth. "He will sleep, I have made sure of it." He looked around him, alert for anyone who might appear.

It had been a fiveday since she had sent Rusadka to him, and she had worried that he thought her supposition about her power was foolish.

"Yevliesza," he said in low tones, "Rusadka told me about . . . root power."

She wished he hadn't named it. This place wasn't completely private. Stepping closer to the archway pillars, she asked, "Do you think it could be true?"

"I do. I think perhaps it could be. But how long can you keep this a secret? If anyone discovers it, if the *fajatim* does . . . I fear how she would twist it to her ends. To discredit you."

"More than she already has."

"Yes. Far more."

A sound came from the opposite side of the arcade. A window opened above it, one with heavy shutters. A face peered out, then disappeared.

Tirhan drew closer to her. "Yevliesza, I could take you with me. We might find our way through the crossings. If not to Alfan Sih, then to another land, one that would be more welcoming. Where I could persuade a different court to join me against Volkia."

"But the boundary fort. How could we even persuade them to let us enter?"

"They cannot stop an envoy from returning home. An envoy and his lieutenant."

He meant her. That she would take Caden's place.

"Nashavety would notice I'm gone! Come after us."

"Not if we leave at night. With a dactyl." He frowned as she shook her head. "I am leaving soon. Come with me. You will be under my protection. It may not be enough, but it is better than here. And Yevliesza . . ." He hesitated. "What if you could find a new entrance into Alfan Sih? Or create one?"

"I don't even know how to begin!"

"Perhaps not. But I am leaving here whether you have the gift of the crossings or not. You could find sanctuary in one or other of the realms."

"Would they take me in, someone who ran from the princip's decree?"

"They would have to." He paused. "If you were my wife."

That stopped her dead. *I won't run from Numinat* was easy to say. But *I won't marry you* was an utterance she couldn't even comprehend, much less say.

"Wife?" was all that came out.

"For convenience. For your protection. Nothing need be promised. Nothing."

A groan came from across the garden. Jeder was waking up.

Tirhan brought her close to him as he lowered his voice. "When you decide, send your maid Annady to me with a piece of paper torn in half. No writing on it. But I will know."

She placed her hand firmly on his forearm to delay him a moment so that she could give him her decision. There was no need for a torn paper.

"My lord. I can't go with you. I'm already accused of hating Numinat. This would put an end to debate. It would be proof of disloyalty. I can't do it. I won't run."

He searched her face. "Think about it, Yevliesza. Think carefully."

"Tirhan, no. I won't run. But I know you have to leave. I hope you find happiness. And a true wife."

Jeder's voice came to her, mumbling something. Hearing him stir, Yevliesza slipped away from the Alfan lord and returned to collecting rocks. The gardener rubbed his forehead, and took another drink from the water skin and poured a little for the cat who wisely ignored it.

Jeder nodded off again. Tirhan's potion might eventually be blamed. But they couldn't punish him. He was leaving.

※

FROM THE WINDOW OF HIS STUDY VALENTY WATCHED THE SUN rise, a blur on the edge of the world. Eventually the thick clouds lightened, and when the sun was over the edge of the eastern arm of the palace, he saw a few flakes of snow drifting down like feathers from a bird struck in mid-air by a hawk.

A grim mood was upon him and had been for days. Yevliesza was still in the clutches of the Raven and Anastyna would hear nothing from him on the subject. Dreiza had still not returned from Zolvina. He drove women from him, despite his attempts to the contrary.

A pulse of light flashed from the great bookcase.

Anastyna summoned him. In the small cavity between two books was a small mirror. Hard to detect unless one looked carefully, this mirror enabled the princip to transmit secret signals. People distrusted mirrors, but in her modern way Anastyna did not and regularly had one of her manifesters summon him with one. Reaching in, he retrieved the mirror, seeing in its polished surface a falcon with grey forehead and buff-colored throat, a yellow ring around its dark eyes in the likeness of the princip's *sympat*. When he saw the falcon in the mirror, he knew to attend Anastyna immediately.

Lighting a candle from the embers in the fireplace he left for the scriptorium, empty at this hour. Once there, he pushed aside a tapestry that disguised the hidden passageway. He used a strong warding to push open the heavy stone door and, lighting a torch from his candle, entered the tunnel. He hoped that the woman had had a change of mind about Yevliesza's punishment. But he doubted she would be up at dawn over such a matter.

Arriving at the princip's secret meeting chamber, he found Lord Chenua with her. When they turned to him, they looked as though they had been in a heated discussion.

Valenty bowed to Anastyna and then to Chenua, receiving in return barely a nod from the envoy. Anastyna was dressed in a long robe edged in ermine and stood behind her chair, clutching the garment close around her neck. Her falcon crouched in the half-open window, still as a statue.

"Valenty," she said. "You are swift. Could you not sleep?"

"Who sleeps well in these times, Lady Princip?" he replied.

Anastyna smirked at his retort but Chenua narrowed his eyes at this impertinence. He was not only a strong man, but tall, a commanding presence, not one to banter with. By the envoy's casual dress—a shirt and jerkin over loose trousers, Valenty assumed that he and Anastyna had spent the night together. Their liaison was a palace secret, meaning that everyone knew but no one was free to bring it up.

"We have news of Volkish intimidations," Anastyna said. "Extortion this time." She glanced at Chenua for him to explain.

"I have had a report from the Lion Court," he said in his rich, bass voice, "that the Volkish demand tribute of my people." He added in a sneering tone, "A regular sum of gold that would deliver them of the necessity of taking my kingdom by arms." He tossed a small rolled parchment on the table, offering it to Valenty.

He read the amount of the tribute. A stunning sum.

"And they have made the same demand of Arabet."

Shaking her head, Anastyna took a seat. "You shall not give them what they ask."

"Never. But it is a call to arms, my lady." His dark face tightened with the effort to control his outrage.

"Lord Valenty, what do you think they can hope to accomplish?" Anastyna asked.

"A warning. For the realms not to interfere. They know that each kingdom is considering a response to Alfan Sih."

But Anastyna had already waited too long to send help; nothing could happen now until spring. The army could not march over a land devoid of gleanings, or not easily, or not a large force. By the time the land greened again, the Volkish would have strengthened their control.

Chenua nodded. "If my king refuses tribute, the Volkish will consider us enemies. Eventually Volkia will have to act against Nubiah."

Valenty turned to the princip. "Have we received such demands?"

"They would not dare." She fingered her torc as though it were strangling her. "But since they know Lord Chenua is at our court, they are sure we will know their demand of Nubiah. They provoke me, Lord Valenty."

"They believe we will not act," he responded. "Their Prince Albrecht must feel secure in this, knowing that the *fajatim* lean toward isolation and would not support you."

"The army," she snapped, "is at my sole command. It shall be my decision and mine alone."

Chenua's voice came softly, like distant thunder. "Yes, that is true. But perhaps not for long."

Left unsaid, that the *fajatim* could replace her. If one more Hall went with Nashavety. The count, they were quite sure, was Raven Fell, Storm Hand, Wild Hill, against Red Wind and Iron River. The speaker of Red Wind was neutral, if not leaning toward Anastyna. Iron River was harder to read. In replacing a princip, there could be no more than one dissenting voice.

They sat in silence for a few moments, each of them calculating, considering the odds.

Adding to the instability, the sixteen-year-old son of the Iron River *fajatim*, Oxanna, had run off to join the partisan fight in Alfan Sih, what there was of it. Whether this would tip Iron River for or against Numinat intervention was hard to judge. Valenty's operatives said that Oxanna could go either way. If the boy died, the outrage could turn the *fajatim* toward an armed response.

Anastyna looked at Chinua. "What about Nubiah's ties to Alfan Sih, my lord? Would they join a campaign with us?"

"I have received no word, but someone must take the first action. If you give me your decision, I will have it before the Lion Court in two days."

Anastyna now had both his own opinion and Chenua's. Valenty strongly believed that the Volkish beast must be stopped. The *fajatim* might try to topple Anastyna for going to war, so her very torc was at risk. But if the Volkish pierced Numinat's defenses, her torc was gone in any case. She might be retained as a surrogate monarch. But she would be under the Volkish boot. He had told her this.

"If, if!" she had responded. She could not imagine such aggression. Or did not want to imagine it.

Chenua picked up the scroll from the table. "My lady, I leave you to your counsellor. Unless you wish me to stay." He smiled at her, and a moment of tenderness passed between them.

She wished him to stay with her on many levels, Valenty knew. It was another game piece that might come into play. He thought that Anastyna would not be influenced by love. But if the *fajatim* chose to retire her, he knew where she would go. The Lion Court.

Chenua bowed and left.

Valenty waited on her pleasure. He wanted to press her for

Yevliesza's release from Raven Fell, but it was not the time to bring up another issue.

With a flick of her hand the princip summoned Evalanja from her perch. The bird flew to the band on her lower arm where it dug its talons into the thick leather. Once settled, it looked at Valenty with pitiless eyes. He had never understood how one could love a bird.

Anastyna stroked the falcon's head feathers, saying, "I am besieged by opinions."

"The price of the torc, my lady," he dared to say.

Anastyna glanced up at him, her eyes no softer than her falcon's. "If I fall, Valenty, you know who will replace me."

They did not need to speak her name.

It was a cold walk through the passageway. He held the torch that he had left in a stanchion on the wall, but it sputtered and died. In the darkness he found his way.

CHAPTER 32

I
n her room, Yevliesza peeled off her dress, hoping that she had spent her last day in the muddy garden. The temperatures had dropped at least fifteen degrees from the day before, but still, there had been rocks to remove and now her hands were mud-caked and her face streaked.

A knock at the door. That would be the maid bringing water for her basin. Warm water, she hoped, which sometimes Annady made an extra effort to bring. When she called for her to enter, the girl had empty hands.

"Annady?"

"There will be no washing in the basin today, miss." She looked at the floor. "I am sorry. Nor any day, so I am to tell you."

"Who tells you this?"

"The lady *fajatim*, it is."

It was not Annady's fault, but Yevliesza found herself throwing out, "Then I will come to supper with dirt on my hands."

"Nay, miss, you are to use the household bath like everyone."

Her stomach prickled with warning. So far she had managed

to never use the public baths. First, because she felt self-conscious about her burns, and now . . . out of more crucial concerns.

Worried, the maid held her gaze.

"Fine then, I will wash at the baths. Thank you, Annady, that will be all."

"But should I accompany you for the buttons?"

"Thank you, but I can wash my hands and face at the baths without help."

After the maid left, she sat at the window seat even though the shutters were closed and warded against the cold. Not for the first time, she wished that more of the castle windows had glass so that she could see outside, and set her mind free at least for a few minutes. She imagined flying on a dactyl's back, Tirhan riding in the forward saddle, his cape streaming behind him. A man who might have freed her. Married her.

She thought of primal root power and what it might mean for her future. How, when she had earned her place in Numinasi society, she would find a way to be of use, whether to announce her power or keep it hidden.

Shortly before supper, she made her way to the baths. As she entered a warm mist met her, rising from the large pool heated by the elementalist on duty. On the far side several women sat naked on the submerged steps rubbing their bodies clean. Yevliesza bent beside the water and dipped her filthy hands into its lovely warmth.

It took a long time for the mud to dissolve. She scrubbed her hands together and pried under her fingernails, finally getting clean enough to bend even lower to wash her face. She had forgotten her towel. As she looked around for one, she saw someone enter, standing in the back and hard to see in the misty room.

"You do not approve of my baths?" Nashavety said.

"Lady *fajatim*," she managed to say, though the sudden appearance of the woman alarmed her. "The waters are very pleasant."

"But you are unhappy to no longer have your private ablutions?"

"No, my lady."

"You have a manner of making a point without seeming to, so you cannot be corrected. But it does not fool me." She came forward, emerging from the fog like an evil fairy.

"You will immerse yourself." She gestured at the other women. "As they are doing. Once a fiveday you will bathe as everyone else does. Your station is no higher than these others, despite the special privileges you have been used to."

The baths, the baths. Why hadn't she seen what could happen? Instinctively, she looked around for escape.

Nashavety had turned to a bath attendant, a thin girl with her long hair clasped at her neck. "Assist this woman with the buttons of her dress."

As the girl approached, Yevliesza thrust out a hand. "No."

"No?" Nashavety said in a soft voice.

"No."

"Come now. It is a small matter." Frowning, Nashavety appeared surprised. "Is it not?"

"It's not the custom . . . the way . . . in the place where I was raised. It's a strong custom to bathe alone. Please, my lady." God, was she begging?

The *fajatim* indicated with a tilt of her head for the attendant to move away. "Fetch a guard," she murmured. The girl fled the baths.

Yevliesza had made a bad mistake. If she had followed orders at first, she might have entered the pool facing Nashavety, might have found a way to hide her back, might have . . . But it was no use, this thing was happening, her unmasking. She kept her gaze on the tiled floor, unable to bear Nashavety's presence, the woman's power over her life, her body.

In another moment the door slammed open and a guard entered, a burly man and armed with short dagger at his belt, though he would need no weapon to enforce Nashavety's wishes.

"Strip her," Nashavety ordered. "Tear her garment down the back."

"Stop." Yevliesza said. "Let the attendant unbutton me." Otherwise the guard would rip off her dress and with it, her shift.

To her surprise, Nashavety said to the guard. "Leave us."

As he did so, she nodded to the attendant, who was thoroughly shaken, but managed with trembling hands to unfasten the buttons of her gown. Yevliesza stepped out of the gown and quickly passed it to the girl so that her hands were full. Then Yevliesza backed up a few steps and removed her shift, still facing Nashavety. She shuffled to the edge of the pool to move down to the first submerged step.

"No," Nashavety said. "You will not separate yourself from others." She indicated the other women who had been watching all this. "Down there."

It was over, then. She was naked and never more helpless before the malwitch. Instead of moving to the other end of the bath, she slowly turned around so that her back was exposed. There was a long pause before Nashavety moved closer to her, examining her. Yevliesza could feel the woman's breath on her neck.

"What . . ." Nashavety hissed. "What is this?"

IN HER SMALL CELL, DREIZA SAT NEXT TO HER LAMP WITH A BOOK of meditations. They had been painstakingly copied by the renunciates in fine indigo ink, and they were lovely, but she found it hard to concentrate.

Her thoughts were on Valenty. Was it because of him that she was so unsettled? A fiveday ago she had told the High Mother that their marriage was good, and she thought that she had been honest. But in fact back at Osta Kiya before she left, Valenty had been distracted by the Volkish crisis. When he made time for her, his thoughts were elsewhere. But did she need his reassurances? Like most Numinasi women, she had always been fiercely independent. Or so she had thought.

She was tired. The unaccustomed exercise of a full day in the fields gleaning the last of the potatoes had taken its toll. She blew out her lamp early and climbed into bed, abandoning herself to sleep.

The room creaked. Zolvina was an ancient place, and its stones were settling in for winter. She turned in her bed. And heard the sound again.

There came a light. A candle flickering. Someone had come in. "Yes?" Dreiza asked sleepily. "Is all well?" She propped herself up on an elbow, peering at the *satvar* who stood by the door.

"No," her visitor whispered, "Not well."

In the flickering light she saw that it was a very young woman. Ah. Kassalya, it must be. She pushed aside her blankets and found her heavy socks, since the floor had a bite of frost. "What brings you, my dear?"

"What brings *you?*" the girl threw back.

"I came to the *satvary* to collect my thoughts. There are so many distractions out there."

The girl shuddered, but whether it was the mention of the larger world or the deep cold of the room, she did not know. She patted the bed. "Sit, and have my blanket."

Kassalya stepped back. The flame from her candle played on her face as though reflecting the girl's scattered thoughts.

"You must dress," Kassalya said. "Leave us. Go now, go tonight." Her voice rose in pitch and frowns of worry pinched her face. "Go, I say! Kirjanichka told me he would not mind going in the dark."

What a very bizarre thing to say. "But, Kassalya, does not the *satvary* welcome all?"

"It is the girl from the origin world."

"What? What of her?

Kassalya looked at her suspiciously. "You have the gift, do you not know?"

Dreiza's foreknowing had seldom been more than glimpses, often contradictory. "No, I do not know. Please tell me."

"Nashavety cast her net. She caught an innocent."

"It is her imposed sentence."

"No! Listen: She must not be with the *fajatim!* Could you not see what will happen, do you not see?"

"I see that she will change our lives, but my powers are small." In her chest, a tight fist of anxiety pulled at her. What was happening at Raven Fell?

"A woman dies, all untimely. I *plucked* this from the future. A sour fruit."

Dreiza stood in agitation. "Do you mean Yevliesza?"

"Dies . . ." Kassalya put her hand to her head, moaning, "Dies, terribly dies."

Dreiza stood, reaching out to grip the girl's arm. "You must tell me. Who dies?" They stood very close now, close enough for her to see tears sliding down Kassalya's face.

"One," the girl moaned. "One or the other of them." Her voice broke. "Ah, and sometimes both, from a great fall."

She blew out the candle. They stood in the dark as a thin trail of smoke snaked between them.

"A fall in status?" Dreiza said in desperation.

The whispered response came as Kassalya slipped through the door. "A fall from a great height."

CHAPTER 33

She stood in the darkest room of Raven Fell, on a floor beneath the underway of the kitchens and storage rooms. The door leading down the stairs to it was small and unremarkable, grimy with apparent disuse. But it was the door to her heart. It led to the darkling room, a spacious and immaculate chamber that had once been part of the nethers, but with palace alterations over hundreds of years, had been cut off. It was hers alone, the place where she never lit a candle.

It was a room in which to discover the truth. Sometimes, to contemplate the mysteries of the Mythos. And sometimes the mystery of her own being.

Nashavety went there now to sort out the meaning of what she had seen on Yevliesza's skin.

A single, uncomfortable chair furnished the room. Made of dense stonewood and unpadded, it assured that her thoughts would not stray from the object of her contemplation: Today, it was Yevliesza. And the impossible, embroidery-like design that adorned her back and neck.

It was a configuration that suggested a flourishing vine, or a river with branching tributaries.

Though she sat in stillness until her back flared with pain, she found no insight into what it signified. In the profound darkness, thoughts stirred and hovered, just out of her grasp. What were these darkling impulses that would not show themselves? She did not want to welcome them.

For the first time in her adult life she was afraid.

Gripping the arms of the stonewood chair, she forced herself to embrace the wraith-like thoughts. "Come," she whispered. "I accept you. Come."

They obeyed, the tittering, malevolent specters. Of jealousy. With a gasp of despair she let them flood over her. They gnawed at her mind, finding it succulent. Her back slumped against the chair, seeking its support. Insatiable, pitiless, envy. Envy of this girl of the mundat. No matter that she was a twice-gifted Numi-nasi and a *fajatim*, this unwelcome girl had surpassed her.

It was what she had guessed from the moment the girl had stood naked before her. The

configuration on her back was impossible, made more so by the fact that it had sprung from terrible burns. She had seen the scars the night that the girl had lain unconscious on the healer's table. Suppurating wounds covering the right side of her back all the way to her chin. A fitting welcome for a stranger who despised Numinat and flouted its ways.

So Nashavety had thought.

Whether the pattern represented a specific thing or symbol, she could not imagine. But one thing was undeniably true. The design was an emblem of dominion, bestowed on her—of course, how could she have misunderstood—bestowed on her by the deep Mythos. And it had installed in her this power during her ride on the dactyl. It had ridden down on the lightning and saved her life with its mitigating hand.

The world had preserved this girl and set her apart from all others. She did not know why. But the knowledge sucked away all joy into the bottomless chasm of her heart. Sitting there in her private nethers, she knew her obligation was to herald Yevliesza and love her.

But that was not going to happen.

৬✿৬

YEVLIESZA DIDN'T APPEAR FOR SUPPER. SHE COULD BARELY SIT still, much less eat. Pacing her chamber, she tried to walk off her anxiety. Tirhan had warned her that no one could know, and she had thought her secret was safe. Until this evening. What would Nashavety make of the tracery? And what would she do? Her thoughts chased each other round and round.

Absently, she moved her left hand around her to her back to touch the altered scars. Would they always proclaim her as disfigured, the outsider who was marked for isolation and contempt?

After hours of these ruminations, she turned to the tray of food one of the kitchen staff had brought for her. Famished by now, she sat at her small table and ate a bowl of cabbage and barley soup.

There she fell asleep, slumped over the food tray.

She wondered why her pillow was so hard. She turned her head so that her cheek and not her forehead pressed against the soup bowl.

Then someone picked her up. Her head lolled against the person's chest. She tried to open her eyes. When she did, she could see nothing but blackness.

At last she was laid down on a stone floor. Someone said, "Leave us."

After awhile she found herself leaning against a wall A flask of water came to her lips, and she drank thirstily.

A hand came under her chin lifting it. Nashavety's long, implacable face stared down at her. "Wake up."

A spike of fear pierced her heart. She was in the Tower, facing the East door. That meant at her side was the Trespass door. Behind the crouching Nashavety, keeping watch, was the thrall.

Yevliesza looked wildly around, taking in her surroundings. The three of them were alone. A sickle moon shed a wan light on the *fajatim* and her beast.

"Let me go, you have no right . . ." Yevliesza began.

"I will let you go, but first we will come to an agreement, you and I."

"That will never happen. I will never agree with you, you . . ."

"Yes?" The woman's mouth moved into a bemused smile. "You think me unfair? Perhaps evil?"

"You walk hollow. You're dark, vicious, and twisted."

"*I* am twisted? How strange that you are the only one who thinks so. I am afraid it is *you* who are twisted. Oh, disfigured beyond repair. Have you seen your back? No, I do not think so, but I am sure you know what is there." Nashavety stood, her face collapsing into a sneer. "Have you thought what it means?"

"I don't know."

Nashavety kicked her savagely, sending Yevliesza sprawling. "Tell me!"

Another kick. The thrall made little gulping noises as though trying to swallow too much saliva.

The pain in her hip and stomach took her breath away. "I don't know anything. The burns stopped hurting, that's all, that's all I know."

"Here is what it means, mundat. It means that when you burned from the lightning your body tried to deny it by creating patterns. It could not accept the punishment of the Mythos for transgressing our realm." Nashavety faced away from the East door, bringing her face into total shadow.

"The princip *brought* me to the realm!"

"Yes, she did. Her transgression, one that she will pay for. But the Mythos does not want you here. You have disrupted and poisoned everything you have touched. You have killed people, betrayed the very ones who offered you succor. You seduced Valenty."

"That's a lie."

"Oh yes, yes you did. Did you think no one knew? Those frantic kisses in the dark places of his household? Here is a man who can have any woman, and he chooses you? You? Scrawny and cross and always advancing yourself over others." Nashavety yanked her to sitting position, kneeling beside her, the violet in her eyes coiling in the blackness. "You are a ruined soul. Can you not see the truth?"

Yevliesza was shaking her head over and over.

"No of course you cannot. But we are here for you to discover it."

The woman's voice turned tender. "Look closely at yourself. You cannot accept failure, cannot accept correction. You exploit your friends. Pyvel, to lead you into the dangerous nethers, Sofiyana to help you in arcana, Rusadka to run your errands. Everyone who opens to you is sucked dry. You even killed a dactyl, which broke the hearts of its trainers." Her hand came around Yevliesza's neck and again she forced her to look into her captor's face. Yevliesza was in the embrace of the malwitch, her limbs still weak from the drug potion.

"And you killed your father, you know."

When Yevliesza started to protest, Nashavety shouted, "Silence! Be quiet and learn." Her voice dropped to a murmur. "And then we will have our agreement."

"What agreement?"

Nashavety yanked at her hair. "Be. Quiet. I do not want to bruise you. But I will."

Standing up, Nashavety elicited a little yelp from the thrall. It pleaded with its eyes for her to let him come at his victim.

"Back!" she shouted at it. "Back!" That gave her room to pace and she began to do so.

"Your father did not die of his wasting brain. He died of a broken heart when he saw what you had become. That you left the mundat, leaving him alone and confused. That you made a place in Valenty's household with no thought for his care . . ." She paused, seeing the expression of denial on Yevliesza's face. "Because did you not wear a small machine on your wrist, flouting our laws, proving that you could not behave honorably?" A gouging kick lashed out, hitting her in the ribs.

"Help!" Yevliesza screamed. Crawling to the east doorway, she screamed again, "Help me!"

Nashavety dragged her to her feet and threw her against the wall. "No one can hear you. I have had that door warded. You belong to me." She held her arm against Yevliesza's neck, forcing her to remain standing.

"Here is the agreement I offer you. You will never go down those stairs where Gorga watches. Never again. But I will let you go. You will jump from the Tower."

"The doors are warded! You haven't got warding power to remove them."

A smile told her that this was not an obstacle.

"Yes, all but the Trespass Door."

Nashavety dragged Yevliesza across the small space of the Tower, but she twisted away, going to her knees, managing to kick at the woman. She was crunched up along the wall, inches away from the Trespass Door. A frigid breeze curled through it.

"There are two ways to leave. One is that I push you, the final humiliation. The other is that you gather your courage and do what a true Numinasi would do after judgment. Step into the air."

Nashavety stood over her. "Jump. Do it before you lose your courage. Do it before you lose your last chance at honor."

"No, you raging bitch!" From her position on the floor she

launched herself at Nashavety's legs and, throwing her off balance, sent her sprawling. "No!"

Nashavety was stronger than Yevliesza, and grappled with her until she was on top of her. "You came into the world in violence, killing your mother." Astride Yevliesza's body she moved them both in a scrunching motion across the floor toward the opening. With a last thrust Yevliesza's head tipped a few inches over the ledge. "Here is your chance to set things even."

Yevliesza stared up at the black sky. Stars winked in and out as tattered clouds moved across the sky. Below her lay the gulf of the two thousand-foot fall to the plains, a drop past the castle and past the rock formations on which it stood.

"Jump," her captor hissed. She crawled off Yevliesza and hauled her to her knees to face the empty hole of the door. "Do it now. Jump!"

"Give me something first!" Yevliesza rasped.

"I give you your honor. It is enough."

"One thing more."

"You have no standing for demands."

"One thing!"

"What, then?" Her hands on Yevliesza's back softened their hold.

Yevliesza moved back from the door, rounding her back to look beaten, keeping her eyes on the stone floor. "That you don't tell anyone about my back. I'm done with disgrace." It was a testimony to the *fajatim's* delusions that this gave her pause.

"There are others who saw you in the baths."

"Four women. Who didn't get a close look. And who can be persuaded that they didn't see anything."

The *fajatim* flattened her lips, thinking. Then: "Very well. No one will know."

"Swear it."

"Swear? But on what?"

"Swear on the First Ones and all the powers of the Mythos."

In the pause that followed, Nashavety got to her feet. Perhaps even she had to consider whether she could make such a vow. But: "Yes, agreed," she said. "I swear on the First Ones and on the Mythos."

Slowly, Yevliesza inched up the wall so that now they both were standing. "So when you said you would let me go, this is what you meant."

"Of course."

Yevliesza stood in front of the door. She knew, and now acutely sensed, the align that pierced the Tower, and she adjusted her position so that Nashavety would fall along that path. She wasn't sure it would help her attack on Nashavety, but she decided to believe it. Even the possibility of align power helping her was enough to fuel her exhausted muscles.

"You have my oath," Nashavety said. "Now jump. Jump!"

Summoning the last of her strength, Yevliesza lunged at the woman, and Nashavety crashed like a felled tree against the wall on the other side of the door.

Yevliesza fell with her, lying across the *fajatim*. Nashavety moaned. Yevliesza skittered off her, heart hammering. Nashavety lay helpless, blood trickling from the side of her head.

Remembering that she had one more adversary, she slowly turned. The thrall took a step toward her. She smelled its wild odor and knew it was no illusion. But she didn't look at the beast. She kept her eyes on Nashavety, still semi-conscious on the floor. Then she backed up, letting the thrall approach its mistress. It bent over Nashavety.

And began licking the blood that was trickling down her face. The horrid thought came: The creature was used to a snack around Yevliesza.

She crept to the stairs. Out of the corner of her eye she could see the thrall still lapping the seeping blood.

The stairs lay engulfed in darkness. Slowly, so as not to draw the thrall's attention, she began her descent. Once out of view of the landing, she hurried her steps, trying for quiet, trailing her hand along the outside curve of the wall to steady herself.

At the bottom, having made her way through the dark, abandoned Tower chambers, she emerged into the lit corridors of Osta Kiya, and ran.

❧

THREE HOURS LATER, VALENTY WAS RUSHING TO RAVEN FELL, having roused Grigeni to join him. In the pre-dawn, the corridors of the palace were dimly lit. He moved quickly but, as in a dream, his movements seemed intolerably slow as though he were moving through deep water.

Earlier, Dreiza had come to disclose a foretelling. Not from her own foreknowledge, she had said, but from a woman of Zolvina, one in whom the High Mother had great confidence and who predicted that through Nashavety's machinations Yevliesza would fall from the Tower.

Hearing this, he had taken Dreiza directly to Anastyna, wasting precious minutes convincing the mistress chamberlain to wake her. Once the story was heard, Anastyna ordered Valenty to remove the girl from Raven Fell and to do so immediately, although she would not insult the *fajatim* by sending palace guards.

Kassalya's prophecy might be wrong. As ever, Anastyna considered all sides, including the foretelling of the court practitioners who said that Yevliesza would be crucial, but not that she would step through the fatal door.

Now he raced to the Hall, clutching a sealed writ from the princip with a hurriedly penned message: You will give Yevliesza into Lord Valenty's care.

AT A SLOWER PACE, DREIZA FOLLOWED, UNABLE TO BEAR STAYING behind.

When she arrived at Raven Fell, she found the forecourt brightly lit from many windows as though the whole household was awake. She knew Valenty must be inside, perhaps confronting the *fajatim*—or finding that the worst had come to pass.

Winded, she sat on a bench and waited, watching the doors of Raven Fell. Sooner than she had expected, the doors opened and Valenty and Grigeni emerged, faces so grim that Dreiza's heart shrank in her chest.

"What is it?" she cried, rising to meet them.

Valenty was giving instructions to Grigeni, who rushed away.

Valenty approached Dreiza. "I have sent Grigeni to bring word to the princip, that the *fajatim* of Raven Fell has fallen ill. She is tended by healers and cannot be disturbed. Lady Sofiyana, Nashavety's Right Hand, now conducts affairs of Raven Fell."

"And Yevliesza?"

"She is gone."

He had been speaking in a flat tone, as though the fire had gone out of him. By his expression she feared that Yevliesza was dead. But his next words changed everything.

"The envoy of Alfan Sih left a few hours ago with his lieutenant, taking a dactyl and saying that he was returning to his court."

If he would not get to the point, Dreiza would pin him to the wall and force it from him.

"But Dreiza, Lieutenant Caden is still in quarters." When he went on, he kept his voice under tight control.

"It is Yevliesza who left with him."

PART IV
THE HAND OF POWER

CHAPTER 34

The dactyl took them into the night. The moon—only a sliver—had set, leaving the land below them in black sleep. Tirhan handled the great dactyl, so he rode in the forward saddle behind the creature's head. Yevliesza rode her own saddle secured in the middle.

It was brutally cold, though she wore Lieutenant Caden's sheepskin chaps and flying jacket. Her relief at escaping Nashavety kept her spirits high, despite the discomfort of her perch where the straps that held her bit into her bruised ribcage. The dactyl, being so massive, was warm-blooded, its scales throwing off heat against her legs and cheeks as she hugged its frame.

Tirhan said they would use the Causeway Gate and they headed northwest on what was to be almost a quarter of a night ride. Lowgate, he had said, was too obvious a choice, being closest of the three boundary gates to Osta Kiya. The Numin Pass Gate was the most remote, but at too high an elevation this time of year.

Now and again Tirhan looked back, shouting into the wind, "Are you well?"

"Yes" was always her answer, because she *was* well—compared to fighting off Nashavety in the Tower.

৩৫৯

IN HER BED CHAMBER, ANASTYNA SAT BEFORE A CREDENZA crafted from silverwood and replete with jars of ointment and vials of perfume from Arabet. A maid dressed her hair as Valenty and Lord Michai consulted with her on the night's events.

"My Lady Princip, I urge you to let her go," Valenty said.

Anastyna tossed her head in impatience, causing the hairdresser to drop her hair pins. She knelt on the floor to retrieve them. "She has gone because she was involved in the *fajatim's* injury." She glanced at Lord Michai. "Is it not likely? She has fled in the middle of the night."

Valenty bit back anger. "She ran because we treated her without mercy or welcome." He added, rashly, "We *all* did."

Lord Michai's face was deeply etched with age and the night's revelations as he said, "The *fajatim* may die, My Lady Princip. Or live with grievous injury. Judgment is premature, but our visitor of the mundat must be put to questions." The princip's High Steward had just returned from Raven Fell where he had seen Nashavety. No one could deny Lord Michai entrance, though healers surrounded the *fajatim's* bed. She had whispered to him unintelligibly, but Lady Sofiyana confirmed that her fall was an accident.

Anastyna spoke slowly, always a sign that she was angry. "It was my will that Yevliesza submit to training in our ways. If it was not a vicious attack, at the least she has defied me."

Lord Michai coughed.

"And so?" Anastyna snapped at him.

"Lest she disappear into the crossings, we must hasten to inform the garrisons."

By a sending in the mirrors. To all three of the boundary forts.

Valenty wished that Yevliesza had shared her plan with him so he could have dissuaded her, wished that he had brought more pressure on Anastyna to temper what were likely Nashavety's harsh methods of instruction. Wished . . . wished. And now she was gone, because Osta Kiya had failed to help her, because her disruptions were too great to bear. Because they had demeaned and degraded her. And he was not without blame, either.

The maid finished pinning Anastyna's dark hair into a jeweled net. The princip rose to face the day though it was still the middle of the night. Her face was pinched with displeasure. "Who must I see before I break my night's fast, Lord Michai?"

He listed the personages who should be informed.

The princip kept them standing for a long while as she gazed into the unlit fireplace. Finally she said to Michai, "Send the messages."

Valenty closed his eyes.

"But," the princip added, "wait long enough that it will be too late." Still speaking to Michai, she turned to Valenty, her face softening. "Let her go."

⚜

THE GARRISON AT THE BOUNDARY GATE SAW THEM COMING AND carried torches into a small field for the dactyl to land. They came in low over a lake and Yevliesza braced herself for the touch-down, but to her surprise it was almost a gentle landing. The dactyl had been trained well.

As soldiers approached, she prepared for a rough reception. If they saw through her disguise she would certainly be detained. In her woolen cap and heavy clothes and cape, she looked shapeless enough, she thought. She jumped quickly down before one of the soldiers could assist her.

As Yevliesza and Tirhan were accompanied into the fort, she saw that it was built on a narrow causeway over a wide lake.

Inside the fort walls, a quick conversation made clear to the *harjat* commander that Tirhan was in haste to return home. Warm broth found its way into Yevliesza's hands and a packet of bread and cheese, although the pack she carried on her back scarcely had room for even that small meal. She knelt to busy herself with the pack, keeping her face averted, while Tirhan received reports of activity in the local crossings.

Tirhan led her to the latrine where they had to hope no one else was using the ditch. Keeping watch at the entryway, he gave her some privacy. She was still so stiff from the frigid ride that she could barely crouch. Her knees screamed, and her arms ached from clutching the saddle, but the aftermath of Nashavety's savage kicks were the worst.

Then they were led to the crossing doors, hammered with iron plates and a heavy cross beam.

As they left Numinat, the memory of the Trespass Door came to her as it had through the night. Lying on her back, with Nashavety on top of her. The icy air hitting her face from the gaping hole of the door. Her head stretched out on the door lintel as though waiting for an axe. Or a very long fall.

She and Tirhan descended the steps of the boundary gate. Down, down, much further than she remembered the access at Lowgate.

During the steep descent, the stairs became more uneven, and instead of grey stone, started to morph into an odd, fleshy texture. The passage down, at first narrow and murky, gave way to a soft light that gradually brightened. She smelled the familiar brew: warm, half-musty, half-sweet.

They reached the tunnel which, by its size, must be the major one. Tears gathered in her eyes for no reason at all, and she fought to dispel them. She was safe. And most importantly, warm.

Here was the first moment that she felt completely free of Raven Fell. But new dangers loomed. Volkish soldiers might come through at any moment, but they found the crossings utterly quiet.

Tirhan took the pack from her shoulders, hefting it on to his own. Their eyes met in a long gaze as they shared this moment of accomplishment. "You are safe from her now," he said.

"Yes." Her voice came out shredded from disuse. "You saved my life."

"I think rather you have saved mine," he said.

"Not yet," she whispered.

Unpacking the garments they had carried in the knapsack, they quickly stripped to change into their new disguises: that of a Numinat lady and her servant. If they were stopped, he couldn't appear to be a prince of Alfan Sih. But in her case, she would likely be allowed passage to one of the kingdoms, since Volkia and Numinat weren't on a war footing.

She pulled a hair net over her hair and fixed it in place with hairpins. Tirhan buttoned her gown up the back.

As he did so, she asked, "Which direction should we go?" All that she knew of the routes was from the brief journey on her way from the mundat and having looked at schematics of the crossings with Grigeni.

"This way," Tirhan said, leading her to the left, down the wide, bright tunnel. She trusted that he knew his way home, but that route couldn't take them to safety. They had to find an alternate route. To a new gate. That was Tirhan's main hope.

"Where are the side recesses?" she whispered. "Are they on this tunnel?"

"Yes. Up ahead."

Back at the castle there had been only a few hurried moments for them to consider a plan. Small recesses existed in the crossings, Tirhan had said, indentations that were the starts of branch-ings. They would stop at one of these and let Yevliesza test her affinity.

The question was whether Yevliesza could bring a power to bear in these nodes and also, if she could sense the direction to Alfan Sih. The closer she came to the test the more unlikely it seemed. Could a person with primal root power—if she even had it—change this mysterious tunnel at all? Back in Osta Kiya it was an untested idea. Here in the crossings it seemed more like a delusion.

But whether they found a way to Alfan Sih or to whatever kingdom accepted them, it would be to her just another strange land. She'd had so little time to think about her future outside of Numinat, a future where she might be a fugitive from a charge of murder. She wouldn't be pursued as far as Earth, she felt sure.

The vision of her old house on the wide basin of Barstow County tugged at her. Her father was gone, but the house no doubt remained with its small garden and her well-loved old car. Numinat had rejected her—perhaps with good reason—but still, she didn't have any welcome there. They had demanded that she come to them, but her attempts to learn and abide by their ways had failed. Now she had fled Anastyna's command that she submit to a teacher. A sadistic one, but the princip didn't know that. Osta Kiya wasn't home. Probably it never would be.

If the mundat was a bad option, at least it was a familiar one. But for now, she had promised to aid Tirhan.

As they walked, the smell of the crossings came at her with a load of memory, that unmistakable smell of yeasty biomass. Through her boots, she felt the path give slightly to her weight as though she walked inside a living thing, or across the hide of a great beast.

Tirhan stopped and pointed. "Here." It was a small cave, hardly more than a scoop in the wall.

She stared at the recess. "What do I *do,* my lord?"

"Can you not drop my title?"

Anger came out of nowhere. "I have no idea what I'm supposed to do! This is nothing but a small dent, don't you see?"

He put his hand on her arm, his voice calm. "Yes, of course. I know this hollow is small, but try falling into your power. See if it might come to you."

"I'm sorry . . . Tirhan. I'm just tired, not thinking straight."

He gently took her hand and led her closer to the wall. There she crouched down to enter the recess, not quite as high as she was. Stabbing pains radiated from her ribs where Nashavety had kicked her. She sank to one knee, gasping.

"What is it?" Tirhan asked.

"Stiffness from the ride."

They took a few steps into the shallow recess, and she knelt, touching the back of the node. Closing her eyes, she tried to concentrate. Nothing came to her except the urge to lie down and sleep. Unconsciousness reached for her. She got to her feet. "Let's keep going. Is there a deeper one?"

They pushed on down the path. So far they had encountered no one. But, after all, it was the last quarter of the night. The day's business of conquest and bloodshed had not yet begun for the Volkish.

"Tirhan," she began. "There's something I need to tell you."

He looked at her, waiting.

"It's Volkia. I know about it. From . . . the mundat."

"So you said before. They are a dark influence?"

"Yes, very dark. I think they are what we called Nazis. And they have—*had* an ideology on my world. A vicious one. It was a mix of dark, hateful ideas. They were fanatics about being a superior race. It brought my world to war. Millions died."

"Terrible indeed. But this . . . mix of ideas. It is a myth in the origin world?"

"Maybe like a myth, except this one was evil. They had

destructive, ugly ideas about racial purity and domination. A pure nation and a pure race. It wasn't just . . . an idea. It was a sick, powerful craving, and it wove many ordinary people into its spell. And then, at the end of the war, it subsided."

"It was not a long-lasting myth?"

"Maybe not like some. But it lived on, underground. It must have, because now they're here."

He frowned. "You think this is Volkia?"

"Maybe. A version of Nazism."

"What did they want? Riches, resources?"

She searched her memory of history. "Dominance, revenge. And land. They wanted room to grow."

"So do the Volkish," he said. "Because their realm is the smallest. Their primordial lands are expanding, but being new, they are not as vast as other realms."

"I'm afraid," she murmured. "Afraid for the Mythos."

"Whoever they are," Tirhan said, "I swear they will not subjugate us."

A faint sound stopped her. It was eerily familiar, a strange clicking sound like a box of glassware being carried, or shards of rock shaken in a bowl.

"Something?" he quietly asked.

"The clicking. Do you hear it?"

He shook his head. "The crossings are silent. In themselves, they make no sound."

That was wrong. The sound was one she had heard before. They went on. After a time, Tirhan stopped to retrieve food from their pack. He passed her a hunk of cheese and tore off a portion of bread for her.

Her full concentration went into eating. After she inhaled the food, strength returned. They continued on.

A corridor came into view on their right, but Tirhan shook his head. "The way to Volkia." After passing the cutoff to Volkia, every step they took would be in the direct line of troop movements.

The tunnel stretched before them, curving now and then like the graceful arcs of the tracery on her skin.

At her side Tirhan asked, "What happened in the Tower? With Nashavety." She had not had time to tell him much, except that the *fajatim* had tried to kill her.

The tunnel narrowed for a time, then bulged out again. She heard the odd clinking from a far distance now. It was a sound she had heard several times during her first journey through the crossings.

"Can you not tell me what happened?" Tirhan asked.

She didn't want to say how it had been. The memory of it came to her fractured, each one a specific terror. The shadows in the tower, the famished thrall, Nashavety's face, contorted in rage, the door, always the door.

But the words spilled out. "Nashavety was in a rage," she began. "Threatening me with her thrall, saying she would throw me from the Tower. She told me I had killed people. That I sucked people dry who tried to be near me. That I . . . poison everything I touch."

"You cannot believe her, Yevliesza."

"I don't, except . . . is anyone completely blameless? I've made mistakes." Her heart felt like a rock in her chest. Telling him made it more vivid. It was in the air around her, little black shapes flapping in and out of sight.

"Here," he whispered, pointing to the side. "It is a node, a better one."

The indentation in the crossing wall was narrow but deep.

"Let us try here," he said, "to see if you have the affinity to coax it." They entered, stooping. With his hand on her back, Tirhan pressed her forward, until they were at the end of the cave which had narrowed so much the two of them were shoulder to shoulder.

The temperature dropped, as though the nub extended into some kind of sub-zero space, and the walls could not insulate them.

She whispered, "What did you tell me before? What you said when you urged me to connect with my power?"

He thought for a moment. "Let yourself fall into it."

Closing her eyes, she let her mind empty. The first thing she felt was the pull of sleep. She fended it off, and tried to relax without losing alertness. But nothing around her was changing. If this tunnel was growing, it was doing so without her.

Her eyes snapped open. "Hear that?"

"What? What is it?"

"Someone's coming. People are coming," she hissed. They tucked themselves back, but anyone who looked in could easily see them.

She and Tirhan were cramped so close together she could feel his heart beating. They waited. The clicking sound began again, but in the background she heard the voices drawing nearer. This place could not hide them.

Fear drove her to concentrate, sending her intention into the cave walls, into the nub of the crossing. *Close*, she told it, *close*, touching the ceiling with her left hand.

"I will meet them," Tirhan said. "They need not find you." Before he could move or she could protest, a flap of hard skin began growing down from the roof of the cave. Within moments it had come halfway over their refuge.

"Move back," she whispered. They scrunched themselves into the cavity, just large enough for them and the knapsack.

Seeing the flap moving down in front of her, she closed her eyes as a sense of falling overcame her. It was as though she had climbed a very steep hill and now was drifting down the other side. A slow-motion, relentless fall into a spacious, warm dark. The clicks were emanating from the walls and rose in volume. She felt—*perceived*—that the recess was growing.

Opening her eyes, she saw that the opening had closed all the way down.

Through the barrier they heard voices and the tramping of heavy feet.

Breathing as quietly as she could, she thought she heard someone just outside their hiding place, next to the flap that shielded them.

A gruff voice came to her ears, a foreign language.

Moments later, the tramping of feet faded. It began to be very cramped in their small enclosure, but as soon as the awareness of its restriction registered with her, the tunnel began to enlarge. Slowly, but noticeably, and as it did, light surged.

"They have gone," Tirhan said. They were now able to separate enough that they could look at each other.

He smiled. It was a beautiful thing to see, and it almost took her breath away. He was looking at her with a strange intensity. "Your power has come to you," he whispered. He lightly put his hand on the back of her neck. "The crossings listen to you."

She looked at the end of the enclosure, knowing that it was tunneling forward. And, somehow, she knew it was to Alfan Sih. The niche was pushing into the darkness, brightening as it went, lengthening with energetic clicks like fingers snapping in time to some inconceivable music. She had deepened into her primal root power.

"This is the way, Tirhan."

"Is it?" he whispered.

Click click, like small pods of something popping. The confining niche they had been in was now expanding in height. They sat up.

"This is the way," she said again, as though reporting something that had happened long ago. "The way to Alfan Sih."

"By the Mythos . . ." he breathed.

"The sounds I hear, they're the sounds of the roots growing. I hear them." She leaned against the tunnel wall, exhausted. Peaceful. "I could always hear them."

Tirhan reached for her hand, clasping it. Barely audible, he whispered, "My lady of crossings."

They turned to watch the path forming in front of them. The bright tunnel was still growing.

CHAPTER 35

Four women stood around the *fajatim's* bed. Even with the heavy drapes closed against the midday sun, a crack of light escaped and pierced her eyes like a cat's claw.

"Close off the light, I beg you," Nashavety groaned, and Vajalyna of Wild Hill went to the curtains to fix them. She had to sidle by Gorga as it sat rather closer to the circle of women than any of them might wish. They must wonder if, considering the *fajatim's* infirmity, the creature could be under control.

Even Nashavety did not know.

"Do you suffer?" asked Oxanna of Iron River. Her plump, round face creased the expected amount, but Nashavety doubted the woman cared for her suffering.

"No, my sister. I am much better today." Despite having fallen down the stone stairs at the end of the hallway. A fall so terrible she could hardly remember the details, she had said. But not as great as could have happened. She ground her teeth at the memory of how the mundat had attacked her at the very lip of the Trespass Door. "I am better today," she repeated.

Vajalyna intoned, "By the grace of the Mythos."

Next to her, the slim and handsome Ineska of Red Wind. And

then diminutive Alya of Storm Hand, who had positioned herself as far from the thrall as possible. Always cautious, that one. As though Nashavety had called them to her bedside to slaughter them. Though there had been times when she had considered it.

She closed her eyes just to rest them but sleep took her away. She startled awake. Vajalyna laid her thin hand on Nashavety's brow. "Perhaps, my sister, we should return when you have rested."

"No, let us proceed . . . and have this done and behind us." The matter of her successor, should she die. "You know that I have made Lady Sofiyana my Right Hand. She is my proper heir." In the murky room it was difficult to see the reactions of the four.

"A highly promising young woman," Vajalyna said.

Nashavety bit her cheeks as a heavy cloak threatened to fall over her mind and drag her down again. "Lady Sofiyana has been in . . . strict training. And proves herself worthy by force of temperament and care for our realm." As she bit harder, she tasted blood. But she must carry on. Sofiyana was a poor candidate for the rigors of Raven Fell, but she had the right convictions. In days like these, that mattered most of all.

Ineska spoke. "She comes from the outland, far from court. Although she does comport herself well."

A cunning woman. Undependable.

"What is your will in this matter?" Lady Alya asked, in that ever-calm voice of hers.

Now was the time to say it clearly. "It is my will that Lady Sofiyana succeed me if my recovery fails. It is my will that she be greeted by all as speaker for Raven Fell."

The group fell silent. Nashavety called upon her thrall to make a small noise.

It arrived in the next moment as a slow, rumbling growl. *Ah, Gorga*, she thought in affection.

In spite of the thrall's warning, Oxanna said, "She is so young, sister. Surely your steward Daraliska . . ."

Vajalyna interrupted. "We cannot gainsay our sister of many years. Her judgment has ever been a faithful guide."

"There was, however, the matter of the midnight excursion to the doomed sky bridge," Ineska said in her forthright manner.

If Nashavety lived she would have her revenge for that utterance. "An unusual departure for my niece, usually so circumspect. But we must not tally the mistakes of youth. What matters is to groom our charges to maturity."

Vajalyna looked at Lady Ineska. "Surely you would not deprive our sister of Raven Fell her choice, should the worst come to pass."

"It would be unseemly," Oxanna murmured.

Alya quickly agreed. "She must have Raven Fell. I urge us to concur."

The thrall trotted to the bedside, and Nashavety placed her hand on its great head. "It gives me such comfort to see our circle in agreement." She smiled at Ineska, and managed to elicit a short bow of her head.

Unanimity, if she was counting correctly. Nashavety closed her eyes to stop the nail that seemed to be penetrating her forehead.

When she opened them again, Sofiyana was bending over her in alarm, her violet curls hanging down. It brought to her mind the tendrils of the mundat's terrible back.

"Sofiyana. You will bring your hair under control if you have to flatten it with grease." Sofiyana ducked a nod. "The *fajatim* agree that you will be my successor. Come the day when I am gone."

"My lady . . ." Sofiyana whispered in what seemed a touching concern.

"But I do not plan to die. I will recover." And even through her weakness and pain she knew, suddenly knew of a surety, that this was true.

"By the Nine, may it be so," Sofiyana dutifully said.

Nashavety held up her hand to display her amber ring. It was large and flawless, except that it held within its honeyed depths the claw of an immature dactyl. "You will someday have this ring. It was a gift from old Princip Lisbetha. You will wear it in remembrance of me." She locked eyes with Sofiyana. "And you will carry out my wishes. Beyond death."

"Yes, always, my lady *fajatim*."

"That is well. Because even in death I will be watching you."

VALENTY STOOD ON THE BATTLEMENTS, LOOKING NORTHWEST IN the direction of Causeway Gate. Word had come that this was the boundary gate where they had departed. Yevliesza and Tirhan. Tirhan, at least, had shown her compassion. Unlike his hosts. They had all worked together, however unknowingly, to drive her away. Like some infernal machine that, once wound up, worked at ruin until the job was complete. Valenty had been a spoke in that machine. How could he be surprised that she was gone?

He had been holding the side of the stone parapet so hard his hand felt frozen in its grip. He pulled away and resumed his walk along the battlements. Sometimes he thought he saw a figure on the plains, very far in the distance. It looked like a horse and rider. But as he watched, he saw it was only the shadow of a twisted tree.

Odd, how it was only when she had gone that he saw Yevliesza clearly. Her qualities that had at first been disturbing had eventually become interesting, then appealing. She pushed against restraints, absorbed everything that Grigeni could teach her, delving deeper into questions taken for granted by her teachers. She adapted to change to a degree that few Numinasi could. He thought of her on the horse that day when they went riding together. Though she had never been on a horse before, she pushed it into a gallop, seemingly for the pure joy of speed. She had fierce loves; perhaps she had even loved *him*.

He thought of Tirhan's role in her departure. Had Nashavety threatened Yevliesza, and had Tirhan attacked the *fajatim* in her defense? If it had come to that, then Tirhan and Yevliesza may have bonded.

The thought burned in him. But if Tirhan had caused Nashavety's injury, why did Nashavety claim she had fallen? Maddeningly, he only knew pieces of that night: at the dactyl pens Tirhan had claimed an envoy's right of transport; then at the boundary gate he told the *harjat* commander that he was returning to Alfan Sih. Yevliesza, dressed in a man's clothes, had posed as his servant. In retrospect, the post commander had admitted the servant was slight of build.

If Tirhan planned to enter at an Alfin Sih gate, it would mean certain arrest by the Volkish, so perhaps they had gone instead to the Jade Pavilion or the Lion Court or elsewhere. In any case, Yevliesza had found a powerful ally, one that he had not guessed. He tried to be glad for her, but the sentiment was beyond him.

In truth, he could never have been with her. How common a story it was, that the one you found was seldom the one you wanted. His people did not live well together, men and women. There had been a time when they lived separately, children raised in all-female households and men keeping to other concerns. Even these days the idea of fidelity was foreign to the Numinasi. But with Dreiza, it was different.

She had suffered under Lisbetha, might even have been cast out of Numinat, and he owed it to his brother to protect her. With her bright and strong mind, he had grown to love her. She had become his adviser in the convoluted life of service to Anastyna, endorsing his disguise of the superficial lord, careless of who he took to bed. But because Dreiza had come to him as a woman of middle age, he wanted to assure her of his care. Thus the vow. Which he had kept, by all that was Deep. He had kept it.

Dreiza had returned to the sanctuary, saying she would stay a little longer. But it was time for her to come home. He did not mind if she wintered in Zolvina, but if she felt he did not care, he would have to make that right. He could not demand, but he might carefully suggest that she return. If he did this, he must do it with a full heart.

Since his heart felt like stone, that would be difficult. To show his sincerity he would make his plea in person, if the old Devi Ilsat would even allow him through the door.

A last glance at the plains. His agent had been gone nearly eighteen days, carrying out his assigned mission. He had great faith in Andrik and also in his best horse, which would serve him well on his journey. He hoped for good news. Even if it was too late for the matter to affect Yevliesza in the way that he had planned. But some things could still be done.

If Nashavety did not die of her injuries, he would make her wish that she had.

TIRHAN AND YEVLIESZA MADE THEIR WAY UP THE SIDE OF A heavily forested ravine.

"We're here, aren't we?" Yevliesza asked. "Alfan Sih?"

"Yes, Yevliesza." Tirhan reached down to hand her up over a rocky outcropping. "How did you know . . . the direction?"

"I didn't know. I still don't. You intend that the roots reach for a place, and they go there."

As they climbed, their boots crunched on the brittle undergrowth and fallen leaves stiffened by frost. When they were out of sight of the tunnel that had pierced the forest, they paused and she exchanged her dress for sturdy clothes from their pack.

"Lights," Yevliesza whispered, looking to the top of the hill. "Lights up there." The hill glowed as though a carpet of molten light lay across it.

"The sun," Tirhan said. "It is dawn."

At the summit, they found themselves in a grove of trees where the interlacing branches caught the morning sun in a subtle glow.

"Silverwood," he said, noting her look of wonder.

She ran her hand along the smooth bark. Under it lay the prized wood for which Alfan Sih was famous.

From their vantage point they looked down on a wide valley filled with mist roiling gently in the morning breeze. And trees. A world of trees, stretching forever. Silverwood was rare, but the ravine was full of balsam and fir and pine in dark greens marching down from the hill and disappearing into the sunken cloud beneath them.

"Tirhan," she asked, staring at the vista. "Is this your world? Endless forest?"

"Yes. Home," he murmured, gazing into the valley.

"That's good." She was so tired she couldn't find all her words. No words for the beauty of the forest or for what it meant for both of them. Return. Allegiance. Relief. Also, and most importantly now, a place to sleep. She sank to her knees, overcome.

He crouched down, looking at her with narrowed eyes. "You are exhausted. But we cannot stay here." He helped her to stand. "We can rest soon."

As he led her along the crest of the hill, she asked, "Where are we going?"

"Away from the boundary gate."

The boundary gate. There was a new one now, of course. *I*

created it, she thought as they trudged along. *I have two powers. One of them is very big.*

When they had descended the hillside and traversed a stream, Tirhan at last stopped.

He led her to a huge evergreen tree where the lowest branches allowed them to walk beneath. In a few minutes he had gathered pine boughs and laid them on the ground, urging her to lie down. Gratefully, she sagged into them.

When she woke up the sun shone through the woods at a new angle. Tirhan was offering her a drink from a water skin. A rich aroma came from a small fire nearby, making her ravenous.

As he led her to the fire she spied a lean-to. "You've been busy. Breakfast hunted down and a house built."

He grinned in pleasure. "My world. And not breakfast, it is mid-day."

"No bagels, then?" she joked. Seeing his expression, she shrugged and said, "Everyone eats them back home."

Sitting by the fire they ate strips of cooked rabbit and the rest of the bread, now hard as stone.

"Tirhan. When we left Osta Kiya, when I came to you that night and asked you to take me with you, you weren't surprised, were you."

"I had prepared for it in case you changed your mind. I had asked Rusadka to find me the garments of a house servant so I could act the part if we were confronted in the crossings."

"Rusadka helped you?"

"You said you trusted her. The only one you trusted." He murmured, "And not Lord Valenty. Though I had thought better of him."

The fire had burned down and collapsed with a last lick of flame from the embers. She watched them cool and then flare in the low wind. How to say the truth. How to even find it. "He toyed with my affections." She had read that phrase somewhere and thought it worked in these circumstances.

"He wanted you."

"By his actions, yes. But then, later, he said he owed his allegiance to Dreiza."

"Did she object to you? That would be uncommon for a Numinasi woman."

"I don't know. He had second thoughts."

He murmured. "And left you with a bruised heart." He paused. "Forgive me. I have intruded."

"Nothing to forgive." To leave the topic behind, she stood up to begin putting things back in the pack. But the movement caused her to wince.

He rose to take her arm. "Let me look at your injury."

"Anyone would be sore after what we've been through."

He calmly responded, "Lie down in the lean-to and we shall see if that is all it is."

She left the fire pit and, after relieving herself behind a tree, she did as she was told.

When she removed her shirt, she lay half-naked, seeing for the first time a huge bruise welling at her side.

Tirhan knelt beside her. "She beat you."

"We beat each other."

He placed his hands gently against her aching ribcage and down to her hips where she still wore her trousers.

"You have two broken ribs," he finally said. "Valenty must hear of this. The princip must hear of it."

She almost laughed. "I think I may have *killed* Nashavety." She doubted they would see her as the victim.

He continued pressing his hands gently against her ribcage, softening the pain. "Sleep now," he said at last. He helped her into her shirt, vest, and jacket.

Before he left, she asked, sleepily, "How are we going to find your followers?"

"We are only a few days' walk from lands I know well."

"What if the Volkish find the new tunnel? We should put out the fire."

"I have already done so. But you needed meat."

"Burn my dress. If they find it in our pack . . . they'll know me for Numinasi. I'd be arrested for helping you."

"They will suspect you in any case, no matter what you wear. Most Alfan are light-haired." She hadn't thought of that.

"Sleep. I will be gone for a short while to hunt."

Of course that's what he would do. Off to the hunt. Bow and arrow, pure Alfan.

As she lay on her bed of boughs she thought about the ninth power and how it wasn't what inhabitants of the Mythos had always thought. The idea that primal root power might be a gift related to all the powers, was wildly wrong. Primal root power meant simply that the crossings could be altered with intent.

Still, it would be unsettling to a lot of people that she appeared to be the only one with this power. It might even be intolerable.

❧

DREIZA WOKE AS MORNING BELLS CHIMED SOFTLY FROM THE communal hall. She donned her shift and wool socks and padded to the basin that the *satvars* had filled for her last night. She splashed the sleep from her eyes. And spied something on her bed. It looked like a dragon beetle, it was so large, but as she drew closer she saw it was a leaf, dripping wet. She twirled it by the stem, wondering how it had gotten there.

A soft knock on her door, and in came an aged attendant who assisted her into her gown. Looking at the woman's tunic and trousers, Dreiza thought how foolish she, a woman of Osta Kiya, must look to one who could dress quickly and without assistance. Some traditions needed changing. It was the kind of notion that compelled one when in sanctuary and which would never come to mind in Osta Kiya.

As the *satvar* accompanied her to the dining hall, Dreiza thought about the leaf on her bed. She guessed that it was from Kassalya, but what did she mean by it? Perhaps nothing, given the girl's tormented mind.

This morning a man sat at table next to the Devi Ilsat. He wore the pale, so he had come from another sanctuary. It was unusual for a man to be at a women's *satvary*. But sometimes a renunciate might come for the High Mother's counsel, or to share a gift of food from distant fields. He and the Devi Ilsat were laughing about something. There seemed to be a lot of laughing from that woman, and it led Dreiza to think how she herself did not laugh much. Strange that renunciates seemed so happy. True, it was peaceful here, but she was already thinking of returning to the palace where things were a bit more lively.

As she helped to clear the porridge bowls, Kassalya interposed herself between Dreiza and the cookery.

"You came back," she said, her voice so neutral it was not clear if this was a good thing or not. Still, it was a relief to see the young woman free of obvious distress.

"Thank you for warning me that night, Kassalya. No one died at the Tower, but I think it was a near thing."

"I was upset. Falling happens." A frown appeared in her youthful face. "You go down and down and you know the ground is coming."

By the First Ones, did the girl not only see the future, but *experience* it? Dreiza glanced at the Devi Ilsat across the room, understanding more keenly why Kassalya must be sheltered. The Devi Ilsat met her eyes and raised a hand slightly. A summons.

"You did not save them," Kassalya said, still blocking her way. "No one saves anyone, or we would all be free because I would walk to all the places of sorrow and save them."

Dreiza's chest clenched in dismay at this summation of the pall that foreknowing had cast over the girl's heart. But the question formed: "If it does no good, why did you urge me to go?"

The girl dropped her gaze to the porridge bowls Dreiza held. Her face grew more serene, as though a simple thing like a used food bowl could anchor her mind. "I need to keep learning. When I foresee things it is only . . . to teach me things. So that I may become better."

Foreknowing was to teach her things as though she needed betterment more than others? If that was how Kassalya saw her strange power, it was a sad gift.

The Devi Ilsat came to join them, along with a helper who took Kassalya gently by the arm.

As she departed, Kassalya turned to ask, "Did you like my present?"

Ah. The leaf. "Yes, thank you. I think you brought it from the numin pool."

Kassalya nodded. "We do not allow leaves there. We keep it unsullied." Then she allowed herself to be led away.

"Do not be troubled," the High Mother said at her side. "She has all she needs amongst us." She cocked her head at Dreiza. "Do you?"

"Yes, Mother. I cherish this time at Zolvina."

The old *satvar* took one of the bowls from Dreiza and led her into the cookery.

Upon her return to the sanctuary three days ago, she had filled in the Devi Ilsat on events. How she had left so suddenly because of Kassalya's premonitions. The disturbing departure of Yevliesza and the injuries to Lady Nashavety. The Devi Ilsat seemed untouched by Dreiza's report. She was always interested to hear of palace goings-on, just as she was keen to hear about the barley harvest and Zolvina's mouser, Lord Woe.

The world was far away to these *satvars*, and while Dreiza had found the sanctuary peaceful, it was perhaps too much so.

They sat at a rough-hewn wood table and the Devi Ilsat pulled a large bowl of chestnuts toward them. "Do you mind?" she asked. "We have such a bountiful harvest this year."

Dreiza was happy to have the High Mother all to herself, and they passed the time scoring the nuts and talking of the visitor from a far sanctuary who was taking a tour of Zolvina's fields. The Devi Ilsat asked about Dreiza's plans for the winter.

"Of course you are welcome to stay with us as long as you like, my dear." Her gnarled hands made quick work of scoring the chestnuts with a knife and setting them in another bowl. After a long while, she added, "However, if you stay, my daughter, what of your husband?"

"I would not like to be long separated from him." She did miss him, but he was preoccupied with court concerns. "What happens to the chestnuts after we make the cuts?"

"We boil them. Then, shelling them is easier." The Devi Ilsat nodded happily. "It is a long process for such small meat."

Hells, was everything to be a lesson? One thing about court life, no one would ever think of giving advice in parables.

"Yevliesza will be in Alfan Sih by now, I should think," the *satvar* said. "I hope she will be happy there. It is a gentler land."

The topic was unwelcome. Dreiza was fond of Yevliesza, but the girl disturbed her. Her next cut into a chestnut slipped and cut into her thumb. Not a deep cut, and it was soon wrapped.

"The subject draws blood, Dreiza," the High Mother said softly.

Dreiza took another chestnut to score. She had forgotten that the Devi Ilsat had healing power, and of course it was not just for physical ailments. That was the problem with people who had the healing gift. You were always looking for someone to fix. She grabbed another chestnut and then another, working faster now to keep up her side of the work.

Finally the Devi Ilsat set her knife aside and pushed the chestnut dish away. "Had he grown too fond of Yevliesza? Possibly his consort?"

Dreiza stared at her bandaged thumb. No, he had not been intimate with Yevliesza. And that was the problem. Valenty admired the girl of the mundat. But he had not taken her to his bed.

She knew what that meant, but she had been pushing it away. When she thought of it at all, it was in a fleeting way, obscured by all the problems Yevliesza had brought to Osta Kiya and to the princip's court.

Now she stared at the hard truth. Valenty loved Yevliesza. Even if he did not know that he did.

But she knew it, and that was why she had come to Zolvina. To try not to hate Yevliesza and to cease being such an embarrassment to her Numinasi sisters by clinging to a man.

"I am . . . unhappy, Mother," she confessed.

"Ah. The owl has come for a visit. I am sorry, my child."

The owl of dark thoughts. She glanced up to see if the Devi Ilsat would expand on the expression. She thought she would send the bowl of nuts crashing to the floor if she did.

But the woman was already carrying the chestnuts to the wood stove.

Now Dreiza was left with just her own company. It was annoying how the High Mother brought up difficult questions but never told one how to solve them.

CHAPTER 36

Alfan Sih was a wildness of trees. No wonder Tirhan had sought refuge in the rooftop Verdant. To one raised in never-ending forest, the stony confines of Osta Kiya might be suffocating.

They descended into valleys, then up again through gaps in wooded ridges. There was always the next valley and hill. Trees bare of their leaves now appeared among the evergreens. Earlier in the day a veil of snow filled the air like the frosty breath of the land.

Once she saw a dactyl overhead, its dark silhouette massive and graceful, no rider visible from so far a distance. Tirhan had murmured, "Here, no Alfan owns such beings. Dactyls fly free." She had never heard him imply criticism of the Numinasi. Maybe now, in his own country, he would be less guarded.

At the crest of the steepest hill they had yet encountered, they paused to rest.

"Here is a thing you may never have seen," Tirhan said. Holding out his hand, he raised her from her seat on the ground. He pointed in a northerly direction.

It was a vast, crumpled tundra, flat, except for regular, rolling hills the shape of sand dunes. Nothing grew, nor did any stream flow or mountain rise.

"It's a wasteland," Yevliesza said, disturbed to see such devastation.

"Well, but look more closely. See how in the near distance small trees and grasses form a transition?"

She did see. The demarcation at the start of the no man's land had spots of green.

"The primordial lands," Tirhan said. "Alfan Sih grows."

"Into nothingness?"

"In another hundred years, forests will spring up and spread. Hills will rise, and when rain falls, streams will form. Then rivers. In five hundred years, it will look like the land we are passing through."

The realms grew. She had known that. Slowly, but not in geologic time.

"So it's not a wasteland," she said, relieved.

"It is new land."

"Would going into it be dangerous?"

"It could be, at times. If you go to the end, there is a land of mist. No one ever emerges from that place."

Yevliesza squinted into the distance, trying to see the wall of mist, but it was too far away.

"We are the arisen worlds, Yevliesza," he said. "And we keep changing."

Halfway down from the crest, Tirhan halted suddenly, holding up a hand for her to stop. He turned his head, listening.

Just downslope, three wolves loped by a stone's throw away. Black and streaked with grey, they were almost as big as a thrall.

"Wraith wolves," he whispered.

The two of them stood still for several minutes until Tirhan judged the creatures were far enough away.

"I'm glad they didn't see us."

"They saw us, but were on the hunt for something easier. When they find their prey they will become shadows to advance for the kill. Black shadows or grey ones, depending on the terrain."

"They will *seem* like shadows, or they *will* be shadows?" she asked.

"They will be wraiths." He smiled reassuringly. "Gone now. There are many wonders in Alfan Sih. I hope to show them to you."

She pondered that as they continued. Staying with him. It was an intoxicating prospect, but it couldn't just be a question of what she wanted. Her primal root power changed everything. From the moment the lightning visited her on the dactyl and gave her a unique hand of power, she was answerable for how she used it. For a land's defense, for a realm's aggression. She had employed it to bring a rightful king home. And now, how would she know the next right step?

Especially, if Nashavety lived, how to keep this power far from that woman's control. Nashavety would try to force her to shut down the Numinat boundary gates, maybe forever. She might well have support from the other *fajatim* who were either as isolationist as she was, or as afraid as she was.

As they walked, Tirhan told her about his family. His mother from a far-off clan, much loved in the great hall of his father. She had creature power and was the best horsewoman in the clan. Her second power was foreknowing that she vowed never to use, a common sacrifice among his people, though she wondered if the bouts of melancholy that Tirhan described might be because she foresaw the coming of the Volkish. His father and brother were reported to be dead at the hands of the occupiers. But no word of his two sisters nor of any friends or companions.

They crossed aligns. Their imprint in her mind was like perceiving long-vanished rivers, creases in the land, filled with glittering, molten light like a buried sun sending its brilliance through a fissure. If she needed to return to the new boundary gate, she could find her way. The pattern of the aligns would guide her.

On the third night Tirhan fashioned another lean-to in case of snow. It wasn't far to a stream, and there Yevliesza bathed in the icy brook for as long as she could stand it, though she didn't wash her hair lest it chill her while it dried.

Once dressed, she carried her boots to the lean-to and sat at the opening, brushing off her feet.

By the time Tirhan returned from a brief hunt to try to replenish their supplies, she was thoroughly cold.

"My clan never lets me forget how badly I hunt," he said in good humor, since he was empty-handed.

In their hut they shared a few handfuls of nuts and seeds and the last of their meat, a small meal that couldn't warm her. She shivered. He put his arm around her and it did help.

"I think you need a fire," he said, getting up.

"Your arms are just as good." It was true, but it also sounded like an invitation. Heat rose in her face. They had slept close for two nights, saying it was for warmth, but she knew it was for comfort, too.

He sat down and put his arm around her again. "You should not have bathed in the river."

Tirhan's scent, pine and sweat and warmth, stirred her. She remembered the accusation in the Tower that she had seduced Valenty, and though Nashavety did nothing but lie, her words came to her now. She hurt everyone she touched.

Moving away, she said, "That wasn't an appeal for your affection."

He turned to face her. "Nor did I take it that way. But you will surely tell me if you change your mind?"

His teasing attitude angered her. "Don't play games this way," she threw at him.

In response, he reached for her, pulling her close to him and kissed her, beginning gently and gaining force. She leaned into the kiss, into him. Then there was no help for it, clothes must come off, and they were quickly shed. The cold swept over them, ignored. When he pulled her to him again, he blazed with warmth.

He whispered her name. It was a sweet, electric sound, sending her skin zinging with desire. He caressed her breasts and ran his hand down to her waist. Half their clothes were still on. She considered the next step and hesitated, putting a hand on his chest.

As they caught their breath, he whispered, "This can wait. Yevliesza, it can wait."

"Tirhan . . ." she said in a panic. She had no idea what she was doing, or should do.

He pulled her head against his chest. "Shh," he murmured, and she clung to him.

His body tensed. Suddenly he sat up. "Make no sound," he whispered in her ear. Carefully he found his shirt and jacket, handing her own clothes to her. "Get dressed, quickly."

When they had dressed, he handed her a knife. "In your boot," he said, as he left the lean-to.

A long few minutes later, she heard voices, a foreign tongue. Then outside the hut, louder.

There would be no safety in the lean-to. She emerged to find a number of men and women dressed in trousers and leather jackets. A pale moonlight illuminated the scene. They were kneeling before Tirhan.

His people had found him.

This reunion was what they had been seeking, and she was glad for him. But there was a sober finality about this scene.

Because she knew at that moment that she and this prince did not share a destiny. His was clear, for better or for worse.

Hers was a distant vista, illumined by the gleam of aligns and informed by the roots of the Mythos. She wasn't sure what destiny awaited her. But it was elsewhere.

❦

VALENTY SAT NEXT TO ONE OF HIS MISTRESSES ON THE COUCH IN his bed chamber. Elivasa had done up her hair for the occasion, into an elaborate bun adorned with gold clasps. When she left the chamber, her hair would be in disarray around her shoulders.

She gestured to the parchment in her hand. "Two of the Raven's maids are ours. The rest are sucking from her tits."

"Just two," Valenty muttered. "Do they know anything?"

An ironic smile pushed into Elivasa's round cheeks. "Would I be here if they did not? Of course they know things. Annady had the delightful job of emptying her bedpans yesterday, and she says the invalid is stirring. Awake most of the time now, sharpening her teeth on the servants."

"Anything broken?" he asked hopefully.

"No. An ankle twisted. The knock on the head shook some rat shit out, but she is apparently the better for it." While Valenty absorbed the implications of this report, Elivasa reached for her cup of ale with a pale, plump hand that had touched her share of grime and blood in Valenty's service.

Valenty took a deep breath, accepting the news. Nashavety was back. Despite the dramatic little scene of the *fajatim* going to her bedside and being forced to recognize Sofiyana as the heir to Raven Fell, Nashavety was in control.

He got up to pace. "While she was delirious we should have administered a nasty tincture."

"Which her healers would have recognized."

He snorted. "Allow a man his dreams."

The handle of the bed chamber door turned. No one had knocked.

Elivasa was instantly on her feet, her small, everyday dagger in hand. She went to one side of the door, and Valenty tensed for a confrontation.

His man Andrik slipped in and gently pushed the door shut behind him. It was his usual entrance when he did not want to be seen or heard. He nodded at Elivasa as she slipped her knife back into an ankle boot.

Valenty grinned. "At last. I hope you brought my horse back."

Andrik's disordered hair fell in front of his face, and he smelled of horseflesh and a long ride. "Aye. Or she brought me, more like."

Sitting on the couch, he gratefully accepted a cup of ale from Valenty and drank it down.

Elivasa shook out her hair from her bun so that she could look properly ravished. On her way out, she gave Andrik a kiss on the cheek, murmuring, "Get a bath, man."

Valenty sat opposite Andrik, waiting to hear his report, restraining the impulse to hurry him along. He had probably ridden hard and all night as well.

Glancing at the floor, Andrik said, "The man you sent me to find is in the underway." He nodded at Valenty's relieved reaction. "Gave me a long chase, that one, not wanting to be found."

"If you brought him back, then he has a story to tell," Valenty said in growing good humor.

A satisfied smile crept across Andrik's face. "Aye, that he does. That he does."

NASHAVETY SAT BEHIND HER DESK. THE GREAT OAKEN EXPANSE OF wood spread out before her, a barricade against the failed policies of the current princip. Anastyna sat on the other side, looking small and vulnerable. As she was.

Nashavety could take this princip down with a flick of her wrist. And would do so, soon, for the good of the realm. Three of the five *fajatim* stood against Anastyna. When she found one more, she could choose her moment.

Her injuries from the Tower had been harsh. But she had returned, come back from the dead. It gave one perspective, having hovered over one's own grave and not quite fallen in. She was in fact stronger than before, despite a limp from a swollen ankle and a persistent headache that made her want to slap her servants. And the ugly crease in her skull that her worthless healers had not yet coaxed away.

"We are gratified to see the *fajatim* looking so well," Anastyna said.

Looking *well?* She was so thin her dressmaker had spent all night altering her gown for this audience. Her skin felt like parchment, her face as narrow as an axe, her scalp half shaved. Her only consolation was that she had soundly beaten the mundat creature, breaking a few bones no doubt, and driven her from Numinat.

"Thank you, My Lady Princip. And for coming to visit. I am able to walk, but it was gracious of you to attend me."

Anastyna dipped her head in acknowledgement.

"I asked you to come in order to consider the situation we find ourselves in with the untimely flight of our guest of the mundat."

"A situation, still?" Anastyna asked with a little moue of confusion. "I thought perhaps you would welcome Yevliesza's departure from our midst." Her grey silk gown contrasted with the pink flush on her cheeks. Anastyna, as always, was attractively arrayed. Except today the silver torc looked like it was starting to choke her.

"But the possible conflict with Volkia, My Lady Princip, if they capture her in Alfan Sih. It could go hard with us."

"Yes. If they conclude that she is our spy. They may well, but we shall deny it. Do not trouble yourself over this matter, Lady Nashavety." She smiled prettily.

"As a member of your council of *fajatim*, should I not . . . *trouble* myself over matters of state?" She said it in a gentle voice although it was not her first impulse. Eight hells, was she to be coddled by a youngster?

"Speak your mind, Lady Nashavety. One wishes to hear your counsel, as always."

"Then if I do not speak out of turn, it is this: Before Volkia has a chance to protest her interference in the control of Alfan Sih, do you take the initiative to disown her. Let us be swift to distance ourselves from her actions. By condemning her alliance with Lord Tirhan . . . and banishing her from our realm."

Anastyna drew a breath to answer, but Nashavety rode over her. "You gave her every opportunity, Lady Princip. Offered her a household in our palace, approved arcana training, forgave the death of those who died on the bridgeway, provided her guidance from one of your trusted advisors." Nashavety raised a palm to indicate that she had complied in Anastyna's request. "And then she flies out in the dead of night with a foreign prince. Though we would gladly have provided her a more dignified departure, she chose to do so in secret." Nashavety shook her head sadly. "It is an insult to your person. And to me."

Anastyna nodded slowly, looking past Nashavety to the windows overlooking the great courtyard.

"Banishment would be a kindness," Nashavety added to give the woman a final push. "After all, the Volkish might execute her as a spy. One hears they can be harsh. But if she is not to be

considered a Numinasi—if we reject her claim of citizenship—
they may take her actions as nothing more than a foolish affair of
the heart. Although I would not blame you if you let the girl
succumb to her fate. We owe her nothing."

There. Let the woman take the blame for Yevliesza's death.
The girl's jump from the Trespass Door would have been satisfying, but driving her into the arms of Volkia might do nicely. If the
girl lost her life, it would be squarely on the princip's shoulders.
Bringing her out of the mundat to live amongst them had always
been a reckless, misshapen scheme. To embed a foreign influence
in the heart of their realm. From that moment Nashavety had
worked to save her beloved land; from that moment, Anastyna
was destined to become the realm's shortest reigning princip.

Anastyna rose. "Thank you for sharing your thoughts, Lady
Nashavety. I will consider them carefully. Yevliesza does have her
supporters, I do not deny it. Yet the decision is mine."

Nashavety stood to walk Anastyna to the door. Every step
rang like a gong in her head, but she wanted to show herself
recovered. Her strength was returning very fast, much to the
chagrin of others, including even Sofiyana, though she strove to
hide it.

In parting, Anastyna said, "It does my heart good to see you
so well recovered, lady." In her smile Nashavety almost thought
she detected sincerity. It galled her considerably.

❦

IN THE MORNING YEVLIESZA WOKE LATE TO FIND THE WORLD
swirling in heavy mist. She had slept alone that night in the lean-
to, with Tirhan staying up late conferring with his people.

She was welcomed to the cook fire and one of the Alfan band
handed her a cup filled with a steaming infusion, saying something in the Alfan language. Tirhan saw her and dragged a pack

over for her to sit on and made himself comfortable on the ground at her side. He told her that he had learned that his father had been executed outright, and his brother killed in leading a force against the occupiers. It seemed to break open his sorrow anew. His mother and sisters were confined in an as-yet undiscovered redoubt, safe for now, unlike other Alfan of standing who had been rounded up into heavily guarded camps.

As he introduced her to the circle around the fire, she lost most of their names except for the squad leader, Kierach, a broad-shouldered, serious man with a close-clipped beard, his clothes a mix of lavish and tattered.

Across the fire she noted a woman who wore a dagger at each hip. Her blond-white hair was tied back, falling to her waist. Tirhan introduced her as Morwen, and the woman nodded at Yevliesza, her gaze lingering rudely.

The men had bows worn across their backs, and now Tirhan did too. His demeanor had changed. The more deference the group gave him, the more pronounced his stance of self-containment became. It was, she supposed, the habit of royals. But now and then he met her eyes, reassuring her.

After a quick meal the band gathered their things and removed all trace of the cook fire. As they began taking apart the lean-to, she almost stopped them. The thought came, *Where will I sleep?* Because she was not going with them.

At last Tirhan took her apart from the others. "We have to leave. The fog is a good cover for us to join Clan Mid Daihinn down-valley. We do not have an extra horse but you can ride with me."

She smiled. "I don't think Kierach would allow it."

"Then you shall have his horse," he said.

That would be a bad beginning. She was sure it wouldn't suit the ways and customs of Alfan Sih.

He watched her, knowing it was time for her to choose.

"I can't go with you," she finally said. He had offered to marry her for her protection, but she didn't have his heart. His heart was in this land of forest and fog, in the company of his people, the clans, the scattered royals, at war with the Volkish invaders.

"Can you not?" he asked. "It would gladden me if you did."

She looked around at the hills, with their cloudy ridges and huddled trees stretching far beyond sight. "This is a land under siege, Tirhan. If the Volkish find me, my powers would be in their hands."

"We would keep it secret," he protested.

"But it would come out. If I made another gate. Or if they wondered how you got past their guarded boundary."

The warrior-like woman approached. Yevliesza noted she was tall, as tall as the men. Strong-looking, slim and with a harsh beauty. She said something to Tirhan in their language, but the meaning was clear from the impatient looks on the Alfans already mounted. *Time to leave.*

"Yes, Morwen," he said in Numinasi. "Presently."

As the woman turned away, Yevliesza stepped toward her. "Morwen, a moment."

She heard her name and turned to face Yevliesza.

"I have to go back through the crossings. But I need a comb. Might you have one?" She looked to Tirhan to translate, but Morwen answered back in heavily accented Numinasi.

"A comb'll be the least of your needs. The Volkish, if they fancy you, they take you."

"But I can't look like I've been living in the woods. It would be suspicious."

Morwen abruptly walked away.

"By the eight hells, I will find you a comb," Tirhan muttered. But then Morwen came back with something in her hand. A small, beautifully wrought comb made of bone.

Handing it to Yevliesza, Morwen held her gaze. "These days, to go alone in the paths, it takes courage." Her lips flattened into an almost smile, and she handed her the comb.

"Thank you," Yevliesza said. "I hope I can return it someday."

"No. A gift."

The woman walked back to her sleek black horse, perhaps glad that Yevliesza was leaving. There might have been some feelings between her and Tirhan, or at least on Morwen's part.

Tirhan asked, "Where will you go?"

"Home."

"But where is home, Yevliesza?"

"A place called Oklahoma."

"And friends to take you in?"

"You shouldn't worry about me. Please think of me as being happy, as I will of you." She took his hand, but whether it was a goodbye gesture or to cling to him, she wasn't sure.

He brought her hand to his lips.

"You will need your dress." He went to the group of riders and took her knapsack from one of the horses. As he repacked it, he declined help with the task. The group watched, frowning.

Finishing, he brought the pack to Yevliesza, stocked with food and essentials to last her a few days.

"I'll see you again," she said.

"So you now have foreknowing as well?" he asked softly.

She gave him a smile she didn't feel. "Probably." She would have embraced him, but his followers were watching, and he was now heir to the throne, if not already king.

He gave her a confident smile, looking the perfect ruler. "Go with all grace, my lady."

As the riders picked their way into the dense growth of pine and fir, Yevliesza walked in the direction she took to be west, since the morning sun was at her back.

She knew her way.

CHAPTER 37

Yevliesza crouched in the tunnel, the one she had made just days before. It was still quite narrow, forcing her to crawl. Up ahead it might have collapsed, forcing her to turn back and face the wilderness of Alfan Sih.

But she came at last to the small cave where she had discovered her primal root power. Stopping to comb her hair once more, she coiled it into a lady-like twist at her neck.

The main path lay a few steps away. With nowhere to hide, if she encountered Volkish troops, she had to be ready. As she rehearsed her story, it didn't seem like a good one, but it was the best that she could do.

More than anything, her story had to mislead the Volkish about her destination.

She had told Tirhan about her home in the mundat, about the old wood house blasted by the sand and the winds to a shiny grey; the lace curtains that her mother had crocheted; the little town with its one-stop shopping. Not mentioned was Shane, whom she half-loved because he was the only boy who dared to speak to her. She could be there in a couple of hours.

But she wasn't going to the mundat.

She hadn't told Tirhan the truth. If the worst happened to him, and the Volkish questioned him, all he would know was that she departed for the mundat. She hoped they would never look for her in the Mythos.

Because home was Numinat. It had slowly become Numinat, with its far vistas, its great mountain ranges and plains, its city-castle with water running up the hillside, its shaped gardens on the roof, its nethers carved along aligns, and a man whom she either hated or admired, she didn't know which.

What waited for her at Osta Kiya, she didn't know. She would have to answer for having left, answer for Nashavety's death or injury. The woman had tried to push her from the Tower. Would they be able to see what the *fajatim* was, how poisonous and brutal? But even if Anastyna rejected Yevliesza, condemned her, the truth was that she had nowhere else to go. And returning to account for her actions might look like what it was. Innocence.

But she wouldn't give Numinat the gift of her root power. They would only harness her for war. She didn't trust Anastyna. The princip was at the mercy of politics, and she might demand that Yevliesza sever the accesses to Numinat. Or forge a path to Volkia to strike at them. Either way, she would be altering the crossings, either for defense or armed conflict. She wouldn't have any choice in the matter. And she would be responsible for destruction and possibly war. She did want Volkia to be beaten back. But the thought of enabling the realms to kill each other was larger and more terrible than she could embrace.

At the opening to the larger tunnel, she heard a thudding sound. The sound of feet tramping. It grew louder, then mingled with voices. Soldiers on the march.

She shrank back into the recess, then scrambled into the small tunnel.

Crawling frantically down the tunnel, she tried to go far enough that anyone entering the cave wouldn't see her. At the last minute, she thought to try to close the opening. Holding her left hand against the wall and concentrating, she was able to bring a flap of the roof to close off her hiding place. There she lay quietly, listening to the muffled passage of what she took for troops.

When she ventured out, the thudding had receded.

Her face dripped with perspiration, and her hair hung in ropes around her shoulders. She wiped her face clean on the inside of her skirt and, using the comb Morwen had given her, rearranged her hair.

Looking out onto the main passageway she found it empty and quiet. There would never be a perfect time to show herself. It had to be now.

With her pack on one shoulder, she slipped out into the larger tunnel. The danger of more soldiers was now more acute. Perhaps she should try to create a new route to Numinat, but every use of her new power risked exposing her ability. And there was no telling how far from help her Numinat emergent point might be. Her pack didn't carry supplies. She had left them in Alfan Sih, in case a patrol searched her and asked why she carried food.

After a few minutes she walked faster, restraining the urge to run. The sooner she was out of the vicinity of Alfan Sih, the better.

A clopping noise. It sounded like a horse, and in the next moment she saw that she had come upon the side path to Volkia. It was occupied.

Soldiers approached. It was no good to hide, they'd seen her. Someone shouted at her. A foreign language, but the meaning was clear. She stopped to face a group of five soldiers, one of them leading a horse.

They approached. Black uniforms with breeches tucked into high boots. Long coats, slit on the sides for their swords in scabbards.

The lead soldier, broad-faced with keen, suspicious eyes,

stood before her. "Madame." He gave a curt nod. "Numinasi, I think?"

"Yes. Good day to you." She thought her heart was beating loud enough for him to hear.

"Please wait," he said in heavily accented Numinasi. "My lord will be wishing to speak with you."

She had just met her first Nazi. Her stomach began to digest itself. *They are Volkish*, she told herself, *Volkish. We are not at war. They do not know me. All will be well.*

The soldier walked back to confer with what looked like the officer in charge. He approached, taking off his hat and placing it under his arm. His uniform, unlike the others, was soft grey and embellished with gold braid and a sash secured with an elaborate pin. His hair, sandy brown, was slicked back from a tall forehead and a face with aristocratic planes.

"Allow me to make myself known to you, madam," he said. His accent was vaguely German, but softly so. "I am Prince Albrecht von Treid. I may have your name as well?"

"Yevliesza of Osta Kiya, House Valenty. An honor to meet you, my lord." She made the sort of bow she had seen women make to the princip. Her voice had broken and she knew her lower lip was trembling. She tried breathing deeply, but nothing helped.

Meanwhile this prince of Volkia was taking in her hair, her dress, her face, which might still be streaked with mud. His eyes were a pale blue, his manner, casual, as befit someone who didn't feel threatened. That was how she must act, she realized, and stood taller, meeting his eyes and waiting.

"You are on your way home or coming from home? Forgive my questions, but in these times it is necessary to know why one is traveling." His relaxed manner didn't fool her. He was a man who expected obedience and got it.

"I am on my way to Numinat, having come from the Lion

Court. I expected it to be a short journey, but I was mistaken as to the path."

"Yes, you are mistaken, madam. In this region, there is only Alfan Sih."

The other soldiers were now gathered behind the prince, as well as a tall white horse with a fancy sword attached to its saddle. The soldiers regarded her with grave expressions. In their finely tailored black uniforms they were clearly of high rank, serving the prince. She had to match them in arrogance. At the very least she needed to stop shaking.

She answered, saying, "I realized I was lost, so I retraced my steps. I'm clear on the way now."

"I see. But why do you travel unaccompanied, madam, without even a maid?"

"My hosts at the Lion Court offered me a servant, but I thought with the current state of unrest I shouldn't put a citizen of Nubiah in danger." She looked at the prince's men. "To be stopped and questioned. It's upsetting, and where relations are in doubt, it might be dangerous."

"You have my apology for the inconvenience," he said without a trace of apology. "But I believe you were even more inconvenienced by the detachment of Volkish soldiers that just passed. Yes? They had questions for you?"

In the pause that followed, he raised an eyebrow.

"I hid," she admitted.

Prince Albrecht cocked his head in mock confusion.

"I didn't know what soldiers they were, and what they would make of me being there alone. I turned into a small crevice, and they passed by."

"Curious behavior. Surely there is no need to hide from honorable men."

"If they were honorable."

His mouth tightened. "I must assume you do not mean to say

that." He waited for her to apologize, but even as the words formed in her mind, she found she didn't want to utter them.

"At the Lion Court what was your business?" he snapped. His gentlemanly behavior had dropped like the mask it had been.

"I went to meet a man who offered an arrangement of marriage."

He frowned. "With a man of such a . . . far country? A Nubian?"

He meant, with a Black man. A swell of anger drove her to say, "Does not the Mythos hold us all in the palm of its hand?"

"Yes, of course," he said genially. Then coldly: "But not equally." He turned to one of his men. "Search her pack."

"I protest," she quickly said. "That is an insult to my person, my lord."

The ghost of a smile came to his face. "Be glad we do not insult your person more thoroughly. If you have nothing to hide?"

A soldier took the pack from her and looked through it. She was glad she had given Tirhan's knife back to him since it might be recognizable as Alfan.

When the soldier shook his head, Albrecht regarded her for a few seconds before saying, "You may go, Yevliesza of Osta Kiya. Your realm and mine may soon settle on an agreement of mutual benefit. Therefore we are anxious not to offend."

In vast relief, she nodded in as lofty a manner as she could muster.

"But, Yevliesza," he said in a way that chilled her, "I will remember you."

ॐ

YEVLIESZA ENTERED NUMINAT ON A BRIGHT, FRIGID DAY WHEN the sun hung low in the sky, a white ball of ice. She couldn't see the land beyond the fort's walls or past the soldiers who surrounded her, but she knew the region she was in, having been there before, the day she had first seen the rolling hills of Numinat and laid eyes on a dragon.

As they marched her across the yard to the commander's billet, she recognized a sentry on the wall. Rusadka. Her friend raised her chin. If she was surprised by Yevliesza's appearance, she hid it.

The guards had her firmly by the arm, but not too harshly. They likely couldn't be sure whether she was a criminal or just an errant aristocrat who would be forgiven by the princip. She wasn't sure, either, but it soon became clear when the captain, thin and stern, kept her standing before his desk for some time before addressing her.

"You are to return to face Princip Anastyna," he said, cutting to the chase.

She had heard those words before, when they had first been uttered in the crossings by her escort, but this time it had a different effect upon her. She had chosen to face Anastyna.

"Are there specific charges against me?"

"That you will discover soon enough." He glanced at the guard. As she was marched to the door, the captain relented and said, "In fact, the charge is treason."

She turned to face him. "Treason?" She had been ready to hear murder, but this could be worse.

The captain went on. "You have given aid to a kingdom at war, endangering our neutrality."

Given aid? Did they know of the new path to Alfan Sih? Had Nashavety figured out her markings?

They took her to a building made of timber badly caulked together. In her small room, the wind whistled through the chinks. The blanket on the cot was welcome, though it was like donning a sheet of ice. She huddled there through the day, hoping to see Rusadka. A window gave out to the horse paddock, empty of the fort's mounts which were no doubt seeking the warmth of the stable.

She thought about the charge of treason. It went to the question of neutrality and Yevliesza being in company with an Alfan Sih prince. Tirhan had foreseen the difficulty, and that was why he had offered to make her his wife. Then she would have been Alfan by marriage and would have had every right to fight as a partisan. But she hadn't fought, that at least was on her side.

In the morning a female soldier brought her warm clothes, fur-lined boots and gloves of heavy wool.

When she had eaten a breakfast of boiled eggs and hot oats, she emerged from her cabin to find three soldiers waiting for her with saddled mounts.

Among them, Rusadka. Their eyes met, and it was like an embrace.

As the other two guards finished loading supplies on the horses, Yevliesza whispered,

"What are you doing here?"

"Sofiyana had me assigned here for the winter. And made sure my promotion did not happen." Rusadka shrugged. "Holds grudges, that one."

"Because you're my friend. How is it you were picked to guard me?"

"I asked. The captain thinks I have been unfairly disciplined. He did not like Sofiyana's interference."

"Is Nashavety dead?"

Rusadka shook her head. "Sofiyana is now her Right Hand."

A young malwitch rising in power. She wondered if Sofiyana had ever been her friend and whether her betrayal grew out of jealousy over Tirhan. But Sofiyana was ambitious. She had come to Osta Kiya to be in the precincts of royal power. How could mere friendship stand in her way?

Rusadka whispered, "Why did you leave? What happened?"

But the guards were now mounting and ordered Yevliesza to do so. There would be time to answer. It was a four-day ride.

The group rode out in single file. The folded hills were dotted with low trees and in the distance buttes rose steeply, crowned by grasses, yellow in the morning light. The snow-clad Numin Mountains loomed to the north, beautiful and harsh, like the Numinasi themselves. A breath filled her chest, feeling like the first one in many days.

Looking at Rusadka on her mount, she felt her spirits lift. Though the wind was merciless and she faced a long journey by horseback, it took a very great effort to suppress a smile.

⚘

WELL BEFORE DAWN, DREIZA SAT AT THE NUMIN POOL, ITS LOW stone wall just wide enough for a comfortable seat.

The night was still, leaving the pool's surface calm. She had awakened in the third quarter of the night and, after lying awake too long, had bundled herself in her warmest garments and walked outside.

The moon had set, but the stars gathered above in their millions. And, as well, in the glassy plane of the numin pool.

The Devi Ilsat's figure of speech kept coming back to her: *The owl has come for a visit.* And it had. So much so that when she looked down at the pool, she almost expected to see the creature perched on her shoulder. What Dreiza had taken for serenity during her stay in Zolvina was no such thing. It was a determined retreat from her life.

It was a life she had loved and which had made her happy, but it was changing. It was time to see clearly.

She looked into the still water and plucked out a twig that, under some unseen current, had been making its way to her. Now the stars were in their pristine state, with no twig floating through the heavens. It was the true dome of the sky, housing the far-flung worlds.

What were her true thoughts? What was her pristine state, that place of wisdom that she had been avoiding?

When the first *satvars* awoke they found Dreiza watching the pool. They let her tend it, because they judged she was doing a good job.

☙❦☙

By the time Yevliesza and her escort reached the plains in front of Osta Kiya, her mood had darkened. The fortress jutted from the land like a giant's fist. From a couple miles' distance, she could just make out the battlements and the slim Tower from which she might have stepped into the air, or been pushed.

She didn't want to die that way. Almost any other execution method would do, but she had looked down that two-thousand-foot fall and thought it was far too slow a death.

In her carefully thought-out plan, she would be exonerated. Surely Anastyna would feel shamed to have put her under the *fajatim's* control in Raven Fell. She would tell the princip about Nashavety's torture and her attempt to kill her in the Tower that night. Nashavety had not accused Yevliesza of causing her injuries, Rusadka informed her. In fact she had tried to erase the events in the Tower by claiming she had fallen. Therefore the only crime of which Yevliesza could be accused was aiding Prince Tirhan. And they had no evidence of that, nor was it true in any way that they could imagine.

Over the course of their journey, Rusadka had been urging her to reveal her primal root power, the gift of altering the crossings.

It would be a startling admission, changing everything, perhaps making her too valuable to be labeled treasonous. But they would also use her to their ends. Her will would no longer be her own. She could destroy things of value, things that in their fear, they would forget to protect: the crossings.

She wouldn't be the one who shut down a path or who forged new routes for war.

If that much was clear, there was one question that coiled in her mind, unanswered: Why was she the recipient of the ninth power? For a time she had taken comfort in Tirhan's suggestion that the Mythos approved of her. But it was not alive and conscious even if sometimes people seemed to regard it that way. So she doubted that she possessed some kind of bestowed destiny with this new power. There was nothing foretold or inevitable. It was just her predicament that she had more power than she wanted or felt capable of using. The real question: Why would she be the only one, if in fact she was the only one? There was a mechanism at work, surely. And it wasn't lightning.

As they approached Osta Kiya, she could see people standing on the battlements, watching. *Now it begins*, she thought. Pyvel might be there and her tutor Grigeni, perhaps Dreiza. Perhaps Valenty.

And Nashavety.

CHAPTER 38

G rigeni sat with Valenty in his study, going over the
precedents for royal proceedings in a case of treason.
As the household Keeper of Books, Grigeni had taken
on the task of scrutinizing the rules for a princip's judgment on
high crimes. If Yevliesza had acted against the Volkish in any
way, it would not go well for her.

Valenty tried to banish thoughts of what Anastyna might do if
that were the case. But he knew that she could not do otherwise
than impose the harshest penalty—as Nashavety had been urging,
marshalling castle opinion. The matter was Anastyna's to decide,
but if she lost the confidence of the *fajatim*, she risked being
deposed. Then the twisted creature who feared and hated the
outside worlds would wear the torc and become the dark heart of
Numinat.

The housekeeper appeared at the door. "Miss Yevliesza is
rested, my lord, and is waiting upon you."

He nodded for Grigeni to accompany him. His presence might
help with the awkwardness of the reunion. And he did need to
secure her cooperation for her defense. He had no reason to think

that Yevliesza would be glad to see him. Much the contrary, as he very well knew.

‎𐫱𐫲𐫳

YEVLIESZA STOOD WHEN THE TWO MEN ENTERED THE ROOM. SHE had been given quarters in Valenty's household, a consideration that might show that Anastyna didn't condemn her outright. A fire burned in the fireplace, and the windows had been warded against the outside.

Departing from his usual attire, Valenty wore dark colors, his quilted vest a deep grey, his trousers black as well as his shirt. He looked cruelly handsome, but his face was neutral, with no hint of the displeasure he must feel at her fleeing Osta Kiya. If that's what he felt. She really must give up trying to predict what he would think or do.

"My lord," she formally said. "And Master Grigeni."

"Yevliesza," Valenty said, gesturing her to sit. She took a seat on the divan and Valenty and Grigeni sat in chairs opposite her. "I am glad to see you looking well."

"Thank you for your hospitality."

"You have everything you need?"

She wore one of her dark blue everyday gowns, but the bodice, which normally snugged tight to her frame, hung loose from the weight she had lost over the last few days. "I'm chilled. A cloak would be welcome."

Grigeni rose to his feet.

"Stay, Grigeni," Valenty said. "I will send someone."

As he went to the door to call a servant, Grigeni said, "I am happy to see you, miss. We have been . . . worried."

"Thank you. But did you worry that I had disgraced the princip?"

He smiled. "That has not been foremost in our minds."

Valenty reseated himself. "Yevliesza. Grigeni is here to advise on how best to conduct your defense. Tomorrow Princip Anastyna will formally question you."

So soon. She nodded with a stab of foreboding.

"By our custom, someone of standing must assist you by presenting evidence. That will be me if you have no objection."

"OK."

Valenty cocked his head. "You are saying yes?"

She felt herself growing impatient with him for no other reason than his formal bearing. Of course, she wouldn't welcome any familiarity from him, either.

Grigeni murmured to Valenty. "She is saying yes."

Valenty paused, letting a potent silence take over the room. Finally he said in even tones, "To begin, let me ask the most important question. Did you enter Alfan Sih, is that where you went? Did you take up arms with Lord Tirhan?"

"I never fought for him." That was true, even if it wasn't all of what Valenty wanted to know. Suddenly, she had the urge to share her discovery of her second power with Valenty, but he was Anastyna's man first and last. If she couldn't trust the princip, then she couldn't trust him, either.

She went on. "Tirhan and I went there because he needed to, and I had nowhere else to go, unless it was back to the mundat."

Valenty exchanged glances with Grigeni. "That at least is on our side." He turned back to her. "How did you avoid the Volkish sentries?"

She had prepared her explanation. "Tirhan knew methods of stealth. Some gates have less fortification than others, and his helpers in Alfan Sih created a diversion." She hoped her face looked more innocent than she felt.

Grigeni murmured. "That is very well, then. But your actions could have gone otherwise."

"Will I be given the chance to tell why I had to leave, what happened to me in Osta Kiya?"

"Yes," Valenty said. "And why did you leave in that manner? We have greatly wondered."

"I ran because Nashavety tried to kill me."

A silence descended. Valenty murmured, "Perhaps a longer version."

"She drugged me that night. When I woke up, I was in the Tower facing her and her thrall. It was late, not long before dawn." As she described what happened next, she gazed above the heads of the men facing her. She remembered every move, every blow. The thrall dripping saliva, Nashavety dripping venom, striking and kicking her.

When she got to the part when Nashavety straddled her as she lay on the floor, shoving her head over the threshold of the Trespass Door, Valenty stood up abruptly, striding to the fireplace.

Grigeni asked, "Do you have wounds on your person? Bruises?"

She shook her head. "Tirhan is a skilled healer. He told me I had two broken ribs."

Valenty's fist crashed down on the wooden mantel. Turning toward her in fury, he asked, "She beat you, tried to push you from the Tower?"

Grigeni intervened. "Nashavety will deny it." He locked gazes with Yevliesza. "Can anyone confirm the *fajatim's* actions?"

"Well, someone carried me to the Tower. I don't think Nashavety could have managed it. Then Tirhan administered to my hurts, especially my broken ribs. Rusadka saw the bruises from the torture of my right hand, but with Tirhan's care, they're almost gone now." She held up her right hand, where the discolorations had lightened under Tirhan's ministrations. "Nashavety had Daraliska use a little vise to improve my attitude."

Valenty paced to the nearest window, throwing off the warding and letting in a river of frigid air.

"You said she urged you to jump," Grigeni said, trying to continue in a methodical manner. "She urged you to kill yourself, saying it was your only hope to redeem your mistakes. What mistakes?"

"That I went into the nethers without permission to see my father. That I put Pyvel in danger of reprimand. That my interference at the Bridge of the Moon caused deaths . . ."

"And?" Grigeni urged.

"That I seduced the man who offered me boarding in his household."

Grigeni dropped his gaze, examining his hands.

Valenty swung around to face them, his face in deep shadow. "I will kill her."

"Nay, do not say so," Grigeni blurted.

Valenty sneered, "I will kill the beast of Raven Fell. So I swear."

"My lord, do not, do not swear!"

"Should I not? The woman is a demon of hell. She will take everything good and turn it to blood and ashes."

Yevliesza rose. Had Valenty just crossed a line? Why was Grigeni so agitated? "Grigeni, what's going on?"

Now standing as well, Grigeni threw her an alarmed look. "If he swears twice, he must take combat either with the challenged person or with her chosen fighter. I am witness. You are witness. A second time, and it cannot be undone."

"What, Grigeni," Valenty harshly asked, "you are sure I would lose?"

Before Grigeni could respond, Yevliesza moved past him to face Valenty. "Don't you dare swear this. Don't you dare try to interfere with some big vow when you did little all this time, let me fall under the *fajatim's* control, abandoned me!"

"Abandoned? I always worked for your release. I did everything in my power to keep you safe, Yevliesza. But I did not know how things stood with you. You did not tell me." He looked at her a long moment. "Why did you not say something to me when we rode out together from the stables? Did you think me so careless of you?"

"Yes, I did! You were afraid of the princip's displeasure when, after the fall of the Moon Bridge, she needed to punish me. You might have wished for me to be safe, but you did *nothing*. You toyed with me, then pled your marriage when most Numinasi don't care about bedmates. You took lovers by the dozen. But even after I said yes, you said no. I couldn't expect you to love me, but wasn't there at least affection? Wasn't there at least *something*?"

Grigeni had almost reached the door when Yevliesza raised her voice. "No, stay, Grigeni. Someone should know the truth in this damn castle."

A knock at the door and a serving man came in with a cloak for Yevliesza.

"Get out," Valenty commanded. The servant fled.

Valenty grabbed her by the arm, drawing her close to him. "Aye. There was affection, Yevliesza. You have that from me. You have everything from me. My mind, my heart, my body." He turned to Grigeni. "That is why the fiend must die."

Yevliesza pulled away from his grip. "I forbid it. I'll face Nashavety myself and test whether Numinat can ever see me for what I am. Don't you swear, goddamn it!"

They were staring at each other with such heat, she wasn't sure whether he would strike her, or she would strike him.

Grigeni coughed. "The problem, though, my lord."

"Problem?" Valenty hissed. "Have we not problems enough?"

"Yes, but we have the princip's questions tomorrow. And, Yevliesza . . ." He turned to her. "Your claims will not be believed, or if believed, cannot be proven. The story of the Tower is too extreme to credit. It may appear a ploy to distract the court from the crime you must answer for: treason."

Yevliesza pulled away from Valenty. Grigeni appealed to them to resume their seats, and they all did so.

She was stunned by what Valenty had said, but she was still so mad she was shaking.

After a decent pause, Grigeni asked her, "Why did you come back to Osta Kiya?"

She took a deep breath, trying to bring her mind to the matter at hand. "After I recovered from my injuries, I decided to come home because I didn't have anywhere else to go. I admit I hoped Nashavety would die. If she had, I wouldn't have to fear being murdered."

"And that is our defense," Grigeni said.

"What?" Valenty asked, annoyed. "That she hoped Nashavety would die?"

"No, my lord. That she *came home*. Because she has found herself to be Numinasi even after rejection and torture."

Slowly, Valenty nodded. "You are right. By the Deep, Grigeni, this is the thing Anastyna has hoped for from the beginning."

"She has a strange way of showing it," Yevliesza murmured.

"Best not to say so in public," Valenty cast back.

"There seems to be a very long list of what I can and can't say."

Grigeni broke in. "But above all you must not tell of what happened in the Tower. Say it was the vise torture. That is cause enough to discredit the *fajatim* of Raven Fell."

Yevliesza cut a glance at Valenty. "She tried to kill me."

"There is no witness," Valenty said. "Grigeni is right. It will never be believed."

Finally she nodded.

Grigeni gathered his notebooks, taking great care to put them in a neat stack.

Yevliesza stared at the floor. She was vastly confused. A moment ago Valenty had declared his love for her. And she wasn't at all sure it was welcome.

CHAPTER 39

S he wore her finest dress, the deep grey with shimmers of lavender that she had worn at the Ninth Moon festival. Back when her father was still alive, back when she had for a brief evening felt like a Numinasi, not yet despised by all, not yet a prisoner of Raven Fell.

That night at the festival Valenty had warned her against being seen with Lord Tirhan. Had he begun to admire her—as the Numinasi put it—to care for her, then? She liked to think he had been jealous of Tirhan. It showed something of his hidden feelings, even if so little else of his behavior did. But he was a man who had conflicting sides: the spoiled noble with too much time on his hands, indulging his passions; and the more fair-minded, thoughtful one who seemed to have the princip's favor.

But no matter her doubts about him, he was going to help her defend herself. She thought she could count on him at least that far.

As she waited for the summons to the royal presence, a knock on her door, and a guard entered to announce that someone was here to see her, "by appointment."

"Who is it?"

"Says his name is Pyvel."

Soon the boy was standing before her, his face full of pleasure.

"We had an appointment, did we?" she said fondly.

He shrugged, grinning. "You look very good, my lady. Like one of the high folk."

"But do I look Numinasi?" She tilted her head up, looking down her nose at him.

"Aye. Now you look like a *fajatim*."

"Are you well, Pyvel? Do you believe the stories they've been telling about me?"

"Never, not a word of it."

"I've made mistakes, Pyvel, I admit it. But treason isn't one of them. If things go badly, please remember I never meant you harm. You were a friend to me when there was no one else."

"Do not talk like that. They will release you, they have to."

"Well, I did take a dactyl without permission . . ."

"You did not! Lord Tirhan took one as was his right, and you . . ." He paused, uncertain.

"Went along for the ride?"

"Aye. A good way to put it. But why did you come back? We thought you went with Tirhan . . . to be with him."

"No, I escaped with Tirhan because I couldn't bear Lady Nashavety's instruction. And no one had forbidden me to return to the mundat. Which I considered doing. But I decided to come back and tell how Nashavety treated me and clear things up. If I can."

"Well then, it will soon be over," he said hopefully.

Yes. With a charge such as treason, it might soon be all over.

Another knock, and Valenty entered. He narrowed his eyes at Pyvel, and the boy slunk out.

"Are you ready?" he asked.

All she could do was nod because words stuck in her throat. She hadn't been truly afraid until this moment.

As he stepped toward her, she pulled back, but he took her by the upper arm and bent to whisper in her ear: "Do not be afraid. Anastyna favors you."

She hung onto those words as they walked under guard to the royal wing.

Anastyna's judgment was to be given in the great Audience Hall, her formal reception room with the tallest windows Yevliesza had ever seen, glazed in real glass. The floor was a mosaic of flagstones, highly polished, and far above, the ceiling vaulted in a series of arches. In the back center of the room, two chairs on a dais.

Spread out on either side, hundreds of onlookers, nobles and plain citizens, and everyone in between. On one side of the dais, the five *fajatim* representing the great houses: Storm Hand, Red Wind, Iron River, Wild Hill and Raven Fell. Behind them, Sofiyana, her violet hair glowing in a shaft of sunlight from the windows. But instead of a profusion of ringlets, her hair was pulled severely back. Already she had begun to look like Nashavety: thin, severe, and sure of herself.

Valenty had led Yevliesza to the side of the dais opposite the *fajatim*. Nashavety stood among the leaders of the great houses, looking hunched over and worn. She thought the woman at last looked like the evil crone she was: bony and decimated, her cheeks hollow, her nose the most prominent feature. Nashavety did not shrink from her gaze, but watched her with an unnerving calm.

Anastyna arrived, accompanied by Lord Michai, High Steward of the Court, who seated himself beside her.

Behind Yevliesza and Valenty, Grigeni stood, giving Yevliesza a reassuring nod.

Ever since she had come to this land, this kingdom, Yevliesza had expected to go on trial. Her father had broken with law and custom by keeping a daughter in a foreign land. Such a choice was considered criminal because children must take their powers when young, and people feared that if a birthright gift came late, it would be distorted if it ever came at all. Nashavety believed that Yevliesza's align power had come deformed and that the girl from the outside would never be normal.

Now came one last accusation of unnaturalness: treason to her land. She wished they'd get on with it.

Lord Michai opened a scroll, and the room quieted.

"Princip Anastyna," he intoned, "finds cause to address questions to Yevliesza, given refuge in House Valenty. Is she ready to answer for herself?"

Valenty spoke up. "She is, my lord."

"Then let us begin." The high steward wore a midnight-blue velvet robe, a great silver belt at his waist, and a dagger in a scabbard. His white hair looked like it had never been combed, and puffed around his face like a cloud.

He described Yevliesza's departure from Osta Kiya, in company with the Alfan envoy. Having been sent to the Hall at Raven Fell, she did not receive permission to leave, nor had she completed the instruction that Anastyna required Lady Nashavety to provide. Was this recital true?

Valenty responded that it was.

Lord Michai went on, describing that the boundary gate commandant said that she was disguised as a male attendant, and that they had departed, Lord Tirhan had claimed, for Alfan Sih.

Michai turned to Valenty. "Why did Yevliesza find it necessary to disguise herself?"

Anastyna held up a hand to stop Valenty's answer and gazed pointedly at Yevliesza.

Yevliesza answered, "I was afraid Lady Nashavety would pursue me and prevent me from leaving."

At this, Nashavety gave a silent laugh.

"And why would she have," Lord Michai asked, "given that she was doing you the favor of clarifying Numinasi ways and customs, and you abandoned her instruction?"

When Yevliesza hesitated, Valenty said, "Because Lady Nashavety had applied torture during her instructions, using a device that crushed her fingers. This convinced her student that her instructor meant her harm."

A few of the *fajatim* looked in distress at Nashavety, who emphatically shook her head at them.

"Does she bear evidence," Lord Michai went on, "of torture on her person?"

Valenty responded. "Finding her injured, Lord Tirhan, a healer, used his arts to quicken her recovery."

Lord Michai turned to Nashavety. "Did you or any in your household use such a device, harming Yevliesza?"

Nashavety's voice quavered, but carried with conviction. "Nothing of the kind ever happened. Although my guest made it clear that my instruction itself was odious."

"Did you insult Nashavety in this manner?" Michai asked Yevliesza.

"No, I did not. Sometimes I cried out in pain. Sometimes when asked to repudiate my father and mother, I hesitated to do it."

Michai sat quietly for a few moments. "Someone is lying to this royal inquiry. It is a grave offense." The audience was as quiet as the flagstones.

Anastyna leaned forward. "Did you, Yevliesza, travel to Alfan Sih and work against Volkia? Speak plainly."

Valenty put his hand on her back to steady her, but she stepped away from him. This was the treason charge, and she meant to answer it clearly.

"I went to Alfan Sih because I had nowhere else to go.

Lord Tirhan offered protection to me after all I had suffered. But I did nothing against Volkia. I didn't take up a weapon, or aid those with weapons. I won't deny I wished him well. But I never accepted a role with his followers, and once we found them in the wilds of the Alfan Sih forests, I left the kingdom."

"And were not stopped by the Volkish?" Anastyna asked. "Questioned, perhaps?"

Yevliesza hesitated. They might find out what happened on that score. She had to tell them. "Not until I was back in the crossings. There I ran into Volkish soldiers who did question me. I said that I had been in Nubiah. They accepted this, and I was free to go."

"They accepted this?" Anastyna asked in obvious doubt. "But they would certainly have told their superiors of the encounter when they had a chance."

"It was a superior officer who questioned me. Prince Albrecht of Volkia."

A wave of murmurs swept through the chamber.

Valenty whispered to her, "Why did you not tell me!"

But Anastyna had drawn back into her chair, frowning, and Lord Michai was speaking.

"So you came very near to creating an incident that would have jeopardized relations with Volkia."

Valenty spoke up. "Coming near to an action cannot be a crime. Prince Albrecht accepted her explanation, and no incident occurred."

"That is true," Anastyna said.

Nashavety interrupted. "May I have permission to tell of something, Lord Michai? I have a confession to make."

Anastyna raised an eyebrow. She nodded to Michai, who said, "You may speak."

Nashavety stepped forward. "There is one thing I have not

told. One thing I kept to myself, even to the point of dissembling."

"You have lied to the court?" Michai asked, leaning forward.

"No, my lord, but I did dissemble to you when you questioned me at my sickbed."

His face stiffened and he waited like a storm hovering.

"As I lay on the verge of death, an understanding came to me. That I had failed as a guide to the girl of the mundat. When you came to me, Lord Michai, I had decided that I did not want Yevliesza to have to face the consequences . . . of having pushed me down the stairs."

Shocked murmurs raced through the Audience Hall. Several of the *fajatim* reacted with astonishment.

Yevliesza threw out, "That's a lie! She'll say anything to destroy me!" She stared at Nashavety, outrage rising. She didn't think she could bear this. This distortion of what had happened, an event that had terrorized her every moment since it had occurred. The Tower, the malwitch's beating, the sight of the long fall to the valley floor.

Michai held up a hand. "Let Lady Nashavety speak."

Yevliesza prepared herself to hear that she had tried to kill Nashavety and not the other way around.

"It was very late at night," Nashavety said in a reasonable tone, tinged with sadness. "She came to my chamber to complain of her low status in my household and lack of privileges. She had basic chores which she deemed beneath her station. I sent her away, following her into the passageway. She turned on me and shoved me down the stairs."

Anastyna said, "This is an alarming—a grave—accusation."

Yevliesza knew that she brought forward this story because she thought that the trial wasn't going in her direction, thought that Anastyna was going to absolve her.

Anastyna went on. "We were not aware nor apprised that

animosity had arisen between you."

"My Lady Princip, she was ever a discontented, prideful young woman, but I had no idea that she harbored murderous intent."

Yevliesza turned to Valenty, whispering murderously, "We should have told my story of the Tower! Now it's too late."

Valenty put his hand on her arm, "We can yet win. Trust me."

She jerked away, considering whether there would be a right moment to tell her side.

Lord Michai went on. "Were there any witnesses, Lady Nashavety?"

"How could there be? It was very late at night. She had awakened me when no one else was present."

Valenty had to restrain Yevliesza as she tried to step forward to protest. He whispered harshly, "She has no proof! This is a desperate ploy, and it sounds like one."

He raised his hand, and Michai nodded to him.

"This is a complete fabrication. Yevliesza has never in her life been violent, and she knew her time with Lady Nashavety was limited. Why would she risk all with such a desperate crime? Why, indeed, would she come back if she knew herself to be a murderer?"

The crowd by this time could not be silenced, despite Michai's attempt to restore decorum.

Anastyna rose from her chair, and slowly the room quieted. In a soft voice she said, "As to coming back to Osta Kiya, to Numinat, Yevliesza. You were in the crossings, driven there by what you claim was cruelty. You could have gone to the place you were born. But instead you willingly came back. Why?"

Yevliesza took a deep breath. "Yes, I came back. I returned because I didn't commit a crime and I was willing to answer for myself. And because Numinat is my home."

"At last!" she heard Grigeni whisper behind her.

Nashavety's voice rang like a gong in the hall. "Numinat is home? Numinat, which you have insulted and despised from the very beginning?"

Yevliesza answered in suppressed fury. "What you see as despising was honoring. I've tried to be worthy of this realm by learning to read, studying your ways and customs, taking arcana training, accepting my father's untimely death. All for the hope to be considered one of you, no matter my birthplace." Her voice cracked as she said, knowing it was still true, no matter what happened in this room, "Because I am Numinasi."

Anastyna leaned in to Michai, saying something, and he nodded.

Turning to Valenty, he asked, "Does Yevliesza have any further information that could assist the princip's decision?"

Valenty took Yevliesza's arm to prevent her from answering. "Be still," he whispered. "This is my opening."

"What opening?"

"My lord," Valenty said, "we have a witness who can shed light on the true attempted murder."

"A witness to Nashavety's fall?"

"No, a witness to an attempt to kill Yevliesza."

Nashavety staggered forward. "What is this? Are we to hear outlandish stories from a man who wishes to excuse a woman he lusts after?"

Lord Michai said, "The witness may speak."

Grigeni brought forward a young man in peasant's clothing. Yevliesza took a close look at him. Tall, a hawkish face. She didn't know him.

But when he frowned, she did. It was the courier who had come for her in the mundat. She had never learned his name or ever seen him in Osta Kiya.

Valenty urged him forward, his hand on the man's shoulder. "This is Fador of Molga Polity, formerly a *harjat* in service."

"I do not know this man," Nashavety exclaimed, "nor have I ever seen him before. He cannot testify about events that he has not witnessed."

Watching Anastyna take her seat again, Yevliesza thought she looked serene and unmoved. The princip wasn't surprised in the least. She had known that this man would come forward. But to say what?

Anastyna slightly raised her hand, allowing the man to speak. "And so?"

Valenty turned to Fador. "Please tell our Lady Princip of the terrible thing you witnessed."

Nashavety raised her voice. "Lies, it is lies upon lies!" She turned to her *fajatim* sisters. "It is a conspiracy to ruin me. You see how the Hall and honor of a *fajatim* is nothing to this princip, nothing!"

"Silence," Michai intoned. "Fador, you may speak."

Fador stood two steps in front of Yevliesza, wilting before Nashavety's glare and the rapt attention of the crowded hall. "I brought . . . I was commanded . . ." He turned to Valenty, who nodded to encourage him.

"It was my mission, on behalf of Princip Anastyna . . . to bring this woman's father from the mundat. He asked for time to organize his papers, saying that he would return within a fiveday. I brought his daughter back." He swallowed. Avoiding Nashavety's black stare, he looked at the dais and finally found an anchor by speaking directly to Lord Michai.

"From Lowgate Fort we took transport to Osta Kiya on a dactyl. Then a storm arose, coming suddenly from the direction of the Numin Mountains, as though it had been hiding there, because it came without warning."

Nashavety lost her rigid pose of outrage. It was the first time Yevliesza had ever seen her look at a loss: her skin deadened, her form hollowed out. She knew what the *harjat* was going to say.

Fador went on. "Lightning stabbed around us like a warrior trying to slash past defenses. The sky became a molten sea and I guided our dactyl quickly onward, trying to pass through the storm. That was when I saw it."

The man's voice grew in confidence as though he was reporting to a superior officer. "A faint outline of a hand in the sky. The small finger of the left hand pointing at us from a clenched fist. And on that hand, a large amber ring glowing with each flash of lightning. Within the golden stone, what looked like a claw."

Nashavety staggered backward, and Vajalyna of Wild Hill rushed forward to support her as she swayed.

Yevliesza knew that ring. She had kissed the hand that bore it at Raven Fell on the day she had been accepted into arcana training. Nashavety always wore the amber ring.

Fador saw that Lord Michai was waiting for him to continue. "Then a stab of lightning pierced the dactyl's side near the middle saddle where my young charge rode. We were not far from the city palace, and our mount . . . the dactyl, was wounded, mortally wounded, and it struggled to remain aloft until it reached the city-palace. I sat with it as it died. Afterwards I resigned my post. I carried a great weight from that night. I thought the Mythos had passed judgment on me, trying to kill me. That I had shamed my *harjat* order. I left for my father's polity. I did not know that the ring meant anything. Then Andrik —Lord Valenty's man—found me." He turned to Valenty for confirmation.

Valenty said, "I sent him to find Fador to determine whether he left the city-palace so suddenly because of some threat. Whether there was more to the event that nearly killed Yevliesza." He paused. "I accuse the *fajatim* of Raven Fell of Trespass of Reach and Trespass of Person for sending the storm and lightning to kill Yevliesza."

Nashavety shook Vajalyna off and stood on her own, her face rigid with fury.

Valenty continued. "Trespass of Reach, because she extended her elemental power out of sight into a far distance. And Trespass of Person in causing grave injury with the intention to kill."

Anastyna leaned forward. "Show me the ring you wear, lady *fajatim*."

Nashavety walked up the two steps to the platform and held out her left hand.

The princip's voice was just loud enough for those closest to the dais to hear. "Do you deny that you extended your power in this way? That you tried to inflict great bodily harm or death on Yevliesza's person?"

"Everything that I did," Nashavety said, "has been for the protection of our kingdom. To keep at bay the poisons that have crept amongst us. Crept in because of you, Princip Anastyna!"

"Enough!" Anastyna cried. She nodded for guards, and they took Nashavety by the arms, pulling her back from the dais. "I find that Lady Nashavety of Raven Fell has committed Trespass of Reach and Person. She is sentenced to fall from the Tower."

The room exploded with cries and jeers, but for or against the sentence, Yevliesza didn't know.

Nashavety turned to the other *fajatim*. "This princip has brought dangerous foreign influence amongst us! As evidence, this pathetic, altered creature"—she pointed to Yevliesza—"who despises our ways and customs. And Chenua of Nubiah, whom Anastyna has taken as a paramour. Listen to me well. Anastyna is poised to intervene in the Volkish war. She will bring Numinat to ruin. I call for the *fajatim* to remove the princip's torc." Nashavety turned to the other *fajatim*. "Who sides with me in my call?"

Vajalyna of Wild Hill, Alya of Storm Hand, and Oxanna of Iron River stepped forward.

Nashavety swung around to look at the dais. "Four of the five *fajatim* have now spoken against you. You must relinquish the torc."

Pandemonium erupted in the room. Guards stepped in front of the dais to fend off the crowds that pressed forward.

Lord Michai was shouting, but no one could hear him in the uproar.

Finally, when a circle of guards had surrounded the dais, Michai intoned. "Hear my judgment! Hear me! Four *fajatim* voices are needed to dismiss a princip. But Lady Nashavety is no longer a *fajatim*, having been condemned to death. We have only three *fajatim* voices against Princip Anastyna."

Nashavety rushed toward Sofiyana and pulled her out of the crowd. "This is my successor!" she hoarsely shouted. "She will be the speaker of Raven Fell!"

"Nay, Lady Nashavety," Michai said in ringing tones. "Lady Sofiyana is your Right Hand. For her to be installed as your successor requires confirmation by the princip. Which she refuses."

Nashavety raised her hand to the sky. The windows of the hall grew dark. In the distance, thunder whispered.

"Bind her hand!" Anastyna shouted. The guards held Nashavety, pinning her arms to her sides.

Yevliesza found herself holding onto Valenty. Somehow she had gone to him, and his arms had come around her.

A braided leather rope was brought, and the soldiers wrapped it around Nashavety, binding her arms to her torso.

Before she was led away, she pinned Yevliesza with her gaze. "I consign you to the eight hells. May you hang over the jaws of darkness all your days, and at the end may they devour you. So I conjure the Mythos."

Grigeni shouted. "Your curse has no power! Your left hand is bound!"

Nashavety smiled. "You will see my power. I vow it will erupt from my broken body." She turned to the crowd. "You will see the destruction Anastyna brings. Save Numinat while you are still able." The soldiers pulled her away, taking her toward a side door of the Audience Room.

"Yevliesza," Valenty whispered into her hair as she held onto him. "You are safe now. It is over."

Her gaze remained on Nashavety as the guards led her away.

"She cursed me." A terrible curse that Nashavety claimed would erupt from her bloody corpse. Yevliesza shuddered.

"No," Valenty said, holding her tightly. "Her curse can mean nothing, Yevliesza, because her hand was bound and nullified."

She pulled back to look at him. "Why didn't you tell me about Fador? You could have spared me the worst of it, the fear."

"You needed all your passion to move the princip and everyone assembled here." He smiled in a way she hadn't seen for a long time, and it stirred her heart despite her anger at what he had withheld.

Valenty took her hands, holding them gently. "You were magnificent."

AT SUNSET, EIGHT PEOPLE ASCENDED THE TOWER STAIRS. ONLY seven would descend the stairs.

Nashavety led them, as was her privilege, her left arm bound behind her back. Three guards followed her, one for each of the Tower doors. Behind them, Princip Anastyna, who had chosen to witness Nashavety's death. Lord Michai followed her. Then Yevliesza and Valenty, whom Anastyna had asked to bear witness. The princip had heard from Yevliesza what had really happened to her in the Tower that night, and her anger had been quiet and terrible.

Valenty would not rest easy until Nashavety was dead. She
had broken every vow and had nearly caused Yevliesza to fall
from the Tower. The woman's brutality surpassed anything he
could have ascribed to her. She had also called for Anastyna to be
deposed. The *fajatims'* loss of confidence in Anastyna was
dangerous. But that was tomorrow's worry.

He watched as, in front of him, Yevliesza climbed the stairs.
She looked beautiful even in the plain gown she had chosen to
wear and despite the last fiveday and its exhaustions. Now her
relief at the outcome in the Audience Hall had given way to a
sober mood. It was no time for satisfaction, or so she must have
thought. In one way she still was not wholly Numinasi. Not hard
enough. Perhaps that would come in time.

Valenty had planned to speak to her about Dreiza, but after the
judgment Yevliesza wanted to be alone. He thought she had softened to him, but there was still a barrier, one that had begun to
come down when he explained to her how long Andrik had been
searching for Fador. She had thanked him, had even said that she
had misjudged him. But she spent the next hours in her quarters
alone, except for a time with Rusadka.

In the small circular room at the summit of the Tower, the
group assembled, Anastyna standing well back from the doors.
Valenty placed himself between Yevliesza and Nashavety, who
was standing in front of the Trespass Door staring out. Brave, he
had to admit. Michai stood next to her.

Nashavety wore a plain dark gown. Her black hair hung loose,
falling below her shoulders. It was Anastyna's will that she wear
no finery or jewels and that her hair be unbound as an emblem of
her fall from honor. She trembled. These moments were the hardest, but it would soon be over with. Valenty would gladly volun-
teer to push her if she would not walk into the air herself.

At a nod from Anastyna, Lord Michai read out her crimes. At
this, Nashavety turned to face the group. Michai intoned: *Trespass*

of Reach, in sending the storm across a distance; Trespass of Person for bringing a lightning strike down on Yevliesza.

Valenty wanted more added to the list, but those two crimes were more than sufficient.

Lord Michai asked the *fajatim* if she was ready.

Nashavety nodded. One by one she gazed at each person in the room, lingering on Yevliesza. "I am ready. I will show you how it is done, Yevliesza. For when your time comes."

Anastyna looked cut from stone. Not even seeing a woman walk through the Trespass Door could move her, not after all that had transpired, not the least of which was the woman's call for the *fajatim* to depose her.

"May I speak?" Yevliesza asked. Valenty turned to her. He hoped she would not lower herself to taunt Nashavety.

Anastyna nodded.

"I ask for this sentence not to be carried out."

Valenty put a hand on her arm. "No, Yevliesza. You cannot stop this."

She did not look at him. "I haven't asked anything of Numinat since my return. I haven't asked for apology or recompense from anyone who disregarded me and put me at risk." Here her voice lowered. "And it wasn't just *fajatim* Nashavety."

Michai frowned at her for this obvious reference to the princip herself.

"The Trespass Door, Yevliesza," Anastyna said coldly, "is for such crimes as she has committed. It is our way and custom."

"I know. But I'm asking for mercy. You could banish her, which would be a terrible punishment. She would be alone, she would still lose her wealth and position and reputation. It's what I'm asking you to grant me."

Nashavety did not stir, her expression was hidden behind her fall of hair. Valenty tried to get Anastyna to look at him, to pause before answering, but her gaze was fixed on Yevliesza.

Valenty harshly whispered, "Yevliesza, do not do this. Take it back."

Anastyna said in an icy tone, "Do you say that I owe you a benefit?"

"No, My Lady Princip. It would be a favor. An indulgence for the one to whom the harm was mostly done."

Valenty expected Anastyna to respond in anger, and indeed, she looked as though she was having difficulty restraining herself. The Tower room became deadly quiet. Valenty wondered just who would be thrown out the door.

To his chagrin, Anastyna finally said, "Very well, Yevliesza."

She was going to indulge Yevliesza. A colossal error, he bitterly thought, one that was almost unthinkable . . . until he paused to reflect that Nashavety had many supporters who she now had to woo to her side. Still, if he had been able to gag Yevliesza to prevent her from asking this favor, he would have.

He bent to speak closer to Yevliesza's ear. "Why? Why do this?"

She murmured back to him. "I can't be the cause of her death. I know what it is to have killed people. It never leaves my mind."

"But she is a *demon*."

Yevliesza looked at him with a strange calm, almost with pity. "There are no such things as demons."

"Yevliesza . . ." he began, but Anastyna was speaking.

"In recognition of Lady Nashavety's . . . former position and services, I grant your request, Yevliesza." A silent, stunned reception greeted this declaration. Valenty noted a small, cold smile from Nashavety, an image that would remain with him for a very long time.

Yevliesza hung her head, as though vastly relieved. Though how she could be, Valenty could not fathom. "Thank you," Yevliesza whispered.

Anastyna turned to Nashavety. "You will never use your

powers in trespass again, or your death sentence will be carried out."

Nashavety stirred, and one of the guards moved between her and the Trespass Door in case she thought to thwart the princip's decision.

In low tones Anastyna said to the nearest guard. "Bring the board."

The board. So the woman was to suffer more than banishment.

Nashavety's face lost the smile, her eyes narrowing.

As the sun set, torches were lit, and the group waited in silence. Valenty noted that Yevliesza did not look at Nashavety, though the *fajatim* gazed at her rescuer with contempt. Perhaps she thought Yevliesza showed weakness. Or perhaps she would rather have died than suffer the next thing.

They heard footfalls on the steps.

The board was brought and placed on a low table which the guard had also carried in. Tied to the board was a knife, its cutting edge gleaming in the torchlight, its handle wrought with a complex silver design.

Two of the guards unbound the straps restraining Nashavety's left arm. They forced her to her knees in front of the low table, resting her hand upon the board. Her left hand. As one of them placed the knife in her right hand, they closed in around her to prevent her from striking others.

Nashavety took the blade and tested the cutting edge with a finger. Then she raised the knife and swiftly chopped off the small finger of her left hand.

She did not cry out. Blood pooled on the board. The violet drained from her eyes, leaving them fathomless black. Her powers were now curtailed, reduced to small things, abilities that could never be more than crow power.

"Bring a healer," Anastyna said, unmoved.

CHAPTER 40

On a bright, snowy day, the sun streamed into Yevliesza's parlor through tall windows, casting ingots of light on the floor. Her few rooms were cluttered with chests and boxes and stray furniture.

A tenday before, Yevliesza had taken quarters on the far side of the central enclosure of the city-palace. Her view to the west took in the noble side of the palace with the royal wing of the princip and in one corner, the looming Tower. Midway between, Valenty's apartments where she had once had a small room, a time which seemed to be in the distant past. Her new residence, granted to her by the princip, was on the first floor, allowing easy access to the courtyard where she often walked, even on these crisp winter days.

Walking seemed the only way to absorb recent events, including her escape with Tirhan to the forests of Alfan Sih; the near-disastrous encounter with Prince Albrecht; and the trial with its shattering conclusion: Nashavety's downfall and curse. The former *fajatim* had departed Osta Kiya on horseback just before dawn the day after the trial, accompanied by a lone servant and a few days' supply of food to get her to Lowgate, and from there, to any kingdom that would have her.

Sofiyana was now installed as *fajatim* of Raven Fell. Anastyna's shocking decision to approve Sofiyana was, Valenty said, due to pressure from the *fajatim* who supported Nashavety. But though the princip decided to respect their demand, she secretly had an understanding with Oxanna of Iron River Hall, whose son had run away to join the Alfan Sih. Anastyna promised to judge him lightly should he ever return—but only if Oxanna agreed to support her as princip. Her position was precarious, with the majority of the *fajatim* openly opposing her, even if Oxanna was apparently an ally. But Anastyna, despite her dainty stature, could be fierce in her own defense. No doubt she had plans to erode or co-opt her challengers.

So Sofiyana was a *fajatim*. A steep rise for the witless girl who preferred pranks to studies in the arcana and who shared with Nashavety a penchant for self-serving lies and vindictive, if not murderous, intent toward rivals.

Heavy footsteps announced Rusadka as she entered the parlor, carrying a prodigious chest. "Where does this go?"

Yevliesza didn't recognize the piece. "I don't know. What is it?"

"Books and folios from Master Grigeni, which will soon crash onto the floor if you do not make up your mind."

"Well then, in the corner. That'll be my study area."

Rusadka brought the chest to its resting place. Yevliesza was grateful for her friend's unflagging support, even after she had lost her promotion for befriending the girl of the mundat.

"Let's stop and I'll make us a sandwich," Yevliesza said. They had been working since dawn, and she was famished.

"Sandwich?" Rusadka asked.

Pyvel ducked in from the small cookery, munching on a carrot. "I will make them!"

"You're not a servant, Pyvel," Yevliesza admonished him. "I'll do it."

"I am to be in training for a steward," he proudly informed Rusadka, whose military uniform and bearing greatly impressed him.

Rusadka gave a stern nod. "Then you should speak when spoken to."

"Yes, ma'am," he said, abashed.

"Pyvel," Yevliesza said, "while I make sandwiches, you can organize your room. And let me know what you need."

"What does a steward need?" he asked. Seeing Rusadka's frown, he disappeared into his bed chamber.

"Have you never been around young people?" Yevliesza asked.

"Not since I was one. The boy needs discipline."

"And I hope you will help him acquire it," Yevliesza said, knowing that Rusadka was not as dour as she pretended to be.

Entering the tiny kitchen she retrieved a packet of sliced mutton from its place in the cold keeper, a compartment in the outer wall. She sliced fragrant bread into pieces and slathered them with butter and herbs.

Through the small window she looked across the central compound. In her habit of looking at Valenty's den windows, she thought of the room where he had taken her the night the *zemya*, the manifestation of the thrall, had stalked her. The night he had sat with her to offer comfort and then had kissed her. More than once. And wished he hadn't.

Rusadka came in to help. "What is out there? You look lost."

"I *am* lost. I don't know what will become of me. Now that I can choose."

"It would be clear if you admitted your . . . new power." Rusadka couldn't see the logic in hiding what she was. The *harjat* thought in military terms, but that arena was exactly Yevliesza's fear.

"I can't. There's a majority of *fajatim* who fear the outside, all the more now that they know Volkia's ambition. I won't be responsible for . . . maiming the crossings."

"A strange word to use. As though the paths were a living thing."

"They are. They grow and change." She picked up two of the plates, but stood immobile, thinking, overcome with an insistent question. "Why me?" She looked at Rusadka, a friend who seemed to know the answers to most things. "Why am I the only one with the Ninth?"

Rusadka was silent. She knew the question underlay so much of Yevliesza's uncertainty about the future. Then she responded, "Because you are the only one who has ever come late to the Deep." At Yevliesza's blank stare, she added, "It explains nothing, does it."

"No, it doesn't." She smiled at seeing Rusadka stumped. "But keep trying."

Plates in hand, they headed for the parlor. "It has to be a secret," Yevliesza said. "Otherwise they'll turn me into a weapon. Or force me to block access. And that includes to the mundat. They don't need to send envoys to earth if they can protect themselves from small machines by cutting off contact."

"Perhaps we would be better off without the mundat." Rusadka saw her friend's unhappy reaction. "Why should we be open to them?"

They settled themselves at the long table that doubled for meals and a desk. Yevliesza was challenged by Rusadka and grateful for her. "I don't know why. But I can't carry that responsibility. And I don't trust Anastyna to, either."

"How can we protect you from being . . . taken by Volkia if the palace guard does not know you need protecting?"

Pyvel appeared at the door to his room eyeing the sandwiches. Yevliesza murmured, "By no one knowing what I am." She beckoned Pyvel to join them.

She smiled at her friend. "Except for you."

※

VALENTY MET YEVLIESZA ON THE VERDANT. SNOW FELL IN A soft cascade across the roof of Osta Kiya, with the sun a yellow smear in the west. Yevliesza had agreed to see him, but the note she sent in response to his invitation was pointedly short: *Yes. At sunset.* It was better than a no, but not by much.

"Would you accept a gift?" he asked when she arrived. He held out a fine wool cloak with fur-lined hood and sleeves.

She eyed it skeptically. "What kind of fur is that?"

"Rabbit."

She paused so long he wished he had not brought a gift at all. It was too much, too soon. He was determined to win her over, but apparently it must go slowly, something that, concerning women, he was not accustomed to.

"Thank you, Valenty," she finally said, exchanging her plain cloak for the fur-lined one. He carried her old cloak as they walked.

"I brought Pyvel."

"So you thought you needed a guard?" he said playfully.

"He's been cooped up for days."

A doubt began rising, even after his deft handling of Anastyna's hearing, that he could win Yevliesza over. He would not blame her for rejecting him, but it was a stark idea. They walked through the Verdant, its benches and plantings mantled with snow. No one else was there, leaving the three of them to leave their tracks in the first long snowfall of winter. Pyvel walked behind them like the chaperone that Yevliesza probably intended.

It was time to tell her everything.

"If I am on trial," he said, "will you hear my defense?"

The crunch of their boots on the snow was the only sound as the sun set and the snow took on a bluish cast. "You may speak," she said, mimicking Lord Michai with the hint of a smile.

He nodded. Turning to Pyvel, he said, "Go to the parapet and see if the courtyard is full of snow yet."

The boy took the hint and veered off to another path.

"Yevliesza," Valenty began, "there are things you do not know about me, things that I have had reason to keep secret. Now you will be part of my secret, and by the princip's command, you cannot reveal what you hear." He looked at her, but her face was hidden behind the hood of her new cape.

"Yes, all right," came her voice.

"I am, and have been for some time, Anastyna's chief spy. I control a number of people who seek out information for the princip. As my father did before me." He gave her a few steps through the snow to absorb this. "I divert suspicion by assuming the role of a lazy noble with low tastes. Until I met you, I enjoyed the . . . requirements of the role."

"So Anastyna forced you to have lovers. How convenient."

"Yes, I suppose so. But it eased my wife's mind, to know that I had my pick of younger lovers. So that she did not feel that she held me too closely."

He heard Yevliesza make a scoffing sound. Valenty plodded on. "Those years ago when I offered marriage to Dreiza, she felt our ages were too far apart, that it could never be satisfying for a young man—which I was at that time—to be yoked to an older woman. I tried to persuade her. She needed protection after my brother died. The old princip hated her and would have ruined her.

"I offered a compromise."

He told her of his vow, which he had honored for years, but

which meant that he could not have a relationship with Yevliesza. Explaining what had gone through his mind the night that the *zemya* threatened her, he admitted his actions had been unfair. But he could not tell her about his vow, because it was not widely known in the palace, and would undermine the role he had nurtured. Thus he was trapped by his good intentions, by vows and politics.

Then Dreiza saw past the pretense. He had taken Lusiana as a lover to try to reassure Dreiza, but she had not been fooled. And in the end, it had driven Yevliesza away.

The two of them had made a circuit of the Verdant. Pyvel was nowhere in sight. And still the snow fell, without any wind or sound. In this white silence, he waited for Yevliesza to say something.

She made her way to a small gazebo and they found themselves out of the snowfall. "You slept with Lusiana to prove to Dreiza that you cared for her? It's a strange reassurance."

"It worked for us. Until now."

Valenty looked down at her as she sat on a bench. The fur of her hood had collected enough snow to give Yevliesza the look of a winter princess. "Most couples agree to have lovers, but with Dreiza, I wanted her to know that she always came first, that she would never have a rival in my heart. And then . . . she did. You."

He sat down next to her. "Yevliesza, this is why I acted as I did. It is the truth."

Outside the gazebo, flakes drifted down relentlessly, lacy white against the darkening sky. In the elegant silence he imagined they might stay there until the world and their small refuge were buried in snow.

"Valenty," she murmured. "I didn't know. I thought . . ."

"I know what you thought, and it tore me apart."

"I blamed you. Unfairly."

"It was fair by what you knew. But now I hope you will give me a chance."

Wariness fell over her face. "A chance?"

He reached under his cloak to remove a scroll from his jacket. "I was to give this to you, if you ever came back." He nodded for her to open it. She did and began to read.

৩৵৹

Yevliesza, my daughter, listen: Numinat has not been kind to you, I know this with a certainty. Where we should have opened our arms to you, instead we closed off our circle, though we pretended otherwise, soothing ourselves with the sly thought that we had allowed you home and into our ways and customs. I do not know if you have gone back to the origin world or to another, more welcoming, kingdom than ours. If you return, here is a thing I wish to tell you.

From the beginning of my life with Valenty, we had a pact, one that we never should have made. Valenty will have told you of this. If you have come back. I feel you will return. The High Mother tells me that the fajatim who hounds you will be bound and gagged. She has her ways of knowing, and I hope she is right.

And now, the vow. Valenty's vow.

It is not our way to bind freedoms between men and women. When I accepted Valenty's promise, I thought it was a vow of love, but I think it came rather from compassion, to protect me from further sufferings given all that had happened to me. How strange that a woman—one as strong as I believed myself to be—accepted his proposal.

Because it is not our way. First, because couples know that attraction—and admiration—is never exclusive. And also because a Numinasi is seldom afraid of others and certainly not in matters of the heart.

You resisted our devotion to custom. But until you understand how strong it is in us, you will always be perplexed. The ways of the Numinasi are like the aligns that course through the rocks of the land. The ways run through our bones. I am not saying it is always good. And I am not saying you should accept all the ways. Sometimes change is wise. I leave you to challenge our more rigid customs. One thing that needs changing is having gowns that button up the back. Here in Zolvina, I wear a tunic and trousers.

Yes, my daughter, I will be taking the pale.

One reason is that, though I believe I could convince Valenty to abandon the vow, you would not by your own customs accept the role of consort. It would never bring you happiness. Well, perhaps one day when you became more used to us. But there is a better reason for me to adopt the path of the satvar.

I have found peace here. It is my time to consider inner things and I look forward to it with great joy. Our hearts are like a still pond that reflects the sky in all its changes. We see what is real through the reflection, for no one can know what the world really is. Everything comes to us through our perceptions. I am old enough to know when leaves have drifted in and how to restore clarity to my heart.

Sometimes even one leaf can bring us to that vital work.

My first step is to release Valenty from the vow. When he came to visit me here we spoke of these things and agreed. He wanted to know how he could help to make me happy, and it is this: For him to release me. Though we will always care for each other, we each also hope that the other finds new happiness.

I trust you will find yours, my daughter.

—*Dreiza*

YEVLIESZA AND VALENTY FOUND PYVEL AT THE BATTLEMENTS throwing snowballs at crows. He had surrounded himself with a glow manifestation so they could find him.

"Pyvel," Valenty called out to him. "You will never hit a crow."

The boy turned around, his cheeks bright red from the cold. "But my lord, they are daring me to try."

"More likely they are plotting revenge."

Pyvel grinned at that. "Miss, may I go inside now?"

"Oh, Pyvel, I didn't mean for you to wait. You're not a servant."

He frowned. "Do I not serve your household?"

Valenty put a hand on her shoulder to stop her answer. "Pyvel," he said, "you are a servant in her household, but she is also your patron and in that role, she will indulge you as she pleases." He nodded at the boy. "But your fortitude is to be commended."

"Go get warm, Pyvel," Yevliesza said, accepting Valenty's small lesson in patronage.

Pyvel brushed the snow from his hands and headed for the warmth of the palace.

When he was out of sight, Valenty took Yevliesza's hand. She gently disengaged from his clasp. "We're not going to hold hands," she said. "I haven't made up my mind."

He looked taken aback, and she almost smiled at how he presumed himself already in possession of her.

"Then can I earn your admiration?" he asked.

"You already have my esteem. You had it once, and it's more than repaired."

"Esteem. That was not what I had in mind."

They stood at the parapet looking over the central compound of Osta Kiya. The lights of the palace blazed from every window except those in the Tower. Youngsters with burgeoning element power had lit a thousand fireplaces, as was their nightly chore.

Each person had their duties and knew what they were. Now it was Valenty's turn.

"Where I come from, a man courts a woman. Or the one who is strongest in admiration pursues the other, to allow a bond to grow."

He smiled a devastating smile that made her want to trash the idea of courtship and go straight for admiration and its benefits. But she'd had too much change lately and needed time to be sure.

"Are you going to tell me how that is done," he asked in good humor, "or am I to discover this myself?"

"I haven't ever been in a courtship," Yevliesza confessed. "But you might start with sharing with me who you really are." She smiled at him, feeling like her face, frozen from the cold night air, would break apart. "It might take awhile. If you have the time?"

"That I do." He cocked his head at her. "How stubborn do you plan to be in this . . . courtship?"

"As stubborn as necessary," she murmured, "to finally know you."

ACKNOWLEDGMENTS

Especially with this foray into high fantasy, I want to thank all those who encouraged and assisted me in ways large and small. Foremost among them, fellow writer Anthea Sharp, whose counsel and support assured that I could—and would—finally tell this story and envision it as a four-book series.

Particular thanks to Sharon Shinn and Marilyn Holt for early reading and advice. For his finely-tuned ear for story and phrase, I could ask for no better than my copyeditor, Jim Thomsen. My appreciation goes out to my advance readers who helped me avoid many mistakes: Chris Bachman, Michele L. Casteel, Charles Hirst, Morgan Mead, Marisa Miller, Lisa Montoya, Eric Morris, Janet Smith, and Leeann Smith.

And most of all (with this sixteenth novel!) so many thanks to my husband and first reader, Thomas Overcast. His belief in me and in my story has made all the difference.

STRANGER IN THE TWISTED REALM
BOOK TWO OF THE ARISEN WORLDS
IS COMING IN EARLY FALL, 2023.

~ HERE IS A SPECIAL PREVIEW. ~

PROLOGUE

P rince Albrecht and his men had ridden hard from the boundary gate deep into Volkia. It was nearly evening by the time they rested their horses on the edge of a plateau within view of the great manor house of Duke Tanfred Wilhoffen. In the violet haze of dusk, the wide plains stretched before him, an expanse that seemed to fill his lungs with cool relief after the tight forests of Alfan Sih.

Behind the prince a horse snorted, impatient to reach the stables. The creak of saddles was the only other sound. It was not until this moment that Commandant Prince Albrecht von Treid felt completely at peace after the lurking violence of the rebels, hiding in glens and thickets, striking fast to kill before fading into the dense woodlands.

Albrecht loved these plains, broken sometimes by canyons that sliced the flats like gaping aligns made visible. Far away, the great Mist Wall, at this distance merely a hands-breadth tall. It trembled with the pangs of birth as it slowly extended the realm. He breathed in this power, or felt that he did.

Looking at the expanse before him, Albrecht felt a powerful

love beyond what he had ever known with parent or lover. *Volkia now and forever*, the thought came, surprising him with its fervor.

But his party must move on without delay to meet Duke Tanfred who had sent a message that an urgent piece of intelligence had come to him. If it affected the war, Albrecht was keen to hear it.

His gelding knew the way down the slope to the valley floor. Wilhoff Manor, forming a square with its three wings and court-yard wall, beckoned with the gentle light of torches. As they approached, the wrought iron gate swung aside under the warding power of the gatekeeper, and they passed into the spacious court-yard. Stablers were waiting to take the horses, and the house steward stepped forward to welcome them.

Noting the duke crossing the courtyard toward him, Albrecht handed the reins of his horse to one of the servants and turned to greet his host. "How good to see you, my lord."

Duke Tanfred bowed. He bristled with energy, his patrician face barely containing some hidden excitement. "Prince Albrecht. Welcome to Wilhoff, welcome indeed." He led the way into the massive brick manor with its gabled and pitched roofs, leaving Albrecht's officers in the charge of the steward.

They entered a reception hall with a high wood-beamed ceiling where manifesting globes hovered, shedding a pleasant glow. A servant took Albrecht's cloak, and Tanfred accompanied the prince deeper into the manor.

"Your rooms are ready, sir," the duke said as they walked. "Refresh yourself after your long ride. Dinner will await your convenience, and the cook has something special planned." He pushed a lock of sandy brown hair back from his forehead, a boyish gesture at odds with his formal jacket and trousers.

Albrecht waved the idea away. "I would rather hear your news first. Food can wait."

They made their way through the rich, dark halls, the stone floor tiles echoing with their footsteps.

"You have news that could not be trusted in a packet," Albrecht said.

"Not in a packet, no. I would have come to the front myself, but I did not want to distract you. How do things go with the Alfan?"

"They are under control. Pockets of insurrection, but like moths around a fire, when they come into our light, they die."

Tanfred remained silent and Albrecht was not surprised. The duke disapproved the war, though he kept his opinions to himself. He was young to have come into his ancestral title, merely twenty-nine, and he had odd leanings, centering around primordialist beliefs. Tanfred's attachment to the legend of the ninth power was an embarrassment, but harmless enough. Prince Albrecht did not allow his command staff to belittle the duke. The man was a patriot, and a dependable contributor to the general coffers. Given that, Tanfred could dance naked under the full moon or have conversations with his horse, and no one would even notice.

Tanfred led him out of the manor through a back door and across a formal garden toward a copse of trees with branches lit up with small manifesting lights like fallen stars.

"This is all quite mysterious, Tanfred."

"I do not mean it to be. But it is—an occasion—that should be given respect." He looked out the other side of the grove, where an opening among the trees gave a view to the Mist Wall. "My prince, in the eleventh month of last year, I had an unsettling experience. A distant tremor ran through me, as though echoing a sound I could not hear. It came from the crossings.

"A few days later it happened again. Something of great import happened there."

Albrecht doubted that Tanfred had sensed anything in the

paths between the realms. "We heard nothing of tremors or vibrations, Tanfred."

"But only a verdualist could detect it, sir. As you know, my affinity is very keen. It is said that the closest power to the crossings is verdure, the gift of growing things."

"It is also said," Albrecht pointed out, "that the most related power is aligns." A gift Tanfred did not have.

"But in the prophecy, it is an individual with verdure . . . verdure . . . who will detect a presence in the crossings. When a time of need arises."

By the First Ones, he was on about primordialist lore. The ninth power saving the Mythos, the favored one, and so on. Albrecht sighed, regretting that he had delayed dinner for this painful conversation.

The young duke rubbed his arms as though remembering the vibrations. "It is my duty to report this to you, sir. I have never noticed any perturbations in the crossings. And twice within so short a time!"

"And nothing since."

"No. But is it not possible that when someone passed through the crossings at those times, I sensed them? And would that not be an extraordinary event?" He paused. "I believe that we may live in a time of the *Eibelung*. The one with the primal root power that can effect a profound change in the Mist Wall."

"These ideas—" Albrecht began, but Tanfred made bold to interrupt him.

"I know what it sounds like. Like a man raving, but might it not be true that in this time of upheaval we have been sent assistance? This individual has been in the crossings twice, and if he comes again, I will know it. And we must welcome him."

"We should welcome this person," Albrecht skeptically said, "because he will expand our lands beyond what we could ever see in our lifetimes, or the lifetimes of our children. . . ."

"Yes, my prince. Indeed yes." In the distance, the Mist Wall was merely a dark band on the horizon. It was slowly growing Volkia even at that moment, leaving new land in its wake.

The cult of the ninth power was small, but even a few thousand of such believers could be a bothersome minority opposing the war. It was very pretty to think that the realm's growth, its natural growth, could intensify and provide more living space and resources. But it was nothing more than mysticism. Now that Albrecht had taken Alfan Sih, he meant to keep it. Volkia's acquisition of that realm had happened in merely three days and with no help from prophecy.

But as Albrecht sat in the deeply shadowed grove with Tanfred, something gave him pause. He recalled that around the time of Tanfred's experience of the tremor, Volkish soldiers found a new path in the crossings. A path by which Lord Tirhan must certainly have returned to his kingdom, since otherwise he would have been apprehended at any of the heavily fortified gates in Alfan Sih.

"You said that the event occurred on the first day of the eleventh month and five days later?"

"I noted the dates in my diary."

Albrecht recalled that he himself had been in the crossings on the latter date, the sixth day of the month. That was the day he crossed to Alfan Sih with a battalion of fresh troops. The day he encountered a Numinasi woman. She was young and unaccompanied, looking slightly disheveled and claiming to have come from a visit to Nubiah. He searched his memory for her name.

Ah. Yevliesza. House Valenty, she had said. He had since learned that early in the autumn she had been brought to Numinat from the origin world by order of Princip Anastyna.

And several months later, she had been in the crossings on both days when Tanfred detected a perturbance. Coincidence? He recalled his strong impression that the reason she had given for being in the crossings was a lie. Perhaps she had brought some kind of small machine with her, and Tanfred had picked up on an alteration that it had caused. If there was the slightest possibility that the woman had something to do with the new path to Alfan Sih, he must find her, question her. And not about mystic prophecies.

After the insolent way she had behaved . . . what had it exactly been? Ah, yes. She had suggested that his troops might lack honor. It was an insult he would not have endured from a man, and had barely restrained himself with the woman of House Valenty. Now he would find her, and this time he would show less restraint.

"I must give your information more careful thought," he told the duke. "But now, sir, come." He put his hand on the duke's shoulder and led him from the grove. "I find that I suddenly have a ferocious appetite after all."

CHAPTER 1

Dreiza, at age seventy-eight, was a *satvar*. From her many years of life and from her handful of days in sanctuary, she knew how to release things. Like beauty, ambition, husband. Life—at least in the *satvary*—was about releasing, and it was not a bad path, since it did eventually prepare one to relinquish life. All this being true, how could she now sit in her small room and refuse to face the day and the loss it would bring?

When Dreiza had taken the pale the previous month, she had given up her fine apartments in Osta Kiya and her life as the cherished wife of the lord of House Valenty. She had given up fine dresses, court life, and old friends.

Now she sat in her oaten-colored tunic and trousers, her hair braided and coiled, and stared at her hands imagining that her heart lay in their clasp, struggling to beat.

A knock at the door. The High Mother came in, a gentle smile on her lips.

The Devi Ilsat might have sent a renunciate to fetch Dreiza, but she came herself, almost making things worse. Dreiza would not fall apart in front of her.

She sat down on the bed facing Dreiza's chair. "The rider is ready, my daughter."

They sat quietly a few minutes. Then Dreiza rose and, making a small bow to the High Mother, walked by herself out of the domicile and through the courtyard gate to the pen.

Kirjanichka was squinting at the rider from Osta Kiya who stood a stone's throw away. Her beloved dactyl knew she would be ridden because the saddle had been strapped around her body.

She must give Kirjanichka back to the princip. The *satvary* could ill afford to keep her permanently, and it would not do for Dreiza to have such a privilege in the simple life she had chosen.

Kirjanichka's whiskers rose and fell with her breath as she gauged the new woman's fitness to ride. Dreiza hoped she would accept her and not be recalcitrant, but the narrowed eyes did not bode well.

Dreiza approached the woman and handed her a small pouch. "She enjoys a few figs," she told her.

They would not have sent a man. Although many dactyls would eventually accept a male rider, Kirjanichka was not usually in a mood to do so, especially since she had been retired from service and had been gifted to Drieza.

As she stood next to Kirjanichka, she rested her hand on the great crest of the dactyl's head. Dactyls did not love to be touched, but Dreiza felt she must have something of her in these last moments.

Her large yellow eyes met Dreiza's. And she had thought the hard thing had been to relinquish her husband! She had bequeathed Valenty to Yevliesza, the young woman who came to the realm after growing up in the mundat, a world of few powers, and of those that remained, only small ones. Yevliesza had come to Numinat lacking her birthright power, and there was no end of trouble over that. But her power had found her at last—the aligns, it turned out to be—and it helped to persuade her to stay amongst them. Dreiza was glad that she would. For Valenty had grown to admire her and must have her. It had been time for Dreiza to lose him, the second husband she had lost. So she knew about renunciation. Or thought she did.

As a gust of wind hit them, Kirjanichka lifted her wings. She had not flown for days, and missed the sky, feeling the breeze in her broad, lovely wings.

"Yes, you must go, my dear," Dreiza whispered. "The day has come to fly high and strong. Remember me, Kirjanichka. I will never forget you."

She sang a parting song to soothe her friend.

Take the days and moments, they are
Yours to keep.
Take the journeys and laughter, they will
Stay with you.
Take my care and devotion, may they
Protect you.
Take my heart, for it goes with you
Now and forever.

And then they were gone, circling once over the *satvary* complex. Dreiza tried to keep them in view but the sun cut into her eyes, and soon they had disappeared into the brightness of the afternoon.

☙❧

SHE WENT FROM CHORE TO CHORE, RAKING THE COURTYARD, filling coal buckets for the *satvar* cells, folding laundry, and her favorite task, washing dishes, the never-ending dishes. When the cooks came in to prepare dinner, she took a few morsels of cheese up to Lord Woe's perch on the west wall, where he slept with slitted eyes, half-watchful for mice.

On her way, she noted that Kassalya's door was ajar.

After feeding the *satvary* cat and returning from the wall of the compound, she saw old Videkya coming out of Kassalya's room.

"How does our sister?" Dreiza asked. She hoped that Videkya noticed that she had been on an errand and had not come to try to see Kassalya. Dreiza felt she had a certain bond with the girl, but the High Mother had given strict orders for her—her especially—not to talk to Kassalya. The girl had lately been in an agitated state, visited as she was by unbearable foreknowing. Kassalya was the youngest member of their community—a wounded being, cared for by the renunciates. In fact, cared for by the Devi Ilsat's close circle, the *satvadeya*, one of whom was Videkya.

The woman closed Kassalya's door and turned to look at Dreiza knowingly. Videkya had lost weight during her long illness, but her eyes were still bright and keen. "She does well enough today. Few have found reason to use this corridor, and thus we preserve her peace."

Dreiza disliked being upbraided indirectly. She had been used to the city-palace of Osta Kiya where people generally said exactly what they meant. "Then I will be on my way," she said with forced calmness.

"My sister," Videkya said, her face softening. "We are all so sorry that your Kirjanichka has gone."

Suddenly not in command of her voice, all Dreiza could do was nod, her throat tight, her face hot. Walking away, she considered how it was that she had maintained her equanimity perfectly through the day, only to have it collapse when someone was kind.

CHAPTER 2

Thirteen-year-old Pyvel rode his new horse at a trot, kicking up clods of snow from the trampled ground. Yevliesza watched him from outside the corral, happy that she could afford such a gift for him, her first friend in Osta Kiya.

He was longing to try a gallop, but a trot was the fastest that his instructor, the *harjat* warrior Rusadka, would allow. Her flawless black skin was set off by the trim of ocelot fur on her cape. Strongly built, she carried off military dress impressively.

Pyvel was often too full of energy to be strictly obedient, but if there was one person he feared, it was Rusadka, a woman who didn't hold with children, but managed to tolerate Pyvel because he was Yevliesza's steward. Or steward-in-training.

"Sit up straight!" Rusadka bellowed across the paddock. "Keep your feet in the stirrups!" She gave Yevliesza a long-suffering look. "Seems he cannot do both."

"You're making him nervous," Yevliesza said, amused that Rusadka had agreed to teach the boy, whom she now treated like a raw army recruit.

"He is nervous?" The *harjat* snorted. "What will he do when faced with enemy horsemen?"

"But we are in the paddock now," Yevliesza chided.

"Keep the reins low!" Rusadka called as the boy came by again, bouncing in the saddle and grinning widely.

Yevliesza enjoyed seeing her friend in the role of an instructor. She was one of only a handful of women to achieve *harjat* rank, much less pass arcana training in her power of aligns. They had been in the arcana triad together, and Yevliesza hadn't graduated, but the training had been worth it, because that was how the two of them had become friends. Rusadka, the only one who knew what Yevliesza really was. Not a master of aligns, but something far more imposing.

The burns on her shoulder and back occasionally pinched, as though the tracery embedded there was growing larger, or deeper. Or just clamoring for attention. She would like to see them for herself, but there were no mirrors in Numinat.

Rusadka turned to note a horse and rider coming up the draw from the valley. Her eyes narrowed. It was Valenty, riding a tall black stallion.

He joined them at the corral, greeting them, his eyes tender on Yevliesza, as hers were on him. She couldn't stop looking at him under ordinary circumstances, but on a horse, commanding it so well as he did, he looked smashing.

"May I join you?" he asked Rusadka, giving her deference since she was the teacher.

"Of course, my lord," she dutifully said. Valenty was a high noble, even if her opinion of him was low.

"I'll bring my mount to the stable," he said when Rusadka turned away. He exchanged glances with Yevliesza, his small smile making light of the woman's disdain and how he earned it by pretending to be less than he was. Rusadka took him at face value, as a spoiled aristocrat with no decent trade and an indecent number of lovers. And now he was courting Yevliesza, and to Rusadka's annoyance, her friend encouraged him.

Pyvel came round again, appealing this time to Yevliesza. "A steward should know how to gallop, mistress!"

Rusadka muttered loud enough for him to hear, "A steward should not have a horse in the first place."

Yevliesza had taken the role of Pyvel's patron, including his room and board and his education. She possessed a small stipend from her father's estate, a reputation as the person responsible for the dread Nashavety's downfall, and the tentative favor of Princip Anastyna. Tentative, because Numinasi politics were ever-shifting, especially in this time of Volkish aggression.

Valenty, having given over his mount to the stable boys, walked down to join the two women. Yevliesza was used to seeing him in court garb, but today he wore a padded jacket trimmed in fur and leather breeches tucked into mud-smeared boots, and he stirred her with his dark good looks and the way he met her eyes. But she was still learning to trust him. He was in a trial period. She had made clear that she would accept his courtship—even after all that happened between them—but conquest was not guaranteed.

It greatly amused Yevliesza to have a lord of the realm accept patience and make an effort to show himself worthy. Or at least sincere. Or at least not craven. With her hard-won place in this land, she wasn't about to be seen as just another of Valenty's bed partners.

"Why Valenty, of all the men who admire you?" Rusadka asked with Valenty still out of earshot.

"No one else admires me!"

Rusadka smirked. "I assure you that is not the case."

"He loved me but he was married. And then Dreiza released him. And he has set aside his . . . stable of women."

Rusadka muttered. "He better have." She looked up at the

palace commanding the hilltop, perched atop the great massif of stone which held the seat of power and the thousands of inhabitants of Osta Kiya. "I think that is Sofiyana on a balcony, looking our way." She spat into the muddy snow.

It might be Sofiyana, scowling down on all the people she considered enemies: Yevliesza, Rusadka, Valenty. But surely the three of them couldn't be any threat to her now that she'd taken Nashavety's place at the head of one of the five great houses of Osta Kiya.

And yet Yevliesza knew that Sofiyana would never forgive her for bringing Nashavety to die in the Tower. And she *had* brought Nashavety to the brink of death. But at the last moment she had persuaded the princip to pardon her. The *fajatim's* sentence had been transmuted to banishment. Nashavety was sent away on horseback with only a small purse of coins. She was at the mercy of whoever would take her in, which might not be anyone since she had been found guilty of high trespass, and should have been condemned also for treason and murder.

Valenty saw them gazing in the direction of the balcony. "Strange, but I think I perceive a frown on that woman's face. But it is too far to be sure."

Rusadka smirked. "Except it is her usual expression."

Valenty said in a bored-noble tone of voice, "And here I thought she rather fancied me."

Of course, Valenty always had to ruin moments by playing this game. Rusadka held her tongue with difficulty. Yevliesza couldn't disabuse Rusadka of her ideas about Valenty. It was his role to play, a rich noble of no account. One who was actually the princip's chief spy. She had promised never to reveal this fact, never to reveal how few lovers Valenty had really taken—and all of them with the full knowledge and approval of Dreiza. His secret was now open to her.

But she hadn't returned the favor. Valenty had no idea who she really was, and she couldn't tell him. Because he worked for the princip, and that put Yevliesza in clear danger.

ABOUT THE AUTHOR

Kay Kenyon is the author of sixteen fantasy and science fiction novels. Her work has been shortlisted for the Philip K. Dick Award, the John W. Campbell Memorial Award, and the American Library Association Reading List award. She lives in beautiful eastern Washington State in the foothills of the Cascade Mountains with her husband Thomas Overcast.

Visit www.kaykenyon.com and join the author's newsletter for a free story, and find out about upcoming releases and reader perks.

9 781733 674638